WHISPERS IN THE TOWN

By Pamela Evans and available from Headline

A Barrow in the Broadway
Lamplight on the Thames
Maggie of Moss Street
Star Quality
Diamonds in Danby Walk
A Fashionable Address
Tea-Blender's Daughter
The Willow Girls
Part of the Family
Town Belles
Yesterday's Friends
Near and Dear
A Song in Your Heart
The Carousel Keeps Turning
A Smile for All Seasons
Where We Belong
Close to Home
Always There
The Pride of Park Street
Second Chance of Sunshine
The Sparrows of Sycamore Road
In the Dark Street Shining
When the Boys Come Home
~~Under an Amber Sky~~
~~The Tideway Girls~~
Harvest Nights
~~The Other Side of Happiness~~
~~Whispers in the Town~~
On her own two feet
Distant dreams

WHISPERS IN THE TOWN

Pamela Evans

headline

First published in Great Britain in 2012 by
HEADLINE PUBLISHING GROUP

1

Cataloguing in Publication Data is available from the British Library

ISBN 978 0 7553 7485 4

Typeset in Bembo by Palimpsest Book Production Limited, Falkirk, Stirlingshire

Printed and bound in Great Britain by
Clays Ltd, St Ives plc

Headline's policy is to use papers that are natural, renewable and
recyclable products and made from wood grown in sustainable forests.
The logging and manufacturing processes are expected to conform
to the environmental regulations of the country of origin.

HEADLINE PUBLISHING GROUP
An Hachette UK Company
338 Euston Road
London NW1 3BH

www.headline.co.uk
www.hachette.co.uk

To Bella, with love.

Acknowledgements

Many thanks to Leah Woodburn and the team at Headline, including the designers who produce such lovely jackets time after time. Thanks also to my agent Barbara Levy, and my friend Rita Ford who provided me with some information I needed for this story.

Chapter One

It was a cold Saturday afternoon in February 1957 and shafts of winter sunlight poured through the shop window, glinting on the glass sweet jars with a pale, luminous yellow. The sunshine was deceptive, however, and a bitter draught accompanied every customer who entered The Toffee Shop causing the Storey sisters Sal and Ann to shiver, despite several layers of clothing and fur boots. They were both in position behind the counters at either side of the shop, one for confectionery, the other stocked as a tobacconist's.

'Flippin' 'eck, it's nippy out there,' greeted Hilda, who had been a regular customer here for many years and had known the sisters since they were little.

'You're telling us; we get the full blast of it every time anyone comes in,' said Sal, a twenty-one-year-old redhead with lively blue eyes and freckles.

'Bit of a drawback in cold weather, a shop door, ain't it?' cackled the middle-aged woman, who was wearing a brown coat and woollen headscarf with curlers poking out of the front. 'I bet you don't half curse it.'

'We do and all,' admitted Sal lightly, 'but Mum and Dad would soon be out of business if the door stayed closed during opening hours, wouldn't they?'

'That's a fact. I don't suppose it opened often enough when the rationing was on. Thank Gawd the hard times seem to be behind us now that more people have jobs and can afford a few luxuries again. Heaven knows we waited long enough,' the customer said cheerily. 'Anyway, it's nice to see the two of you doing your bit behind the counter. You're good girls to stand in for your mum and dad on a Saturday afternoon so that they can have a break.'

'There's nothing good about me,' responded Ann, who was a brown-eyed brunette like her mother with the same forthright manner. 'I only do it because there's no blinkin' choice.'

Her sister Sal threw her a disapproving look because her remark could give the false impression that she was mean-spirited. Ann could be a bit bolshie at times and she often spoke without thinking but she had a good heart. 'Take no notice of her, Hilda,' she said. 'It's just her cold feet talking. She doesn't really mind doing a stint in here, do you, Ann?'

'She does it – whether she likes it or not – that's the important thing,' declared the customer, giving Ann an encouraging smile.

Both sisters had full-time jobs outside of the family business which was in Perry Parade, a row of shops in a working-class residential area on the outskirts of Hammersmith. But it was a tradition in the Storey household for the daughters of the family to look after the shop for a few hours on a Saturday afternoon to give their parents some free time together.

Their mother was a stickler for family duty and had brought her daughters up with her own values, at times ramming them home to a tiresome degree. Sal rather enjoyed her stint in the shop as a change from her office job but it wasn't always convenient for either of them and Ann often had a grumble about it.

Now Hilda turned to Sal who was behind the sweet counter. 'Two separate quarters of sherbet lemons for my young 'uns, please, luv. I'll have to have 'em in separate bags if you don't mind or there'll be all-out war when the little perishers share them out.'

'Certainly.' Sal smiled, lifting the jar down from the shelf and transferring the sweets to the scales with a scoop. 'I bet they'll count the actual sweets to make sure they are equal. I know Ann and I used to do that when we were children.'

Hilda let out a raucous laugh. 'Kids eh. They'd count their cornflakes one by one if they could, to make sure one hasn't got more than the other.'

She went on to buy bull's-eyes, pear drops, Storey's home-made toffee and a variety of chocolate bars before moving to the other counter to purchase cigarettes for herself and tobacco for her husband's pipe.

'This little lot should keep 'em happy in our house over the weekend and if it doesn't I'll bang their heads together,' she said, her shopping bag loaded with goodies for her family. 'Thanks girls and ta-ta for now; be good.'

'Fat chance we'll have of being anything else while we're stuck in here every Saturday afternoon,' Ann complained after the door had closed behind her.

'Don't go on about it, Ann, it's only a few hours out of the week,' Sal pointed out. 'I know it can be a bit of a nuisance if you've got other things to do but it's the least we can do for Mum and Dad.'

'I don't see why we should have to do it at all.'

'You know very well why. It's because they've always been good to us so it's only right that we should give something back now that we're adults. The shop supported us until we were old enough to earn our own living, remember.'

'As if I could forget, the number of times Mum has shoved it down our throats and − all right − I accept that we should do it sometimes; but every week is a bit much, you must admit,' she said. 'She only forces us to do it to make a point. Dad doesn't push it.'

'He wouldn't, would he, as Mum's the boss in our family. Dad does what he's told the same as we do,' Sal said. 'Personally, I think she does a good job in her own way. I know she can be a bit of a nag at times but she does her best for us all, organising the household and running the shop with Dad.'

'He pulls his weight too,' Ann said.

'I know he does but Mum just happens to be the one I am trying to defend at this particular moment.'

'Dad's such a sweetheart we never need to defend him anyway,' Ann came back at her. 'Quite honestly I don't think he's bothered about having a break on a Saturday afternoon. He just goes along with her so that she won't give him a hard time.'

'Be fair Ann,' reasoned Sal. 'They're entitled to a few hours off at the same time, even if it is only to put their feet up.'

'And I have never said otherwise,' she conceded with an irritated sigh, 'but I've got better things to do with my time this Saturday afternoon than stand behind this flamin' counter.'

'Such as?' queried Sal lightly.

'I want some new shoes with really high stiletto heels. I saw a pair of beauties this morning in the town but I couldn't make my mind up whether to buy them or not. Now I know I want them for definite and I can't go there to get them because I've got to stay here and I want to wear them tonight.'

'Not more shoes, please,' wailed Sal. 'Our wardrobe is overflowing with your footwear and clothes. There's hardly any room for anything of mine.'

'You don't half exaggerate. Just because you've got your man and you're saving up to get married so you can't have any new things, it doesn't mean that the rest of us have to go around looking like frumps. I still have to get out there in the dance halls of a Saturday night in the hope of finding someone.'

'So I'm a frump then, am I?' Sal retorted.

Ann made a face. 'No, of course you're not. Sorry, Sal. I only said that because you rattled me.' She ran a studious eye over her sister. 'Mind you . . . you're not nearly as smart and up to date as you used to be because you never buy anything new to wear.'

'It's a question of priorities. I'd sooner save my money for things for my bottom drawer.'

'All right, don't rub it in, that you're the younger sister with a shiny engagement ring and a wedding planned and I don't even have a steady boyfriend.'

'I wasn't rubbing it in,' protested Sal who was engaged to her long-term boyfriend Terry Granger, their wedding arranged for the summer of this year. 'Anyway, you've had loads of boyfriends so it isn't as though you don't get plenty of chances.'

'And I let them all slip through my fingers.'

'I didn't say that but you don't stay with any of them for very long, do you?'

'They get on my nerves after a little while so I have to get rid of them,' Ann sighed. 'Maybe it's because I've never found anyone with that something special that everyone goes on about.'

'Or it could be that you are expecting too much,' suggested her sister. 'Blokes are all only human beings. I expect even Tony Curtis and Elvis Presley have their irritating habits.'

'If I was going out with either of them I'm sure I could put up with any amount of annoyance,' Ann laughed, making a joke of it. 'Anyway, I've probably missed the boat altogether now at the grand old age of twenty-two.'

'Now you're just being ridiculous.'

'Maybe I am but nearly all of my friends are married, engaged or courting strong. I'll have no one to go out hunting with before long. But I'm not prepared to settle for someone who doesn't give me that special buzz just to get myself off the shelf.'

'You'll meet your special man soon, I'm sure.'

'It would help if I could get those shoes.'

'Oh come on,' laughed Sal. 'Since when did a pair of shoes ever help anyone get a man?'

'It's all part of the gear that will make me look irresistible.' Ann grinned. 'And it doesn't need the two of us to be here for the whole of the afternoon, does it? I could easily slip out to get the shoes. I wouldn't be gone long.'

'You know how busy it gets later on when everyone comes in for their weekend treats,' Sal reminded her. 'I don't mind you getting the shoes in the least but with the best will in the world I can't serve on both counters at the same time and Mum will go mad if she gets to hear that people have been kept waiting, which she will do because the customers will be very quick to tell her. You know how fussy she is about the shop's reputation.'

'I'll be back before the rush, I promise,' claimed Ann. 'I've only got to pop up to King Street. Even allowing for the time I'll have to wait to get served, this being a Saturday, I won't be gone for much more than half an hour.'

'And the rest,' predicted Sal.

The conversation came to a halt as the door from the

house at the back of the shop opened and their paternal grandmother Dolly came in carrying a tray of tea and biscuits. At her heels was Scamp the family dog, a black and white mongrel with more than a touch of terrier about him, long pointed ears and dark eyes which could be very persuasive when he wanted a bone or a cuddle.

'Hello Gran, how smashing to see you,' Ann gushed with a crafty gleam in her eye. 'What perfect timing!'

'It's only tea and biscuits, dear,' Dolly pointed out.

'She isn't talking about the tea and biscuits, Gran. She's after a favour,' said Sal with a wry grin. 'She's going to ask you to stand in for her here while she goes off to buy shoes.'

'I've seen a pair of stiletto heels I really want. The Italian style that everyone smart is wearing, Gran,' Ann explained.

'Yes, I have seen young women wearing them,' Dolly said. 'So, how long are you going to be?'

'Only about half an hour.'

'Go on then,' she agreed without hesitation. 'Off you go.'

'Oh Gran,' said Ann, hugging her. 'You're the best grandmother anyone could have.'

'Enough of your old flannel,' said the older woman with an affectionate smile. 'I'm not so daft as to fall for it.' She looked at Ann, who seemed about to dash off. 'It's cold outside so go upstairs and get your coat and tell your mother where I am and that I'll have my tea with Sal down here. Oh, and bring my big cardi down with you please. It feels cold down here away from the fire.'

'Will do.' She hurried through the door to the house followed by the dog, who was probably keen to return to his favourite spot on the rug by the living-room fire.

'Now Sal, can you turn that heater up a bit please, dear?' said Dolly, hugging herself against the cold. 'It's proper parky in here.'

Sal went to the electric fire at the back of the shop. 'It's already on the highest setting, Gran,' she said. 'Why don't you stand close to it while you're not serving?'

'I think I shall have to,' she said. 'You know what a cold mortal I am.'

Only in terms of body temperature, thought Sal, because she knew of no one with a warmer heart than her grandmother.

Ann didn't return in half an hour which was no surprise to Sal because her sister was always pushing her luck. But Ann also had many virtues and it wasn't in Sal's nature to begrudge her. Anyway, she enjoyed working with her gran who had lived with the family since she was widowed when Sal and Ann were little. Both sisters adored her. She was shrewd, kind and had a keen sense of humour. Now in her sixties, she wasn't traditionally elderly in appearance and was rather a striking figure, her hair still red though peppered with grey, the freckles she had passed on to Sal now more pronounced with age. She had clear blue eyes, a predilection for bright lipstick and a fondness for a glass or two of stout in the evenings.

'Is there any more toffee in the stockroom do you

know, Sal?' she asked now as she checked the counter display to see which items needed to be replenished during the lull, though the shop had been busy until now.

'No we're right out of it; we put the last of it out on the counter earlier and that's all gone now,' she replied.

'I shall have to get busy with my pots and pans then, won't I?' Dolly made all the toffee for the shop from her own recipe. Storey's Home-made, as it was known, was their biggest seller, drew people from outside of the area and gave the Storeys an advantage over other confectionery retailers. 'We can't have our customers being disappointed, can we?'

'They can't get enough of it,' remarked Sal. 'It's everyone's favourite, including mine.'

'That's nice to know,' said Dolly with a smile. 'As long as there is still a demand I shall continue to make it.'

The shop door opened and Ann burst in, pink-cheeked and breathless and carrying a paper bag printed with the name of a well-known shoe shop.

'You got them then,' observed Sal. 'Let's have a look.'

Ann didn't need a second bidding and out came sheer elegance in the form of black patent shoes with winkle-picker toes and pencil-sharp stilettos.

'Aren't they just the loveliest things you've ever seen,' sighed Ann, pushing her feet into them and parading around swinging her hips.

'They are gorgeous, I must admit,' agreed Sal. 'I'd like a pair like that for my going-away outfit.'

'Are you sure that you can walk in them, Ann dear?'

asked Dolly with the sort of practical concern more typical of her generation than her granddaughters'.

'The shoes that I can't walk in haven't been invented yet, Gran,' giggled Ann.

A blast of cold air heralded a flurry of customers, glad to get inside out of the weather. This was the usual last-minute weekend rush before closing time because, in common with most other shops, The Toffee Shop didn't open on a Sunday. Now the adults were eager for their weekend cigarettes and a crowd of exuberant children were jostling for a position close to the sweet counter, all talking at once.

'All right, Gran,' said Ann, hobbling to the other side of the cigarette counter in her new shoes. 'I'll take over now.'

'Okey doke,' agreed Dolly and headed for the door into the house.

The Storey property was an old, traditional building on three floors with sash windows and stone sills. At ground level was the shop, the stockrooms and a small, basically furnished sitting room for those on duty to take a break. From here there were doors to a small garden with a shabby wooden shed-cum-garage at the bottom. The first floor consisted of a kitchen, sitting room and living room and the top floor had three bedrooms and a bathroom.

It was on the first floor that an argument erupted between Ann and her mother that evening at the meal table.

'You had no right to go off and leave your grandmother

helping Sal in the shop,' Joan Storey admonished, her brown eyes bright with anger. 'Especially in this cold weather.'

'Oh not that again,' Ann responded as her mother had already reprimanded her on the subject at length. 'Gran didn't mind standing in for me. She likes working in the shop. I wouldn't have asked her if she didn't.'

'God knows, I ask little enough of you,' Joan carried on as though her daughter hadn't spoken. 'I never ask for help with the domestic chores apart from a little assistance with the dishes now and again. But I do like you to show your appreciation by looking after the shop on a Saturday afternoon.'

Ann emitted an eloquent sigh. 'I know that, Mum, and I'm sorry,' she said dutifully.

'She wasn't gone for long, Mum,' fibbed Sal in her sister's defence. They had their differences and plenty of them but she and Ann were basically devoted and always united against others.

'That isn't the point and I told her that when she came upstairs for her coat before she went.' Joan stared at Ann coldly. 'Your grandmother shouldn't have to fill in for you unless there is an emergency. It's draughty down there and she's an old woman.'

'Hey, steady on, Joan,' objected Dolly. 'I'm still capable of dishing out a few acid drops you know.'

'Please don't side with her, Dolly,' snapped Joan.

'Gran's done nothing wrong,' said Ann, her voice rising angrily. 'So there's no need to speak to her like that. Anyway, she isn't old in her ways. You don't seem to think so either when you want her to help *you* in the shop.'

Joan looked about to explode, eyes bulging, plump cheeks strawberry-coloured with rage. 'Horace, speak to your daughter please,' she demanded, glaring at her husband.

'Er . . . I can't actually see the problem in her slipping off for a short time, dear. You could even say it was a tea break,' he said to his wife in his usual mild-mannered way. 'So long as Mum didn't mind, there's no harm done.'

'It's the principle of the thing,' Joan ranted. 'This shop has provided well for us as a family, even if we did have to subsidise our income during the war when you had to work on munitions and everything was so short we couldn't make a decent living from it. The girls have had the best we can give them and now they must make a contribution. It's called family spirit.'

A tall, angular man with gentle blue eyes, his ginger hair beginning to recede and turn white at the edges, Horace heaved a sigh of resignation and turned his attention to Ann.

'So . . . young lady, what was it that was so important you had to go out suddenly?' he asked.

'Shoes,' she replied defiantly, as though daring him to object. 'I needed new shoes so I went to get them.'

'Shoes,' snorted Joan. 'You got your grandmother to stand in for you while you were out buying yourself shoes.'

Watching her sister flush with fury, Sal braced herself for the outburst she knew would come. Explosions weren't unusual between Ann and her mother, both being outspoken and hot-tempered.

'Yeah, that's right and if you don't like it you'll just have to lump it.' Ann burst out, surpassing her usual level of disrespect when in a temper. 'I pay you for my keep every Friday when I get my pay packet.' Her eyes were wet with angry tears, cheeks flaming. 'I don't owe you anything so I don't have to spend every Saturday afternoon stuck behind the counter in your rotten shop when I've been out working all week in a flamin' factory office. The shop is yours and Dad's, not mine and Sal's.'

'Well, that's gratitude for you,' huffed Joan, red blotches suffusing her face and neck. 'I'll remember that the next time you are short of money and we help you out with our income from the shop.'

'Do what you like,' said Ann thickly and rushed from the room.

'Don't even think of going after her, any of you,' ordered Joan, giving the three remaining family members a warning look. 'You stay where you are and eat your meal before it goes cold.'

Sal had completely lost her appetite but she dared not leave a morsel of the sausage, beans and chips her mother had cooked so she stayed where she was and the four of them finished the meal in silence.

'It's very disloyal of you to take Ann's side against me, Horace.' Dolly and Sal had made a diplomatic exit after the meal and were in the kitchen washing the dishes with the door closed while Joan and Horace went at it hammer and tongs in the other room. 'I am deeply hurt.'

'I didn't deliberately take sides, dear,' he explained. 'It was just that I honestly couldn't see anything so terrible in her going out for a short time.'

'Well I was upset about it so you should have backed me up whether I was right or wrong. It's your duty as my husband,' she said in a strident manner. 'Anyway, you are far too soft with the girls.'

'Maybe I am less vociferous in my approach to them than you are,' he admitted. 'But they know they can only go so far with me. I have my limits.'

'You let them get away with murder.'

'Look, Joan, the fact is that they are both grown women now,' he tried to reason. 'They have their own lives and their own opinions. There isn't much we can do about that.'

'You *are* taking Ann's side.'

'No, not exactly. She was very rude to you and I shall have a few strong words with her about it. But the truth of the matter is that we can't force either of them to work in the shop now that they are adults and paying their way.'

'We shouldn't have to force them,' she snapped. 'They should do it with a willing heart out of gratitude.'

'In a perfect world they would and most of the time they do do it willingly.' Horace sighed. 'But they are young and eager to get on with their own lives outside of us. They didn't ask to be born so they shouldn't have to be grateful to us all the time. It was our job to do our best for them when they were growing up and we did it out of instinct, not because we wanted anything from them later on. It's what decent parents do. One day when they are married and have children of their own, they will see things differently.'

'Ann doesn't seem to have any respect for me at all.'

'She did overstep the mark just now but I do think that the two of you spark each other off.'

'It's no wonder she never keeps a boyfriend, with a temper like that,' she persisted.

'From what I can work out, it's the other way round,' he said. 'It's her who gives the boyfriends their marching orders.'

'She would say that, wouldn't she?'

'That isn't a nice thing to say about your daughter, Joan,' he said sternly. 'It's a good job I know that you don't mean it.'

'No, I don't mean it,' she admitted, looking sheepish. 'Because she's upset me I don't know what I'm saying.'

'That works both ways,' he said. 'I'm sure she didn't mean any of those horrible things she said to you. Anyway, I shall speak to her about her attitude.'

'I should think so too.' She looked at him and for a moment there was bitterness almost to the point of hatred towards him in her eyes; she was full of resentment and disappointment.

Catching the full force of her sudden contempt, he winced; they stood either side of the fireplace locked in silence as tension unrelated to the current issue rose around them. 'I shall speak to her right away,' he said hoarsely. 'And please try and calm down, dear. Don't spoil the weekend for yourself by being miserable. I know how you enjoy Sundays.'

'All these family rows, Horace,' she sighed. 'It didn't used to be like this.'

'It's just the rough and tumble of family life now that we have grown-up children,' he said kindly as though her fleeting moment of malice hadn't happened. 'I doubt if we are any different to any other family. There are bound to be differences of opinion when the children become adults because they have their own views on things. We have lost our influence over them.'

She shrugged her shoulders, looking dejected

'Cheer up, dear. It's a day off for us tomorrow.'

'Mm, there is that I suppose.'

'I'll go and have a word with Ann right away,' he said and headed for the stairs, a knot of anxiety tightening his stomach. He loved his wife dearly but he did wish she would let go of the past and accept things as they were; acknowledge him as he was.

'I've really blown it with Mum this time, haven't I?' said Ann, full of remorse when Sal went to see her in the bedroom they shared as soon as she'd finished helping her grandmother with the dishes.

'You were a bit explosive,' agreed Sal.

'I know. It was awful. I lost my temper completely and the words came pouring out. But Mum gets me to the state where I don't know what I'm saying,' she said. 'She can be very annoying, you must admit.'

'Yes I do admit it but she has her standards, especially about the shop.'

'Does she have to inflict them on the rest of us?'

'You know what she's like. But you also know that there isn't anything she wouldn't do for her family,' Sal pointed out. 'She likes us all to muck in, that's all.'

Ann sighed heavily. 'Yeah, I suppose you're right.' She put her head in her hands despairingly. 'Oh dear, all those terrible things I said. So I suppose I shall have to apologise.'

'And the sooner the better,' advised Sal. 'Otherwise there'll be a terrible atmosphere in the house all weekend.'

'There was a tap on the door and their father called out. 'Are you decent in there?'

Ann opened the door to her father and Sal slipped out, leaving them alone to settle their differences. It was time she started getting ready to go out with Terry anyway.

'I suppose you've been sent to give me a trouncing?' Ann said to her father.

'I would have come anyway,' he said in a stern manner. 'It really isn't right to speak to your mother the way you did. It was horrible and I was thoroughly ashamed of you.'

'I'm sorry, Dad,' she said. 'I didn't mean what I said, especially about not owing her anything.'

'It isn't me you need to apologise to.'

'I know,' she readily agreed. 'But Mum does treat Sal and me like kids sometimes. She still thinks she can tell us what to do and it makes me so mad.'

'So what if she is a bit hard on you at times. She's

your mother, no matter how old you are, and she deserves respect.'

'Yeah, yeah, I know.'

'Look Ann, your mother is keen on family together-ness and there is nothing wrong with that,' he said in a persuasive manner. 'It doesn't really hurt you to look after the shop on a Saturday afternoon, does it?'

'I only popped out.'

'I'm not only talking about that,' he said gravely. 'I'm talking about your rudeness to your mother just now and your general attitude towards doing anything that doesn't suit you.'

'I'm at work all the week, Dad,' she reminded him. 'I don't have all that much chance to do my own things.'

'I realise that and I shall point this out to your mother but just take it easy on her in future.'

'I'll try.'

'In the meantime I would like you to go and apologise to her right away.'

'OK.'

He turned to leave then looked back into the room. 'And do try and look as though you mean it, dear. She really didn't deserve that tongue-lashing you gave her.'

'All right, Dad,' she said following him from the room, feeling his strength and noticing the upright way he held himself, his back ramrod straight. Dad's personality was something of a paradox. He seemed weak in that he allowed his wife to dictate to him but there was some-thing very strong about him too. There was a sense that he could cope with any emergency that might arise and that his judgement was never flawed. Mum ruled the roost but he was the backbone of the family; a quiet and wise presence. What would any of them do without him?

Terry was far more interested in the letter he'd received from his older brother Charlie in Australia than the trials and tribulations of the Storey family as related to him by Sal in the pub that evening.

'Charlie is doing really well, Sal,' he said with blatant envy, having handed her some photographs of his brother and his wife standing outside their house in Adelaide beside a smart-looking car. 'He went out there as a welder five years ago and he's a car sales executive now and enjoying the standard of living that goes with it.'

'It does look nice, I must admit,' said Sal, studying the picture. 'Lovely house.'

'I know. It's all possible out there.'

'He seems to have made a go of it anyway,' she agreed.

'It's the land of opportunity,' Terry continued, waxing lyrical as he sipped his beer. He was twenty-three; a tall man with brown curly hair and hazel eyes; not outstandingly good-looking but well set up and presentable. He was a skilled metalworker by trade and like many men who worked in overalls, he took care with his appearance outside the factory and was smartly dressed in a suit and tie in a traditional style. 'All that lovely sunshine and chances to better yourself. No wonder it's got that name.'

'Mm.' Sal was wearing a blue sweater that enhanced the colour of her eyes and a black pencil skirt, her shoulder-length hair worn loose in a simple style similar to that of Grace Kelly, 'I have heard people say that sort of thing about Australia.'

'This country is no good at all,' he went on. 'Absolutely finished.'

'I don't agree with you,' she said defensively. 'Things are better now than they have been for years and likely to improve into the future, according to the papers. We have had the war to contend with, remember. It was bound to take a while to get things goings again. But goods are plentiful now and there are more jobs around.'

'There's still a terrible housing shortage,' he reminded her. 'And there isn't any scope for ordinary people here, whereas in Australia there is. It's a young country with lots of space and not enough people to fill it which is why they are putting a lot of money into their immigration scheme.'

'I suppose it makes sense.'

'I mean, take me for instance, I'll probably still be slaving away in a factory when I'm sixty-five whereas Charlie will be rolling in dough. By then he'll have a swimming pool in his garden, I reckon. They have the weather for it.'

'Do I detect a note of jealousy?'

'Maybe you do,' he admitted. 'But inspired is more the word I would use.'

'Inspired to do what?'

'Go out there and join him.'

She felt as though she had just hit a wall at high speed. 'You want to go off to Australia and leave me. But . . . we're supposed to be getting married in the summer.'

'You as well, of course, you daft thing,' he made clear. 'I want us to emigrate to Australia. Both of us.'

The relief was sweet and the idea exciting. 'Us go abroad?' she said with awe.

'Yeah, why not? Plenty of people are doing it. Ten pounds is all it costs. The Australian government pays the rest because they need people from outside to work in their booming industries and set up home there. The journey takes a few weeks on the boat. So you get a holiday as well. Oh Sal, isn't it a great thing to do?'

Anywhere abroad was glamorous to her, having never been further than the South Coast. She'd heard about the ten-pound scheme, of course. Ten-Pound Poms they called the people who went to Australia that way. In fact, a woman from work and her husband had emigrated a few years ago. All Sal could think about was sunshine and bright modern housing such as was in the photograph she had just seen. The pictures in her mind were like scenes in a Technicolor film.

'Yes, it is, Terry,' she agreed.

'In fact, it's more than just an idea, Sal,' he said, enthusiasm rising with every syllable. 'I'm serious. I really want us to go.'

'Hey, slow down. We can't go just like that,' she objected. 'It won't be that easy.'

'It can't be difficult or so many people wouldn't be doing it,' he pointed out. 'I've made a few enquiries and the first move is to approach Australia House, apparently. So I'll go sick one day next week and get all the information from there.'

Infected by his zeal, she sipped her gin and lime and said, 'All right then.'

Terry put his drink down on the table and stood up. 'Come with me,' he said, taking her hand. 'I want to show you something.'

He led her across the crowded, smoky bar and out into the wet and windy weather.

'Look,' he said waving his hand towards the street, the pavements glistening with rain in the amber glow of the lamp-posts. 'What do you see?'

'Houses.'

'What else?'

'People walking along.'

'Carrying what?'

'Umbrellas.'

'Exactly. Rain, cramped houses and grey dismal streets, that's what we'll see for the rest of our lives if we miss this opportunity.'

'It rains there too, I expect,' she said. 'They have winters, don't they?'

'Not like ours,' he said, 'and they have proper summers when the sun actually shines so people can get out of doors.'

'Must be lovely.'

'The ten-pound scheme won't last for ever, Sal. Anyway, now is the time to do something like this, while we are young and fit and ready for a challenge.' He opened the door of the bar which was a traditional London pub with dark furnishings and fittings, people standing because there weren't enough seats, a piano player in the corner and a group of people singing around it. 'See how old and gloomy everything is. We've got the chance to make something of our lives. So let's do it.'

'You'd better get the information then, hadn't you,' she said excitedly

'Did you have a good night?' Sal asked of her sister when Ann crept into the bedroom carrying her shoes after midnight. Sal was settled in bed with her book.

'Yeah, not bad,' Ann said casually, undoing her suspenders and rolling her stockings down. 'Had a bit of a laugh with the girls.'

'Did you meet anyone nice?'

'No, I didn't click with anyone tonight,' she said. 'Must be losing my touch.'

'The shoes didn't work their magic then.'

'No, but I enjoyed wearing them.'

'I've got some exciting news.'

'Really.' Ann looked at her and grinned wickedly. 'What happened? Did you and Terry go all the way?' she chortled.

Sal giggled. 'Trust you to say something like that. Miss One-Track Mind.'

'Let's face it kid, the full works in the *you know what* department is the most exciting thing that's ever going to happen to us, I reckon,' Ann said.

'As thrilling as that prospect is, there are other things,' Sal said eagerly. 'Terry wants us to emigrate to Australia.'

'Blimey, Sal. Now that really is exciting. Is he serious about it?'

'Very. He's going to Australia House next week to get all the details.'

'Lucky you. I'd love to do something like that,' said Ann dreamily. She finished undressing quickly, shivering as she pulled on her pyjamas and ran a comb through her hair that was worn short in the popular Italian style. 'I won't half miss you though.'

'Oh yeah, there is that,' said Sal, a sharp pang of reality encroaching into the sunshine and excitement of her imagination. 'Still, I don't suppose it will come to anything. The idea only came up because Terry had a letter from his brother who is out there and doing well. He'll probably have forgotten all about it come Monday.'

'Oh well, only time will tell. I'm going for a wash, a quick one in this weather,' said Ann and hurried from the room, muttering about the icy temperature.

Far from forgetting about the emigration idea, Terry's enthusiasm for it grew with every day that passed, especially after his visit to Australia House where he obtained all the relevant literature and application forms which he was eager for both him and Sal to fill in to start the ball rolling. The proposed move to Australia became his sole topic of conversation and any chance Sal had of keeping it from her parents at this early stage was shattered because he couldn't stop talking about it.

Her mother's reaction was as she expected.

'It's the other side of the world,' said Joan

despondently after Terry had broken the news and left and she got Sal on her own. 'We'll never see you again.'

'I haven't even filled in the forms yet, Mum,' Sal reminded her.

'But you're going to, aren't you,' she surmised. 'Terry seems determined to go.'

Sal nodded. 'Yes, he is very keen and I am too,' she said. 'But the last thing I want to do is hurt you and Dad.'

'And you think you can walk out of our lives and not hurt us.' Joan was becoming tearful.

'No I suppose not. I hadn't thought that far ahead. It's just that there are such good opportunities there. We could have a better life.'

'Without your family around you,' exclaimed her mother. 'How could that possibly be better?'

'I know. That's the bit I don't like,' Sal said.

'All the sunshine in the world and better standard of living won't be worth anything without people you love around you.'

'We can come back after two years if it doesn't work out.'

'That isn't the right attitude to have,' Joan told her. 'If you are going to go all that way, you must have a positive attitude and be determined to make a go of it. That's the whole idea.'

'Yes, of course. I must admit that I haven't seriously considered the drawbacks yet,' she explained. 'It's just that it seems so exciting and I don't want to spoil it for Terry. Obviously he wouldn't go without me and I know how much he wants this.'

'Oh well, I have had my say and I am not going to try and stop you,' said Joan, her manner strengthening and tone becoming softer as she remembered what her husband had said recently about her domineering attitude towards her daughters. 'It's your life and I must stand aside and let you live it as you wish. I know I haven't been very good at letting go where you and Ann are concerned up until now but I will try my best to be better. If you decide to go ahead, you will have my blessing.'

'Thanks Mum.' Sal burst into tears. The last thing she had expected was for her mother to be nice about it, and somehow that really hurt.

'It's a bit late to take the dog out, isn't it dear, especially as I've already taken him for a walk,' said her father as Sal got Scamp's lead and headed towards the stairs with the dog at her heels.

'He can't get enough of outings, can you boy?' she said, fondling the dog's head. She needed to get out of the house to clear her mind and calm down because her emotions were in chaos after her chat with her mother. 'And it's only just turned ten o'clock. Terry went home early tonight so that he could pore over the Australia stuff some more.'

Her father managed a smile but it wasn't heartfelt. 'He's like a kid with a new toy over this proposed move abroad, isn't he?' he said.

'He certainly is.'

'Don't go unless you're absolutely sure it's what you want, Sal,' he advised.

She thought this over. 'How can anyone be sure about a thing like that? Because you can't possibly know how it's going to turn out.'

'You can't know but you can have a feel for it,' he suggested. 'Just make sure you want to do it because *you* really want to, not just because Terry wants to go.'

'It's such a big thing, Dad,' she said. 'Naturally I have a few doubts whereas Terry doesn't seem to have any at all, not at this stage anyway. Perhaps it's different for men because they don't show their emotions as much as women. Anyway, you've seen how eager he is. How can I spoil it when I can see what a marvellous opportunity it is?'

'I'll go in your place if you're thinking of dropping out,' said Dolly, coming out of the kitchen and immediately lifting the atmosphere. 'All that sunshine and good living. I wouldn't mind some of that. Cor, not half.'

'Oh Gran, you are a case,' said Sal. 'You wouldn't last five minutes outside of London.'

'I've never had a chance and I wouldn't mind giving it a try,' she chuckled.

'Do you fancy coming for a walk with me and Scamp?' asked Sal. Her grandmother was about the only family member whose company she could tolerate while she was feeling so emotional though she'd really rather have some time on her own.

'In this weather? Not bloomin' likely,' she said, pleasing Sal. 'This isn't Australia you know.'

'It certainly isn't,' Sal responded, doing her coat up

and wrapping her scarf round her neck and making as
though to leave. 'I'll see you both later.'

The wind whipped across the road, blowing the litter
about and whistling around the corners as Sal walked
along the shopping parade which was at the centre of
the community, a variety of stores including a butcher's,
baker's, grocer's, draper's, newsagent's and dry-cleaner's.
They all knew each other around here and many a trouble
or a joke was shared.

Heading past the shops along the residential street of
terraced houses, the weather felt less cold as she got into
her stride and she began to feel exhilarated, realising that
since the emigration idea had arisen she had been excited
and terrified in equal measures. Now she just felt sad.
Everything seemed very dear to her suddenly: the dismal
streets, the elderly lamp-posts, the little houses with their
tiny front gardens beneath the lit windows.

She passed a house where the curtains weren't drawn
and she could see the television set in the corner, a bulky
wooden box with a rather snowy black and white picture,
the family sitting around watching it. A lot of people
were getting the television now. Mum and Dad had
bought one recently. Sal still hadn't quite got over the
wonder of having a mini cinema screen in the house.

Reaching the Broadway the noise and activity increased
as buses roared through the town; there were quite a few
cars around too, another thing that was on the increase.
There was the usual bustle near the station but people
were hurrying with heads down against the weather.

'Come on then Scamp,' she said, halting in her stride and turning. 'I think we've had enough of this very fresh air so let's go home.'

Before she came out she had felt traumatised and indecisive. Now she knew exactly what she had to do.

'You've just got a bad attack of cold feet, that's all it is,' opined Terry the following evening after the family had gone to bed and Sal finally got the chance to speak to him alone. They were sitting together on the sofa in the living room and she had given him her decision. 'It's perfectly understandable but it will pass.'

'I wish I could believe that but I know it isn't just a passing thing,' she told him shakily; she'd been dreading telling him ever since she'd made up her mind. 'I hate to do it to you but I can't go to Australia and that's all there is to it.'

'So your family have been putting pressure on you to stay here, have they?' He was still not taking her seriously.

'No they wouldn't do that; even Mum's given me her blessing,' she told him. 'It's my own decision.'

'Look, Sal, I get scared about it at times,' he confided. 'Anyone planning to do something this big would. I feel bad about leaving my folks too, especially as my brother has already gone. But we're young and we have our own lives to lead and we'd be mad not to take this opportunity.'

'There'll be other chances for us, here at home. We

can still have a good life, Terry. As long as we're together, that's the important thing.'

Terry got up and paced around the room, finally coming to a halt by the fireplace with his back to the hearth, only dying embers now left of the fire. 'How can you have gone off the idea just like that when you've been as keen as I am all along?'

'The reality of it hit home, I suppose,' she said. 'It isn't Australia I have gone off. It sounds like a great country. It's leaving here I can't cope with. I realised that I didn't want to be all those miles away from the people we love.'

'We love each other,' he said, becoming belligerent. 'At least we are supposed to, though you are showing precious little sign of it at the moment.'

'This has nothing to do with my feelings for you,' she told him. 'I know how much you want to go and I feel terrible for spoiling it for you but I just can't do it, Terry. So it's best I tell you now before things get seriously underway.'

'This is crazy. You're young and healthy,' he said, his voice rising. 'Where's your spirit?'

'Just because I don't want to emigrate doesn't make me feeble,' she said, standing her ground. 'All right, maybe I'm not as adventurous as you are but that isn't a crime.'

'Come on, Sal, it will be all right,' he said, his manner becoming persuasive. 'Together we can do anything. We'll have each other. You'll have me to look after you.'

Seeing the enthusiasm he exuded from his every pore she was consumed with guilt and tempted to make him happy by changing her mind. But she knew it would be a mistake.

'I really am very sorry,' she said, getting up and going over to him. 'I'd only make you miserable if I was unhappy. But I'll make it up to you, I promise. I'll be the best wife a man can have.'

He stared at her with contempt. 'If you don't come to Australia you won't,' he said coldly.

'That sounds like a threat.'

'Not a threat; just a reality,' he told her. 'Because I am going whether you come or not and I intend to make my life there so there will be no point in us getting married as we'll be living on different sides of the world.'

'Now you are just trying to manipulate me,' she accused. 'It won't work, Terry.'

'I am not trying to manipulate you,' he came back at her, his tone harsh and definite. 'I am just stating facts. I intend to move to Australia and I really want you to come with me. But if you don't, it won't stop me.'

Now Sal really was hurting. 'So this emigration thing means more to you than I do.'

'That works both ways,' he said. 'I could say that your family mean more to you than I do.'

'You know that isn't true.'

'Then come with me,' he urged her.

'It isn't just the family, it's everything. I like it here and I don't want to go abroad to live. Surely I'm entitled to an opinion on something as vital to our lives as this.'

'I am entitled to an opinion too and I want to go,'

he stated. 'So take your courage in your hands and say that you'll come with me.'

She went back to the sofa and sank down on to it, feeling physically weakened by the shock of his reaction. She'd thought they could talk about it; had expected him to understand. 'It isn't about courage. It's about the fact that I really don't want to go, Terry, so it would be a recipe for disaster for both of us since if I wasn't happy neither would you be. I feel sick with misery every time I think of leaving here for good. It has to be something we both want to do for it to work.'

'All right; you don't want to come, so you stay here. But I shall go ahead. So long as I meet all the criteria required by the Australian government, that is where my future lies. I'm going, Sal, with or without you.'

There was a terrible calmness in his manner. This wasn't just a tactic to get her to change her mind. He really meant it, which spoke volumes about his feelings for her. After four years together she was seeing another and unsuspected side to him. She twisted the diamond solitaire ring off her finger.

'There's nothing left to say then, is there?' she said, handing it to him, still hoping that he would persuade her to take it back and say that he wouldn't go abroad without her.

But he took the ring and said gruffly, 'No, Sal, I don't suppose there is. So I'll get off home now and leave you to live your life as you wish, without me. Don't bother to come to the door. I can see myself out.'

She didn't move as he left the room and she heard

the front door close behind him; she just stayed where she was, trying to take in what had happened. Part of her wanted to go after him and tell him she had changed her mind and would do anything for him. He had been a part of her life for a long time. Surely something so vital to both their lives couldn't just end like this.

But in her heart she knew that it had. She didn't know exactly what had happened but she did know that their feelings for each other had been put to the test and had not proved to be strong enough on either side for something as huge as emigration. She'd always thought that there was nothing she wouldn't do for Terry and vice versa. Now she knew different. They had failed each other. She felt almost too sad to cry. It was as though her whole sense of purpose had been stripped away. What on earth would she do without him?

When she realised that the room was freezing now that the fire was out and she was shivering, she got up and went upstairs to bed. She still hadn't properly taken it in but she knew there was an awful inevitability about it.

Chapter Two

'Waterloo Station please,' said the man who flagged down a taxi in Regent Street and then clambered into the back of the vehicle while the driver set the meter. The passenger then leaned forward and spoke to the driver through the open window of his compartment. 'I'd be much obliged if you could step on it, old boy. I've got a train to catch and I'm cutting it a bit fine.'

'I'll do my best, mate,' said the obliging driver, a twenty-five-year-old man with the stunning combination of dark hair, deep blue eyes and a broad grin. 'The traffic is heavy though. But if anyone can get you there in time, I'm your man.'

'The London traffic seems to get worse every time I come into town,' observed the man, who looked to be in late middle age and was well spoken and smartly dressed in a dark overcoat and trilby hat. 'I don't know how you cabbies cope with it.'

'It's our job, and you do get used to it after a while,' said Bob Beck as they came to a stop in a hold-up at one of central London's ubiquitous sets of traffic lights. 'You need to have steady nerves, though, because it's every driver for himself around here. No one gives way in the West End so you just have to take your courage in your hands and be as daring as everyone else.'

'I've noticed that the drivers seem rather aggressive,' said the man. 'I wouldn't be brave enough to bring my car into central London these days.'

Experience had taught Bob to judge whether his customers wanted conversation or silence. As this one seemed to be in the former category he said chattily, 'Are you in town on business then?'

'That's right. I had to come in for a meeting at my head office,' the man replied. 'But I'll be glad to get home to Guildford where I work locally. London is too hectic for me nowadays so I'm glad these meetings don't come up very often.'

'I'm just the opposite. I absolutely love the place,' Bob told him as the traffic began to move again. 'I was born and bred in the country but I'm a Londoner through and through now.'

'Do your people still live in the country?'

'Oh yeah, they would never move away from there. Mum and Dad and my younger brother are all still in the family home, in a village near Exeter in Devon,' said Bob whose deep gravel tones still had a hint of a West Country accent despite a strong cockney influence. 'I go down to see them as often as I can.'

They lapsed into silence and the man looked out of the window at the crowds with umbrellas up and heads down against the wind, rain running down the cab windows.

'Miserable weather again,' he remarked conversationally.

'Yeah, it is a bit dismal. It's always dodgy at this time of the year though,' responded Bob. 'March winds and all that. We all start to think the winter is over but it's a bit too soon to see the end of the cold weather.'

'We could all do with some sunshine to give us a lift.'

'Too true,' agreed Bob heartily. 'But I'll be getting plenty of that soon anyway.'

'Are you going on one of these foreign holidays that are getting to be so popular these days?'

'No. Actually, I'm emigrating to Australia later this year.'

'Are you indeed?' the passenger responded with surprise. 'That's a very bold step. Still . . . you're young and you're fearless then, aren't you?'

'I don't know about that but I suppose it is the time to be a bit adventurous,' Bob told him.

'You get set in your ways when you're older and you don't want to up sticks,' said the man.

'I enjoy a challenge. I had my first adventure when I was sixteen and I came to London from Devon not knowing a soul here. I did any job I could find to keep myself then.'

'You thought the streets of London were paved with gold, like so many before you, I suppose.'

'No, not exactly, but I did know that I wasn't cut out for country life so London seemed the obvious place to head for,' Bob explained. 'After doing my National Service

I decided to make it my permanent home and settled in Fulham.'

'And now you're off to the other side of the world. Are you going on your own?'

'Oh no, I'm going with my girlfriend,' he replied. 'She'll be my wife by the time we leave though.'

'Very nice too,' said the passenger. 'How do your folks feel about you leaving?'

Bob's mood took a sudden dive as he recalled telling the family about his plans. His mother, bless her, had pretended not to mind but he'd known that her heart was breaking. A strong and courageous woman, it wasn't in her nature to try to hold her sons back. She had always believed that a child was loaned to you for a short time and would eventually go their own way, which he'd done as a teenager. Of course, his leaving for London was a whole lot different to the forthcoming departure. London to Devon was a stone's throw in comparison.

'My younger brother thinks it's quite exciting to have a brother living abroad; something to tell his pals,' he said now. 'Mum and Dad are being really good about it though I don't expect they are very happy.'

'You can bet your life they're not,' declared the man. 'I'd hate it if any of my children went abroad to live. But I wouldn't try to stop them if that was what they really wanted, of course.'

'Nearly there,' said Bob, steering the conversation away from the emotive subject as they went over Westminster Bridge with the stunning views of the river and the

Houses of Parliament. Even on a wet day like this the sight still gave Bob a thrill.

The man looked at his watch. 'I'll be in time for my train after all,' he said as Bob pulled up outside the station. 'Thanks very much for getting me here so swiftly.'

'Thank *you* very much,' said Bob when the man paid him and included a healthy tip.

Picking up another passenger from the taxi queue outside the station, Bob set off for north London. This fare didn't seem to want to talk which suited Bob because his dark mood worsened as he reflected on how much he was going to miss this city he had grown to love. The place was downright decrepit in parts; even now there were still areas that hadn't been put right after the war. But that was an element of its charm, the diversity and the rich in close proximity to the poor. He liked the vibrancy and the cosmopolitan feel, the anonymity which created privacy and was very different from the claustrophobic nature of growing up in a small country village.

There was a feeling here that anything was possible. An avid reader, Bob usually had a few library books about the history of London by his bedside. He had a voracious appetite for the subject and, because of his occupation, he knew the geography of the city off by heart.

In a reflective mood he recalled how he'd come into the job in the first place. After the strict regime of the army during his two years' National Service, when he'd been taught to drive and some useful engineering skills, he'd wanted to be his own boss but had no idea how he could make that happen without substantial financial resources.

Just by chance he'd got talking to a taxi driver in a pub one night; the man had told him how the taxi business worked and that no capital was required if you worked as a driver for a taxi firm. What had appealed to Bob was the idea that he could work for as long or as little as he liked with no one breathing down his neck. However, the procedure wasn't straightforward. As well as in-depth police checks, the application process also required that potential drivers learn London until every single street was ingrained in their memory. It had taken Bob almost a year.

During that period he'd earned his living doing any job he could find and had learned The Knowledge by riding around London on a bicycle, memorising every street. When Scotland Yard finally issued him with a licence, to start with he got a job driving for a taxi firm but worked every shift there to get enough money for the deposit on a hackney cab of his own which he was now buying on hire purchase.

Of course it was all about to change. His beloved cab would have to be sold and he'd need to start again in Australia though he doubted if he would be driving a taxi for a living there because his fiancée Kate wanted him to have an occupation with more class.

Who could say what would happen when they got there? Skilled men in particular were most needed, so at first he might have to use the basic engineering skills he'd learned in the army to make a living and move on from that later. He was certainly going to work hard and make the most of every opportunity.

So, enough of sentimentality about leaving people and places he loved. His future lay with Kate in Australia and he would do his very best to make a success of it for them both. They were very lucky indeed to be able to go for ten pounds each.

But even reminding himself of that didn't dispel the heaviness of heart that had come upon him. He knew it would pass. As soon as he saw Kate all doubts would fade.

'So you're working again tonight then, Bob,' remarked Kate Reynolds when he called at her bedsit in Fulham in the early evening of that same day during a rest break before he started the late shift.

He nodded. 'The more hours I work, the more money for us,' he told her.

'I thoroughly approve of that,' she enthused. 'But it does get a bit lonesome in the evenings without you. Still, it won't be for much longer will it? In a few months' time you'll be out of the taxi driving game altogether and evening work will be a thing of the past.'

'We don't know what I'll be doing out there yet,' he reminded her. 'Whatever happens we'll have to work hard. Nothing comes from nothing.'

'You certainly won't be driving a taxi if I have anything to do with it,' she said firmly. 'We're going abroad to better ourselves, not stay the same.'

'We might have to do any job we can find for a while

until we find our feet,' he suggested. 'We can't expect everything to fall into our laps.'

'That isn't the right sort of attitude to have, Bob,' she said in a tone of mild admonishment. 'To be successful you have to be positive and think big.'

'I'm just being realistic. Anyway, I enjoy my job and wouldn't mind doing it there.'

'I know all that but you're better than taxi driving, Bob. You're the sort of man who can do well for yourself. You and me together; the sky is the limit. Immigrants can achieve great things out there and we are going to be one of the success stories.'

'It will take time though, Kate,' he pointed out, hoping to inject some sort of reality into her impossibly high expectations. 'Obviously I'm not going to get a top notch job in the first week.'

'No, I suppose not,' she agreed with reluctance. 'But you have to aim high from the minute we get off the boat. Determination, and plenty of it, is what you'll need.' She paused. 'Anyway, would you like something to eat to save you going home before you go back to work? I can do you some spaghetti on toast with an egg on top. I quite fancy that myself so we can have it together.'

'Lovely,' he said.

'Coming up.'

Sitting at her small, well-worn dining table watching her work in her cupboard of a kitchen, which was just a compartment in the main room, her slim figure clad in a black sweater and tight black skirt, he thought not for the first time, how different she was to the other girls he'd been out with. Not many single women in their early twenties lived away from home. But, although she had been brought up in London and her parents still lived here, she preferred to have a place of her own and had somehow made this cramped and shabby bedsit, with its limited kitchen facilities and shared bathroom, seem stylish.

She was very independent, enormously confident and stunningly glamorous in a completely different way to her peers. Not for Kate the hair cut and permed into the latest Italian style and face fresh with youthfulness. She had dramatic black straight hair worn long and her make-up was lavish and expertly applied. Because she oozed self-confidence she seemed older than her years. Although she was young and extremely feminine, there was nothing girlish about her.

He'd met her a year ago at a dance hall and the chemistry between them had been instant and overpowering. Even now he found it hard to believe that someone as sophisticated and beautiful as Kate would give him a second glance. A switchboard operator in a local factory office, she was determined to better herself and the emigration idea had been entirely hers.

As she so often told him, 'You have to take your chances while you can and this ten-pound emigration scheme is the perfect opportunity for us.' They were already engaged but would leave England as a married couple. The wedding date was set for August which was just a few weeks before their expected departure date in September.

His morbid sentimentality had dissolved in her company as he had known it would. A new start in a different country with Kate by his side. What more could any man ask for?

Stirring tinned spaghetti in the saucepan on her gas ring with an oven no bigger than a biscuit tin beneath, Kate thanked God that she would soon be leaving all this behind. Her plan for a new life abroad didn't include a cubbyhole of a kitchen with a stained sink and practically no cupboard space or facilities. She intended to have a sparkling new electric oven in a house with plenty of room and modern amenities, probably even a fridge.

For all that this wasn't a palace, though, she didn't regret leaving home. The parents were all right but only in very small doses. This might just be a bedsit but she came and went as she pleased, something she couldn't do if she was still living under the parental roof. When a girl turned twenty-one she needed her independence and didn't want to account for her movements.

She and Bob were two of a kind in a way. He'd left home when he was sixteen and that really impressed her. With him, though, it had been a geographical change rather than a need to strike out on his own away from home and family. Apparently he hadn't enjoyed country life. But he seemed very fond of his family. She'd met them a couple of times and, although she had found them intolerably boring, Bob seemed very close to them which had been a drawback when she'd been trying to persuade him to emigrate with her. He'd had doubts about being so far away from them, whereas she didn't give a hoot how far she was from her parents. It wasn't that she didn't feel affection for them exactly; just that they were superfluous to her needs now.

She suspected that Bob was going to require more than a little encouragement from her to start the essential climb up in the world when they embarked upon their new life together. But she would pile on the pressure because she had no intention of being married to a taxi driver for the rest of her life, and neither did she intend going out to work herself once they were established. They would probably have to live in a hostel for a while at first, they had been told that, but as soon as they'd found their feet she wanted to start making her dream into a reality. She had no career aspirations for herself; her aim was to be the wife of a successful man. Bob had been enterprising enough to leave home at sixteen and make a life for himself in London – he was intelligent too; always reading some book or other – so she was damned sure he had enough savvy to rise above taxi driving, with a great deal of persuasion from her, of course.

He was a lovely bloke, though, and met her physical requirements perfectly with his dark hair, gorgeous blue eyes and fabulous physique. With plenty of support from her he should soon suit her in more material ways too. Oh yes, Bob Beck taxi driver would soon be a thing of the past.

Spooning the spaghetti on to the toast on plates balanced precariously on the plank of wood the landlord referred to as a draining board, she turned to Bob and said, 'Just the eggs to do now. Two minutes.'

'What did I do to deserve you?' he said lovingly.

'I think your good looks might have something to do with it,' she laughed.

Bob was overwhelmed with love and desire for her.

'Will you cheer up and stop going about with a phizog like a castrated pig, Stan Beck,' said his wife Mavis one Saturday evening in high summer when the couple and their youngest son Joe sat around the table in their cottage kitchen eating their meal.

'Ain't nothin' wrong with me,' said Stan, a burly man with wild dark hair tinged with grey.

'Don't you tell me fibs,' shot back Mavis, a plump, fresh-faced countrywoman who was devoted to her husband and family but made sure they knew that she was in charge. 'Your chin has been in your boots ever since our Bob told us about his plans to emigrate. Well, there isn't anything we can do about it. He's moving to Australia and that's all there is to it. So get used to it and stop bein' such a misery about the place.'

'There isn't any need for it,' persisted Stan who, like Mavis and Joe, had a pronounced West Country accent. 'The boy moved to London when he was barely out o' short pants. Isn't that far enough away for him?'

'He's a young 'un who wants to make more of his life,' Mavis pointed out. 'Anyway, he's a grown man and has every right to do what he wants.'

''Appen he has but he's got no right to break his

mother's heart, and don't tell me you're not fretting 'cause I know very well that you are.'

'So what if I am. I shall have to put up with it,' she said. 'He isn't tied to us. He's free to do as he pleases.'

'He might come back after two years, Ma,' suggested Joe, who was twenty, dark-haired and good-looking like his brother but rather immature for his age. 'Even if he doesn't he'll write to us. It'll be exciting getting letters from somewhere foreign. There'll be photos too, I reckon. I don't know anyone else who's got someone abroad.'

'You should be thinking of your mother's feelings, not rubbing it in,' scolded his father.

'Oi, that's enough, Stan,' Mavis said. 'It isn't Joe's fault so don't take it out on him.'

'Sorry, my luvver.'

Mavis knew that her husband's anger and despair was born mostly out of love and protectiveness for her though he had been devastated by Bob's news at a personal level too. He was quite right, of course, their son's decision to emigrate had all but flattened her. But she had pretended otherwise because she believed that her sons should be free to fly the nest without guilt. If their destiny took them out of reach then so be it, no matter how painful for their parents.

As Bob had left home at a young age they'd had plenty of time to get used to his not being around all the time. But as it was now he came back to see them on a regular basis. There would be no visits when he went abroad. What ordinary person could afford to travel to and from Australia?

'It's that woman he's got hooked up with,' Stan went on miserably. 'This is all her doing.'

'Her name is Kate and she is your son's intended so show some respect, if you please.'

'She didn't show us much respect when she was here, did she?' he reminded her. 'She made it obvious that she wasn't partial to our company. Moving to Australia is all her idea.'

''Appen it is but I think we both know that our Bob isn't the sort to be forced against his will to do anything. It he didn't want to go he wouldn't, it's as simple as that. Anyway you're a fine one to talk. You're always wanting to make more of your life than you already have; even now you've turned fifty you are still chasing something else.'

'What's age got to do with it? You don't give up trying just because you get a few grey hairs. Anyway, everything I do is to make some decent money for us,' said Stan, who was a farm labourer cum painter and decorator, odd-job man and would-be entrepreneur. He was also very skilful with wood and tried his hand at carpentry but only as a hobby. 'And at least I don't go rushing off to the other side of the world to try and do it.'

'Bob's always been the daring type,' she reminded him. 'He likes a challenge and there's nothing wrong with that.'

'All I'm saying is that a woman can influence a man, persuade him into things without him even realising it.'

'Oh yeah, like you are influenced by me, you mean,' she said with irony. 'That's a good 'un.'

'Pack it in, you two, before it ends in a slanging match,' said Joe, who was accustomed to lively differences of opinion between his parents though there was never any real malice no matter how heated they became. Joe wasn't the type to analyse the finer points of human nature but even he had realised that the fact that they were both very strong characters created an explosive combination. 'Can I have some more pie please, Mum?'

'Yeah, help yourself, son.'

'I suppose you're off gallivanting, this being a Saturday night,' said Stan.

'Naturally,' Joe replied.

'You going to a dance, son?' enquired his mother pleasantly.

'No, not tonight, Ma. Me and the boys have found a pub in Exeter where they have entertainment on a Saturday night and we are going there. They usually ask the punters to get up and do a turn so I'll get up and give 'em a song.'

'Good for you,' encouraged his mother. 'You've got a lovely singing voice.'

'It earned me a few free drinks last time, anyway, so I can't be too bad,' he told them. 'They loved my version of "Heartbreak Hotel". Even the old codgers gave me a cheer and they're not supposed to like Elvis Presley.'

'Who's he?' asked Stan.

'An American singer, Dad.'

'Never 'eard of him.'

'That's 'cause you're old. But, to be fair, neither had anyone else heard of him until last year,' said Joe. 'Now

49

he's really famous. Even us country bumpkins know all about his music.'

'Never mind Elvis Presley, you watch it on that motorbike of yours if you're gonna be drinking,' warned his mother.

'There's no law that says how much we can have to drink, Mum,' he reminded her.

'Maybe not but it's not right to be incapable in charge of a vehicle on the road.'

'Oh do give over. I won't be incapable. 'Appen I'll have a couple o' beers but that's all. I've got to let my hair down a bit on a Saturday night.'

'Don't forget we're working on that fencing job tomorrow,' his father reminded him. 'I don't want you moping about with a sore head and being no damned use to me whatsoever.'

'It's Sunday tomorrow, Dad,' groaned Joe, who worked with his father. 'I thought it was supposed to be a day of rest.'

'If a customer wants a job doing on a Sunday we do it on a Sunday because we are self-employed so we never turn work away when it's around because we don't know when we'll have a slack patch,' Stan lectured. 'Anyway, there's no such thing as a day of rest when you've got livestock and land.'

'We've only got a few chickens, a goat, cats and dogs and a couple of acres,' Joe said.

'Still livestock isn't it?' The Becks rented the cottage and the two acres of land that went with it and Mavis and Stan – who were both originally from the village – had moved in there as newlyweds. 'They have to be fed and looked after and the vegetables in the ground have to be taken care of as it's them as feeds us.'

'All right, don't go on about it. I'll take it easy on the booze so that I'll be in a fit state for work tomorrow,' he said with an irritated sigh, tucking into his second helping of meat pie.

As it happened Joe was so busy enjoying himself by singing to the punters that night that he had very little to drink; he didn't even finish his first pint. He'd had such a good time he was in very high spirits, though, as he and his pals gathered outside the Exeter pub after closing time singing the Elvis hit 'Don't be Cruel'.

'A good night, wasn't it, boys?' said one of them.

'The best,' agreed Joe who was dressed in a black leather jacket and narrow trousers.

'All we are missing is some girls,' said another.

'Where are we gonna find any at this time of night?' queried Joe.

'We ain't,' said someone.

'We'd better go to a dance next Saturday; that's where all the girls go,' suggested the first speaker. 'You don't get decent crumpet in pubs.'

'Dancing next week then,' said Joe.

'Meanwhile give us a song, Joe. It went down well in the pub.'

Joe let rip with 'Blue Suede Shoes' and the others joined in. Some passers-by told them to stop making such a noise or they would call the police.

The young men ignored them and carried on regardless for a while.

'Might as well go home,' said one of the group eventually. 'There's nothing doin' 'ere.'

'I've got to go to work tomorrow,' said Joe. 'So I'd better be off too.'

The crowd dispersed and Joe walked over to his motorbike parked by the kerb.

'See you lads,' he yelled above the engine noise as he revved up.

As he roared away into the night he let out a loud and joyful cry of 'Yahoo.' He was young and free, it was Saturday night and life was great!

'What was that, Stan?' asked Mavis, waking up with a start and nudging her sleeping husband. 'I heard a noise downstairs.'

'Whasamatter?' he grunted drowsily.

'I heard banging.'

'It's probably Joe getting himself a sandwich or somethin',' he said. 'Go back to sleep and let me do the same.'

Then Mavis shot up in bed as they heard a loud knocking. 'It's the front door, Stan,' she said shakily.

'Aye, it is an' all,' he agreed, sounding none too pleased.

'Who's calling on us in the middle of the night?' Mavis said worriedly.

'It'll be Joe, forgotten his key,' grumbled Stan, getting out of bed and putting his slippers on. 'I'll give him what for, waking us up like this.'

Mavis followed her husband down the creaky narrow stairs to the front door and stood beside him as he opened it.

'Evening, Stan,' said the village policeman.

'It isn't evening, it's the middle of the night.' Stan was always on the defensive when the police were around as he sometimes flew close to the wind when trying to make his fortune. 'So what do you want with us at this hour? Getting decent people out of their beds. It isn't right. I'm as clean as a whistle. You've got nothing on me.'

The constable looked serious. 'It's not you I'm here about, Stan. It's your Joe,' he explained gravely. 'I'm sorry to have to tell you but there's been an accident.'

Mavis grabbed her husband's arm as her legs almost buckled beneath her.

'Hello Bob,' said Kate, ushering him into the bedsit when he called unexpectedly in the afternoon of the following day. 'This is a nice surprise. I wasn't expecting to see you until later on.'

'I can't see you later,' he said, looking pale and worried. 'That's why I've come round now. I thought it would be better to tell you to your face rather than on the phone.'

Her expression darkened. 'Oh no! Don't tell me you're working again,' she said irritably. 'You promised to take me out somewhere nice tonight.'

'I have to go to Devon right away. I'm on my way there now,' he explained. 'My brother has had a serious accident on his motorbike.'

'Oh . . . that's terrible,' she said unemotionally. 'Is he badly hurt?'

'Dad wouldn't have phoned me asking me to go home if he wasn't. But I don't know any of the details except that Joe is in hospital. My father was in a hurry to get back to Mum at the bedside.'

'So . . . when will you be back?'

He looked at her in astonishment because, obviously, he could have no idea at this stage. 'I haven't even thought about that yet, Kate,' he told her. 'I won't know until I get there and find out what the situation is. I'm far more worried about what I'll find than when I'll be getting back, to be perfectly honest.'

'Don't forget we have to go to Australia House next week for a final interview to make sure everything is in order,' she reminded him sharply. 'You really mustn't miss that because we both need to be there.'

Australia was the last thing on his mind. 'It depends how things are with Joe,' he said. 'I can't promise anything.'

'But it's all arranged, Bob,' she persisted, her voice rising with anger.

'Then it will have to be rearranged if I can't get back in time,' he snapped, a combination of concern for his brother and Kate's callous attitude towards the accident making him short-tempered.

'After all the time and effort I've put into the move abroad, you can't even be bothered to attend a pre-arranged meeting.' She was fuming. 'God knows I've asked little enough of you. I've made all the effort, done all the work.'

'Kate, how can you be like this?' he asked, shocked by the fact that she had shown not so much as a smidgeon of interest in his brother or how his parents might be coping at this worrying time. 'I have a family emergency on my hands and all you can think of is the bloody emigration thing.'

'It might be nothing to you but the *bloody emigration thing* means a lot to me.'

'Tell me something I don't already know.'

'What's that supposed to mean?'

'It means that for the past few months I have heard of nothing else from you but Australia, Australia, Australia.'

'I'm very sorry if I've been boring you,' she said huffily. 'But it's a big thing. There is a lot to organise; not to mention the wedding beforehand as well.'

'I realise that but there are other things in life, and right now my brother's condition is my main concern.'

'Oh well, if you want to be like that you'd better bugger off to Devon then.'

'I will,' he said and turned on his heel.

He was at the bottom of the stairs, about to leave through the communal front door, when she came after him.

'Sorry Bob,' she said, looking sheepish. 'I've behaved like a selfish cow.'

'I'll say you have,' he agreed.

'Of course you must go to Devon.'

'I know that,' he said tartly.

'It's just that the Australia thing is so hugely important I got my priorities confused for a while back then,' she explained. 'Obviously if you can't get back in time I'll rearrange the appointment.'

He gave her a hard look. 'I didn't realise you could be so heartless, Kate.'

'I didn't mean it, honestly. You know I'm not like that really,' she said persuasively, sliding her arms around him. 'I really am sorry, so am I forgiven?'

'Yeah, I'll let you off this time.'

'I hope your brother will be all right,' she said.

'Me too, but thanks.'

'Will you ring me on the house phone to let me know how things are?'

He nodded, kissed her rather absently and left, pre-occupied with thoughts of his family.

As Kate turned and went back up the stairs, her expression was one of fury. She took a dim view of having her arrangements interfered with. Bob's family's problems were his parents', not his. He shouldn't have to go rushing off to them. Damn the stupid people to hell!

Bob arrived at hospital in Exeter to find his brother in a coma having hit a tree in a country lane at high speed on his motorbike. The doctors wouldn't be able to assess the extent of his injuries until he came round. Although deeply affected by the news, Bob knew he mustn't show how worried he was to his parents who suddenly seemed old and frail. The intensity of his feelings for them took him by surprise, maybe because it was the first time they had been seriously tested.

'He'll come through this, Mum,' he said to Mavis who was distraught but desperately trying to appear strong as was her way. 'Us Becks are fighters, you know that.'

'The doctors won't say for definite if he will come round at all,' she told him shakily, looking whey-faced, her eyes red and shadowed.

'They won't want to commit themselves at this stage,' said Bob. 'Doctors are always a bit cagey but they are obviously expecting him to wake up or they would have told us to be prepared for the worst.'

''Appen you're right,' she sighed. 'Thanks for coming, son. We thought we ought to send for you just in case.'

'Of course I must be here.' He gave her an affectionate hug, feeling choked with emotion. 'I would have been very upset if you hadn't sent for me.'

'Course he would,' added Stan, who was pale and unusually subdued.

'I know you've got a lot going on in London, Bob, what with your work, the wedding and the move abroad, so we don't expect you to stay for long,' said his mother.

'I shall stay for as long as you need me,' he assured her from the bottom of his heart.

One evening a few days later a long-distance call from Devon came through from a phone box for Kate on the communal house telephone.

'How are things, Bob?' she asked, on hearing his voice.

'The good news is, Joe has come round,' he said.

'Oh, that's fantastic . . .'

'Yeah, it is a relief.'

'So you can come back to London now then?'

'Not exactly no,' he told her. 'The bad news is, he's injured his pelvis and it's affected his spinal cord and he's lost the use of his legs.'

'He's out of danger though?'

'Well yeah, but it's a very serious injury and he'll be in hospital for a long time.'

'Still, as long as his condition isn't critical now, that's the important thing,' she said.

'Of course but his life will change dramatically because even when he comes home he'll be in a wheelchair and we don't know if he will be permanently disabled.'

'That's really sad. Have they given you any sort of hope as regards that?'

'They haven't ruled out the possibility that he might walk again,' he explained. 'But it really is too early to say. Still, at least he's alive so we are all very grateful for that.'

'Yes, that's the main thing,' she agreed. 'So now that the crisis is over you can come back to London, can't you?'

'Not yet, I've just told you,' he said. 'I'm still needed here for the time being.'

'But there's nothing you can do and you're losing money while you're not working,' she said, not bothering to hide her impatience now.

'I can't worry about that at the moment. This is more important.'

'When *will* you be back then?' she demanded.

He wanted to scream at her persistence. Why couldn't she understand the gravity of the situation he was in here? 'I can't tell you that now Kate . . . oh, there's the pips going; the money's running out and I've no more change,' he said and the phone went dead, rather to his relief.

He was shaking slightly as he came out of the phone box and walked slowly back to the hospital to collect his parents and take them home to the cottage. It had been a harrowing few days and pressure from Kate hadn't helped matters one little bit.

'You must get yourself off back to London soon, Bob. You can't afford to lose any more work, especially with the wedding and the move abroad coming up,' said Mavis one evening a week later. 'Your dad and I will be all right now, honestly.'

'Will you though?'

'Course we will. We've got the van so we can get to and from the hospital and there's nothing you can do here. Joe is being well looked after in hospital so you can rest easy knowing that.'

'I will have to be getting back at some point soon to earn some money,' he said, knowing that he must be realistic but also aware that the trouble would really begin when his brother was discharged from hospital. How did a twenty year old come to terms with being disabled, especially someone as lively and energetic as Joe had been? 'But I'll come down here as often as I can and you make sure to ring me from the phone box and reverse the charges to let me know what's going on. Any problem and I'll come right away.'

'We'll keep in touch, don't you be worrying,' said his

mother, who looked absolutely drained from the stress of the last week. 'I think I'll go to bed. At least I can sleep now, knowing that he's in safe hands.'

'G'night Mum,' he said, hugging her and kissing her cheek. 'Sleep well.'

'Night son.'

'I think I'll go up too,' added his father. 'I've checked on the animals so I'll say goodnight, Bob.'

The stairs were in the living room and Bob watched them leave together, tired and subdued but obviously devoted. It was strange to see them so quiet. He was used to warfare between them but the noisy banter had been completely absent since he'd been here this time.

He looked round the room with its old oak beams, well-worn but cosy furnishings, abundant ornaments and copies of trading magazines such as *Exchange and Mart* that always littered the place because of his father's search for business opportunities. The room hadn't changed since he was a boy but it was as though he was seeing it for the first time. He could feel its essence; smell the familiar scent of furniture polish and fresh-baked pastry from the pie they had had for supper.

It was the smell and feel of home which he couldn't get away from quickly enough when he was sixteen, so eager was he to explore life beyond the village and broaden his horizons. It was the natural thing for a grown offspring to be eager to flee the nest but he'd always known that all of this was here for him to come back to.

Rising, he went outside into the yard which was bathed

in moonlight and silent; the livestock settled down for the night, the two dogs following him out and sitting at his feet. The summer air was warm and balmy and his nostrils were invaded by the freshness of the country air tinged with the sour farmyard pungency of animals: a smell he'd grown up with.

Even out here he noticed evidence of his father's entrepreneurial aspirations. There was an old car he was in the middle of doing up with the idea of selling it. Dad was a tryer; no doubt about it. But somehow you knew that, although he would always earn a living, he would never be a rich man because he had neither the guile nor the ruthlessness that created millionaires from the wrong side of the track.

Ironically the one real talent he did have, for carpentry, he did for very little financial gain. Completely self-taught, he crafted beautiful doll's houses in his spare time with meticulous care but he couldn't produce enough of them to make a living out of it so kept it as a hobby. Usually he made one here and there to order from people in the village and he didn't charge much more than the cost of the materials. He claimed that if he were to allow his woodwork to become commercial it would no longer be his way of relaxing.

The tranquillity out here had soothed Bob and clarified his troubled mind. When he went back inside he knew with absolute certainty what he must do. He anticipated it with dread but it had to be done.

Chapter Three

'That's the daftest thing I have ever heard in my life, Sal,' declared Ann one Saturday afternoon in September when the sisters were doing their usual stint in the shop. 'Why on earth would you want to go all the way to Tilbury Docks next Friday to see a man off to Australia who is no longer a part of your life?'

'Terry was very much a part of my life once, and for a long time too,' Sal reminded her. 'We were friends as well as everything else.'

'But you fell out so badly when he chucked you,' said Ann whose tactlessness was a by-product of her concern for Sal.

'He didn't chuck me, as such,' Sal disagreed. 'I could have kept him if I'd been willing to go to Australia with him.'

'Huh! Some choice,' snorted Ann, then realising that she was being insensitive added in a gentler tone. 'Look, Sal, I know how much he hurt you so why put yourself out for him at this late stage?'

'Why shouldn't I? I don't hold a grudge against him. I'm well over all of that now.'

'But it's a weekday so you'll have to get time off work.' Ann said.

'I have some annual leave owing to me so getting a day off won't be a problem.'

Ann had seen her sister devastated by this man once; she didn't want to stand by and see it happen again. 'But won't it be rather a pointless exercise?'

'Practically speaking, yes absolutely. But I'd like to do it anyway. It's as much for my sake as his,' Sal tried to explain. 'I want him to know that I have no hard feelings towards him now. Whatever you think of him, it's a huge challenge he's taking on, and it takes real courage to emigrate on your own. Not many people would have the guts to do it. I want to give him some support; to wish him well and wipe the slate clean for us both.'

'You can do that by going round to his house the day before. That's only a ten-minute walk.'

'That wouldn't be the same thing at all.'

'I suppose not,' Ann agreed. 'But what's put this idea into your head anyway?'

'I happened to meet his mother in town the other day and she mentioned that he was going next Friday and they are all going to Tilbury to see him off. She gave me all the details and I realised then that I want to go too for old times' sake. I feel that I *must* go, Ann. Apart from anything else I need to bring that chapter of my life to a close.'

'I thought you already had done.'

'I have but . . . oh, I can't explain why I want to go because it's personal, so leave it at that and stop going on about it.'

'Do you think he's going to promise to come back to you or something?' Ann persisted, tactless again in her concern.

'Of course not,' Sal replied with exasperation 'What do you think I am, stupid or something? It's a new start for me as well as him.'

'It ended between you in early spring and it's now the autumn,' Ann reminded her, 'and you've made no effort to make a new start by finding someone else.'

'I don't want anyone else at the moment.'

'It's the only way you're going to get over him.'

'The answer to everything doesn't lie in the arms of a man,' Sal said. 'I am having a perfectly happy life without one for the time being, thanks very much.'

'I'm your sister, I know you inside out and I know that you're still pining for that heartless worm Terry Granger.'

'Don't talk about him like that! We wanted different things from life, that's all. The fact that he's going to Australia on his own shows how much he wanted to emigrate. It isn't as if he chucked me for another woman or went off me or anything. He probably felt just as let down by me because I wouldn't go with him as I did by him for going ahead without me.'

'Mm . . . there is that I suppose. But he isn't in your life any more so why go traipsing across London to see the back of him?' Ann queried. 'I've done my very best to help you get over him but all you want to do is to stay at home of an evening and read your books. I mean that's no way for someone of your age to carry on. You should be out enjoying yourself.'

'You call standing in the ranks at a dance hall hoping some bloke might fancy me enjoying myself? I call it hell.'

'It's what single girls like us have to do. I mean, how else can we meet men? We're not in the upper classes where you get introduced to eligible ones.'

'It's a cattle market and I hate it, that's why I won't let you talk me into going with you any more.'

The past few months had indeed been hellish for Sal. Terry had been at the centre of her life for so long, her confidence as well as her heart had been shattered by what had happened; her purpose in life stripped away. She had thought she and Terry would be soulmates for ever, completely in tune with each other, so the shock of discovery that she had been wrong had left her deeply traumatised.

Her sister only had her best interests at heart by trying to encourage her to go out dancing, she knew that, but Sal could only take so much of that sort of torture. So her social life now consisted of the cinema once a week with her friends from work. Since the break-up with Terry, Sal had become one of the library's most regular customers and was currently working her way through Dickens. She also enjoyed the works of Agatha Christie and John Steinbeck as well as those of younger authors. Perhaps she was afraid of further rejection; maybe she just wasn't ready for another relationship. She didn't know. But she was sure that she wanted to see Terry off next week. Crazy maybe, but she felt compelled to do it.

It was a cool and misty autumn morning and Sal stood on the quayside at Tilbury Docks staring at the ship that would soon take her ex-fiancé to the other side of the world. The docks were a hive of activity; people coming and going, luggage being shifted, foghorns sounding and the gangplank crowded with boarding passengers.

She had said her final farewell to Terry in the reception hall in the passenger terminal and then slipped away quickly so that he could be alone with his family for what would be a very emotional parting. With her intellect she knew that coming here today had been an act of sheer futility. Time off work and a long journey for just a few minutes with someone she had once thought she had known and would never see again. From a feeling point of view, however, it was the best thing she could have done.

The experience had had a cathartic effect, all romantic notions towards Terry finally expelled. He'd seemed like a stranger; had been glad she'd come, he'd said, but she could tell that he was excited and perhaps a little nervous in the face of what he was about to do so his thoughts were all of that. He had already moved on mentally; she was a thing of the past. His relatives, especially his mother, had been tearful but Sal had been oddly dry-eyed. She'd shed all her tears after they'd broken up. Now the time had come for him to go and this gave her a feeling of liberation.

For all that, it was a sad and nostalgic time and she was feeling very tense. She decided to find somewhere she could get a hot drink to moisten her parched mouth. After a final look towards the quayside, she headed towards the station hoping to find a café on the way, her eyes stinging slightly from the mist.

'Is there anyone sitting here?' enquired a stranger.

'No,' said Sal, looking up from her seat in the café to see a dark-haired man indicating towards the empty seat on the other side of the small table.

'Mind if I sit here?'

'Not at all,' she said absently, deeply immersed in her own thoughts.

'Very crowded in here isn't it?' he remarked, unloading his tray. 'This is the only seat left. Otherwise I'd have left you in peace.'

'That's quite all right,' she assured him politely. 'I don't mind in the least.'

'The crowds are from the docks,' he mentioned chattily, sitting down with a cup of tea and a bun. 'It's a busy place.'

'It certainly is,' she responded, taking a perfunctory glance around the crowded café which was basic, steamy and infused with the smell of frying.

'I've been to see my ex-fiancée off to Australia to a new life,' he blurted out, having no idea why he was telling her. 'God only knows why I bothered to make the journey since she wasn't in the least bit interested in my being there.'

'Oh dear,' said Sal politely.

'I should have been going with her you see; that was the original plan,' he continued. 'I must be mad to have come here today.'

The similarity of their circumstances aroused Sal's interest almost despite herself. 'If you are then so am I.'

Up went his brows. 'No! Really?' he said.

She nodded. 'My fiancé wanted to go, I didn't. So he said he would go anyway and we split up.'

'Snap.'

'Well at least I'm not the only one.'

'It doesn't hurt any the less for that though, I suppose.'

'Naturally it was very painful when he said he was going without me,' she said. 'But it's quite a while ago now so I've had time to get used to it. Coming here today has brought down the final curtain; so to speak.'

'It's more or less the same for me though I hadn't got round to putting it into those words,' he said. 'I just wanted to see her one last time.'

'What actually happened then?' she asked, noticing what lovely blue eyes he had.

'My fiancé and I were planning a new life abroad together but, in the end, I couldn't go for family reasons. She was furious. She broke off the engagement, cancelled the wedding and went ahead with her plans alone. I was shocked to think she would do that and saw her in a whole new light. At first she thought she could persuade me to change my mind but as soon as she realised she couldn't she gave me the push; said she wasn't going to let me hold her back from a better life abroad.'

Intrigued, Sal asked, 'Did something in particular happen in your family to make you change your mind about going?'

'Yes, my brother had a motorbike accident and was seriously injured,' he replied.

'How awful,' she said with genuine sincerity. 'So you had to stay home to look after him?'

'Oh no, Mum and Dad do that,' he explained. 'I don't even live at home. My mother told me I should carry on with my plans to emigrate. In fact she spent ages trying to persuade me. She's like that. Always wants the best for her boys even if it does break her heart.'

'So why did you pull out then?'

'The accident made me realise how much the family means to me I suppose, and I just couldn't cope with the idea of not seeing them ever again. I live in London and they live in Devon so I don't see them every day but I do go down when I can,' he told her. 'Kate and I were going to Australia with the idea of putting down roots so the chances of my seeing the family again were practically nil and I couldn't bear the thought of that.'

'So you made the sacrifice.'

'Oh no, it wasn't a sacrifice.' He sipped his tea and looked at her over the rim, noticing her clear blue eyes that were lit with interest, which encouraged him to confide in her. 'Looking back, I'm not even sure that I wanted to go that much. It was all Kate's idea. She had great ambitions, and I kind of got swept along with them.

I am quite an adventurous type so if it hadn't been for my brother's accident I probably would have gone and I'm very glad that I didn't because I know I would have regretted it. So let's just say that my priorities were clarified by an unexpected tragedy.'

'You lost her, though, so that could be counted as a sacrifice,' she suggested.

'It was a blow, of course, but an eye-opener too. It was painful to realise that she wanted a new life abroad more than she wanted me. Her attitude to my brother's injuries was a shock too. She didn't give a damn. Just as well I found out what she was really like when I did because with such shallowness on her part, the relationship couldn't have lasted. So, no, I don't class it as a sacrifice at all.'

She was tempted to tell him more about how shocked and traumatised she'd been by Terry's behaviour but decided not to dwell on old wounds. She was more interested in him than herself at the moment, probably because it was a diversion. 'So, how is your brother now?' she asked.

He made a face. 'Not very good. He's out of hospital now and trying my poor parents' patience to the limit, especially my mother. He's having trouble coping with the fact that he can't walk and making their lives hell. I can understand it up to a point. He is only twenty so it must be hard.'

'It wouldn't be easy at any age but I know what you mean.'

'He won't cooperate with the doctors or anyone who

tries to help him. He's supposed to make an effort to get his legs moving and to do special exercises which will help but he won't do anything, not even attend the physiotherapy sessions they organised for him. Nothing! He just sits in his wheelchair all day feeling sorry for himself and having Mum run around after him.'

'Have the medical people said there is a chance he could walk again then?' she enquired.

'They seem to think it might be possible,' he said. 'In cases like his it *is* possible but it will involve a great deal of painful effort on his part and it might not work. The longer he is out of action, the harder it will be because everything will seize up.'

'Is that why he won't try, because it isn't sure to work so he's afraid of having to face the worst?'

'Yeah, I think there is a lot of fear as well as pain involved,' he replied thoughtfully. 'He says he just can't get his legs to move and none of us can possibly imagine what that feels like because we haven't experienced it.'

'Which is true of course,' she said. 'It must be hard for him; the poor thing.'

'Exactly and that's why we try to stay patient with him. But he's doing himself no good by just sitting there complaining all day long. I get upset because I want things to be better for him and I feel so powerless.'

'Did he not do the physiotherapy at all?' she asked.

'He tried it when he first came home from hospital but, because it was painful and there were no immediate results, he stopped going. He's looking for a miracle cure, I think, and there isn't one.'

'I suppose his confidence must have taken a knock.'

He nodded. 'No doubt about that. He sees his mates going out enjoying themselves and it depresses him. That bloody motorbike of his; he always has been a bit of a speed merchant on it. He swears that he only had half a pint of beer that night, though some local gossips are suggesting that he must have been drunk because he was on his way home from a pub. He reckons that someone ran across the road in front of him causing him to swerve to avoid hitting them and he hit the tree instead. But no one has come forward so maybe it was just his imagination or a shadow or something. It happened in an unlit country lane. Anyway, it makes no odds what caused it. The bike is a write-off and my brother seems doomed to spend the rest of his life in a wheelchair. Thankfully no one else was involved. The lane was deserted.'

'These things have a habit of working out, even if he does have to accept the worst,' she said. 'Everything passes and this will too. And at least he's alive. He's young; he'll come through this dark time whichever way it goes.'

'I hope so,' he said. 'I mustn't be so gloomy about it. Sorry to have given you such an ear-bashing. I don't know what's got into me, going on about it to a stranger. It isn't like me to do that.'

'Don't apologise,' she urged him. 'I've enjoyed listening. It's taken my mind off my own troubles.'

'That's something then,' he said. 'So, is there anyone new on your romantic horizon?'

'Absolutely not,' she declared. 'I'm completely off men at the moment.'

'I feel the same about women,' he said with a wry grin. 'No offence meant. You've been brilliant. Thanks for allowing me to let it all out.'

'Likewise. It's because we are strangers we found it easy to confide. Sometimes it's better than talking to friends and loved ones because you know you're never going to see your confidant again so you can really let rip and have a good moan.'

'And I certainly have.' He looked at her enquiringly. 'Can I get you something? Tea . . . coffee?'

'It's nice of you to offer but no thanks,' she said. 'I must be on my way now.'

He shrugged in a good-natured way. 'All right then.'

She got to her feet, gathering her handbag. 'I really hope things work out for your brother,' she said earnestly. 'And for you, too.'

'Thanks,' he said with an uncertain smile. 'I hope the same for you; take care of yourself.'

'Will do. Ta-ta.'

'Cheerio.'

Watching her go, a slim figure in a blue coat, her bright hair falling to her collar, Bob realised how much more cheerful he felt for having talked to her. There was some comfort in knowing that he wasn't the only one who had been jilted for another country. But she was so nice; so interested, especially in his brother; a complete contrast to Kate who had regarded Joe's accident merely as a nuisance and a threat to her plans.

The blue-eyed redhead – he now realised he didn't even know her name – had had a special warmth about her; pretty too, with those lovely eyes and stunning hair. Under other circumstances he might have wanted to know more about her but this wasn't the time. They were just passing strangers and it would be best left that way. He sensed, somehow, that she would agree with him about that.

Sal sat on the train feeling better than she had in ages. The chap in the café had had an uplifting effect on her somehow. She felt less of a freak knowing that she wasn't the only one who had been cast aside by someone who valued ambition more than her. He'd been nice and good-looking in a wholesome sort of a way, with such lovely blue eyes.

It was surprising how you could have such a personal conversation with someone you knew nothing about except their current problem. She didn't know his name or what he did for a living. But that was why it had worked so well. Just a one-off meeting that had been good for them both. No complications, no future; just a brief respite from a sense of rejection that tended to linger despite the confident front she showed to other people.

Oh well, home now to face the inquisition she knew would come. Being part of a family meant that privacy was almost unattainable. Any change in routine had to be accounted for no matter how personal, so she'd had to tell them where she was going this morning when she left home earlier than usual.

★   ★   ★

'I hope he appreciated your going all that way to see him off,' said her mother over their evening meal which was shepherd's pie with carrots and cabbage.

'Yes, I'm sure he did,' fibbed Sal to protect her parents and grandmother. They had all been very upset about the way Terry had treated her. Fiercely defensive of their own and unable to see the situation from any other angle than how it had affected Sal, they had been incensed at the time of the break-up. It was as much as Sal could do to stop them from storming round to his house to tell him to his face what they thought of him. So now there was nothing to be gained by telling them about his somewhat indifferent attitude towards her at Tilbury, and stirring them up again.

'He wasn't worthy of the gesture,' declared her mother.

'He certainly wasn't,' agreed her husband whole-heartedly.

'I would have shoved him over the side if I could have got on the boat,' said Joan.

'I'm sure you would but I didn't go anywhere near the boat,' Sal explained. 'I said goodbye to him in the reception hall in the passenger terminal. Anyway, he's entitled to emigrate if he wants to. It isn't a crime.'

'It is when he's engaged to my daughter,' Joan came back at her sharply.

'Anyway, he's gone now and it's all over,' said Dolly, who could see that the discussion was upsetting Sal. 'Time to forget all about him. Let's talk about something else.'

'Yeah, let's do that,' agreed Ann.

'I still think—' began Joan.

'We know what you think dear,' Horace cut in. 'But there's no point in dwelling on it.'

'There's something far more important for us to discuss than Terry Granger,' said Dolly, looking at Joan and Horace with a twinkle in her eye. 'It's a certain couple's silver wedding coming up in November.' She turned to her granddaughters. 'Your mum and dad will have been married for twenty-five years. Isn't that lovely?'

'Yeah, that's really nice,' agreed Ann.

'Well done,' added Sal. 'Are we going to have a great big knees-up?'

'Certainly not,' replied Joan.

'Oh come on dear,' coaxed Horace, smiling at his wife affectionately, 'we can't let something as important as that pass without a celebration of some sort.'

'You know I don't like parties.'

'Just a small festivity to mark the occasion,' he urged.

'Why not do something with just the two of you if you don't want to make a big thing of it,' suggested Dolly. 'You could go out for dinner at some posh place in the West End.'

Joan looked doubtful. 'If we're going to do something special I'd like the rest of you to be there,' she said.

'Goodho,' said Ann with approval. 'Some posh nosh in the West End would be just the job for me.'

'It's for Mum and Dad, Ann, not us,' Sal reminded her.

'Yeah, I know but since Mum wants us there, we might as well enjoy ourselves.'

'Exactly,' agreed Joan.

'You girls will have to dig deep into your pockets,' their grandmother told them. 'Because you'll have to buy them something made of silver as a gift.'

'There'll be no need for anything like that,' said Joan, who wasn't a materialistic woman.

'Course there will,' disagreed Sal. 'Ann and I will club together and get you something really nice.'

'You must have a new frock, too, Mum, for such a special occasion,' added Ann.

'I don't think so,' began Joan, who rarely spent money on clothes and had no interest in fashion.

'You must, Mum. Ann and I will take you out and help you choose something really special. We'll go to Oxford Street on a Saturday morning,' said Sal excitedly. 'Dad and Gran won't mind looking after the shop, will you?'

'Course we won't,' said Dolly.

'There you are dear,' said Horace affectionately. 'You'll be the belle of the ball.'

'It won't be a ball,' said the down-to-earth Joan, embarrassed by flattery.

'The most glamorous woman in the restaurant then,' he insisted.

Joan looked flushed. 'Oh go on with you,' she said but was clearly enjoying the attention.

'So choose a restaurant you fancy and I'll make all the arrangements,' said her husband.

'There really isn't any need for all this fuss,' she protested mildly. 'But if you insist on going ahead, we'll all decide where we want to go. It will be a joint family decision.'

Sal smiled. After such an emotional day, it was cheering to see her parents looking so happy together. It didn't happen nearly often enough.

'Well this is all very nice,' said Joan as the five of them settled at the table in Simpson's-in-the-Strand.

'Very posh,' observed Ann.

'Yes, it is classy. Your father and I came here once before you two were born,' said Joan. She wore a smart black cocktail dress her daughters had helped her to choose with a silver pendant with a small diamond centre her husband had given her as an anniversary gift. Sal, Ann and Dolly had pooled resources and bought the couple a silver fruit bowl.

'We certainly couldn't afford it after you two arrived,' laughed Horace, nicely turned out in a suit and tie.

'You should go out to nice places more often,' suggested Sal, looking attractive in a cream long-sleeved blouse and black pencil skirt. 'You both work hard. Ann and I are off your hands. You ought to treat yourselves now and again.'

'You know me. I'm not one for nights out,' said Joan. 'Anyway, if you do this sort of thing too often, it loses its specialness and becomes commonplace.'

'I meant only occasionally,' explained Sal. 'As you never go anywhere nice at the moment, now and then would probably be enough.'

'We'll see,' said Joan. 'In the meantime let's concentrate on enjoying this evening.'

It really was splendid here, thought Sal, observing the beautiful wood panelling and chandeliers. The restaurant was very traditional and, according to the leaflet she had picked up on the way in, known the world over for its British cuisine.

Watching the waiters glide by wheeling silver-domed trolleys containing joints of meat to carve at the diners' tables, she remembered something else she had read in the brochure.

'Apparently this place originally opened as a chess club and coffee house in the eighteen hundreds,' she informed the others in a conversational manner. 'They used to wheel the meat to the guests' tables to avoid interrupting the chess games in progress, and they've kept the tradition going ever since.'

'That's interesting and what a nice idea,' said Dolly.

'So let's get some drinks organised,' suggested Horace, 'and you can all study the menu and decide what you're going to have to eat. I shall have the beef. They're famous here for their Scottish beef on the bone.'

The wine began to flow and the meal got underway with the waiter carving the most succulent of meats at the table. Horace made a simple but moving speech after the main course.

'Your mother and I have our ups and downs the same as every other married couple,' he said. 'But we're basically solid and I want to thank her for giving me twenty-five wonderful years.'

'Likewise dear,' said Joan, beaming.

Glasses were chinked and Sal said, 'On behalf of myself and Ann we'd like to thank you for giving us such a sound upbringing and a nice life.'

'Hear hear,' cheered Ann.

'Even if I do make you work in the shop on a Saturday afternoon,' added Joan with a chuckle.

'Yes, even then,' said Sal, thinking how lovely it was to see her parents' affection for each other. It wasn't usually evident; in fact there were often undertones of tension and resentment between them for some reason, so this was a real treat. 'Isn't that right, Ann?'

'Yeah, it is,' agreed her sister, who was flushed and more than a little tipsy.

Her mother was apparently heading that way too because she said, 'Ooh, the wine must have gone to my head.' She hadn't mentioned it to the others because she hadn't wanted to spoil the celebrations but she had been plagued with a crippling headache for the past few days. The wine must have aggravated it because she suddenly felt dreadfully ill. Sick and dizzy and her head was splitting. 'I feel quite light-headed.'

'Here, have some water, Mum,' said Sal, pouring her a glass from the jug.

'Oh dear, I do feel strange. Perhaps I need some air,' she said, rising to her feet.

'I'll go outside with you,' said Horace, getting up and pulling her chair out for her.

But before he had a chance even to take her arm she crumpled and fell to the floor while her husband and daughters looked on in horror.

'The wine must be more potent that we thought,' said Horace worriedly, and went down on to his knees to his wife who was lying on the floor with her eyes closed.

'She isn't used to it, that's probably why she's passed out,' said Sal nervously; there was something utterly terrifying about seeing your mother in an unconscious state.

'My wife has had a funny turn,' Horace explained to the waiter who came over to see what was going on. 'She's fainted and I can't seem to bring her round.'

A hush fell over the restaurant as staff gathered around them. A doctor who happened to be dining there rushed over and offered his assistance. But, despite his very best endeavours, he couldn't bring her round either.

Joan never regained consciousness though she remained in a coma for the best part of twenty-four hours. The result of the post-mortem was a brain haemorrhage; apparently one of those rare things that very occasionally happens out of the blue. She would have known nothing after she passed out so wouldn't have suffered. But, while they were all glad that she died peacefully, it didn't help her poor stricken relatives to come to terms with the tragedy. They were all in deep shock at her untimely demise.

It was Sal's first experience of death at close hand and the suddenness left her reeling. There had been no warning and Mum had only been in her fifties. This bereavement was so traumatic it made any bad thing that had gone before seem incidental. The awful, aching void was so intense she couldn't imagine it ever going away.

Her heart went out to her poor father who was magnificent the way he carried on; being strong for them all as he coped with the ghastly administration of death and arrangements for the funeral.

They closed the shop on the day of the funeral, which was the biggest ordeal of Sal's life. People said she might find the service a comfort but her sorrow was all-consuming. It must have been even worse for her father. But while the mourners wept all around him, Dad stood straight and brave throughout the dreadful interment then hosted the wake at the house with dignity.

'I bet you're glad it's over aren't you, Dad?' said Sal when the last guest had finally left and she and Ann and Gran were clearing up. 'I know I am.'

'Yes, it was something of a trial,' he admitted wearily. 'It's a very sad day.'

'You go and put your feet up and I'll bring you something to drink,' she offered warmly. 'Would you like a cup of tea?'

'I think something stronger would be more appropriate just now,' he said. 'I think there's some whisky we got in for the guests left in the bottle.'

'You sit down and I'll bring it to you.'

'Thank you dear,' he said. 'I might have an early night after that. I'm whacked.'

'That's a very good idea,' agreed Sal. 'You must be absolutely worn out.'

Sal and Ann had been on compassionate leave from work until after the funeral but were both due to go back the next day so were up early. It had been decided that Dad and Gran would run the shop between them but take on a full-time assistant as soon as they could find someone suitable.

'Dad's having a lie-in then,' observed Sal when her father didn't appear for breakfast or by the time she was ready to leave for work. 'He deserves it too. He was exhausted last night.'

'I'll open the shop and manage on my own until he comes down,' said Dolly. 'The customers will just have to wait that bit longer to get served on their way to work. It's mostly cigarettes and tobacco early on. At least that doesn't have to be weighed so you can get the queue moving quicker.'

'I'll call in and see him before I go,' said Sal, heading for the stairs. 'Just to say cheerio. I won't wake him if he's still asleep.'

'Tell him I'll manage in the shop until he comes down so there's no need for him to rush,' said Dolly.

'Will do.'

A few minutes later Sal came down the stairs a lot quicker than she'd gone up. 'Dad isn't there,' she said in a tone of disbelief.

'He must be in the shop then, filling up the shelves or something,' suggested Dolly.

'No, Gran, he won't be in the shop,' Sal told her gravely. 'He's gone. Some of his drawers have been left open and are empty, and there aren't many of his clothes left in the wardrobe either. He must have packed a suitcase and gone while we were all in bed.'

'No,' gasped Dolly, who adored her only son. 'That can't possibly be right.'

Sal went over to her grandmother, who looked pale and unsteady. 'Sorry, Gran, to have thrown that at you,' she said, taking her arm supportively. 'It was such a shock I just came out with it. But I think it will be best if you come upstairs with me and see for yourself. Mum and Dad's bedroom, well just Dad's bedroom now, of course, has been abandoned.'

'Oh, my Lord, whatever next,' said Ann, holding her head.

Together the three women went up the stairs.

'Why would he go off like that, I wonder,' asked Sal that evening when she and her sister and grandmother were sitting by the fire in the living room trying to make sense of her father's disappearance. Ann had been to work but Sal had stayed home to help Dolly in the shop. 'He's gone without a word, leaving the business as well as his family.'

'He's gone because he wants to get away from us of course,' declared Ann who had always been closer to her father than her mother and was desperately hurt by his action. 'What other reason could there be?'

'I'm sure it isn't quite as simple as that, dear,' said her grandmother. 'Anyway, he wouldn't want to get away from us; we're all he's got now that Joan has gone.'

'We've just lost our mother and our father walks out on us when we need him most,' Ann went on miserably. 'That doesn't seem like the actions of a man who gives a damn about his family to me. The selfish sod. I hate him.'

'Something must have made him decide to leave so suddenly,' said Dolly.

'He's probably got another woman if the truth be known,' decided Ann, angry and sad and wanting to hit out. 'That's why men usually leave home, isn't it?'

'Not Dad,' Sal disagreed ardently. 'He isn't the type. Anyway he never went anywhere without Mum so how would he have met anyone else?'

'He used to go down the pub sometimes on his own and there were those Chamber of Commerce meetings. They were probably just a cover for what he was really up to. Mum was very cold towards him at times if you remember.'

'Now you're just being ridiculous,' admonished her sister. 'Never in a million years would Dad do something like that.'

'Where is he then?' asked Ann, close to tears. 'You just tell me that.'

'You know that I can't.'

'His place is here with us and he buggers off and leaves us! That's a terrible thing to do.'

'We *are* both adults, Ann,' Sal reminded her. 'It isn't as though we're little kids who can't look after ourselves.'

'Even so, he should be here,' Ann insisted. 'Well, he can stay away for all I care, the unfeeling pig.'

'Shut up Ann. You'll upset Gran. He is her son as well as our dad, remember.'

'Sorry, Gran,' she said thickly, 'and I know you must be upset too but I just don't know how he could do something like this. There is no excuse, *no excuse at all*.'

'I know you are hurting dear,' said Dolly. 'We all are.'

'He'll be back,' said Sal.

'Of course he will,' added Dolly.

'Oh yeah, and that's why he's taken his clothes, is it?' said Ann. 'Because he intends coming back.' She was thoughtful for a moment. 'No wonder he was so chirpy at the funeral. He knew he was going. Probably had some tart waiting for him.'

'Now you are going too far,' snapped Sal. 'I won't have you talking like that about Dad. He adored our mother and you know that as well as I do.'

'We thought he loved us but he obviously doesn't,' Ann insisted. 'We thought we knew him but we didn't know him at all. While we've all been falling apart since Mum died, he's been quite cheerful. He's probably even glad she's dead.'

'That's a terrible thing to say,' Sal told her, her voice rising. 'He was being strong for our sakes. It was all an act to hide his broken heart.'

'I'm not so sure.'

'Take it all back,' ordered Sal.

'Only the bit about him being glad . . .'

'All of it . . .'

'Girls, girls,' Dolly intervened. 'We are all upset and shocked by your father's disappearance and I know, Ann, that you are only saying these awful things because you're hurt. But he's taken his clothes so he obviously doesn't intend to come back, for the time being anyway, so we have to work out what to do about the shop.'

'We shall have to close up or sell it or something,' said

Ann dismissively. 'Since you can't run it on your own, can you, Gran?'

'With the best will in the world, no I can't,' she agreed. 'It's too big a job for one person.'

'I think we owe it to Mum to keep it going,' said Sal, making a sudden decision. 'That's one thing we can do to keep her memory alive. She and Dad loved the shop.'

'Do we get staff in to help Gran then?' asked Ann.

'No, we run the business between us,' announced Sal in a moment of unexpected inspiration. 'The three of us working together until Dad comes back.'

'There's just one flaw to that plan,' Ann pointed out to her sister. 'You and I both have full-time jobs.'

'Then let's give them up and work in the shop,' Sal's enthusiasm was rising. 'It's a family business so let's keep it that way. It gave Mum and Dad a decent living and Gran too part-time, so it will do the same for us. There will be things to sort out as regards the bank account and so on but once we explain the circumstances it shouldn't be a problem.'

'I already have authority to write cheques,' Dolly told them. 'Your dad arranged that for your mum and me just in case we ever needed to pay a shop bill if he was out for any reason.'

'So, I say that The Toffee Shop carries on under new management but still stays in the family,' said Sal.

'I'm not at all sure that I want to give up my job,' Ann mentioned uncertainly.

'You're always saying that the work is dead boring,' Sal reminded her.

'Yeah, well, everybody says that about work, don't they? And yes the actual work is tedious, but the girls are nice and we do usually have a laugh at some point in the day. Standing behind a counter in the family shop will be even more boring than what I do now.'

'Not if we are involved in the business,' said Sal. 'It won't be the same as when we stand in on a Saturday afternoon. There'll be other things to do as well.'

'Such as?' Ann wanted to know.

'There will be all the paperwork to do and the ordering and we could try and build the business up with new lines. We'll have a personal interest so we'll feel entirely differently about it; we'll want the shop to do well.'

'Mm, I suppose you might be right.'

'You can still see your workmates in the evenings and Sundays,' said Sal. 'Just think. No fares; lunches at home and no travelling time. More time in bed in the mornings.'

'Who would take responsibility?' asked Ann. 'Someone will have to be in charge.'

'You if you like.'

'No thanks,' she said without hesitation. 'I don't want something like that to worry about.'

'You, Gran?' asked Sal.

'I'd rather not at my age, dear,' said Dolly.

'Looks like the job is going to fall to me then,' said Sal. 'So are you in or out, Ann?'

Her sister still seemed uncertain. 'Er . . . I'll have to give a week's notice . . . but yeah, I think I'm in.'

'Good. Well, there'll be a lot of sorting out to do and

I shall have to give a week's notice too but they might let me off that for compassionate reasons.'

'I know which wholesalers your mum and dad dealt with and other things that might be useful,' said Dolly, her interest rising.

'Well done, Gran. From now on the three of us will be a team,' announced Sal. 'When Dad does come back, he'll find a thriving family business.'

'And if you believe he'll be back you'll believe anything,' snorted Ann with contempt.

Sal and her grandmother exchanged glances. They both knew that Ann's words weren't meant. For a few minutes the pain of recent events had lessened as they had been distracted by plans for the business. But nothing had changed. Mum had died and Dad had left. That was the awful reality of the situation.

Chapter Four

'Brass monkeys' was the way The Toffee Shop customers would describe the weather, pavements patched with ice, privets white with frost, people out in extra layers of clothing with scarves and hats in abundance. But the Storey kitchen was warm and fragrant with toffee in the making one Sunday afternoon during the cold snap of February 1958, its occupants oblivious to the elements outside. Sal was busy studying her grandmother's technique as she created her mouth-watering item of confectionery. Now that Sal was running the business she had deemed it wise to be au fait with every aspect so that she could step into any task if the need ever arose.

'You stir the butter, sugar, water and syrup over a medium heat stirring constantly to melt the butter and dissolve the sugar,' said Dolly, also explaining that she was wiping the sides of the pan with a wet pastry brush to avoid crystallisation.

'Do you bring it to the boil?' asked Sal.

'Yes, then test it with a thermometer until it reaches

exactly the right temperature,' Dolly explained. 'This batch is going to be our original creamy toffee but the next lot we'll dip in dark melted chocolate and then do some with almonds.' She continued to stir, eventually lifting the large saucepan over to the kitchen table where she began pouring the contents into flat square tins already prepared with greaseproof paper. She spread the toffee with a spoon to create a smooth, even surface. 'We'll let that set a little then you can score it into small squares with a greased knife.'

'It smells delicious, Gran,' said Sal. 'Can I have a bit when it's ready please?'

'I don't suppose I'll be able to stop you, will I?' She grinned. 'I never have before. You and your sister have been helping yourself to a first piece of a fresh batch since you were nippers. You always used to hang around the kitchen when toffee was being made.'

'I remember how much we used to love it,' said Sal, smiling at the memory. 'We missed it during the rationing when you had to stop making it because you couldn't get the ingredients.'

'Yeah, those were tough times for us all,' Dolly sighed. 'But they are well behind us now, thank Gawd. Prime Minister Macmillan says that some of us have never had it so good and I agree with him. I can remember the really bad old days, you see; the terrible depression of the nineteen thirties. Of course then came the war and the long austerity years after.'

'The good times have been a long time coming but let's hope they're here to stay,' said Sal.

'Not half.' Dolly wiped her brow with the back of her hand. 'I'm glad you're learning how to make the toffee, Sal. It would be a comfort to me if I were ill at any time, knowing you'd be able to stand in for me temporarily. Your mum learned for the same reason. Waste of her time as it happened . . .'

Her words tailed off and they both fell silent. It was three months since Joan's death and there were still frequent moments like this, when sadness and breath-taking disbelief suddenly engulfed them and they needed a few moments to compose themselves.

'It makes sense for someone else to be able to step into the breach.' Sal knew better than to suggest that she take over the job permanently if Gran found it too much at any time because Dolly's toffee was her pride and joy and nothing short of incapacity or death would prevent her from making it herself. 'Our home-made toffee is what makes us stand out from other confectioners.'

'It is indeed,' Dolly said proudly, casting her eye over the filled tins. 'There, that should keep the customers happy, for a little while at least.'

'Are you going to do the chocolate toffee straight away?' Sal enquired.

'We'll have a break with a cup of tea first, shall we?' Dolly suggested.

'I'll make it and get these pans washed while the kettle boils,' offered Sal. 'You sit down and take the weight off your feet for a while.'

'Thanks luv.' Dolly sat down at the table with a sigh. 'You're a good girl.'

'I'm only washing a few pans and making the tea, Gran,' was Sal's reaction to her grandmother's praise, which she considered to be unnecessary. 'It's the least I can do after all your efforts.'

Watching her granddaughter working at the sink, slim and nimble and full of life, Dolly said, 'You've done ever so well these past few months and I'm very proud of you.'

'Really,' said Sal in surprise, 'and why is that?'

'Because you've taken over the business with such a willing heart and you're making a good job of it.'

'Well, thanks, Gran,' she responded. 'But there are three of us working here remember. You and Ann as well as me; we make a good team.'

'But you're the energy and the brains behind it. You're the one with the really keen interest. I like to be involved in the shop but not to the same extent as you are. I love you and your sister equally but as far as the business is concerned you are the star and Ann would agree with me about that if she was here. She does her fair share but she does just work here and she would be the first to admit it because she doesn't want more than that from it. Take this afternoon for instance, you are here with me learning how to make toffee and she is out at the pictures with her friends.'

'There's nothing wrong with that, Gran.' Sal was quick to defend. 'She's entitled to have Sundays off.'

'I know that and I am not criticising her in the least; I wouldn't do that behind her back,' Dolly made clear. 'I'm just saying that you are eager to know every aspect of the business, whereas Ann isn't bothered and she has been honest about that from the start.'

'Learning how to make toffee isn't a chore for me,' said Sal. 'It's a pleasure.'

'I can tell that,' said Dolly. 'You've taken over the management of the shop as though born to it and the place is a credit to you.'

'I enjoy the work, that's probably why.' She poured boiling water into the teapot and swilled it around. 'I think maybe I'm using it as a crutch to take my mind off other things. You know, first I lost Terry then Mum died and Dad left so it's all been very distressing. But, for whatever reason, I am happy in my work and it's the last thing I expected when I suggested that we take the shop on. It feels entirely different to those Saturday afternoons when Ann and I used to cover for Mum and Dad. I didn't have any interest then. It's strange how it's worked out because I only wanted us to keep the shop going as a gesture to Mum but in doing so I found a job I enjoy heaps more than working in an office. It isn't just a job, though, is it? It's a way of life. I think I must have inherited some of Mum and Dad's entrepreneurial spirit. I really do want to make the shop a success.

'And you are doing.'

Looking back over the past three months Sal could see that running the shop had been therapeutic for her. It didn't change anything, of course, but when she saw the place nicely stocked, smart and polished, she felt enormously proud. Customer relations came naturally to her. There were a few who thought themselves superior to anyone her side of the counter, especially now that things were plentiful again, but there weren't many of those; not around here. And when the takings were healthy at the end of the week it gave her satisfaction, something she had never experienced in her office job.

Sal and Ann worked full time in the business; Gran, from choice, looked after the housekeeping and did part-time hours in the shop as well as making the toffee. She was always willing to do a few extra hours if they needed her.

As products of a secondary modern school, career aspirations had been non-existent for Sal and her sister and a job merely a bridge between school and mother-hood with marriage in between, it was hoped. But now Sal felt as though she had a career of sorts and wouldn't want to do any other kind of work. It was a pity such tragic circumstances had given her this opportunity. Of course, when her father came back, as she was still sure that he would some day, he would probably want to resume his position but she would cross that bridge when she came to it.

They had heard nothing from her father and still had no idea where he might have gone, if he was well, or even alive. She and her grandmother still had faith in his return but Ann disagreed entirely and said she wanted nothing to do with him if he ever did turn up. She was enraged every time his name was mentioned. They kept his room clean but it wasn't used; the idea of one of the girls moving in to save sharing a bedroom would be tantamount to giving up hope so remained tacit.

'Here you are, Gran,' said Sal now, putting a cup of tea on the table in front of Dolly then one for herself and a plate of biscuits.

'Thanks dear.'

Sitting here in the cosy kitchen sipping tea and nibbling a ginger nut, Sal realised that she was actually enjoying the taste; probably the first time she had actually noticed the flavour of anything since her mother's death. So it was true what they said: life really did go on despite the most unbearable tragedies.

There was a queue in the butcher's on Saturday morning when Dolly went to get the weekend meat.

'Morning Dolly,' said the middle-aged woman in front of her who was local as were most of the regular shoppers in Perry Parade. Passing trade had never been a significant part of the turnover here but was beginning to increase with the growing number of cars on the road.

'Morning Ada,' responded Dolly.

'How are you now, dear?' asked the woman in a manner to suggest that Dolly was seriously ailing.

'As fit as I'll ever be, thanks,' she replied brightly, her guard up because she knew what the other woman was hinting at. Dolly had become accustomed to sudden silences when she entered a shop and knew that gossip about Horace's disappearance was rife. 'How about you?'

'I get me aches and pains like everyone else but I don't complain,' she replied sanctimoniously. 'Not much point is there, since no one listens?'

'I'm sure they would if there was anything seriously wrong with you,' suggested Dolly.

'Yeah, I expect so,' said Ada, keen to move the conversation on to a juicier topic. 'Any news from that son of yours yet?'

Dolly frowned at her. 'That's my business,' she said sharply.

'All right, keep your hair on,' Ada retorted. 'I was only asking. There's no need to be nasty. It isn't like you, Dolly.'

A hush had come over the shop and Dolly knew that all the women were listening.

'She's got a lot on her mind,' said one of them. 'It's bound to take its toll.'

'Shame,' said another sympathetically. 'It must be such a worry for you, Dolly, dear.'

'Disgraceful more like,' added Ada forcefully. 'Going off and leaving you and the girls at a time like that. It's downright disgusting. We are all behind you, Dolly. If there's anything we can do you only have to ask.'

'There is something as a matter of fact,' Dolly told her.

'Anything at all,' offered Ada, 'just tell us what it is.'

'You can stop your spiteful gossip about my son,' she said in a firm tone. 'I know you are all saying that he has left his family and gone off with another woman, well he hasn't, so put a sock in it.'

'We're just concerned because you're a neighbour and well thought of round here,' Ada said, adopting a self-righteous air. 'We know how close you and Horace were.'

'Well, show your solidarity and stop making up stories

that have no truth in them,' Dolly snapped. 'When he comes back I'll let you know; until then I'd appreciate some silence on the subject.'

'Oo-er,' said one of the women.

'We didn't mean to upset you, Dolly,' said Ada.

'I'm not upset,' Dolly said, 'just very angry. And if I catch you gossiping about my family again, then you'll see what I'm like when I really am upset.'

'Sorry luv,' said someone and there was a murmur of agreement.

'Anyone seen the new Doris Day film?' asked one of the women in an effort to ease the uncomfortable atmosphere,

There were murmurs in the negative.

'Then get yourselves down to the Odeon,' said the filmgoer. 'It's a real treat.'

The queue moved along and the conversation was all about the film. Dolly was a sensible woman; she knew that in a close-knit community like this one gossip was inevitable. Similarly there was always plenty of help on offer in times of trouble.

But wild speculation about her son she couldn't take and her spirits were low as she finished her business in the butcher's and made her way back to The Toffee Shop just a few doors down. The truth was that she missed Horace and worried about him constantly. The fact that he was middle-aged didn't diminish her maternal feelings. He was still her boy and she knew instinctively that there was no other woman involved in his disappearance. She was also certain that there must be a very good reason for him to take off as he had. But what was it and where the hell was he?

'What's the matter, Gran?' asked Sal when Dolly came back into the shop. 'You look a bit down in the dumps.'

'Nothing to worry about, dear. Just people gossiping,' she replied.

'About Dad?'

She nodded.

'Who was it?' asked Sal, immediately defensive of her grandmother. 'I'll go and tell them where to get off. I'm not having you upset. Blinkin' cheek.'

'Calm down, Sal,' urged Dolly. 'There's no need for you to do anything at all. I've told them what I think about their gossip in no uncertain terms so they'll be careful what they say when I'm around in future. But I don't like to be on bad terms with my neighbours.'

'And you won't be,' Sal assured her. 'They've all known you a long time and think a lot of you. They understand that you will react to talk about Dad. It will blow over.'

'They'll still gossip no matter how long they've known you,' put in Ann. 'It's only human nature. And they've got a nice spicy topic to chew over. Ooh I could kill that man for doing this to you, to us. Selfish bugger.'

'Don't start, Ann,' warned Sal. 'You'll upset Gran even more than she is already.'

'I'm not the one who walked out,' said Ann heatedly. 'It isn't me who's upset her.'

A flurry of customers brought the conversation to an

abrupt halt. Dolly went through to the house with the shopping and the sisters got busy serving and exchanging the usual casual dialogue with the customers that was part and parcel of the job. Something one of the women mentioned gave Sal an idea of a way to cheer her grandmother up.

'Do you fancy coming to the pictures with me tonight, Gran?' asked Sal as the three of them sat at the kitchen table eating beans on toast for lunch. 'The new Doris Day film is on locally and I know how much you love her films.'

Dolly looked at her in a questioning manner. 'You wouldn't want to go out with an old woman on a Saturday night, surely.'

'Yes I would, I'm a great Doris Day fan too.'

'She's got nothing better to do, Gran,' chipped in Ann, teasing her sister. 'She'll only be staying in reading her books if she doesn't go out with you. She's getting to the stage where *Sunday Night at the London Palladium* is the highlight of her week.'

'What's wrong with that?' questioned Dolly. 'It's a very popular television show.'

'It shouldn't be the biggest thing in your life when you're twenty-two, though,' Ann said with a wry grin.

'And it isn't so don't be so saucy,' riposted Sal.

'Well, if you do really want me to come, I'd love to,' said Dolly.

'Do you fancy joining us, Ann?' asked Sal.

'On a Saturday night? Not bloomin' likely.'

'No surprise there then,' said Sal amiably. 'I suppose you're going out dancing?'

Ann looked odd, even a little mysterious. 'Yeah, that's right,' she said.

'Ann,' began her sister with a questioning look. 'What are you up to?'

'Why would I be up to anything?' she asked innocently.

'I don't know why but I recognise that look in your eye,' Sal told her lightly. 'I don't think you're being quite honest with us.'

Ann laughed. 'Why would I lie?'

'No idea,' said Sal with a half-smile. 'But I have a funny feeling that you are.'

Ann shrugged. 'You'll just have to wonder about it then, won't you?' she said. 'Because I'm saying nothing.'

'Come on, spill the beans,' urged Sal.

'I'm going dancing,' she insisted.

'She says she's going dancing and that's all we need to know,' Dolly chipped in. 'So stop badgering her, Sal.'

'Thanks Gran,' said Ann. 'Sorry if I upset you this morning.'

'You're forgiven,' said Dolly at which point Ann went round to her and gave her a hug.

'While you're in a good mood, Ann, do you mind if I take half an hour off this afternoon and leave you holding the fort while it isn't busy in the shop?' asked Sal. 'I want to go to the library. There's a book I particularly want that someone has told me about.'

'Yeah, as long as you're not gone all afternoon.'

'Like you are when you go off to buy shoes,' said Sal with a meaningful grin. 'As if I would.'

'Do you have a copy of *Room at the Top* by John Braine please?' Sal asked the librarian at Hammersmith Library. 'I can't see one on the shelves.'

'All our copies of that title go out as soon as they come in,' said the librarian, a pleasant woman of about thirty with her hair taken back off her face. 'And when you've read it you will understand why. I couldn't put it down.'

'I can't wait to read it,' Sal enthused. 'So will you add me to the waiting list please?'

The librarian thought for a moment. 'They might have a copy at Fulham Library or one of our other local branches. I can give them a ring if you like.'

'That would be lovely,' said Sal. 'Thank you.'

The woman made the call and came off the phone smiling. 'They have just had a copy brought back at Fulham. If you can get over there quickly they'll keep it for you.'

'Thanks very much,' said Sal, 'I'll go straight away. It's only a few minutes on the bus.'

'This is wonderful,' said Sal when the Fulham librarian handed her the much-wanted title. 'I almost wish I wasn't going out tonight so I could start on it. Still, I can read it in bed.'

'I'm sure you'll enjoy it,' said the woman and turned her attention to a man who was waiting to be served.

'Ooh, you've got some interesting reading there,' she said to him as she stamped his non-fiction books. 'Obviously a man with a passion for the history of London.'

'I wouldn't go so far as to say it's a passion exactly,' he said, 'but it is a particular interest of mine.'

Something about the tone of his voice, the deep gravel London tang mixed with a hint of West Country, made Sal turn round.

'Hello there,' she said, recognising him as the man she had chatted to in the café at Tilbury Docks.

Recognition dawned instantly and he beamed at her. 'The redhead from Tilbury. You've managed to survive then, despite your broken heart.'

She nodded. 'You too.'

'Quiet please,' came a voice from somewhere within the library.

Sal and the man made their way to the exit and continued their conversation outside. 'How is your brother now?' she enquired with interest.

Bob frowned. 'About the same, thanks for asking,' he said. 'Fancy you remembering that.'

'I don't suppose I'll forget anything that happened that day, as it was such an emotional occasion.'

'Me neither.'

'Your brother's condition hasn't improved then.'

'It hadn't when I was last at home,' he told her. 'When I speak to Mum on the phone she tries to make me believe that everything is fine and dandy but I know it isn't. I'll be going down there soon to see for myself.'

'I'm sorry there isn't better news.'

'Me too but it's just one of those things.' He gave her an enquiring look. 'Anyway, what about you? Has your broken heart mended yet?'

'So much has happened I haven't had much time to think about it,' she said and went on to tell him about her family problems and her new role at the shop.

'Blimey,' was his stunned reaction. 'You have been having a dramatic time. It's a wonder you're not on your knees.'

'If anything it's made me stronger I think,' she told him. 'Losing Mum and Dad leaving certainly put Terry's departure from my life into perspective.'

'You look well anyway.'

'Thank you,' she said. 'Everything that's happened has made me realise that I'm a survivor.'

'I think I might be one of those too,' he said. 'Do you live round here?'

'Hammersmith. You?'

'Fulham.'

'So this is your local library then,' she said.

He nodded.

'I'm just an interloper from Hammersmith, nabbing one of your titles,' she said, showing him the book.

'Fiction?'

'Yeah, it's about a young working-class man who marries for money and social position but falls in love with an older woman. It's quite emotional and . . . er, sexy apparently.'

He laughed. 'I'd better get hold of a copy sharpish then, hadn't I.'

'You're more interested in non-fiction by the look of it,' she said, glancing at the books he was carrying.

'Yeah, London history mostly. I'm fascinated by the place,' he informed her. 'I'm a taxi driver and it's handy being able to point out the sights and tell people something about them if they seem interested.'

'A history lesson while you ride eh,' she joked. 'A captive audience.'

'I hope not,' he said. 'People would avoid my cab like the plague if that was what it was like.'

'Do you go to classes to help increase your knowledge?' she enquired with interest.

'Oh no,' he replied in a definite tone. 'I finished with the classroom the day I left school.'

'As you have a particular interest you might enjoy a class now that you are an adult and would be doing it from choice,' she suggested.

'Nah.'

'Oh well,' said Sal, deciding to leave it at that. 'I only ever go in a taxi for very special occasions but I know they are in demand in central London so you wouldn't have a lack of customers whatever you talked about.'

'Things are better for most people nowadays; they have money in their pockets to spend on enjoyment – theatres and so on, so there's usually plenty of business about in the West End for us cabbies. Plenty of competition too, though.'

'I'm sure,' she said, hugging herself against the cold. 'But I'd better be off. My sister is holding the fort in the shop on her own.'

'Nice to see you again.'

'You too. Cheerio.'

'Ta-ta.'

Watching her swing off down the street then break into a run and jump on the bus, he realised that he was smiling because it had been such a pleasant interlude. He also realised that he still didn't even know her name. 'You're slipping there, mate,' he told himself then turned and walked back towards home.

'At last,' said Ann disapprovingly when Sal rushed into the shop. 'Nice of you to come back at all.'

'I'm ever so sorry Ann. I got held up,' explained Sal. 'Have you been busy?'

'In patches, yes . . . very,' she replied. 'Where the hell have you been? It isn't like you to be late back.'

'I went to Fulham Library to get a book I particularly wanted,' Sal explained. 'Then I met someone and got talking.'

'Who did you get talking to?'

'Just someone who was taking some books out on loan.'

'Why are you being so mysterious?'

'I'm not. I can't tell you who he is because I don't even know his name.'

'Oh so it's a he is it?' Ann said, giving her sister a studious look. 'Tell me more.'

'There's nothing to say and if there was I wouldn't tell you,' she said, laughing. 'You're not the only one around here who can be secretive, you know.'

The shop bell rang as the door opened heralding a group of children who came in and clustered around the sweet counter all talking at once.

'You take a break, Ann, I'll see to this,' said Sal to her sister.

'Two ounces of aniseed balls please,' said a boy of about ten. 'No, make that two ounces of pear drops.'

'Are you sure that's what you want?' she asked. 'No changing your mind when I've weighed and bagged them.'

'I'm sure,' he replied.

Sal got busy with the scales as the other children lined up with their money. She was thinking of the man she'd met in the library and how nice he was. In another life she might have harboured romantic notions about someone as good-looking as he was. That would have been at a time when she had considered a boyfriend and marriage as essential for a girl like her. She still wanted those things at some point but the urgency had gone out of it, thank goodness. It would have been nice to know his name though . . .

'Did you enjoy the film, Gran?' asked Sal as she and her grandmother made their way out of the cinema with the rest of the crowds, having seen *The Pajama Game*.

'Not half,' she said. 'Did you?'

'I absolutely loved it.'

'You can't beat a Doris Day film to give you a lift.'

'She's so gorgeous,' sighed Sal. 'That lovely fresh complexion and blond hair. She looks good in anything whether it be factory worker's clothes or pyjamas. I wish I looked like her.'

'Film stars have special cosmetics to make them look like that,' said Dolly.

'She's probably beautiful anyway so the make-up artists have a good base to work on; and so talented with that great singing voice and good acting.'

'She is a very good all rounder,' agreed Dolly. 'But don't you go hankering after looking like film stars. You're far too sensible for that sort of carry-on.'

'Maybe I am but we all admire film stars, Gran, even you,' Sal pointed out.

'I suppose so,' she admitted. 'Anyway, shall we stop off and get some chips to eat when we get home?'

'Good idea,' enthused Sal, linking arms with her grandmother as they left the crowds and walked through the less busy back streets. 'That would finish the evening off perfectly.'

'Shall we get some for Ann?'

'I don't think it will be worth it because she probably won't come rolling home until the early hours,' said Sal. 'As she's out with her secret boyfriend.'

'She's gone dancing,' Dolly reminded her.

'And if you believe that you'll believe anything,' said Sal with a wicked giggle.

Sal was in bed immersed in her new library book when Ann came in and immediately started to peel off her clothes.

'How was Doris Day?' she asked, undoing her suspenders,

rolling her stockings down and sitting on the edge of the bed to take them off, careful not to ladder them,

'As lovely as ever' Sal replied. 'It was a really good film. How was your night?'

'I had a smashing time thanks,' Ann said, seeming happy but quieter than usual.

'That's good.' Pretending to go along with the suspected subterfuge Sal added, 'Did you dance every dance then?'

'Something like that,' she replied and Sal couldn't help noticing that there was a new glow about her.

'So do I get to hear about it?' asked Sal because her sister was usually the most garrulous of people after she'd been out enjoying herself. There was no stopping her as a rule.

'I'll make a deal with you, kid,' she said with a grin. 'I won't complain about you having the light on to read your book when I'm trying to get to sleep, if you don't ask me any more questions about tonight.'

As they had a regular battle about the light being on most nights and Sal was engrossed in her book anyway, she said. 'All right, it's a deal.'

'Good,' said Ann, slipping into her nightdress and heading for the bathroom.

Sal returned to her book but she couldn't help but be puzzled because it wasn't like Ann to be cagey. Oh well, if there's anything to tell she'll let me know about it in her own good time, she thought, she's entitled to her privacy. Sal took out her bookmark and concentrated on the riveting story she was reading.

Chapter Five

It was a tribute to the human spirit, thought Bob, that his mother could behave as though everything was perfectly normal in the Beck household when nothing could be further from the truth.

'Your father has been up to no good again, Bob,' said Mavis in the tone of jovial disapproval she only ever used with regard to her husband.

'What have you done this time, Dad?' asked Bob, who was staying for a couple of days; they were gathered, as usual, in the kitchen.

'Nothin'. Well, nothin' that isn't above board anyway.'

'He brought home a washer with an electric wringer,' she announced.

'Well . . . that's a good thing isn't it, Mum?' said Bob. 'It must make life easier for you.'

'If he got it so cheap with no receipt, who did he buy it from, that's what I want to know?' she said. 'It'll have dropped off the back of a lorry, you mark my words.'

'That's all the thanks I get,' said Stan, looking peeved.

'I bring 'ome a lovely machine to take the drudgery out of washday for her and all I get is accusations. Most women would have been tickled pink. But not Mavis. Oh no, she has to throw it back in my face.'

'Aren't you even using it, Mum?' asked Bob.

'Course I'm using it,' she told him. 'No point in having it as an ornament, is there?'

'If you feel so strongly about it why don't you make him take it back?'

'I asked him to and he wouldn't,' she replied, 'so sooner than have it stuck there doing nothing, I started using it.'

'And is it good?'

'Nothin' short of a miracle. It's got paddles inside that wash the clothes without any help from me. Clean as a whistle and the electric wringer is a dream.'

'Isn't it a bit hypocritical to be enjoying it if you're suspicious about its origins?'

''Appen it is,' she admitted. 'But I'm not perfect.'

'So why not just be glad of it and not worry where it came from,' suggested Bob.

''Cos I'm afraid a copper is going to come knocking on the door to accuse your father of receiving stolen goods, that's why,' she explained.

'How many more times must I tell you woman, I bought it off a bloke I was doin' some work for. His missus is having a new one, an expensive contraption with some newfangled kind of spin-dryer attached to it, twin-tub I think they call it, so he was letting this one go for next to nothing.'

'If it's second-hand there's no problem, Mum,' Bob assured her.

'Looks new to me,' she said.

'It's been well looked after, that's why,' Stan insisted crossly. 'But I'm sure if you were to take a closer look you'd find the odd scratch or two which would prove I'm telling the truth if you can't take my word for it.'

'All right you two,' said Bob. 'That's enough. I've come to enjoy your company, not to listen to you scrapping.'

This banter would have been perfectly normal in the Beck house were it not for the fact that there was another person present in the room, Bob's brother Joe, who barely uttered so much as a syllable these days. He just sat in his wheelchair all day in moody silence.

'Sorry Bob,' Mavis apologised. 'You've come all this way to see us, so stop your arguing, Stan, and let the boy drink his tea in peace.'

Bob's hands flew to his head in despair. 'You're still getting at him, Mum. Stop it, both of you. I know this is the usual way you carry on but give it a rest for once, will you.' Turning to his brother, he added, 'How do you put up with them?'

He shrugged. 'I've got no choice.'

'Mm, there is that.' It saddened and angered Bob in equal measures to see Joe in this sorry state, sullen and resentful, pale-skinned, his hair almost down to his shoulders because he wouldn't go to the barber's. He refused go out anywhere apparently. 'But maybe if you could do some of the physiotherapy it might help. I've heard it can be very good.'

'That is why you're here, is it?' he snapped, his eyes blazing. 'To try to bully me into somethin' I'm not gonna do no matter how much you all go on at me. You've come to try and sort me out, I suppose.'

'Of course not,' fibbed Bob, who had been worried about the situation at home, having heard about it from his distressed mother on the phone. 'I come home every so often as a matter of course, you know that.'

'Well you can save the lectures 'cause I'm not listening,' he said. 'So leave me alone.'

'All right mate,' agreed Bob. 'I'll change the subject. How are you enjoying the television I brought for you the last time I was here?'

'He loves that,' Mavis answered for him. 'It gives him a lot of pleasure, that do.'

'I've lost the use of my legs, Mum, not the power of speech, and I can speak for myself,' Joe objected.

'Don't be rude to Mum, Joe, just because you've got the hump.'

'She's always bossing me about.'

'Of course she is. It's what mothers do. She's looking after you,' said Bob. 'Somebody has to.'

'And I have to be grateful do I?'

'It wouldn't be a bad idea. You could certainly be a bit more civil to her.'

'You try sitting in this wheelchair and having your mother helping you all day long,' Joe said.

'I know it's rotten for you,' said Bob more sympathetically. 'But I don't suppose she likes it any more than you do.'

'I don't mind,' Mavis was quick to assure him. 'He's my son so of course I'm happy to look after him.'

'I suppose now you're gonna tell me that the accident was my own fault because I was drunk,' Joe said to Bob aggressively. 'Come on, let's get it over with.'

'I wasn't going to say anything of the sort,' denied Bob.

'Well I wasn't drunk,' he insisted. 'I didn't have more than half a pint that night. As I keep telling you all, the accident happened because I swerved to avoid someone who ran across the lane. I know no one believes me but it's the last thing I remember before I blacked out and I'm not imagining it.'

'No one is suggesting that you are,' Bob assured him. 'Everyone just wants you to get better. There's no point in going over and over the cause of the accident. It won't change anything.'

'I'm not gonna get better so get used to it. I've injured my spine and you don't come back from that.'

'I don't remember you qualifying as a doctor,' said Bob.

'Don't be sarky,' said Joe sulkily. 'I'm the one with the injury. I know what it feels like.'

'The medical team at the hospital seem to think it might be possible for you to regain the use of your legs and they don't usually give people false hope.'

'"Might be possible,"' he said with emphasis. 'Do you think if that was true I'd still be sitting in this stinking chair? I've tried and it just doesn't work.'

'These things take quite a bit of time, I should imagine,' replied Bob.

'Leave him be,' put in Mavis, mostly to protect her injured son but also because she wanted to avoid another one of Joe's temper tantrums which upset and exhausted her.

'Look mate, I shall be dragging Dad off to the pub later for a quick one before supper,' said Bob. 'Do you fancy coming with us?'

'No thanks,' said Joe.

'You might enjoy it.'

'Stuck in this thing, you must be joking.'

Mavis appealed to Bob with her eyes to drop the subject and he responded. 'Oh well, if you change your mind, we'll be glad to have you along.' He paused, deciding that a spot of humour might not be a bad thing. 'If Mum will let Dad go, of course.'

'Since when have I ever had a say in what your father does,' she said predictably.

'Oh I don't know,' responded Bob with a wry grin. 'I think Dad knows who's boss in this house.'

They both laughed and the tension eased a little but it was a very unhappy and unhealthy situation in the Beck household and Bob was deeply concerned.

The village pub was crowded, smoky and resonant with the roar of boisterous conversation, the clientele entirely male in this early evening session. Later on a few of the local men might bring their wives along for an outing but for the moment there were no women around at all, which meant that some of the language was as blue as the willow pattern plates on the wall. The decor was traditional with polished wood in abundance: the solid oak beams, the tables and chairs and the bar counter. As well as the plates, the walls were also decked with brasses and faded photographs of the pub in bygone days.

'The situation at home is still pretty grim then, Dad,' remarked Bob as the two men stood at the bar with their beer. 'There doesn't seem to be any improvement in Joe's condition at all, or his mood.'

Stan shook his head slowly. 'He gets worse if anything,' he confided. 'His bad temper day after day is wearing your mother out. I'm very worried about her, as well as him.'

'Do you want me to move back home?' It was the last thing Bob wanted but he would do it if necessary. 'Only if you think it'll help, Dad, I'll make arrangements right away.'

'No, you mustn't do that, son.' Stan was adamant. 'You've your cab to pay for and you won't get the same money around here as you get in London whatever job you do. Besides, you're established there now. It's where you want to be.'

'I know but I feel bad for not being on hand to give you all some support,' Bob explained.

'You come as often as you can,' his father reminded him. 'That's good enough for us. Anyway, if you were to move back it might make things worse because your brother would feel even guiltier, you having to give up your life in London because of him.'

'Guilty. His attitude seems more like self-pity to me.' Stan took a healthy swig from his pint glass. 'Think about it, son. He's causing his mother a lot of extra work because of his accident. He knows he should be trying but because he found it nigh-on impossible and very painful, he couldn't cope so he lost all his confidence and gave up.' He paused thoughtfully. 'I mean, you and me both know what Joe was like before the accident. Always out and about; a bit reckless maybe but usually ready for a laugh and a joke. This lad sitting in his wheelchair all day isn't the boy we knew and he hates himself for not having the guts to try. No one knows to what degree he could retain the use of his legs. It could be that he always walks with a limp, it could be that he can only get one leg going. It could be that he gets no use in them at all. He's scared to try in case he fails.'

'So what's the answer?'

'If I knew that I would have had him back on his feet again by now,' Stan said.

'Maybe a tougher approach for his own good might be worth a try,' suggested Bob.

''Appen it would.' Stan sucked in his breath, shaking his head slowly. 'But your mother wouldn't allow that. I'd be a dead man if I started getting firm with him. She's far too soft, I reckon. But that's 'cause she's his ma. Us men can stand back a bit. Women actually feel their kid's pain, no matter how old they are.'

'I see,' said Bob.

'They say all things pass but I'm buggered if I know how this one will,' said Stan.

'It will, Dad. One way or another.'

★   ★   ★

The next day while Stan was at work and Mavis outside feeding the chickens, Bob found the opportunity he'd been waiting for.

'I never had you down as a quitter,' he said to Joe.

'Of course you wouldn't, 'cause I ain't.'

'You are at the moment,' said Bob, taking a gamble. 'You've completely given up. The brother I knew would never have done that. He would have had a go, and he'd have smiled now and then even if he failed. The accident happened and none of us can change that so accept it and do your best to make things better for yourself and everyone around you. Maybe there is no way back for you and if there isn't at least you'd know and you can resign yourself and make the best of things with the help of people who care about you. So what's the matter with you? Where's your spirit?'

'Easy for you to say, standing there on two good legs preaching to me.'

'Yeah, I know it's very easy for me. But if you think I enjoy having a brother who spends all his life feeling sorry for himself, you're wrong. I hate to see you behaving like a coward because I know that you're not, not in your heart.'

Joe's mouth tightened in anger and he made as though to get out of his chair but it was only a perfunctory attempt.

'Come on, have a pop at me,' goaded Bob, raising his fists. 'Surely you're not going to stand for me having a go at you. Come on, put your dukes up.'

His brother gripped the sides of his chair, his face

white and moist with sweat, his mouth set in a grim line.

'What are you waiting for?' said Bob, deliberately provoking him and stabbing his fists towards him while feeling like hell about it. 'Bring me down to size. Let me have it, boy. Come on, I dare you.'

Joe tried to lift himself again, his face contorted with pain, and Bob held his breath in expectation but his brother sat down again with a bump. 'Nah, you're not worth it,' he said in a tone of resignation. 'Why don't you bugger off back to London. You're not wanted around here. Not by me anyway.'

Before Bob had a chance to respond, their mother came in through the back door. 'Everything all right, boys?' she asked.

'Yeah, everything is fine, Mum,' replied Bob. 'We were just having a brotherly chat, weren't we, Joe?'

'That's right,' he confirmed, receiving the message in his brother's eyes. 'We're just catching up.'

'Good,' said Mavis because it suited her to go along with them, though she could sense trouble a mile off in her family and knew there had been some sort of an altercation. 'It's nice to see you getting along. Joe needs some company nearer to his own age.'

'I agree,' said Bob, hiding his feelings. Apparently Joe's mates had stopping coming to see him at his own request. He said they made him feel worse, all being able-bodied and enjoying life. Things would be better for him if he didn't push away anyone who tried to help. It was a seemingly unsolvable situation. Bob was apprehensive about going back to London but knew he would only make things worse if he stayed and he did have his living to earn. He would try to come more often though. The biggest problem, as far as he could see, was that no one knew if there really was any hope of an improvement for Joe so it was understandable that he was depressed. Bob's heart went out to him and he cared deeply even though it might have seemed otherwise just now. But too much indulgence wouldn't help his brother and he did get copious amounts of that from his mother. It was hard to be cruel even if it was with the very best intentions.

Bob was still preoccupied with thoughts of the family when he got back to London. As much as he wanted to be here, it was hard to be away from them at this challenging time. But his living was here and he had to get on and earn it, he reminded himself, as he dropped a fare off in Wigmore Street and picked up another passenger.

'Hammersmith please, King Street,' requested the man.

'Righto,' said Bob and headed for Marble Arch en route for West London.

'I'm just going to the night safe,' Sal told her grandmother, who was cooking supper in the kitchen. 'Won't be long.'

'All right dear,' said Dolly casually. 'The food won't be ready for a while anyway.'

'See you later then,' said Sal, slipping into her coat and going down the stairs where she put the takings, all bagged and accounted for, into her shopping bag.

She looked after the administration of the shop single-handed and always did the cashing up, partly because she liked to keep her finger on the pulse but also because her sister didn't want to do it and Gran was busy making their meal at closing time.

If Sal hadn't had a chance to go to the bank and there was a lot of cash in the till after they'd closed on a Friday and Saturday, as was the case this Friday, Sal took the money to the night safe rather than having it in the house over the weekend, just as a precaution, though the dog letting rip was enough to frighten off any burglar. They weren't to know that barking was the most aggressive thing Scamp ever did.

The evenings were getting lighter now that spring was underway, she observed with pleasure, as she headed along the parade and realised that it wasn't dark yet. It was still chilly though, she thought, shivering. The sharp March winds were lingering well into April.

Sal's thoughts turned to her sister as she walked towards the Broadway. Ann had admitted to having a new boyfriend called Thomas but she wouldn't say anything else about him and refused point blank to bring him home. It was most unusual for her to be so quiet about her love life so it was all a bit mysterious and Sal was very curious. Still, Ann seemed happy, that was the important thing.

Turning a corner into a side street that led to the Broadway, Sal let out a yell as she felt someone grab her from behind.

'Drop the bag,' said a gruff voice.

She swung round to see a young man wearing a long jacket and narrow trousers. 'Get off me you animal,' she said spiritedly though she was very startled. 'I'll have you done for assault.'

'Let go of the bag and you won't get hurt,' he ordered.

'Never,' she said, bending over slightly and clinging on to the bag as though her life depended on it. 'If you want money go and earn it. There are plenty of jobs about.'

'Drop it, you stupid cow,' he demanded, taking a rough grab for the bag.

'Get lost.'

'Don't blame me if you get hurt then,' he threatened.

'You'll be the one getting hurt, mate,' she said but she was secretly terrified because she knew she couldn't match his physical strength and was trying to hide the fact that she was trembling. 'So get out of the way before you get it where it really hurts.' She gritted her teeth and held on to the bag. 'Clear off, you thieving toe-rag.'

'Right, don't say you haven't been warned,' he said, overpowering her with his superior strength.

'Thanks very much mate,' Bob said to his fare when he gave him a tip. 'Goodnight. All the best.'

Bob turned the sign to For Hire and headed along the side street towards Hammersmith Broadway on his way back to the West End for the evening's business. Making his way along the road he slowed down. What the hell was going on there? he wondered. A woman was being attacked. God Almighty, the nerve of the bloke. It wasn't even dark.

Pulling into the kerb, he leaped out of the cab and bounded over just in time to see the woman fall to the ground and the man run away.

'He's got the shop takings,' cried Sal as Bob went to her assistance. 'Don't worry about me. I'm all right.'

Bob was after him like a shot, too caught up in his purpose to dwell on the fact that the victim was the girl he'd first met at Tilbury. He caught the thief at the end of the road and wrestled him to the ground.

'Right, you thieving bugger, you're not going anywhere except to the nick.'

'Thanks for everything,' said Sal to Bob a while later when they were sitting at a fashionable Formica-topped table in a cheerful coffee bar with the jukebox playing against the hiss of the coffee machine. They had been to the police station with Sal's assailant, delivered the shop takings to the night safe at the bank and stopped off at the phone box to let her grandmother know she'd be a bit late home. He'd insisted on taking her for some refreshment to give her a chance to calm down a little before going home. 'He'd have got away with the money if you hadn't come along when you did.'

'Never mind about the money,' he said. 'As long as you're all right, that's the important thing.'

'I'm a bit shaken up and my bottom is sore from where I hit the ground when he pushed me over but I'll live.'

'I hope you don't mind my mentioning it but perhaps you should have someone with you in future when you're carrying the shop takings on the street,' he suggested.

She nodded. 'You're absolutely right. I've never given it a thought until now, which is a bit careless I suppose. We're very casual about it, probably because our neighbourhood isn't the sort of place you expect that sort of thing, and it was still light. It isn't as though we have takings on the scale of Selfridges or anything. We're only small fry.'

'Even so, you get all sorts around the Broadway area, the same as any busy town,' he mentioned.

'But this was in a quiet side street.'

'I know. I could hardly believe my eyes when I saw what was happening.'

'The thief was a stranger to me so I believed him when he told the police that he didn't realise I was carrying the shop takings and was just after my personal stuff,' she said.

'He would have been even more disappointed that he didn't get away with it when he realised what was in the bag,' he said with a wry grin.

'Yeah, he probably is a bit miffed.'

'Anyway, let's hope he gets what he deserves now.'

'I'm not after revenge but I did feel duty bound to report him to the police,' she said. 'But knowing that justice will be done doesn't really change the way I feel. It's shaken my faith in human nature. Nothing like that has ever happened to me before.'

'I shouldn't dwell on it too much because most people are decent types. Still, it's only natural that you feel a bit vulnerable after something like that. I'll take you home in the cab to save you walking.'

'Thank you.'

'I wonder why fate keeps bringing us together,' he mentioned casually. 'This is the third time.'

'That's true and two of them have been fraught occasions,' she remarked.

'Still, at least we know each other's names now.'

She nodded and smiled and he thought she was gorgeous. So natural with her blue eyes and bright shiny hair. That fiancé of hers must have been stark raving mad to choose emigration over her.

'It must all be down to coincidence I suppose,' she decided. 'But I must admit it's odd, especially as our first meeting was a long way from home.'

'Do you think we are being told something?' he asked.

'Don't tell me you believe in that sort of thing,' she said. 'You seem so down to earth.'

'Working men can have imaginative notions too you know,' he said. 'I never rule anything out as regards that sort of thing because you just never know.'

'I only meant that you seem so straightforward.'

'We all have our idiosyncrasies,' he said.

'Are you still reading?' she asked.

He nodded enthusiastically. 'You?'

'Oh yes,' she told him. 'I couldn't do without my books. You must be very clued up about London history.'

'I've barely scratched the surface,' he said.

'You'll be able to take people around London as a proper tour guide one day,' she suggested.

'I wouldn't mind but I don't expect there are any openings for someone like me,' he said. 'People's expectations of you are entirely based on your station in life. Because I'm a taxi driver I'm not expected to enjoy anything cultural such as art, classical music or history, but I like them all.'

'Good for you for breaking the mould.'

He smiled and noticing that she looked a bit pale, he said, 'Well I think we'd better get you home and I have to go and earn my daily bread.'

When they drew up outside the shop she said, 'Would you like to come in?'

'Thanks but I can't stop now,' he said. 'I have to go to work.'

'I hope you aren't late because of me.'

'No, of course not. That's why I chose taxi driving because I can be my own boss, even if it does mean working in the evenings sometimes, something that used to drive my ex-fiancée mad.'

'But if you don't work you don't earn.'

'Exactly.'

'Well thanks again anyway.'

He looked at her in the dim light because darkness had now fallen and knew that he wanted to see her again; very much. But this wasn't the time to do anything about it, when she had had a shock and was still upset. Still, now that he knew where she lived all was not lost.

★　　★　　★

'That's the last time you're going to the night safe on your own,' declared Dolly when Sal told her what had happened in a modified version so as not to worry her too much.

'Too right it is,' agreed Sal. 'Next time I'll take Ann with me. I know a man would be better but since we don't have one of those between us, my sister will have to do.'

'Thanks very much,' said Ann jokingly. 'But of course I'll go with you.'

'Dad always used to do it, didn't he, and we never thought anything of it,' said Sal. 'That's probably why we're so casual about it now.'

'Mm,' said Dolly, and a sad kind of silence descended.

'So who's the bloke who caught the thief and brought you home then?' asked Ann eventually.

'He's a taxi driver who just happened to be passing,' she said. 'I've come across him a couple of times before.'

'You should have brought him in so I could have thanked him,' said Dolly.

'He had to go to work.'

'Old young or in the middle?' Ann wanted to know.

'Young and handsome,' Sal replied.

'Married?'

'Not as far as I know.'

'So what are you waiting for, girl?'

'Give it a rest,' said Sal.

'Yes, she's been through an ordeal so leave her alone,' admonished their grandmother.

'I'm going out now anyway,' Ann announced brightly.

'And God help anyone who asks you where you're going,' chided Sal.

'That's right. My business is my own and yours is mine too,' she giggled. 'So long both. See you later but don't wait up.'

With that she swung out of the room.

Sal and Dolly looked at each other. 'I think this romance she's having might be serious,' said the latter.

'That's why she's keeping quiet about him,' said Sal. 'In case he goes the same way as all the others.'

'Not unless he's married,' said Dolly, frowning. 'And I hope to God that isn't the reason she's keeping it so close to her chest.'

'I wondered about that and I asked her but she swears blind he isn't,' said Sal.

'Let's hope she isn't telling porky pies then, for the sake of everyone involved,' said Dolly. 'Anyway, it's time you had something to eat. You must be starving.'

The incident had robbed Sal of her appetite but she'd have to make an effort to please Gran who thought the answer to all of life's ills could be found in a good meal, an attitude which probably had something to do with the long years of food shortages.

One of the advantages of a busy life was the lack of time to brood on things for long. The day after the attempted robbery there was a crisis in the shop when the ice-cream cabinet broke down and all the stock melted.

'I think we should get a new one and the sooner the

better,' said Sal in their lunch break when the three women were sitting around the kitchen table. 'Dad got that one second-hand so we've had the best of it.'

'What about the expense?' queried Dolly.

'By the time we've paid someone to fix it, we might as well buy one.'

'There'll be quite a lot of difference in the price of a repair and the cost of a new cabinet, dear.'

'Mm, there is that,' agreed Sal. 'But I think paying to get it repaired might be a false economy because it could go on the blink again. If we get a new one at least we'll know that we're not going to have summer stock melting and costing us money.'

'Fortunately we didn't have much in there this time because the season hasn't started,' Dolly pointed out. 'So we didn't have too much of a loss.'

'It'll be different come the summer.' Sal turned to Ann. 'What do you think?'

Her sister's thoughts appeared to be elsewhere and she didn't reply.

'Ann,' said Sal.

'What,' she said blankly.

Sal repeated the question.

'I don't mind what you do,' said Ann without interest. 'You look after the books so you know if the shop can afford a new ice-cream cabinet.'

'Well, yes, obviously I would have to look into that side of it but we need to decide what's best,' she told her. 'The three of us.'

'I've told you before, I just work here,' Ann reminded

her. 'You run things and I'll go along with whatever you decide.'

'But it's a family business and you are part of the family,' Sal said. 'It wouldn't be right for us to do things without discussing them with you first.'

'I'm happy for you to do that,' Ann assured her. 'I don't want to be involved in the decisions. I'm sorry if that makes me seem selfish but it's the way I am. I'd rather take a lower wage than have all the bother of running the place. Anyway, it isn't our business, it's Dad's.'

'All the more reason to make a good job of looking after it for him,' said Sal.

'So that when he feels like coming back with his new woman, he'll take over and get rid of us.'

There was a sharp intake of breath from Dolly while Sal stared at her sister with a shocked expression.

'That's a terrible thing to say. I can't believe you really mean it.'

'Look,' Ann began with an eloquent sigh, 'he buggered off without a thought for his daughters or his mother, so if he decides to come back with someone new in his life he won't bother about us then, will he? It's obvious.'

'Oh Ann, how can you say such things,' cried Sal.

'How could he go off without a word?' she retaliated. 'That's what you should be asking. I don't know why you are hanging on to some sentimental idea about him.'

'Because he's her father and she knows that he's a good man,' said Dolly sharply.

'Good men don't walk out on their family, do they?'

There was silence.

'Yeah, I thought that would shut you up,' said Ann. 'There's no answer to it, that's why.'

'I'm not going to argue with you about it,' said Dolly patiently. 'You are entitled to your opinion but I'd rather you kept your thoughts to yourself in front of me.'

'You can be very insensitive at times, Ann,' said Sal. 'So do what Gran says and keep your opinions to yourself.'

Ann shrugged. 'I'll try because I really don't want to upset you,' she said. 'But I can't help the way I feel.'

'Anyway, what about this ice-cream cabinet,' said Sal, moving on quickly.

'Do what you think is best, Sal,' suggested Ann, concentrating on her food. 'You seem to have pretty good judgement as regards shop matters.'

'If you think the business can afford it let's go ahead and get a new one,' said Dolly.

'Right, I'll crack on and see what's about in the way of cabinets then,' Sal said.

Although ostensibly calm, Ann's comments about their father had rattled Sal, even though she knew they were merely the result of Ann's pain and disappointment in their father. Unfortunately some of what she said couldn't honestly be denied. Good men didn't usually walk out on their families. Gran was getting on a bit in years now; surely Dad must be wondering how she was keeping and if she was all right. He'd always been very caring towards her when he was here. How could that suddenly end?

No, she decided, she wouldn't let her trust in him be shattered by her sister's remarks. Faith had no logic. It was profound to those who had it and unfathomable to those who didn't. But nothing would persuade her to lose hers in her father. She was determined.

A couple of days later when Sal was having her break and Ann had popped to the baker's to get some currant buns for them to have with their tea, Dolly was standing in for them behind the counter when a stranger came into the shop.

'What can I do for you, sir?' she asked.

'That toffee looks very good,' he said. 'Can I have a quarter please.'

'There's a man with good taste,' approved Dolly, grinning at him. 'I made it myself.'

'Even better.' He smiled. 'You can't beat home-made toffee and you can't get it in many shops these days.'

'I've been making it for more years than I care to remember,' she said.

'Go on with you,' he joshed, his eyes sparkling with fun. 'It can't be that many years.'

'Ooh you flatterer,' she came back at him light-heartedly. 'It's a good job I recognise soft soap when I hear it.' She gave him a studious look. 'Haven't seen you around here before. Are you just passing through?'

'No. I came over to find out how Sal is,' he explained. 'I brought her home the other night.'

She narrowed her eyes on him. 'Are you the taxi driver who nailed that tea-leaf?' she asked.

He nodded. 'It was lucky I happened to be passing and saw what was going on,' he said modestly.

Dolly put down the toffee hammer and came out from behind the counter. 'Let me shake your hand. Thank you so much for coming to Sal's rescue,' she said, pumping his hand enthusiastically. 'I'm so grateful to you.'

'It was nothing really,' he said, not entirely comfortable with such effusive gratitude. 'It was the least I could do.'

'Well, it was no small thing to us.'

'What about my toffee,' he said, moving on swiftly before she had the opportunity to offer more thanks. 'Any chance of getting it weighed up in this lifetime?'

'You cheeky young monkey,' cackled Dolly and went round to the other side of the counter, picked up a piece of toffee and handed it to him. ''Scuse fingers but that's to keep you going and the rest will be with our compliments as a thank-you.' She opened the door to the house and stepped inside. 'Sal,' she shouted up the stairs. 'Come on down to the shop. There is someone here to see you.'

Chapter Six

'So we finally got together without coincidence or fate having a hand in it,' remarked Bob the following Sunday evening when he and Sal were sitting at a table by the window overlooking the Thames in one of London's most historic pubs, the Dove, on the towpath at Hammersmith.

She nodded. 'We managed this all on our own,' she said. 'Or rather you did, as it was your idea and you twisted my arm.'

'Oh, come on,' he responded with a smile. 'I didn't have to twist it very hard, did I?'

'No, all right, I admit it,' she said, grinning and raising her hands in a gesture of surrender. 'But there was a condition.'

'A condition that suited us both.'

When he'd called at the shop a few days ago and Gran had, somewhat embarrassingly, forced Sal to invite him into the house for a cup of tea while she was on her break, he'd asked her if he could see her again on his next night off and she'd said she would be delighted so long as they kept it casual. She hadn't long regained her confidence after the parting from Terry so didn't want to make herself emotionally fragile again.

'We've both had our fingers burned,' she said now.

'Mine were practically blistered,' he said.

'Do you still miss her?'

'I have my moments, of course,' he replied. 'I expect it's the same for you.'

'Naturally. But it's over a year since Terry and I split up and so much has happened since then I don't have many. I still miss Mum and Dad a lot though.'

'It must be hard.'

'It hasn't been the best of times. The loss of Terry all but destroyed me but losing Mum and Dad gave me strength even though I was heartbroken. I suppose because I knew everything rested on me because Gran and Ann were both in pieces though they were at pains not to show it. My sister pretends to be as hard as nails but she isn't at all. I only suggested keeping the shop going as a tribute to Mum but I'm actually enjoying it and am ambitious for its future.'

'Plenty of job satisfaction then.'

'Exactly. Anyway, that's enough about me and my troubles. Let's just relax and enjoy the evening.' She looked around the pub's ancient interior. 'This place must be heaven for someone like you who is interested in London history. Some famous literary figures have enjoyed a drink in this very room; Ernest Hemingway was a regular, apparently.'

'You're very well informed,' he observed. 'Sounds as though you know it off by heart.'

'I was brought up around here,' she explained. 'So it's common knowledge to me. There's a lovely view of Chiswick Eyot and the swans that nest there but you can't see much in the dark.'

'We'll have to come in daylight the next time,' he said lightly.

She smiled, approving of the suggestion. 'Yeah, that would be lovely.'

'So what sorts of things do you like to do in your spare time, apart from reading?' he asked.

'Nothing very exciting these days. I'm really boring according to my sister and I think she's right. I don't go out much of an evening, not since Terry,' she confessed. 'Ann has given up trying to drag me out to dance halls on a manhunt because I refused to go after a while. She's got a boyfriend now, anyway, so the search is off for her as well, thank goodness.'

'Dance halls eh,' he said. 'I haven't been to one of those in a while.'

Their glances met and she smiled. 'So what do you do on your evenings off then?'

'I sometimes go down to the local for a pint and a chat with my mates, or to play billiards,' he said. 'Occasionally the cinema if there's anything good on though that isn't something I enjoy doing on my own.'

'Mm, I know what you mean. I sometimes go with my girlfriends or Gran because I enjoy a good film too,' she told him. 'There's meant to be a cracker on general release at the moment.'

'Do you mean *The Bridge on the River Kwai*?'

She nodded. 'People say it's brilliant.'

'Maybe we could go and see it together if we haven't fallen out by the end of the evening.'

'We'll have to try not to upset each other then, won't we?' she said. 'Because I really would like to see that film.'

'Meanwhile, would you like another gin and lime?' he asked, rising.

'Yes please,' she said. 'That would be smashing.'

'Well, how did it go?' asked Ann when Sal went into the bedroom later that night.

'It was good,' she replied. 'I really enjoyed myself.'

'At last,' said Ann, who was already in bed. 'You've done it. You've finally ditched your books and moved on from that weasel Terry Granger.'

'I haven't ditched my books; I've merely had an evening out,' said Sal, 'and don't start bad-mouthing Terry again. You know it upsets me.'

'Quite why is beyond me.'

'Because it's unnecessary. Terry emigrated; he didn't murder or rape anyone so stop ripping him to pieces,' said Sal, starting to get undressed.

'All right, keep your hair on,' retorted Ann. 'So are you seeing this new man again then?'

'As it happens, I'm going to the cinema with him on Wednesday night.'

'That sounds promising. He must be keen to want to see you again so soon.'

'No, not especially, so don't make more of it than there is,' warned Sal because although she really fancied Bob she was still cautious and Ann was prone to exaggeration in her eagerness for Sal to be fixed up romantically. 'It just happens to be his night off. He works some evenings, often on a Friday and Saturday because that's when there's plenty of business about on his patch.'

'Good for you, girl. I thought he seemed like a really nice bloke when he was here.'

'He's lovely but don't get carried away at this early stage,' Sal emphasised. 'It's only a couple of dates and neither of us is looking for anything serious.'

'It's a start anyway,' Ann persisted. 'After a year of living like a nun it's about time.'

'All right, don't go on about it,' said Sal because her sister did tend to belabour this particular issue. 'How come you're in bed before me anyway?'

'Because you've been out enjoying yourself and are not tucked up so early.'

'Mm, I suppose so.'

'I wasn't too late home anyway,' Ann said. 'I was feeling tired for some reason.'

'That's what comes of being out every night.'

'You'll be doing that soon, I hope. Out every night and home in the early hours. That's the way it should be for a single girl like you.'

'I won't be out every night.' Sal was adamant. 'Not

even if I was dating someone like the delectable Paul Newman. That isn't my sort of thing at all.'

'We'll see,' said Ann with a knowing look. 'You can have the light on if you want to read. It won't keep me awake tonight because I'm far too shattered.'

'Thanks,' said Sal but she didn't think she would bother with her book tonight because, despite her casual attitude to Ann, thoughts of her evening with Bob were wonderfully distracting and she wanted to curl up with them.

'I could get used to this,' said Sal as Bob helped her out of his cab outside the shop, after the cinema. 'I don't get to ride in a taxi very often.'

'There aren't many perks to going out with a taxi driver; we can't take you to the Ritz every night or anything.' He grinned. 'But we can save you waiting for the bus.'

'Don't sell yourself short,' she said lightly. 'It's a good honest living. Anyway, any woman worth her salt doesn't go out with a man for what he can give her.'

'Some do,' he said. 'Kate only went out with me because she thought I had potential to make something better of myself down under and give her a good life.'

'I'm sure there was more to it than that,' she said.

'Yeah, to be fair, I expect there was and I did enjoy our time together while it lasted. Anyway, that's all in the past. So you enjoyed the film then.'

'I did. Alec Guinness and Jack Hawkins were superb, I thought. I'm not usually a great lover of war films but that was something special.'

'I thought so too.'

'Are you coming in for a cup of tea?' she asked. 'Gran would love to see you.'

Being a normal healthy male and her being a very pretty girl, a cup of tea and some family socialising wasn't exactly his first choice but it wouldn't be nice to make it too obvious so he said, 'Thank you. I'd like that very much.' Then impulse took over and he leaned forward and kissed her. She responded. It seemed right and natural and utterly wonderful.

As spring turned to summer and the new ice-cream cabinet began to pay its way, Sal and Bob's feelings for each other grew and things seemed to be going well for Sal in general, which encouraged her to put the bad times behind her. She and Bob were happy together and she had a more equal relationship with him than she'd ever had with Terry, partly because Bob wasn't at all overbearing and also because she was more confident in herself now.

The shop continued to do well but there was an increasing threat to independent confectioners as more grocery shops went self-service and stocked non-grocery items including pre-packaged sweets and chocolate.

'Business must be good for you, George, with more retail outlets stocking confectionery,' Sal said to the rep from the wholesaler's who'd been supplying The Toffee Shop for as far back as she could remember. He always called on a Monday afternoon because it was usually quiet and Ann was looking after the shop while Sal concentrated on the order. 'More commission for you, I should imagine.'

'Not necessarily,' said George who was a small dapper man of about fifty with dark Brylcreemed hair and a neatly trimmed moustache. 'Those stores with a few branches tend to order centrally and distribute to their shops direct.'

'Don't you get the order for the whole lot then?'

'The company does. I don't. It's done in the office by people higher up in the Sales Department than I am,' he explained.

'Not so good then.'

'I do all right,' he told her cheerfully. 'There are still enough independents around for us chaps on the road to earn a decent living.'

'Do people eat more sweets with them being available in more places, do you think?' she enquired chattily.

'Oh definitely,' he said. 'Especially as sweets were on ration for such a long time and people were deprived. So hopefully there'll be enough business for the supermarkets as well as small shops like yours. Anyway, we'll just have to see what happens to the trade in the future. One thing's for sure, we can't halt progress whether we like it or not.'

'You're right there, George, so we'll have to rise to the challenge,' she said in a positive manner. 'One thing I do know for sure, I won't let this place go downhill without a fight.'

'I bet you won't. Your mum and dad would be proud of the way you run things.' He'd known Sal and her sister since they were little and he thought Sal was doing a good job with the business. She was a born shopkeeper like her mother. It had been a shock to him, Joan Storey dying well before her time and Horace going off like that. Nobody seemed to know why he'd gone but there was plenty of speculation, mostly derogatory to Horace. Personally he'd always found the man to be a thoroughly genuine sort so hadn't judged him though naturally he was curious because he'd known the family for such a long time.

'I'd like to think so,' she said, moving on swiftly before any more could be said on the subject. 'Now let's do the order shall we, George? I've got a nice healthy one for you today and it's all written down ready so I'll call it out to you and if you think of anything I've missed just shout. Sherbet Dabs we're very short of . . . sweet cigarettes . . . liquorice chews . . .'

As she reeled it off he wrote it down, enjoying the thought of how it would boost his commission.

Ann was in a foul mood one morning in June.

'About time too,' she snarled at Sal when she came out of the bathroom after her early ablutions. 'You're not the only person living in this house you know, and the rest of us need to use the facilities as well as you.'

'I wasn't long.'

'Yes, you were. You were ages,' she snapped. 'I've been bursting while I've been waiting out here.'

With that Ann stormed into the bathroom and slammed the door so hard it resounded throughout the building.

Sal continued getting dressed and was about to go downstairs for breakfast when her sister came back into the bedroom, scowling viciously.

'What on earth is the matter with you?' Sal demanded. 'You've had a face like a wet floor mop for days. And that outburst just now was completely unnecessary.'

'It was absolutely necessary and there is nothing wrong with my mood that a little consideration wouldn't cure.'

'Rubbish,' insisted Sal. 'You've done nothing but bite my head off, and Gran's, these past few weeks.'

'Well . . . you're both getting on my nerves.'

'Oh I'm so sorry to hear that,' said Sal with withering sarcasm. 'Perhaps you'd like us to find alternative accommodation and let you have this house to yourself.'

'I wish.'

'You can wish all you like but since you do have to live with us you can start treating us decently or we might decide that you should be the one to go.'

'I will go,' threatened Ann, knowing full well that she didn't mean it. 'I'll get my own place and get away from you two nagging at me all day long.'

'Good. You do that.' Sal also knew that none of this was going to happen and was speaking in the heat of the moment. 'And the sooner the better as far as I'm concerned.'

The sisters stared at each other furiously then, to Sal's amazement, Ann's face crumpled and she burst into tears.

Anger was immediately replaced by concern and Sal put her arms round her. 'What is it? What's the matter?' she asked.

'I'm pregnant,' Ann spluttered.

'Ooh blimey,' said Sal, unable to hide her shock. 'No wonder you're crying.'

'What am I going to do, Sal?'

'Well, you can start by trying to calm down,' she said in a kind but authoritative manner, though she herself was rocked by this news. 'Then we'll talk about it. You me and Gran.'

'I can't tell Gran,' she wailed. 'She'll go mad.'

'Gran's been around a lot longer than we have and she will have lived through far worse things than a granddaughter getting pregnant.'

'An unmarried granddaughter,' Ann reminded her.

'Even an unmarried one,' said Sal, determined to stay positive despite the gravity of the situation. 'I presume it's Thomas's?'

'Of course it is; what sort of girl do you think I am?'

'Just asking. You're so blinkin' secretive lately I never know what's going on with your love life.' Sal was hurt that her sister hadn't confided in her about her man. 'Anyway, what does he have to say about it?'

'He doesn't know.'

'Oh . . . but shouldn't he have been the first person you told?' Sal said worriedly.

'No . . .'

'At least give him the chance to do the decent thing,' Sal suggested.

'I'm not telling him,' she said thickly. 'I finished with him the other night anyway. That's why I've been so miserable.'

'Oh Ann, what possessed you to do a thing like that when you need him so much at this time?'

'Because I don't want him to know about the baby,' she explained. 'He wouldn't be able to do anything about it anyway so I'd rather spare him the situation. It's my problem so my decision.'

'So he is married then?'

There was a brief hiatus then she said, 'No he isn't married but we can't be together and that's definite so just take my word for it and don't go on at me.'

'Who is he, Ann?' Sal persisted, 'and why can't you be together?'

'We can't so drop it, will you.'

'Fair enough,' Sal finally agreed. 'But promise me you won't put off telling Gran. The three of us are family and she shouldn't be left out.'

Ann emitted an eloquent sigh. 'I suppose I shall have to,' she agreed with reluctance.

'I'll move out of here to spare you from the disgrace,' said Ann defiantly, having dropped the bombshell on her grandmother over breakfast. 'But I'm not going to have an abortion or go to one of those hostels for unmarried mothers and have the baby taken away from me for adoption.'

'Hey, slow down,' admonished Dolly. 'Who said anything about any of those things?'

'That's what usually happens to women in this situation, isn't it?' said Ann.

'Not always. So you can stop making assumptions and

listen to me, my girl. There'll be no more talk of you leaving here . . .'

'But the scandal, Gran. There's been enough gossip about this family with Dad going; my getting pregnant will ruin our reputation altogether.'

'Remember the old saying about sticks and stones . . .'

'Yeah, I know the one.'

'So keep it in mind and calm down,' said Dolly. 'The locals still come here for their sweets and ciggies, no matter what they are saying about us, don't they?'

'There is that but . . .'

'But nothing,' said Dolly firmly. 'Now what about the father of the baby?'

'She isn't going to tell him,' Sal informed her.

Dolly was in a commanding mood and gave Sal a sharp look. 'You should let your sister answer for herself, you know.' She turned to Ann. 'Still, as she has told me, is it true?'

'Absolutely,' she stated firmly.

There was a pause while Dolly thought this over. 'Well, you obviously have your reasons for not telling him and not letting us know who he is,' she said at last. 'You're over twenty-one and past the age where I can tell you what to do. So let's concentrate on how we are going to cope with the situation.'

'Well said,' agreed Sal.

'It isn't going to be an easy time for you, Ann, I won't make light of it because you're a sensible girl and you know there will be problems. But since your mum and dad haven't been around the three of us have worked well as a team so I think we should carry on that way. Speaking for myself, I will be behind you all the way during the pregnancy and beyond and I'm sure that your sister feels the same.'

'Definitely,' Sal confirmed.

'Bugger the gossips,' said Dolly. 'Let 'em do their worst. We'll concentrate on the things that matter, like getting you through the next few months then giving you some support when the little one arrives.'

'I'll second that,' said Sal wholeheartedly.

Ann started to cry again but this time it was with relief and gratitude.

Washing the breakfast dishes at the kitchen sink while the girls opened the shop, Dolly had tension knots in her stomach. She hadn't been nearly as calm as she'd seemed over Ann's dramatic news. Unmarried mothers were given a terrible time by society in general and when you had a shop at the heart of the community, you were well known and therefore more of a target for talk and abuse, especially as the family reputation had already been tarnished by Horace's untimely disappearance. Toughened by age and experience, she herself was able to let such things go over her head but she wasn't sure how Ann would cope. Even though her manner suggested otherwise, she was actually quite a sensitive girl.

So Dolly and Sal would have to do everything they possibly could to help her through the testing times ahead. She paused, dishcloth in hand, feeling a surge of pleasure at the thought of a baby in the family. Whatever the problems it was something to look forward to. She hadn't expected her first great-grandchild to be born out of wedlock but the baby would get no less of a welcome because of it. Ann said she'd missed two periods so thought she was about three months gone; it would probably be due around Christmas or the New Year, though they wouldn't know for sure until she'd seen a doctor.

It was a good job Joan hadn't lived to see it. She'd been a stickler for respectability and it would have broken her heart, initially anyway. As for Horace, what would he think of becoming a grandfather for the first time under such circumstances? He would have been tickled pink despite everything, she knew that in her heart. She was forced to dry her hands on the tea towel so that she could mop her eyes with her handkerchief as they filled with tears at the thought of her son. She so wished he was here to welcome the next generation.

'I told you Gran would be good about it, didn't I?' said Sal, after the early rush in the shop was over and she and Ann were restocking the shelves.

'Yeah, bless her,' said Ann, putting a new jar of acid drops out to replace the empty one. 'She's the best.'

'Do you feel a bit better about it now that it's out in the open?' said Sal, stacking cigarette packets on the shelf.

'I don't feel quite so alone now,' she said. 'I feel physically sick the whole time though which is all part of pregnancy I suppose, and I'm going to have to spend the next six months or so trying to hide my condition from the outside world. I don't want people talking about me until it's unavoidable.'

'I know it's traditional but hanging your head in shame isn't actually compulsory,' opined Sal. 'I think you should hold your head up high. You're creating a new life and surely that's something to be proud of.'

'Without a husband it isn't and you know that as well as I do.'

'I do unfortunately but I don't think it should be that way,' Sal declared. 'So let's break the rules and celebrate your condition. Let's show 'em, kid.'

'Easy for you to say, you're not the one who's in the condition,' Ann reminded her.

'There is that,' Sal was forced to agree. 'But I'm not going to be ashamed of you and that's definite. If I hear anyone making snide remarks, they'll wish they hadn't.'

Ann opened a new box of black jacks and put them on display at the front of the counter. 'I'm going to miss Thomas like mad,' she said wistfully. 'I don't want to sound soppy but I do love him, you know. The first bloke I've ever really loved and look where it's got me.'

'Is there no chance for the two of you?'

'None at all.'

Sal sensed a profound sadness in her sister and knew somehow that she mustn't pursue the matter further at this stage. But she was very puzzled about the situation as well as Ann's secrecy. Why couldn't Ann be with the man she loved? The awful part was being powerless to help. She and Gran could give Ann support in bucket loads as regards the baby and that must give her some comfort but they couldn't make the pain in her heart go away.

'You seem a bit quiet tonight, Sal,' observed Bob a week or so later when the two of them were out walking by the river with the dog. It was a balmy evening and there were plenty of people about on the towpath. The plan was for Sal and Bob to sit outside one of the riverside pubs with Scamp and have a drink if they could get a table. 'Is everything all right?'

'We've got a bit of a family problem actually,' she replied, having thought carefully beforehand about whether or not to confide in him.

'Nothing serious I hope,' he said, looking concerned. 'Nothing wrong with your Gran is there?'

'No, Gran's fine.'

'That's good . . . but don't tell me if you'd rather not,' he said. 'I don't want to pry.'

'You'll find out soon enough anyway so it's best if you hear it from me,' she said. 'It's Ann, she's pregnant and there's no chance of the father standing by her.'

'Oh blimey,' he said. 'So what will she do?'

'She's keeping the baby,' she replied without hesitation. 'Gran and I are going to help her through it and she and the baby will live at home with us.'

They grabbed a table and he went inside to get the drinks while she stayed with the dog sitting quietly at her feet. She looked at the setting sun shining on the water, upon which there were various craft including some with oarsmen skimming by, Hammersmith Bridge in all its ornate glory completing the picture.

'One of the good things about having a family business is that Ann won't have to lose her job because of the pregnancy,' she said, when Bob came back and they were settled with their drinks. 'She can work for as long as she feels able to and later on she can fit the job around the baby. Gran and I will help.'

'She's lucky to have you,' he remarked. 'A girl in our village at home had her life made a misery when she got herself up the duff. Her parents chucked her out.'

'It's awful the way people treat anyone who finds themselves in that position,' she said. 'Anyone would think it was a crime. I've told Ann to hold her head up. I'm certainly going to on her behalf. There'll be none of this crawling around in shame as far as I'm concerned.'

'Good for you,' he approved. 'I'd be the same if she was my sister. Or if there was any scandal about any member of my family. Things are said in the village about my brother but they don't say it twice when I'm around, even though I might agree with them. I can say it but no one else can.'

'What on earth do they find to say about him?' wondered Sal. 'He's done nothing wrong.'

'Because he doesn't make an effort and hides away at home, leading Mum and Dad, especially Mum, a merry dance,' he said. 'And, of course, there was a lot of talk at the time about him being drunk when the accident happened so some say it was his own fault. He swears blind he was sober and I am taking his word for it. As no one else was involved, to me it's irrelevant anyway. It doesn't alter the situation. He's stuck in that wheelchair and likely to be for the rest of his life unless there's a miracle.'

'I can't believe people would say bad things about someone who is in such a horrible position.'

'It's only a few,' he told her. 'The sort to enjoy a good old gossip though some of the talk is because Mum and Dad are so well thought of in the village and they don't like to see them having such a hard time. Dad has a reputation as a bit of a chancer but he's got a good heart so people like him. Mum and Dad have lived all their lives in the village and that counts for a lot down there.'

'But it must be awful for Joe in his situation and the last thing people should be doing is saying malicious things,' she said. 'I'm sure he doesn't want to be stuck in that chair.'

'Of course he doesn't,' agreed Bob. 'That's why he's so miserable all the time. It's hard for Mum and Dad to live with day after day, though Mum won't hear a word against him, of course.' He paused thoughtfully. 'I must go down there some time soon. I don't like to leave it too long.'

'That shouldn't be a hardship, not in this weather,' she commented. 'Devon will be lovely I should imagine, not that I've ever been there but I've heard about it.'

He gave her a studious look. 'Do you fancy coming with me?' he asked with a smile. 'I'd love to have you along.'

'I wasn't fishing for an invitation,' she said, embarrassed.

'I know that,' he assured her. 'But why don't you come? I'll only be going for a couple of days or so.'

'I'm not sure,' she said, hesitant because it was so unexpected.

'All perfectly legit,' he made clear. 'I can sleep in with Joe so you can have my bedroom. Mum and Dad would love to meet you, I can promise you that.'

'I'd love to come but am wondering about getting the time off from the shop,' she said.

'They can manage without you for a couple of days,' he said brightly. 'If we go early on a Sunday morning and get back late Tuesday night, you'll only miss two days. If we do it that way I don't lose Friday and Saturday's business. A couple of days in the country will do you the world of good.'

'I'm sure it would,' she said, smiling. 'The disadvantage of working in a small family business is that you never get to take regular holidays as you would if you were employed by someone else.'

'I'm self-employed so I have the same trouble. So let's both head for the country the weekend after next.'

'As long as Gran doesn't mind doing some extra hours to cover for me for those days, you're on.'

'Lovely.' He looked thoughtful suddenly. 'I must warn you that it will be very different to what you're used to,' he said. 'It's always a bit chaotic and a far cry from town life. Mum and Dad have their own way of doing things.'

'I look forward to meeting them,' she said.

He nodded thoughtfully then looked at her glass. 'Same again for you?'

'Yes please.'

He glanced down at Scamp who was panting slightly, his dark, adoring eyes fixed on Bob. 'I'll bring some water for his lordship,' he said. 'We don't want to leave him out.'

Watching him stride towards the pub, she thought what a handsome figure he cut in his light-coloured slacks and sports jacket. Having him in her life made anything bearable, even the family scandal they were about to face. Meanwhile a couple of days away from it all would be something to look forward to.

When Bob had warned Sal that life in the Beck household would be different to what she was used to, she hadn't realised to what degree. Here at the charmingly shabby cottage – with its uneven floors, unexpected steps and wooden beams that had seen better days – no one turned a hair when a tortoise made its way across the living-room floor and nibbled Bob's mother's toe, exposed by her sandal, and having a cat sit on a chair at the table with the family at mealtimes seemed to be the norm. Sal couldn't help thinking how horrified her fastidious mother would have been to see a tabby walk across the kitchen table while Bob's mother was laying it for a meal. The furniture at home was strictly off limits to dear old Scamp. Here the domestic animals seemed to have the run of the house. But the atmosphere was wonderfully casual and oozing with warmth.

'So you're in the confectionery trade then,' remarked Stan when they were seated around the large wooden kitchen table eating a Sunday roast which didn't seem affected by the presence of a menagerie. In fact, the food was delicious.

She nodded. 'Sweets, cigarettes, tobacco and all that goes with them,' she told him.

'Your shop must be doing well with people having more money in their pockets to spend on luxuries and no rationing to worry about,' he said.

'The shop does OK,' she responded. 'It isn't mine though. It's my father's.'

'If you run it, where is your dad then?'

'I don't know Mr Beck,' she replied candidly. 'He's disappeared. We have no idea where he is.'

'That's a funny kettle o' fish isn't it?'

'Stan,' cut in Mavis, glaring at him. 'Mind your business and don't go prying into Sal's private family affairs. She's our guest, remember.'

'It's all right, Mrs Beck,' Sal assured her. 'I'm not embarrassed about what happened. Just very saddened by it. My dad left right after my mother's funeral. It broke our hearts but life has to go on.'

'Oh . . . my Lord,' said Mavis sympathetically. 'I'm very sorry to hear that.' She cleared her throat. 'Would you like a bit more meat, my dear?'

'I still have plenty thanks,' she said. 'But this is delicious.'

'I'll have some more, please Mum,' said Joe.

'Might have known you'd want some,' said Mavis affectionately. 'He's a proper gannet.'

Sal smiled politely at Bob's brother, perceiving a likeness between the siblings. 'He's still a growing boy perhaps,' she suggested jokingly, smiling at him in a friendly manner.

'Growing outwards,' said Bob, looking at his brother and grinning. 'Your lack of exercise is beginning to show, kiddo, and you're getting fat.'

'What am I supposed to do about it,' scowled Joe. 'It isn't as if I can go for a five-mile run every day is it?'

'Course he can't so don't be so insensitive, Bob,' scolded their mother.

'There are exercises you can do which might help you get back on your feet.'

'Don't start going on at him the minute you walk in the door,' warned Mavis.

'Bob was only saying . . .' began his father.

'Change the subject, for goodness' sake,' said Mavis, hot and flustered. 'It'll only lead to a full-blown row and I'm sure Sal doesn't want to hear that.'

'Don't worry about me,' responded Sal. 'All families have arguments. You should be in our house sometimes. My sister and I nearly come to blows at times.'

'Just the three of you is there?' asked Mavis. 'You, your sister and your gran?'

'At the moment yes,' Sal confirmed. 'Though we're soon to become four. My sister is having a baby.'

'Oh, I didn't realised she was married,' remarked Mavis.

'She isn't,' said Sal.

A silence ensued then Mavis said, 'These things happen, don't they?'

'They certainly do but Gran and I are right behind her,' Sal made clear. 'We'll do what we can to help her. There'll be gossip of course, but not when I'm around.'

'Sal is a strong lady,' added Bob heartily, hoping to bring some levity into the atmosphere. 'You cross her at your peril. I wouldn't like to try it.'

He was sitting next to Sal and she turned to him and smiled. 'Oh, don't be so horrible,' she remonstrated playfully. 'You make me sound like some awful harridan.'

'I just meant that you know your own mind.'

'On this particular subject I do,' she said. 'I don't see why someone should be made to feel like a criminal when they are not. Yes, she has broken the rules but she hasn't committed a crime against humanity or anything so she shouldn't be punished.'

'There you are, folks,' said Bob. 'Sal isn't one to mess with. I'm scared stiff of her.'

Sal laughed and slapped him lightly on the arm. 'You will be if you carry on,' she said in an affectionate manner. She turned to the others. 'Anyway, let's change the subject. Tell me about this lovely village of yours.'

'Lovely,' snorted Joe. 'It's the most boring place on earth. There's more life in James Dean.'

'Isn't he the young film star who died in a car crash a few years ago?' said Mavis.

'Exactly,' said Joe.

'How would you know what goes on in the village since you never go out?' asked his father.

'I have been out in the past, haven't I? Anyway I hear you and Mum talking about it.' He turned towards Sal. 'The most exciting thing that ever happens is when some girl gets herself into the same state as your sister. That livens things up a bit.' He paused. 'Or, of course, if someone gets smashed up on a motorbike. The gossips have a hell of a time with that one.'

'That isn't fair,' said his father. 'Everyone has gone out of their way to help you. It isn't their fault if you threw every kind gesture back in their faces.'

'I was hoping you would take me on a tour of the village, Joe,' Sal cut in. 'I would really enjoy that.'

'Is that your idea of a joke?' he snorted.

'No, not at all.'

'How can I take anyone anywhere?'

'I'd push your wheelchair of course,' she explained. 'But you'd be taking me in every other way. I don't know the area at all so you'd be my guide.'

'There's nothing to see.'

'I'm sure there is for a stranger with fresh eyes.'

Then to the amazement of the Beck family, he said, 'Yeah all right, if you want.'

'You realise that you've pulled off something of a miracle, Sal,' said Mavis when Sal was helping her with the dishes. 'We haven't been able to persuade Joe to go out to the village since he came home from the hospital. The only time he ever used to leave this house was for

158

his doctor's appointments but he doesn't even go to those now.'

'Yeah, Bob did say you were having trouble persuading him to go out,' she said.

'Is that why you suggested it?'

'It seemed like a good idea and I'd like to go anyway,' she replied. 'I thought it might work, my being a stranger.'

'That was a very kind thought.'

'It seemed too good an opportunity to miss,' she said. 'But we haven't actually gone yet. He might change his mind when it comes to it.'

'I do hope not.'

'Don't worry Mrs Beck,' said Sal, drying a cup and hanging it on a hook on the dresser. 'I'm not one to be easily put off.'

Mavis turned to look at her, smiling approvingly. 'No, I don't believe you are.'

'So this is the village centre then, is it?' said Sal after she had pushed the wheelchair along a country lane and then through narrow streets of whitewashed houses to emerge at a crossroads and signs of habitation: some pretty cottages, a school, shop, pub and a church and village hall, the entire area deserted.

'Yeah. This is it. I told you there's nothing here, didn't I? We don't even have a village green,' he said. 'Not that I'm complaining 'cause at least I'm spared people gawping at me.'

'I think it's absolutely charming,' she said, ignoring the latter part of his sentence.

'Isn't exactly bursting with life though, is it?'

'I don't think much goes on on a Sunday afternoon anywhere,' she pointed out.

'I bet there's plenty happening in London all the time.'

'In the West End there are always people about,' she said. 'But in the suburbs there isn't much action at this time on a Sunday afternoon. The cinemas are open and people go to the park and the river. But I expect that your local cinemas are open in the town.'

'Oh yeah. I was all right when I had the bike,' he said. 'I used to go to Exeter for entertainment. It isn't like London o' course but it's better than this dead hole.'

She sat down on a bench in the sunshine with him beside her. 'I can understand how awful it must be for you, Joe,' she said. 'I really can.'

'But you think I don't try.'

'I didn't say that.'

'It's what you're thinking though,' he said. 'I bet my brother's told you what a waste of space I am. Putting on Mum and Dad and driving them mad.'

'He has not said that,' she said adamantly. 'I'm sure your parents are very happy to look after you.'

'Bob has said that I don't try though, hasn't he?'

'No, not exactly.' She wanted to be honest but also tactful. 'He thinks you've lost your nerve because of the pain and disappointment of trying to get going again, that's all, and he feels powerless to help.'

'He would say that, wouldn't he? It's easy for him to preach about it when he's fit and able.'

'He's concerned because you won't let the hospital help you, I think,' she said.

'All I've got to do is get up off my backside and I'll be able to walk, that's what he thinks,' he said, his voice rising. 'Well it isn't like that at all.'

'I'm sure it isn't.'

'Do you think I'd be stuck in this chair letting a woman wheel me to the village if I could walk?'

She looked into his blue eyes so like his brother's but full of pain, shame and disappointment. She put her hand on his in a gesture of friendship. 'No, I don't think that, Joe. I really don't.'

'When I'm on my own I try to get up but I just can't do it. Everything is stuck,' he went on to say. 'It's as though I freeze up and I can't make my body move. The pain is awful too. They said it would be very gradual but there's no movement at all. Not any! I used to go to the hospital for the physiotherapy regular but it was too hard. I couldn't bear the disappointment of making no progress any more so I stopped going.'

Sal took a handkerchief from her pocket and handed it to him as she saw tears roll down his cheeks.

'I understand,' she said.

There was the sound of voices and people suddenly appeared and headed for the church.

'Quick, let's get out of here,' said Joe urgently, tears wiped away swiftly. 'Hurry.'

'Give me a chance,' said Sal, getting up and grabbing the wheelchair handles. 'I don't know what the rush is all about.'

'I don't want to get caught by the God brigade so hurry up.' He gave an eloquent sigh as a young woman headed towards them. 'Oh no, too late.'

'Hello Joe,' said the pretty, dark-haired girl who was about Joe's age and dressed in a smart dress and jacket. 'Nice to see you out and about.'

'Is it?'

'Yeah, course it is. We miss seeing you around the village.'

'We're just going, Gloria . . .'

'You look well,' said the girl.

'Is that supposed to be funny?'

'No. Of course not. Being in a chair doesn't stop you from looking well,' she said. 'A bit of extra weight suits you.'

'Thanks for nothing,' he said.

'Sorry, I just meant . . .'

'He knows what you meant,' said Sal.

Gloria looked from one to the other. 'Are you two . . . ?'

'No. This is Sal, my brother's girlfriend.'

'Oh I see.'

The two women nodded and smiled at each other.

'Off to church are you?' said Joe

'That's right,' she replied.

'You didn't used to be the religious type.'

'It's a special occasion,' she explained. 'My sister's baby's christening.'

'I thought it must be something special to get a sinner like you there.'

'Oi cheeky,' she said. 'I'm godmother as a matter of fact.'

'Godmother? You? Aren't you supposed to guide the kid along the straight and narrow for that job?' he said.

'Something along those lines, I believe.'

'You're a fine one then . . .'

'Watch it, Beck, before I thump you,' she said jokingly. 'And I won't be put off by the wheelchair neither.'

'I'm trembling in my boots,' he came back at her.

'You will be.'

Someone called Gloria to hurry up and she said, 'Ta-ta then. See you around.'

'Not if I see you first,' he said.

'Suit yourself,' she said and turned and swung away towards the church.

'Let's get going before anyone else spots us and comes over,' said Joe.

'She seemed nice,' commented Sal as she began to push the chair back towards the cottage.

'Nice,' he said, incredulous at the suggestion. 'She's the village prossie.'

'I don't believe you,' she said. 'She's far too young and fresh-looking.'

'Fresh is the word,' he said. 'You ask my mates. She'll go with anyone.'

'Are you speaking from personal experience?'

'No, not exactly, but the boys say . . .'

'Lads are very prone to exaggerate about that sort of thing,' she said, sounding about forty-five. 'So I should

163

take it with a pinch of salt if I were you. She certainly seemed to like you.'

'Don't be daft,' he said. 'She's hot stuff. She wouldn't look at someone in a wheelchair, even if I did fancy her, which I don't.'

'But she did look at you, Joe, in that special way.'

'No she didn't,' he insisted. 'I've known her all my life. We were at school together.'

'Oh well, you think what you like but I know what I saw,' she said and turned her attention to the glorious scenery as they headed out of the village and Joe fell silent. Through the gaps in the hedgerows she could see mile upon mile of farmland, a patchwork quilt of browns, yellow and greens.

When the cottage came into view Joe astounded her by saying, 'Thanks for taking me.'

'You took me,' she said determinedly. 'And I want no argument about that.'

'I'd better keep quiet then, hadn't I?' he said.

'I should.'

It was nothing more than the slightest glimmer of a notion but she did believe that she had made a connection with him. That pleased her very much indeed.

'Sal's family seem a right rum lot, don't they,' Stan said to Mavis that night in bed. 'What with her father walking out before his wife was even cold in the grave and not a word to any of them and her sister up the spout with no man by her side.'

'Mm, they do sound a bit rough, I must admit,' agreed

his wife. 'But Sal seems really refined, doesn't she, as though she's been well brought up.'

'And very good-hearted.'

'Yeah, she seems lovely,' she said. 'She's very good with Joe too, taking him out in his chair like that. I haven't seen him so cheerful in ages.'

'Nor me.'

'I really like her, Stan. I feel comfortable with her. She fits in lovely with us. I hope she comes again.'

'She's certainly a big improvement on his last girlfriend, isn't she?'

'Not half,' she said. 'Let's hope he hangs on to her.'

'Yeah,' he said, kissing her lightly. 'Night, love.'

'Night, Stan.'

Mavis lay staring at the moonlight shining through the lattice windows through a gap in the curtains and forming a pattern on the ceiling, and reviewing the events of the day with pleasure. Bob seemed very keen on Sal which pleased her but worried her too because it made him vulnerable. He'd been badly hurt by Kate. She did hope the same thing wasn't repeated with Sal. She seemed very nice but you just never knew what was going to happen when it came to affairs of the heart.

Chapter Seven

Sal did go to the Becks' again that summer at the end of August into early September, a glorious few days of fresh air and relaxation. The welcome she received from the family was typically warm-hearted and she felt increasingly at home with them. Again she made a special effort with Joe and sensed a bond growing between them. She thought he probably valued an outsider, someone less emotionally involved in his problems than his family, to talk to.

On the last night she and Bob went for a walk in the moonlight and when they lingered by a farm gate, his arm round her, the evening seemed enchanted.

'I'm having such a wonderful time, Bob,' she said. 'Thanks for bringing me.'

'I love having you along,' he told her. 'In fact I love you wherever we are Sal. Here, or in London, everywhere.'

'I feel the same,' she said, melting into his arms.

There were no plans for the future yet; just mutual joy in the moment. A time when they put all problems aside and revelled in each other. She felt nourished and strengthened by his love and confident that she could cope with everything more easily because of it.

Because the Becks paid little attention to news outside of the village and didn't regularly tune in to the national news on the radio or television, Sal and Bob were unaware of the violent race riots that had erupted in west London while they'd been away in Devon and were still in progress on their return, just a few miles away in the Notting Hill Gate area.

'There's been petrol bombs and attacks with milk bottles and God knows what else,' Dolly informed them when they arrived back at the shop just before closing time on Tuesday. 'To make matters worse, crowds of troublemakers have gone there from outside the area to join in. Just for the hell of it. Evil buggers.'

'That's awful,' said Sal. 'Does anyone know what started it?'

'People are saying that a gang of Teddy Boys taunted black immigrants with racial slogans and they retaliated but we don't know if it's true,' said Dolly. 'But both sides have been fighting and still are as far as we know. Apparently the coppers are having a terrible time trying to control the riots.'

'There's been trouble in that area for a while, ever since the Caribbean community started growing so rapidly, so I've heard,' Sal said. 'It's rough round there with poor housing and general dilapidation.'

Dolly looked at Bob. 'Be careful if you have to go

through that district when you're out in your taxi or you might find a broken milk bottle heading your way. When people are that fired up they'll hit out at anyone.'

'The police will have closed the roads round there, I should think,' he said.

She nodded. 'Yeah of course.'

'Where's Ann?' asked Sal.

'Having a lie-down on her bed,' Dolly replied.

'Is it her usual pregnancy rest or isn't she well?' asked Sal.

'She's not ill exactly but she seems a bit down in the dumps so I told her to stay up there for longer if she feels like it. It'll be the extra weight she's carrying that's getting her down, I expect. She isn't six months yet, but she's quite big.'

'That and her hormones running amok.' The shop door opened and a flood of last-minute customers came in. 'I'll see to this, Gran,' Sal offered, 'as I've had the weekend off.'

'We'll do it together,' said Dolly.

'I'll put the kettle on then,' said Bob.

'Good boy,' approved Dolly.

'Not feeling too bright then, Ann,' said Sal, finding her sister lying on her bed.

'I'm OK,' she said. 'I'm getting up now anyway. So how did the weekend go?'

'Smashing,' Sal replied. 'But I hear there's been all sorts of trouble a few miles down the road from here.'

'Yeah, it's a terrible business,' Ann said dully. 'I don't know why people can't live and let live.'

Sal looked at her, sensing that all was not well. 'Gran said you've been a bit miserable while I've been away.'

'I wish she'd stop monitoring my every mood,' she objected, getting up slowly and sitting on the edge of the bed. 'I'm only having a baby; it isn't an illness you know. I don't need to be under constant observation.'

'All right, don't bite my head off. Gran means well, you know that. Anyway you obviously are in a rotten mood.'

'So would you be if you were the size of a house and knew that everyone is talking about you.'

'I think your pregnancy is the last thing on people's minds. At the moment everyone will be talking about the goings-on at Notting Hill Gate.'

Ann shrugged.

'When's your next antenatal appointment at the doctors?' Sal enquired.

'End of next month.'

'I'll come with you.'

'There's no need.'

'I want to make sure you do actually go,' Sal said because her sister was sensitive to her plight and tended to hide away at home if she could.

'Makes no odds to me whether you come or not,' Ann said with indifference, and Sal knew for certain that something other than her pregnancy was bothering her.

'Bob's downstairs so are you coming down to say hello?' she asked. 'He's made some tea.'

'Yeah, might as well,' Ann said, getting heavily to her feet.

Sal knew better than to ask questions when her sister was in this sort of mood but she was concerned and curious as to what had upset her. Something obviously had.

Ann was reduced to tears at the antenatal appointment because the doctor told her that her blood pressure was cause for concern so she must go to bed as soon as she got home and stay there until he told her otherwise.

'I can't do that,' she told him, appalled.

'Oh really and why is that?'

'I have a job to do.'

'I'm afraid you must rest,' he insisted.

'But I'm not ill so why should I have to carry on like an invalid?' she demanded.

He peered at her over his spectacles, his expression grave.

'Because you are an expectant mother and as such you have a responsibility to your unborn child,' he said sharply. 'If you don't do as I say you may harm your baby.'

'Oh, I see,' said Ann, thoroughly put in her place.

'No one is indispensable, my dear,' he went on in a kindlier manner. He'd been the family doctor for years and knew them well. 'I'm sure your sister can manage without you in the shop.'

'Of course,' confirmed Sal. 'How long does she need to stay in bed for?'

'Possibly until the baby is born in two months' time,' he said, shocking both sisters. 'It depends what happens with the blood pressure. I shall arrange for the district nurse to call in regularly to keep a close eye on it. For the moment complete bed rest is essential for the health of both mother and baby.'

'I'll see that she does it, Doctor,' said Sal and escorted her sobbing sister from the room.

'My life isn't my own any more,' wailed Ann as they walked home through the town, many of the shops closed as it was Wednesday afternoon.

'I don't suppose it can be now,' said Sal.

'Thanks a lot, that makes me feel a whole lot better,' she snapped sarcastically.

'I didn't mean to rub it in and I don't know any more about these things than you do but to me it's obvious that life can't be the same as before when you have a baby,' said Sal, 'because the child has to come first. You've moved on to the next stage of your life and you're not number one any more.'

'I feel as though I've lost all control over my life and the baby isn't even here yet,' said Ann. 'God knows what it'll be like when it is.'

'Other women seem to make the transition into motherhood and so will you,' said Sal supportively. 'I expect you'll feel differently when you actually see your baby. It might take a while to get used to being a mum but I'm sure it will all be worthwhile.'

'Meanwhile what about the shop while I'm stuck in bed?' Ann asked. 'You'll be very pushed without me.'

'You let me worry about that,' Sal assured her. 'Gran and I will manage.'

But when they got home to find their grandmother showing the early symptoms of the bronchitis she was prone to in winter which always required a spell in bed, Sal did wonder how she was going to cope with the shop on her own as well as two invalids to look after. 'I'll do it somehow,' she told herself.

'It's getting on for half past eight, Sal, and you've been on the go since early this morning so it's time you called it a day,' said Bob, pouring tea for them both and putting it on to a tray on the corner of the kitchen table. 'Come into the living room with me and sit down.'

'Sorry I'm always working, Bob,' apologised Sal, who was stirring toffee in a saucepan. 'I know I've been neglecting you lately but there's so much to do with Ann and Gran out of action. It is only temporary, I promise you.'

'Don't worry about me. I'm thinking about you,' he told her. 'It's too much work for one person.'

'I have had some help in the shop from a certain good Samaritan,' she said. Bob helped out on the counter when he wasn't out working in his taxi. 'Anyway, the situation isn't going to last for ever.'

'Ann will be out of action for a while yet, though, won't she?' he reminded her.

'Mm, she could be. Gran should be up and about again quite soon though. She'll take over on the domestic front which will make a big difference and she'll give me some help in the shop once she's back on her feet.'

'And make the toffee.'

'Yes, that too,' she agreed. 'I'm very glad she taught me how to do it though. We've sold right out and it's one of our bestsellers.'

'That lot should keep your customers happy for a while,' he said, looking at the trays of toffee setting on the kitchen table.

'This pan is the last one.' She lifted the saucepan off the gas and added some nuts. 'I'll get it into the tin and come in the other room and sit down with you.'

'Shall I take the patients a cup of tea?'

'If you don't mind,' she said, pouring the toffee into its tin and putting the saucepan in the sink. 'I don't know what I would have done without you these last few weeks.'

'Glad to help,' he said cheerfully.

'Could you tell them I'll bring their cocoa up later on?' she asked him.

'Sure.'

The past month had been a very testing time for Sal as she'd struggled to run the shop, the house and look after her sister and grandmother. She'd had to rise early to keep on top of the paperwork as well as the general administration and ordinary day-to-day shop work and the cooking and housekeeping. Gran had had a bad time with acute bronchitis but was on the mend now so should soon be back doing the cooking even if she wasn't strong enough to work in the shop. Ann probably wouldn't be back at work until after the baby was born and her hours would be restricted then because of her new responsibilities.

But Sal was determined not to take anyone on from outside even on a temporary basis. This was a family business and if possible that's how it would stay. Although she was tired and had virtually no spare time, a part of her revelled in the challenge. She had learned a lot about herself since she'd lost Terry and her parents. She had discovered strengths she'd never before been aware of and knew now that she thrived on hard work.

Bob, bless him, had been a wonderful support. As well as helping out in the shop he kept her spirits up with his cheery presence. He'd also been to the new cash and carry warehouse to collect some stock to tide them over until the wholesaler's delivery. This new idea of traders being able to buy stock in smaller amounts on a pay-as-you-go basis was brilliant, though she could only use the service if Bob was around as she had no transport. And that was something else she needed to speak to him about . . .

'Ooh, this tea is welcome,' she said, a bit later, snuggled up on the sofa with Bob and a tray of tea and biscuits. 'When we've had this I want you to come down the garden with me.'

'That sounds interesting.'

'Not that,' she said, slapping his arm. 'I want to show you something in the shed.'

'Promises, promises.'

'Oh Bob, stop mucking about,' she laughed.

'I was being serious,' he said with a wry grin. 'But you've got me intrigued now so finish your tea and let's go to the shed.'

She did as he said and led him down the back garden path, armed with a torch, and opened the door of the shed.

'Oh, so it's a garage, not just a shed,' he said as they went inside and she shone the beam on her father's green Morris Minor.

'I think it was originally built as a shed but as it was big enough for Dad's car and there's an alleyway at the back to get it in and out, he used it as a garage. But we always call it the shed and we use it for the lawnmower and other garden tools.'

'So why are we here in the dark and cold at this time of night?' he wondered. 'I assume you don't want me to mow the lawn.'

'Course I don't,' she laughed. 'I want to know what you think of the car and the idea of putting it back on the road.'

'It's a good motor,' he said, shining the torch over it again. 'Well looked after. But who would drive it?'

'Me. Obviously I'd have to learn to drive first,' she said. 'But it would be so useful for the shop; to go to the cash and carry and the wholesaler's on the odd times when they can't deliver. It isn't a huge car but there would be enough room to carry stock in the boot and on the back seat.'

'It does seem a bit daft for it to be wasting away in here when you could be making use of it,' he said. 'Yeah, I think it's an excellent idea. But wouldn't you need to discuss it with Ann and Dolly before you decide?'

'Yes, of course, but I wanted your opinion before I raised the subject.'

'I'm flattered.'

'Ann won't care one way or the other but Gran might not like it,' she said. 'It is still Dad's car after all and she may think we should leave it alone.'

'But you want to use it to help you run his shop so I'm sure she'll be all right about it.'

'It might be handy for private use as well,' she mused. 'When Ann has had the baby for instance. She might want to learn to drive it so she can go further afield with the little one.'

'From what you've told me about your father he would be pleased to have you use it,' he said. 'He sounds like a really nice bloke who would want to make things easier for you.'

'He is a very nice man but Ann wouldn't agree with you about that, nor would a few others round here.'

'That's their problem. You can't judge a person for one wrong thing they do in their life. From what I've heard he was always a good husband and father. All right, clearing off and leaving you wasn't the best idea but he must have had his reasons. As you have said, you and Ann are both adults and he left you with a good source of income. So I think using his car is perfectly in order.'

'Thanks Bob,' she said, shivering. 'I'll speak to the others about it sometime soon. Let's go inside into the warm.'

With his arm round her casually they walked back up the garden path.

A little later that same evening, while Sal and Bob were snuggled up together on the sofa downstairs, Dolly was sitting on Ann's bed keeping her company while they drank their cocoa.

'I'll be up and about in a couple of days, thank Gawd,' said Dolly. 'I bet Sal will be glad too. It's a lot for her having everything to do and us to look after as well.'

'It is, Gran,' Ann agreed. 'I'm absolutely bored stiff with lying about in bed. I mean it isn't even as if I'm ill. I feel guilty about Sal having to do everything and wait on me as well when there's nothing wrong with me.'

'Sal wouldn't want you to do anything that might put your baby at risk,' said her grandmother.

'I know, she's very good,' she said and burst into tears.

'Whatever's the matter, love?' Dolly asked, putting down her cocoa and slipping a comforting arm round the younger woman.

'Nothing Gran. I'm just being silly. I'm fine really. I don't know what came over me. Must be my hormones playing up again.'

'Pregnancy does make women weepy at times.'

'I feel all on my own, Gran,' Ann said, mopping her eyes with her handkerchief. 'As though me and my bump are isolated from the rest of the world. I know that you and Sal are with me all the way and I'm very grateful but I still feel lonely inside myself, sort of set apart.'

'Is there anything you want to talk about, dear?' enquired Dolly. 'Something that might be causing this lonely feeling that's upsetting you? Something to do with the baby's father perhaps.'

'Nothing that being up and about again won't put right,' Ann said, seeming to pull herself together.

Her grandmother didn't believe a word of it. Ann had been troubled about something for weeks. Looking back Dolly recalled it seemed to have started that weekend that Sal was away in Devon with Bob. Something had triggered her strange mood and it was before she'd been confined to bed.

Oh well, whatever it was she obviously didn't want to share it so all Dolly could do was to be on hand if she was needed.

Both Ann and Dolly thought that bringing Horace's car into use was an excellent idea. Ann even said she might think about learning to drive it after the baby was born. So Sal applied for her provisional licence with a view to booking a course of lessons in the New Year.

Christmas was very quiet that year. Bob felt duty bound to go to Devon to see his folks, Ann was still confined to bed so there was only Sal and her grandmother who was now fully recovered from her illness. They cooked turkey and all the trimmings and ate it in the bedroom with Ann. Sal determinedly tried to create some festive spirit but there were too many missing loved ones so she was glad to see the back of it and overjoyed when Bob returned from Devon.

A few days after Christmas, the doctor became even more concerned about Ann's blood pressure readings and decided to send her into hospital with a view to having the baby induced. But when she'd been in two days still nothing had been done.

Sal and Gran found her in very low spirits when they went to visit in the evening.

'You'd think I was a leper the way some of them in here carry on,' she said, glancing towards the ward where the mothers all had male visitors. 'Talk about smug.

They've all got their babies and their husbands visiting and I've got neither. As far as they're concerned I'm an outcast.'

'They're not all mean to you, are they?' Dolly enquired.

'One or two are OK but the rest are right bitches. There's a clique of them who are self-righteous and full of themselves.'

'You'll have your baby soon, love,' said Sal encouragingly.

'I still won't have the other essential item for acceptance as a parent though will I, a husband,' she pointed out, 'and that's what some people can't stand, though I think they actually enjoy it, being up there on the moral high ground looking down on me while they've got everything they want.'

'Take no notice of 'em love,' said Dolly. 'You won't be in here for ever.'

'It's beginning to feel as though I will,' she said mournfully. 'I came in to be induced but they keep delaying it for some reason. God knows why. They don't tell you anything.'

'I suppose they're hoping it will happen naturally,' suggested Sal. 'You are almost due now.'

Just then a nurse appeared and said the doctor had decided that they would be inducing the baby that evening.

'At last,' said Ann when the medic had gone, by which time visiting hour was over. 'Let's get on with it and get this baby born.'

'Good luck, kid,' said Sal, hugging her. 'We'll keep in

touch with the hospital and come to see you as soon as they'll let us.'

'Ta-ta darlin',' said Dolly, feeling anxious because she knew exactly what her granddaughter had to go through. 'We'll be thinking of you. Next time we see you, you'll have your baby and it will all be worth it, you'll see.'

Sal was on the verge of tears as she and her grand-mother walked out of the ward. It felt wrong leaving her sister there but those were the rules. Visitors out on the dot and not a second later. She did hope that Ann would be all right.

After a restless night and several phone calls to the hospital the next day, Sal and Dolly finally got the news they were waiting for. Ann had given birth to a baby boy. But they were told in no uncertain terms that they couldn't visit until the evening. Only husbands were allowed the privilege of visiting outside of the official visiting times.

Armed with flowers, fruit and chocolates, Sal and Dolly hurried excitedly into the ward and were too busy thinking about the new arrival to notice that all eyes in the ward were turned on them.

'You did it,' said Sal, hugging her sister and putting all the goodies down on the bed. 'Well done. You're a star and we're really proud of you.'

'Let's have a look at him then,' said Dolly, glancing towards the cot beside the bed.

'Help yourself,' said Ann. 'He's fast asleep so don't pick him up just yet.'

Sal and Dolly both peered into the cot from either side and a shocked silence ensued.

'Yes, I thought you'd be lost for words,' said Ann with a wry grin.

'He's beautiful,' said Sal at last. 'Isn't he Gran?'

'Absolutely,' agreed Dolly.

'Even if he is blacker than Nat King Cole?' said Ann.

'Most definitely,' Sal confirmed.

'So now you know why I didn't bring his daddy home to meet you,' said Ann on her first night home, late into the evening when she was feeding Tommy who she had named after his father, the name he used in England because it was simpler.

'You should have done,' said Sal. 'Surely you must have known that he would have been welcome here. We're not the sort of people to bother about the colour of someone's skin.'

'Yeah, I did know that, but not everyone is like you so there was no point in taking things to that level,' she explained. 'I knew we couldn't have a future together. The Notting Hill riots proved that. Black and white just don't mix in this country. We've made no progress whatever as far as that's concerned. If we had, the riots wouldn't have happened.'

Dolly gave her a shrewd look. 'That was what upset you when Sal was away in Devon, wasn't it? I knew there was something wrong but didn't connect it to the riots because we weren't affected in this area, at least I thought we weren't.'

'It rubbed salt into the wounds,' she admitted. 'But it made me even more certain that I'd done the right thing in giving Thomas up, for his sake more than mine. He's got his own culture. His people would have hated him being with a white girl as much as some of mine would hate me being with a black man. But I was very sad and worried about him because he lives around there, or he did when I knew him.'

'Surely there was a way you could have made it work, with a bit of support from us,' said Sal.

'It didn't happen so we'll never know for sure how it would have worked out.' Ann lifted the baby on to her shoulder and patted his back gently to bring up his wind. 'But I have a damned good idea.'

'Shouldn't you tell him about little Tommy, though?' asked Dolly. 'He has a right to know that he has a son.'

Ann shook her head. 'Absolutely not! He'd feel he had to do the decent thing and it would end in disaster. Honestly, things are best left as they are.'

'Where did you meet him anyway?' Sal enquired.

'In a café in the Notting Hill Gate area,' she explained. 'I was in there with a couple of girlfriends one Thursday evening, as the shops on Oxford Street stay open late on Thursdays, so we went straight from work and decided to walk some of the way home, for a laugh. We stopped at a café in a side street round there and he came in with some mates. He looked like Harry Belafonte, absolutely gorgeous, honestly. I was bowled over by him and I could tell that he liked the look of me but before we could do anything about it the café owner threw him out. It was a No Blacks place.'

'So how did you get to know him then?' asked Sal.

'I told the café owner what I thought of him and got chucked out as well, much to my friends' mortification,' she explained. 'Thomas thanked me for my support and we got talking outside, he asked me if he could see me again and . . . you know the rest.'

'All this going on in your life and you said nothing about it to us,' said Sal.

'I knew you would have worried – whether you like to admit it or not there is a lot of racial prejudice around – and I was so nuts about him I didn't want anything to spoil it so I buried my head in the sand and lived for the moment,' Ann said. 'Then when I fell pregnant I knew I couldn't fool myself any longer. So I ended it and broke my heart in the process.'

'His too by the sound of it.'

'Yes, very probably. But he'll have got over it by now. He has plenty of friends and his own way of life in Ladbroke Grove. Though why there has to be such animosity between people, I've no idea. I mean, we are all just human beings.'

'It's probably fear of the unknown,' said Dolly. 'People round there are worried for their jobs with so many newcomers settling in the area. There's housing problems too.'

'Thomas is an intelligent man but he sweeps up on the station to earn a living,' Ann told her. 'Not many white men are willing to do that. And as for their homes!

183

You wouldn't want to live like they do, Gran: several large families packed into one house and unscrupulous landlords charging the earth for a yard or two of sleeping space per person.'

'I've heard rumours about the housing,' said Sal.

'They're more than just rumours,' said Ann. 'I've been there and seen it for myself. There ought to be a law against charging such high rents but if there is one it isn't being enforced at the moment so the landlords can do what they like, especially as blacks are banned in so many places they are grateful for anywhere to live.'

Not being well informed on the details of any Rent Act, Sal just said, 'Anyway, the good news is that you've got your beautiful little boy and you're back home with us and out of that hospital, away from those horrible women.'

'Oh that load of witches; they were in their element when they saw Tommy,' she said with a wry grin. 'I was now the complete outsider, an unmarried mother to a black child. They loved it and were so obvious it would have been laughable if it hadn't been so hurtful. Then a sweet black nurse came on duty and they didn't dare to look down their noses at me while she was around because she was in charge. Anyway, I'm away from all that now, though I suppose I'll be getting a few funny looks and strong comments from the people round here.'

'Bound to,' said Sal. 'But we've all got broad backs so let them say what they like.'

'If you've finished feeding him can I hold him?' asked Dolly. 'Sal will go and make the cocoa won't you love?'

'Course I will.'

'As soon as I've got into a routine with his nibs I shall be pulling my weight again,' said Ann.

'Thank God for that,' said Sal approvingly. 'We've missed you.'

Tommy fitted into the family so easily, Sal couldn't imagine not having him around and the three women adored him. There were broken nights, of course, and days when he was fretful and strained their nerves a little but the joy he brought to the family outweighed the irritations by far.

Although Ann had been none too sure about her suitability for motherhood and had found it difficult to hold her head up during the pregnancy, now that Tommy was a reality she couldn't have been prouder or more confident. She loved showing her son off to the customers who came into the shop and he was such a picture, most of the women of the neighbourhood melted at first sight, especially as he grew and started to smile, his velvet dark eyes shining. There was some verbal abuse from ignorant and spiteful people but once the Storey women stood up to them they had less to say for themselves. With both her sister and grandmother back on form, life became more normal for Sal.

'It's good to have you back,' Bob remarked lightly one evening in March when they walked home from the cinema arm in arm having seen *Cat on a Hot Tin Roof* with Elizabeth Taylor and Paul Newman.

'Have I neglected you very much?' she asked.

'A bit. You've had a lot on your plate and I still got to see you so I'm not complaining but it's nice to go out on my night off.'

'I agree,' she said. 'Ann can't do the same hours as before in the shop because of the baby but she is back working part-time now.' She grinned. 'One thing my nephew will be used to as he grows up is people. We have him in the shop with us quite often and what a fuss the women make of him.'

'So now that your life has reverted to normal are you going to start driving lessons?'

'Yeah, I'm starting next week and Ann is planning on learning later on, which will be handy for the business.' She halted in her step and looked at him. 'You don't mind my having professional lessons as against having you to teach me do you? Only I really do want us to stay friends.'

He laughed heartily. 'I'm relieved,' he admitted. 'I wouldn't fancy sitting in the passenger seat with your hot temper beside me as I show you the ropes.'

'That isn't what you were supposed to say,' she teased. 'You should have said how disappointed you are.'

'We agreed from the start to be honest with each other,' he reminded her.

'I know,' she said, squeezing his arm, 'and I love you for it.'

'Likewise,' he said, thinking he must be the luckiest bloke in the whole of London to have the love of Sal.

'There's another coffee bar opening across the street, I see,' remarked Bob to his cabby pal Trevor as they sat at a table near the window eating bacon sandwiches in Mario's, a café in the back streets near Paddington where many of the London cabbies – men of all ages and types – spent their breaks. This was their social club and college, where they heard what was going on through the taxi grapevine: where one route had been exchanged for another, if a street name had been altered and what police examiners were doing to make life even more difficult for new cabbies. There was an air of animation and camaraderie as taxi drivers pored over maps, arguing good-humouredly over various street names. A fog of cigarette smoke hung in the air mingling with the pungent smell of frying.

'Coffee bars and launderettes are springing up every-where you look now,' remarked Trevor.

'And supermarkets,' added Bob. 'Not that I'm complaining about the launderettes. They're very handy for a single bloke like me.'

'I feel sad to see Charlie's hardware store go though,' said Trevor, looking across the street where the iron-monger's shop had once been and now builders were working and a sign announced Coffee Bar Opening Soon. 'It was useful when you had something that needed fixing at home and wanted nails and things. Charlie really knew his stuff about household repairs and was always ready to give advice.'

'Mm, it's a shame,' agreed Bob. 'The coffee bars are the money-spinners, that's why the entrepreneurs are keen to open as many as they can while they are so popular.'

'It's a shame when the original traders don't want to leave,' said Trevor.

'They get paid a packet to move away, I should think,' speculated Bob. 'And they don't have to go.'

'That isn't necessarily the case,' said Trevor. 'They are led to believe they are getting a good deal though it's usually well below the market price for their business. Some of them are only too happy to take the money and go because it's easier but, if they don't, the big boys pile on the pressure and get the place anyway.'

Bob frowned. 'They use bullying tactics to get them out. Is that what you mean?' he asked.

Trevor nodded. 'That does go on now that the economy is in better shape and businessmen are keen to set up shop in the latest new thing.'

'You hear about these things when you're out and about in London but I don't know anyone who's actually come up against it,' Bob remarked.

'I don't either but there's a regular in our local pub whose brother-in-law is a copper in the Met. He's usually got a tale to tell. Apparently there's a bent businessman called Bernie Fox who's buying up as many sites as he can get his hands on in and around London.'

'How does he operate exactly?' Bob was interested to know.

'Initially he approaches the shopkeeper and offers to buy his business,' his friend explained. 'All very cordial and friendly at first.'

'And if they refuse he turns nasty.'

'Very nasty. Windows get broken, doors smashed in and

the shop interiors wrecked. And if that doesn't work his thugs turn to beating the shopkeeper into submission.'

'What about the police?' asked Bob, horrified. 'Why don't they arrest this Bernie Fox?'

'He's too clever,' Trevor replied. 'He never goes near the places himself. He has his boys do it and the victims are too afraid to stand up to them.'

'Why don't the police pull the thugs in then?'

'They do but there's never enough evidence to make a charge stick because the victims are too afraid to speak out. Bernie and his henchmen are far too crafty to let themselves be vulnerable so the police are powerless to do anything about it. They've pulled Bernie Fox in a few times but have had to release him again.'

'I'd like a few minutes alone with him,' said Bob.

'Wouldn't we all?'

'It's surprising that he got a licence to open a café right opposite this one.'

'Fox has got friends everywhere. Anyway, it'll count as healthy competition. A different clientele too. The coffee bar will be full of youngsters.'

'Let's hope Fox doesn't set his sights on this place,' said Bob, glancing around the café. 'I can't see the boys being happy with frothy coffee and a jukebox during their break.'

Trevor gave a knowing grin. 'You can say that again, mate,' he said. 'I think Bernie Fox really would have a fight on his hands if he threatened any of our watering holes. There are a lot of us cabbies in London. We might not all get along all of the time but we stick together against crooked outsiders. North or south of the river.'

189

'That's true,' said Bob, lifting his large mug of tea and taking a healthy swallow.

Sal was flush with success as she drove herself and Bob home from the test centre having passed her test one sunny day in June 1959. She'd taken the test in the driving instructor's vehicle but Bob had been waiting for her in the Morris Minor in the expectation of good news.

'I'm so proud of you,' he said.

'Thanks,' she responded excitedly. 'I'm proud of myself as it happens but it's nice to know that you are too. I can't wait to tell Ann and Gran.'

'They'll be waiting with bated breath.'

'I won't pretend not to have passed because everyone does that as a joke when they've done some big important thing,' she said.

'Do they?'

'Of course.'

'I don't think I've ever done any big important thing in my life,' he said.

'Yes, you have,' she said. 'Apart from anything else, you did the knowledge and got your cabbie's licence.'

'What's big and important about that?'

'Stop pretending to be this hard-hearted, unemotional man,' she said. 'Because I know different.'

'Getting the cabbie's licence was a means to an end for me,' he told her.

'So was passing my driving test if you look at it that way because I need to drive for the shop,' she told him.

'But it's still an achievement, as is yours.' She paused, keeping her eyes on the road as they went round the alarmingly busy Hammersmith Broadway. 'It's lovely that you are pleased for me, though. I really do love having you in my life, Bob.'

'Oh well, if passing your driving test makes you feel loving towards me, I'll book you another one,' he joked.

'I've got my licence for life now or at least until I'm very old,' she said. 'So you'd be wasting your time.'

'Damn it,' he laughed.

'I shall miss you while you're in Devon,' she said wistfully because he was going to see his family the next day.

'Sure you won't come with me?'

'I'd love to but I need to be around while we get the stocktaking done,' she explained. 'It wouldn't be fair to leave it all to the others, especially as Ann has the baby to look after as well as her shop work. I'll come with you the next time you go.'

'I'll only be away for a few days anyway,' he said. 'But I shall miss you every moment.'

'Likewise,' she said with feeling.

It was the sharing that Sal valued so much in her relationship with Bob; knowing that things that happened to her meant as much to him as they did to her, and vice versa. Her happiness was his prime concern and that gave her a warm feeling inside. She trusted him implicitly and that was life-enhancing.

'I suppose I had better brace myself for a whole lot of female squealing and hugging when Dolly and Ann hear the news, hadn't I?' he said as they turned into Perry Parade.

'Yes, I think you better had,' she said, carefully pulling up outside the shop.

'Sal . . .' he began.

'Yeah,' she said, making sure the engine was turned off and handbrake on.

'Why don't we make it a double celebration?'

'In what way exactly?'

'Well, we've been seeing each other for over a year now. I know we both said we wouldn't . . . that we'd both been badly hurt—'

'But we know now that we won't hurt each other,' she cut in.

'You know what I'm trying to say, don't you?'

'I'm going to be a bit cheeky and take a guess and hope I'm right,' she said, beaming. 'The answer is yes, Bob, I would really love to marry you.'

As he took her in his arms, full of joy, there was a loud rapping sound on the car window.

'Oi, you two, that's enough of that old malarkey for now. Ann and I are waiting to know what happened about the driving test,' shouted Dolly.

They got out of the car, both faces wreathed in smiles as they prepared to tell her both pieces of good news. As they went into the shop with her, laughing and insisting on telling her and Ann the news together, they were unaware that they were being closely observed from a car parked further down the street on the other side of the road.

Chapter Eight

A steady and relentless drizzle fell on to the roof of the cottage, trickled down the windows and swelled the puddles in the yard, the surrounding landscape hidden from view by a rain mist that blended into the leaden grey sky.

'It's just as well Sal didn't come with me as the weather's so rotten,' remarked Bob to his mother who was busy making pastry on the kitchen table while he chatted to her over a cup of tea. 'It's as dark and dismal as November outside.'

'Maybe as it's wet today the rain will stay away on Saturday for the village summer fête for a change. The weather usually manages to put the mockers on it,' she said. 'Anyway, it's us Sal comes to see and she doesn't bother about the weather.'

'That's true,' agreed Bob.

'I am disappointed that she couldn't come, though, because I like to see her,' Mavis confessed. 'I hope the two of you haven't fallen out and that's why she's stayed away.'

'Quite the opposite, Mum,' he said excitedly, unable to keep the news to himself any longer. 'In fact, Sal is going to become part of the family.'

Mavis dropped the pastry she was kneading on to the board, staring at him. 'You mean . . . ?'

He smiled and nodded. 'Yeah, I've asked her to marry me and she said yes.'

'That's proper lovely,' she said, rushing over and putting her floury hands around him. 'Oh my lor, I'm that pleased.' Beaming, she ran to open the kitchen door and yelled towards the barn where her husband was working, 'Stan, come in 'ere directly. Not later on but now, this very minute.'

'Congratulations,' said Joe, wheeling himself over to his brother and offering his hand.

'Thanks, mate.'

'What's 'appened?' asked Stan in alarm as he burst in the door. 'Who's hurt themselves?'

'No one's hurt, Dad, but Bob's getting married to Sal,' explained Joe.

'Is that all?' said Stan, frowning. 'You nearly gave me an 'eart attack, Mavis. Fancy calling me in all urgent like, just to tell me that. I thought one of you was in trouble.'

'Is that all you have to say when your eldest son has just got engaged?'

Stan shook Bob by the hand. 'Well done, son. Sal is a grand girl. When's the wedding?'

'Give us a chance,' said Bob. 'It only happened yesterday. I haven't even had a chance to buy her a ring yet, let alone start making wedding arrangements.'

'Let's hope it gets as far as the wedding this time,' said Stan thoughtlessly but without malice.

'Take that back, Stan Beck,' ordered Mavis. 'That isn't a nice thing to say at all.'

'I didn't mean any harm, I was only saying that last time . . .'

'Well, this is this time and Sal is nothing like Kate,' stated Mavis, rolling out the pastry in an overzealous manner. 'This time it isn't going to go wrong. You and I are going to have a daughter-in-law, Stan. Oh my, I must write a letter to Sal offering our congratulations. You can take it back with you, Bob. As soon as the pub opens, Stan, you must go and get a bottle of something special so that we can drink a toast to the occasion.'

'I won't argue with you about that.'

'No staying down there till they close, mind,' she warned.

'As if I would,' he said, grinning.

'Quite,' she said with irony.

There was a knock on the kitchen door and Bob went to open it to see a pretty, dark-eyed young woman in a bright red plastic mac, headscarf and wellington boots, rain dripping from head to toe.

''Ello my luvver,' she said in a broad West Country accent. 'I'm Gloria from the village. I knows Joe from school and I've come to see if he wants a game of cards as it's so wet and miserable out.' She gave him a critical look. 'Ask me in then, for Gawd's sake. I'm getting soaked out here.'

'Sorry,' he said obediently and ushered her inside.

'Cor, what a day,' she said, shaking her mac and scarf over the kitchen sink then hanging them up in the lobby as though she was completely at home here, her near-black hair falling damply to her shoulders. 'It's enough to give you the pip. The great British summer, eh. It's a joke.' She looked at Joe. 'Fancy a game o' cards?'

'Yeah, I don't mind.'

'Any chance of a cup o' tea, Mrs B?' asked Gloria breezily, 'I'll make it if you're busy, and a few of your lovely cakes or biscuits would be nice. What are you making?'

'A meat pie and some jam tarts,' she replied. 'Not that it's any of your business.'

'A jam tart or three would be lovely when they're ready,' she said. 'I'll be back to make the tea directly. Come on Joe, let's get the cards out.'

She opened the door into the sitting room and without a word of protest Joe wheeled himself out of the kitchen and Gloria closed the door behind them.

'Cheeky young madam,' tutted Mavis. 'Not an ounce of shame in her.'

'She seems very much at home here so she must come regular,' observed Bob.

'She does,' confirmed his mother.

'You didn't say anything on the phone.'

'What's to tell?' she said. 'She isn't anyone important. Just a local girl who comes to see Joe.'

'Nothing going on between them then?'

'Of course not,' replied his mother adamantly. 'She comes round here and takes Joe out for a walk now and again, that's all, obviously.'

'Why obviously?' Bob enquired. 'A girlfriend would be good for him. He can't walk but everything else is in working order as far as we know.'

'Yes I agree, a girlfriend would be good for him but not *her*,' she stressed.

'What's wrong with her?'

'She's common for a start.'

'We're not exactly top drawer, Mum,' Bob reminded her.

'I'm not sure I like that remark, Bob Beck. Are you suggesting that we're riff-raff?'

'Of course not but we're not royalty either.'

'All right, we might be a bit rough and ready,' she conceded, 'but we do have standards. Whereas not only is Gloria as common as muck, she's never heard of morality. She'll go with anyone she fancies, according to village gossip anyway. No holding back with her.'

'It's kind of her to spend time with Joe though, isn't it? He needs company of his own age. And at least he doesn't shut her out as he did with his other friends.'

'He doesn't have much choice because she pushes herself in and won't take no for an answer. You've seen what she's like. She comes barging in 'ere as though she owns the place, demanding tea and biscuits. Honestly, the cheek of the girl.'

'But Joe is in the other room having a game of cards,' Bob pointed out. 'Surely that's better for him than sitting around watching you make pastry; better for you and Dad too.'

'Course it is,' agreed Stan.

'I might have known you'd approve just 'cause she's got a pretty face,' chided Mavis.

'It's got nothing to do with the way she looks. All right, I admit she is a bit pushy but at least she takes the time to spend with Joe.'

'She's after him, that's why,' declared Mavis with a disapproving air. 'She's looking for a husband.'

'Don't talk so soft,' said her husband. 'Do you seriously believe that a good-looking girl like Gloria would cast her net in the direction of a man with no prospects seeing as he can't walk let alone work? She might be a bit rough round the edges but she won't be short of admirers.'

'None that would want to marry her, though,' his wife retaliated. 'Not with her reputation.'

The conversation came to an abrupt halt when Gloria re-entered the room.

'Shall I put the kettle on now, Mrs B?' she asked, not waiting for a reply before taking the kettle off the stove and heading for the sink to fill it. 'I can see that you're busy.'

'Looks like you're doing it anyway,' said Mavis pointedly.

'Yeah, might as well, to save you the trouble,' she chirped, seeming unaffected by Mavis's remark. 'Anyone else fancy a cup? Go on, you might as well all have one as I'm making it. Biscuits will be all right for Joe and me as the jam tarts aren't ready yet.'

'Good, I'm pleased about that,' said Mavis with withering sarcasm.

Dumbfounded, Bob looked on as Gloria – apparently immune to Mavis's hostile attitude – filled the kettle and burst into song with a version of the Everley Brothers' hit 'Bye Bye Love' then proceeded to take the cups and saucers from the dresser and set them out on a tray. He hadn't seen this kitchen so cheerful since before Joe's accident despite his mother's thunderous look.

Bob could hardly believe that Mavis, a forthright woman, was allowing this slip of a girl to undermine her authority so blatantly. Maybe, despite her criticism of Gloria, Mum did actually appreciate the time the girl was giving to Joe and didn't want to frighten her away. Oh well, whatever the outcome, while his brother was occupied it took the strain off his parents and that could only be a good thing.

The Toffee Shop often served as a social centre as well as a retail outlet when locals happened to meet there and stayed for a chat. Such was the situation a few days later just before closing time. The shop was full; all three Storeys were serving and Tommy, now six months old, was in his pram being admired by one and all.

'Isn't he coming on?' said one female customer who was buying toffee.

'He's gorgeous,' said another in the queue. 'Those lovely eyes and such a cheeky smile.'

'These dark skinned . . . brown, er . . . coloured babies,' began a woman uncertainly, 'are often very pretty.'

'I think the term is black,' offered Sal helpfully.

'Sorry, I wasn't sure . . . it's a bit awkward. I mean, I don't know any others,' she said as though Tommy was some sort of rare species. 'Though I've seen some around, of course.'

'That's all right, I'm sure my sister wouldn't be offended if she'd heard.' She looked across at Ann who was serving on the tobacco counter. 'But she hasn't so you're all right.'

The good-humoured dialogue continued until a woman in the sweet queue reached her turn at the counter and made an announcement. 'It's a damned disgrace,' she began, glaring at Sal. 'That sister of yours should be thoroughly ashamed of herself, not putting that baby of hers on show for all to see. This used to be a respectable shop.'

'Do you mind,' objected Sal, instantly furious. 'I don't like to hear criticism of a member of my family.'

'Even if she did sleep with a black man and is a mother to an illegitimate child?' the woman demanded.

Sal threw her a furious look. 'Yes, even then,' she said forcefully. 'My sister's private life is none of my business and it certainly isn't any of yours.'

'Talk about blatant shamelessness . . .'

'Because of the attitude of bigots like you – who make life hell for people like my sister and her baby's father – she's bringing her beautiful son up on her own,' Sal went on. 'So get out of this shop and don't come back. Go on, bugger off.'

The woman was clearly taken aback by the onslaught but she stood her ground. 'I want a quarter of acid drops please,' she said determinedly.

'Well you won't get them here,' declared Sal, coming out from behind the counter and confronting the woman. 'So get out before I drag you out.'

'I've never been so insulted.'

'We're the ones who are insulted, our family, so clear off back to your den, you old witch.'

As the woman turned to leave, Sal took her arm and helped her on her way. 'Get out of here and never come back,' she said as she pushed the woman out of the door and shut it after her with a resounding slam. She addressed the remaining customers. 'Right, who's next to be served? Or does anyone else have anything to say on the subject?'

The shop was only normally this silent when it was closed. Then Ann said, 'Thanks, sis. Well done.'

A murmur of agreement rippled through the room then someone said nervously. 'A quarter of chocolate toffee please.'

'Coming up,' said Sal and the chatter resumed.

There was a man at the end of the queue, a stranger who was well dressed but flamboyant in a light grey suit, Italian-style shoes and a colourful tie.

'Well done for fighting your corner,' he said when his turn came by which time the rest of the customers had left. 'You can do without people like her in your shop.'

'I'll say.' Sal was struggling to calm down as she was still blazing. 'So what can I get you?'

'Half a pound of fruit drops please,' he said. 'I'm very partial to boiled sweets.'

'Certainly,' she said, lifting the jar off the shelf.

201

'The public can be infuriating when you're that side of the counter sometimes, can't they?'

'We don't usually have much trouble here because they are mostly regulars,' she told him. 'But yes, you can get the odd difficult customer every now and again and she really was one of the worst we've had.'

'It's at times like this that you feel like getting out of the retail trade, I expect.'

'Oh no, not me. I love the job.' She looked at him. 'Why? Are you a retailer?'

'No, but I know people who are and they sometimes get fed up with being at the public's beck and call.'

'We all get fed up from time to time whatever we do for a living,' she said, weighing up the fruit drops. 'It doesn't mean we want to change to something else.'

'Speak for yourself,' said Ann who now had Tommy in her arms. 'I get fed up with the sight of this shop sometimes and I'd cheerfully do something else.'

'Take no notice of her,' Dolly intervened jokingly. 'The grass is always greener for my granddaughter.'

'Like that is it?' he said lightly.

Sal took his money and handed him his change, still smarting from the altercation and trying not to show it. 'Enjoy your sweets,' she said, eager to close the shop so that she could relax and stop hiding her feelings.

'I was wondering if I could have a chat with the three of you after hours sometime soon?' he enquired politely.

'Oh so you're a rep are you?' said Sal. 'We're very happy with our regular supplier thank you.'

'No, I'm not a confectionery rep,' he said. 'But I think you'll be interested in what I have to offer.'

'We've got all the insurance we need, thanks,' Dolly informed him.

'I'm not an insurance salesman either,' he told her. 'Half an hour, that's all I ask. I promise you won't regret it.'

'We'll give you fifteen minutes maximum,' said Sal. 'Not a minute longer. By the time closing time comes all we want to do is go upstairs and have something to eat.'

'Fair enough, fifteen minutes it is,' he agreed.

'You'd better come tomorrow night after we close the shop then,' said Sal wearily. She was used to persuasive reps plying their trade but couldn't face having to deal with one this evening.

'Thank you, ladies,' he said, heading for the door. 'I look forward to seeing you tomorrow.'

'It cost him a bag of fruit drops to get the appointment,' chuckled Dolly after he'd gone. 'It'll be some new product that's come on to the market that he wants us to push, I expect.'

'Anyway, it's knocking-off time,' Ann reminded them, 'so I'll go and feed and bath his nibs.'

'I'll just cash up and I'll be up too,' said Sal.

Dolly lingered after Ann had gone.

'Aren't you supposed to be doing the meal, Gran?' asked Sal, taking the pound notes out of the till.

'It's finishing off in the oven,' she said. 'I wanted a quiet word with you because I can see that you're upset.'

'Who says I'm upset?'

'Me. Even if you didn't have the tell-tale red blotches all over your neck, I would know, and I just wanted to reassure you that you did right in throwing that woman out.'

'It wasn't very professional though, was it?' Sal said. 'I could have been more polite about it. But what she said made my blood boil and I just acted on instinct.'

'Your instinct was right.'

'I'd do the same again,' she said. 'I'd sooner have no customers left at all than have that sort of talk in the shop.'

'Fortunately it won't come to that because most people keep their opinions to themselves, when they're in the shop at least. I know Ann has shocked the neighbourhood but most of them are decent people even though they enjoy a good old gossip behind our backs. Anyway, they need us as much as we need them.'

'I don't know for how much longer with all these supermarkets opening up and stocking sweets.'

'We're a community store,' Dolly said. 'There will always be a place for us. They can't get home-made toffee fresh out of the pan in the supermarket, can they?'

'That's true.' Sal looked at her grandmother and tears welled up. 'Oh Gran, you're such a comfort. It hurts me to hear bad things said about Ann and Tommy.' She pointed to her heart. 'It actually hurts and I can't hold back.'

'And nor should you have to in a case like that.' She gave Sal an affectionate hug. 'Right. Now you get on with cashing up and I'll go and see to the dinner.'

'Thanks Gran,' she said and turned her attention back to the cash register, her fingers trembling slightly.

'The King's Road, Chelsea please,' said the young woman with the Audrey Hepburn fringe who got into Bob's taxi outside Waterloo Station.

'What number?'

'I want to go to the Mary Quant shop, Bazaar,' she said. 'I don't know what number it is.'

'Don't worry, I know,' he assured her. 'Every taxi driver in London knows where that shop is.'

'Yeah, it's very famous but I've never been there before,' she said, settling in the back seat. 'But I've heard so much about it and as I've got the afternoon off work I thought I'd go and see for myself.'

'That street is very fashionable,' he said. 'A lot of arty types hang out round there.'

'That's why I'm going,' said the girl, who looked to be about seventeen. 'I'm really excited and dying to buy something from Bazaar. I've got some birthday money to spend which is why I can afford to splash out on a taxi.'

'Do you live in London?' he asked to be sociable, while inwardly cursing the swarms of motor scooters that were so prevalent on London's roads at the moment and needed all his concentration to avoid them.

'No, I live miles out in the suburbs,' she said. 'But we can be just as go-ahead as Chelsea girls.'

'Of course you can.'

'They say that Mary Quant stuff is reasonably priced even though it's posh where it is.'

'Is it really? Women's fashion isn't my strong point, I'm afraid,' he said politely.

He hoped she wasn't going to chatter all the way because he wasn't in the mood. He wanted to gather his thoughts after the visit to the family. He'd got back from Devon too late last night to see Sal so was planning on finishing early today in order to get to Hammersmith in time to spend the evening with her. His thoughts drifted back to his stay in Devon and his brother.

'I wouldn't touch her with a bargepole in that way,' Joe had said when Bob had gently probed about Gloria.

'You seem quite friendly though,' Bob had observed.

'We're mates, that's all,' he'd said.

'She seems like a really nice girl to me.'

'She's as rough as old boots, and you know it.'

'That doesn't mean she doesn't have a good heart.'

'Try telling that to Mum.'

'There's no need,' he'd said. 'If Mum hadn't realised that, Gloria wouldn't get through the door.'

'Mm, I suppose you're right. I don't know why Gloria bothers with me to tell you the truth,' Joe had confided. 'It can't be much fun spending time with a cripple. Especially for someone like her, a girl who likes a good time and is never short of a bloke to take her out. Still, she does all that when she isn't with me, I suppose.'

'Could be but I've no idea,' Bob had said.

Bob's reverie was interrupted by his passenger. 'I think we're there,' she said excitedly. 'I just saw a street sign.'

'Yes, I'll drop you as near as I can to Bazaar.'

'Thanks.'

They proceeded along the street which was fairly quiet. Here and there were traditional grocer's shops, boutiques and small classy-looking cafés. It was all very refined.

'It's quieter than I expected,' said his passenger. 'Because it's so well known I thought it would be crowded.'

'It's a weekday, that's why,' he explained. 'You should be here on a Saturday afternoon. There are plenty of people about then, parading in their fashionable clothes.'

'Ooh look, there's Bazaar,' she squeaked eagerly as he slowed down ready to stop. 'How thrilling.'

He smiled as he watched her trip lightly towards Mary Quant's iconic emporium which had opened in 1955 and was now a London landmark. Oh well, he thought, as he pulled out into the traffic, only a few hours more and he could finish work and see his beloved Sal.

'Make it quick boys, if you wouldn't mind,' requested Ann when the stranger in the suit and his colleague arrived at the shop on the dot that evening. She kissed Tommy's head. 'I've got things to do with my little boy here.'

'And I'm needed in the kitchen,' added Dolly, all three women standing behind the counter. They knew how persistent sales reps could be so were taking a firm line from the start. 'So show us your catalogues of whatever it is you want to sell to us and we can all get on with our evening in peace.'

'We're not here to sell you anything,' said the man they had met yesterday.

'We're here to buy,' added the other one who had whisky-scented breath and his hair styled in an elaborate quiff.

'Why didn't you come when the shop was open then?' asked Sal, a little peeved. 'I've done the cashing up now and we've finished work for the day. So what is it you want? Sweets, chocolate, cigarettes?'

'None of those.'

'What then?'

'Your shop,' he announced calmly. 'Our boss wants to buy your shop and we're here to do the negotiations.'

The women stared at him in disbelief.

'You've had a wasted journey then,' said Sal when she'd recovered sufficiently to speak. 'Even if we wanted to, which we most definitely don't, this business isn't ours to sell. It belongs to my father. You should have done your research.'

The man looked slightly taken aback by this news but he recovered swiftly. 'So, we'll deal with your dad then,' he stated.

'You'll have a job, mate,' said Ann. 'We don't know where he is and neither does anyone else.'

'Mm,' said the second man thoughtfully. 'I can see that that might be a bit of a problem but nothing we can't solve with a little bit of savvy.' He paused, mulling it over. 'We can perhaps arrange to rent the premises from you.'

'I don't understand what you're getting at,' said Sal, puzzled. 'How can we rent the premises to you when we're using them ourselves?'

'You wouldn't be using them,' he explained, keeping his gaze on her while he spoke. 'The shop will be turned into a launderette. Our boss has got a chain of them all over London, and yours is exactly the site he is after, being in a parade away from the main town but in a built-up area where plenty of people won't have their own washing machines. It will be an asset to the community; far more useful than a sweetshop.'

'Not to mention a money-spinner for your boss,' Sal put in.

'Exactly,' said Ann.

'The boss might be willing to consider letting you stay on in the living accommodation,' he went on. 'So if we were to come to a rental agreement, you wouldn't be out of pocket. He'd make sure of that.'

'That' very generous of him,' said Sal sarcastically. 'We're not interested so you might as well leave now.'

The man took a silver cigarette case out of his pocket, lit a cigarette and inhaled deeply.

'I don't think you have quite got our drift,' he said, slowly exhaling a cloud of smoke. 'Our boss really wants this site and what he wants he always gets one way or another. He isn't the sort of man who copes well with obstacles standing in the way of his business plans. In fact he doesn't tolerate them.'

A shiver ran up Sal's spine but she managed to appear calm. 'Are you threatening us?' she asked in a spirited manner.

'Yeah, they flippin' well are,' Ann cut in heatedly. 'The brass neck of them.'

'We are not threatening you,' said the first man smoothly. 'We are simply offering you an excellent business opportunity.'

'Threatening people is against the law, you know,' Dolly reminded him.

Noticing the tremble in her grandmother's voice, despite her feisty attitude, Sal put her arm round her and said to the unwanted guests, 'Look the answer is one hundred per cent no so can you leave now please as you are upsetting my grandmother.'

The men made no move to go. 'We're not ready to leave yet,' announced the one with the quiff and his tone was grim. 'We need to have an agreement in principle to take back to the boss. He won't accept anything less.'

'Well you won't be getting one from us, not now, not ever,' Sal made clear. 'We're not selling or renting or changing anything at all around here. This shop will remain as it is indefinitely. Do you understand me?'

'I understand what you're saying but it isn't acceptable to us,' he told her. 'Believe me, you'd do well to agree sooner rather than later. It will save you a whole lot of aggravation and we'll get our way in the end, I promise you.' He rested his gaze meaningfully on Tommy. 'After all, you do have a little one to consider. I'm sure you don't want anything to happen to him.'

'That's a threat if ever I heard one,' said Sal, 'so get out and leave us alone.'

'I'll call the police,' said Ann shakily.

'And tell them what exactly?' the man asked glibly. 'We've done nothing wrong. Just offered you the chance of a fair business deal and shown a kindly interest in the kid. You'd be done for wasting police time.'

'You threatened my baby,' said Ann, holding Tommy ever closer. 'You need locking up.'

'We'll take a chance on the police's attitude to our allegations,' said Sal and was on her way over to the telephone when there was a tap on the shop door.

'What's going on?' asked Bob when Sal let him in and he saw Dolly looking pale and shaky, Ann on the verge of tears and Sal about to explode.

'We're being threatened by these thugs, Bob, and I'm just going to call the police,' explained Sal, her voice shaking with a mixture of fury and fear. 'They're after our shop.'

'We're not threatening anyone,' said one of the men. 'Do we look like thugs?'

'Flash suits don't hide what you are,' said Sal, 'and I'm calling the police right now.'

'No, Sal, don't involve the law,' advised Bob, astonishing her.

'But we have to . . .'

'Not at this stage,' Bob insisted. 'Just let these gentlemen tell me exactly what their business is with you then we'll see about what action to take. OK boys, I'm a very close friend of the family so tell me what's going on.'

While the women looked on nervously, they gave Bob an adapted version of what they wanted with the threats edited out.

'I see,' said Bob, amazing the women with his obliging attitude. 'Well, it sounds like a fair enough plan to me.

So why not give us a couple of days to work out the finer points of the deal and come back and see us again. Say Thursday night just a bit later than this to make sure the ladies have finished their evening meal and so on.'

'What are you doing, Bob?' demanded Sal. 'They're crooks and they threatened us.'

'I'm sure they didn't intend to,' he said in an even tone. 'They are just offering you the chance to make a change.' He held out his hand to the spokesman. 'Shall we see you on Thursday evening then, gentlemen?'

'Er . . .' began the quiff, sounding uncertain.

'You can tell your boss that the deal is done all bar the shouting,' Bob went on, shaking the other man's hand. 'Just leave the ladies to me.'

'Thursday night then,' said the man and they left.

'Well,' exploded Sal furiously. 'Leave the ladies to me indeed. What a cheek and so much for solidarity. I was sure we could rely on support from you.'

'You can.'

'Sounds like it,' she snapped. 'You were practically ready for us to sign on the dotted line.'

'I shall have to ask you to trust me on this one,' he said, looking from one to the other. 'Please just let me deal with it in my own way. I promise you, you will keep the shop and none of you will come to any harm.'

'But—' began Sal.

'No questions, Sal, if you don't mind,' he said. 'But a cuppa would be nice.'

'Are you eating with us?' asked Dolly. 'There's plenty so you're very welcome.'

'Thanks but I can't stay long.'

'What!' exclaimed Sal. 'I thought we were supposed to be spending the evening together. I haven't seen you since you got back from Devon.'

'I know and I did intend to spend the evening with you, sweetheart,' he said, putting his arm round her. 'But I have other things to see to after all.'

She nodded, guessing that those things would be connected to their present problem. 'Oh I see,' she said knowingly.

After Dolly had gone to bed the sisters stayed up talking about the events of the evening.

'I'm terrified and I don't mind admitting it,' confessed Ann, looking pale and tense. 'Scared for Tommy. I don't know what I'd do if anything happened to him.'

'Nothing will,' said Sal.

'But these people don't know the meaning of decency,' Ann pointed out. 'They'll do whatever it takes to get their own way. They've probably got plans to kidnap Tommy and hold him until we agree to do what they want.'

'Now you're letting your imagination run wild,' said Sal. 'We'll just have to trust Bob.'

'I do trust him but what can he do against people like them? He's just an ordinary decent bloke. They are gangsters. Violence will be second nature to them. They won't care who they hurt. Babies, old ladies, anyone.'

'I don't know what Bob can do or how he'll do it,' said Sal. 'But I do know that he'll get it sorted.'

The sisters were in the living room drinking cocoa. 'Tommy is very vulnerable without a dad,' said Ann sadly.

'He does have a dad.'

'Not one who is involved in his life.'

'Maybe his dad might like to be if he knew of his son's existence.'

'Yeah, I do sometimes wonder what he'd think of him,' Ann admitted wistfully, surprising her sister as she rarely spoke along these lines. 'Especially now that he's getting bigger and developing his own personality.'

'His father would be very proud of him, I should think.'

'Mm.' Ann looked meditatively into space. 'I expect he would too. But we'll never know for sure because I will not be going down that road.'

'I thought you were softening there for a moment,' remarked Sal lightly.

'It isn't a question of that because I love the man to bits and there's nothing I would like better than to be with him. For the three of us to be together as a family,' she said. 'But I am all Tommy has and it's my job to protect him. I'm not having him being split between the two cultures.'

'You know more about it than I do,' admitted Sal. 'I've always been outside of that world.'

'So had I until I met Thomas and then I learned a lot about prejudice on both sides. It's better this way, believe me, Sal. Anyway, Thomas has probably got someone else by now. He's a good-looking bloke. There'll be no shortage of choice.'

Sal thought enough had been said on the subject so she steered the conversation away from it.

'Is Gran OK, do you think?' she asked.

'As far as I know, why?'

'She went off to bed in a hurry tonight. I know she's a strong woman but she's getting on a bit in years to have to deal with threats from bullies like that.'

'She was really scared when they were in the shop, I think,' said Ann, 'I noticed that she was trembling.'

'I was too,' said Sal. 'We all were.'

'But Gran seemed to perk up once Bob had said he'd deal with it, though she will always put up a front however she is feeling. She would never admit to any kind of weakness. It's a shame really,' said Ann. 'Surely when you're old you're entitled to admit to feeling a bit fragile at times.'

'You'd think so, wouldn't you,' agreed Sal, 'and I expect some older people do. But our gran would have to be on her last legs before she'd do that.'

'Oh well, I suppose we'd better turn in or we'll be half dead in the morning.'

'Even if we can't get to sleep we'll be resting.' Sal rose. 'Come on, kid. Let's get up those stairs.'

'I'm right behind you,' said Ann.

Dolly was thrashing about in the sheets unable to sleep or even rest because of tight tension knots in her stomach and a racing heart. The episode in the shop this evening had really unnerved her but she didn't want the girls to know because they looked to her to be strong, especially now that their parents weren't around. That's why she'd gone to bed early so that she could hide away from them under the covers.

Being a positive soul in the normal run of things, she didn't often feel lonely or depressed but she felt very much alone tonight. Even after many years of widowhood, she still missed her beloved husband quite painfully at times. It was the absence of that special partner in her life that every now and again hit her hard; the one person who valued her above all others and knew her so well he could almost read her thoughts. She had the girls, of course, and she loved them dearly and vice versa but there was no one to give her that special cuddle that would make the events of this evening seem less frightening.

She must snap out of this before the morning. She didn't want the girls to worry about her. They had enough problems with the threat to the shop hanging over them. Besides, she was the one they turned to for reassurance; not the other way round. How could she be so self-indulgent as to wallow in her own feelings when poor Ann was worried sick about her baby?

A gentle tap on the door startled her.

'Are you still awake, Gran?' came Sal's voice.

'Yeah, I'm awake,' she replied. 'What's the matter? Has something happened?'

'No.'

'What do you want then?'

'Sorry to disturb you but we are just wondering if you're all right,' said Ann.

'Course I am, why wouldn't I be?'

'We thought you might be worrying about those men.' There was a silence. 'Can we come in please?'

'Come on,' said Dolly, sitting up and turning on the bedside light.

Pyjama-clad, they entered the room and made themselves comfortable sitting on her bed.

'We went to bed but neither of us can settle down,' explained Sal.

'Too tense to get to sleep,' added Ann. 'And we can't talk because we might wake Tommy.'

'So you've come to make sure that I don't get to sleep either, have you?' she asked, kidding them.

'Nothing seems so bad if you're there, Gran,' said Sal. 'Even those awful men.'

'You'd better get into bed with me then, hadn't you,' she suggested. 'Like you used to do when you were little.'

'Can we?'

'Course you can. One of you pop downstairs and make some tea and we'll have that and talk until we're ready to drop off.'

'I'll go down and do it,' offered Sal.

'Just remember girls, that us three are Storeys and as such we're tough. We're not going to let those crooks get us down,' she said resolutely.

'I'll second that,' said Sal, heading for the door.

'Especially as we have Bob to look out for us too,' Dolly added in a strong voice.

'Good old Bob,' said Ann. 'He'll sort something out.'

'Exactly,' agreed Sal on her way out.

As Ann climbed into her bed, Dolly noticed that her own feeling of desolation had lessened. That was what came of feeling needed and cared for, she thought, smiling to herself. Together the three of them could be strong. With Bob looking out for them too, they were nigh-on invulnerable.

'Now don't take up all the bed, Ann dear,' she said gently. 'We need to save some space for Sal and you're not little girls any more.'

'Sorry Gran,' Ann said, budging up.

Chapter Nine

On Thursday afternoon Bob parked his cab near a telephone box, put some coins into the slot sand dialled a number.

'Hello Sal,' he said.

'Bob, where have you been?' She sounded relieved to hear from him.

'Sorry I haven't been in touch, love,' he apologised. 'I've been very busy.'

'Just when I really need you, you disappear into thin air,' she said but she was only kidding because she knew he was genuine. 'As you can imagine, after what happened on Tuesday night we are all feeling a bit vulnerable.'

'I'm sure you must be but don't worry; all will be well,' he said in a warm tone.

'I hope you're coming over tonight,' she said.

'Er . . . yeah . . .'

'You don't sound too sure.'

'I will be over but I don't know what time I'll get there.'

'But those men are coming round, Bob,' she reminded him, her voice rising. 'You arranged it with them so I assumed you would be here when they arrive.'

'They won't be coming . . .'

'Oh, you've rearranged it, have you? So when will they be coming?'

'They won't.'

'Not ever?'

'That's right. So you can forget all about them and their crooked proposition,' he assured her. 'You won't hear any more about it. Take my word for it.'

'Bob . . . what have you done to them?' she asked, concerned for him.

'Nothing.'

'You'll be in big trouble if you've attacked them or anything,' she warned. 'I told you we should leave it to the police. You'll get hurt messing with the likes of them.'

'Whoops, the money is running out Sal, so I shall have to go.'

'I can't hear the pips.'

'I'll see you later,' he said and hung up.

He'd fibbed about the reason for the abrupt ending to the call because he hadn't wanted to explain himself just yet which was why he'd stayed away from the Storeys yesterday. The less they knew at this stage the better. All would be revealed to them but only when the job had been done, later this evening if all went to plan.

He walked back to his cab whistling, but he wasn't quite as carefree as he seemed.

★　　★　　★

'Who are you?' demanded Bernie Fox, a thin man of middle years well suited to his name, having pointed features and dark shifty eyes. His black hair gleamed with a lavish amount of Brylcreem and was worn so flat to his head it looked as though it had been painted on. He was wearing a light grey suit and shiny tie and was sitting at a desk in an office-like room in a house in the leafy suburb of Clapham. 'And, more importantly, how did you get into my house?'

'Your morons let us in,' replied Bob who was accompanied by a dozen or so of his cabbie pals including Trevor. 'They didn't have much choice as there are a lot more of us than there are of them.'

'Where are my men now?'

'Outside. Being looked after by several friends of ours,' replied Bob. 'Your thugs are tough but we are stronger in numbers, Bernie.'

'Mr Fox to you.'

'There are a lot of cabbies working in London, *Bernie*,' said Bob with deliberate emphasis on the name. 'And they all take a dim view when they hear about people being terrorised into letting go of their shop premises.'

'Oh, I've had enough of this,' stated Bernie in an irritated manner. 'I'm calling the police.'

'You won't do that,' said Bob with an air of confidence. 'You won't want to give them the opportunity of coming anywhere near you since they've been trying to put you away for years.'

Bernie gave him a sharp look, his thin lips set in a firm line, 'Who are you?' he asked again.

'My name is Bob Beck. My mates and I are all licensed London taxi drivers.'

'Peasants.'

'At least we earn our money honestly,' stated Bob, holding Trevor back as he moved forward as though to set about Bernie.

'And so do I,' claimed Bernie. 'I pay good money for the shop premises I take over. I'm a fair businessman.'

'Do you call paying way below the asking price and bullying people into selling to you fair business practice?'

The other man shrugged. 'I don't know where you got your information from but you've clearly been misinformed. I own a chain of businesses and all completely legit.'

'We know that isn't true but we don't have time to hang about here arguing about it,' said Bob. 'We have a living to earn and many of our lads are working tonight.'

'So state your business and get out,' said Bernie. 'The sooner the better.'

'We want, or rather we demand that you stop pestering the women at The Toffee Shop in Perry Parade, Hammersmith,' Bob informed him. 'They are not interested in doing business with you so leave them alone.'

'And you are going to make me, are you? A few cabbies.'

'If you look out of the window you will see that there are a lot more of us than just the ones in here. And they will all be willing to come and see you again if we hear that you are continuing to pester the Storey women.

What's more next time they won't be prepared to come all this way without any action.'

Bernie was beginning to look uncomfortable but doing his best to hide it and he didn't move from his desk. Bob walked over to the window and drew back the net curtains with a flourish. 'Come and have a look outside. It's still light.'

With an impatient sigh, the other man went to the window and looked out to see taxis parked all along the street and beyond. Even Bob was impressed by the turnout. Some of these men he'd never met personally but they'd heard through the grapevine that one of their own needed help and they'd answered the call.

'So what,' bluffed Bernie. 'I've got plenty of contacts.'

'Not as many as we have,' Bob told him. 'If necessary every cabbie in London will give us their support. There is a bond between us and we are loyal to each other, something you wouldn't know anything about because you have to buy people's support. We may not have influence individually but together we are unbeatable. Yeah, you've probably got a few louts with plenty of muscle working for you but we outnumber you by about a thousand to one. So leave the Storey women alone.'

The other man was clearly unnerved but wasn't quite ready to admit defeat. 'Oh go away and ply your grubby trade,' he said. 'I've got work to do.'

'And what would that be? Going through the phone book to find more small traders you can frighten into selling, or practically giving their business away to you?'

'Get out.'

Bob moved forward and the others followed so that Bernie was surrounded.

'Right,' said Bob. 'Are we going to do business or shall we rough you up?'

'I'll have you done for assault,' he threatened but a quiver was discernible in his voice.

'No you won't,' said Bob coolly. 'You won't do anything that involves the law. You're far too crafty for that. Now, we are busy people and we are getting bored with being around you. So this is the deal: you erase The Toffee Shop from your list of future acquisitions and we'll go away and leave you alone. If we hear that you've been anywhere near there again, and believe me we will hear about it, we'll be back, and we won't be in the mood to talk. Action will be our purpose then. Now what's it to be?'

There was a brief hiatus. 'All right, we won't go near The Toffee Shop again,' Bernie finally agreed, sounding really peeved. 'There are plenty of other prospects around. A few thick-headed taxi drivers won't stop my business empire from growing.'

'The police will get a case against you in the end you know,' Bob said. 'You won't get away with it for ever.'

The other man didn't say anything; just sat there putting on a defiant front in defeat.

'Come on boys, let's get out of here.' Bob and the cabbies left in a dignified manner.

'So how did you get all those taxi drivers together?' asked Sal after Bob had explained what had happened with Bernie Fox.

'Through Mario's the cabbies' café, that's our club and information centre,' he explained. 'The boys are in and out of there during the day. And those who hadn't gone in heard about it from those who had while they're out on the road. If there's anything important we can spread news quicker than the BBC through Mario's.'

'How did you find Bernie Fox's address?' asked Dolly.

'Mm. I wondered that,' said Sal. 'I doubt if those sort of people would make their personal details known to anyone outside of their own thuggish circle.'

'We intercepted the two morons at the end of your road in their car on the way to see you,' he replied. 'I knew what time they were coming so we were there waiting for them when they arrived.'

'How exactly did you do that?' This was Sal.

'We blocked them in with our taxis. Then some of us forced the information out of them. And don't worry, we didn't use violence. We didn't need to. Our power was in numbers. It took no time at all to frighten them into taking us to see their boss.'

'In their car?'

'No. We made them leave that where it was and we went in my cab with a taxi escort.' He grinned. 'You should have seen us. It was a sight for sore eyes.'

'Thanks Bob,' said Dolly. 'You've done well by us.'

'Yeah, you did a good job,' agreed Ann.

'Hear hear,' added Sal.

'We got a good result, that's the important thing,' said Bob. 'Not for the rest of his victims unfortunately because we can't make a full-time job of it. So we'll just have to hope that the police get him and his helpers banged up eventually.'

'This whole thing makes me feel as though we've led very sheltered lives,' Sal said. 'I mean, you hear about gangsters but if you don't come up against them they seem like the stuff of fiction. Now we know only too well that such people exist. Who would have thought anyone would be interested in a sweetshop away from the main shopping area?'

'Independents are what people like Bernie Fox are after. Shopkeepers they think they can bully. Some of the traders in the main shopping areas belong to big chains and he knows he wouldn't stand a chance with them,' he said.

'I suppose the majority of launderettes we see around are come by legitimately.'

'Oh yes,' said Bob. 'My local one is a godsend to a single bloke like me.'

'Not single for much longer, though,' said Ann.

His face lit up as though a warm glow was spreading within him. 'No, happily.'

'You'll be able to take my washing to the launderette as well as your own after we're married,' said Sal and they all roared with laughter.

'Glad to see she's setting out a few ground rules at this early stage,' observed Ann light-heartedly.

As the atmosphere lifted the Bernie Fox affair lost a little of its significance.

★　★　★

'Well, it hasn't been a very romantic start to our engage-ment, has it?' remarked Bob, later that same evening when he and Sal took Scamp for his late walk. 'First I'm away in Devon then I'm out chasing crooks when I should have been with you.'

'That doesn't matter,' she said. 'You did well by us and I love you even more for it, if that is possible.'

They stopped and kissed while the dog pottered along in front, sniffing around pavement trees and lamp-posts.

'Now that the drama is over, you and I need to go out shopping for a ring for you,' he suggested. 'So maybe you can arrange some time off as soon as you can.'

'I'd love to.'

As they walked on it occurred to Sal that this wouldn't be her first engagement ring; it was a second time for them both. Her stomach lurched as she remembered the pain when the last one had taken such an unexpected turn. That wasn't going to happen again. Her relationship with Bob was much more solid.

She reflected on how different her life had been when Terry had played such an important part in it and Mum and Dad had been around. How she wished they still were and she could share her current happiness with them. She knew instinctively that they would approve of Bob, who was closer to her family than Terry had ever been. She'd always had a suspicion that Dad hadn't been keen on Terry, though nothing to that effect had ever been said. Reminded of her father, she was aware of the nagging knot of worry about him that never quite went away. Some news of him was the only thing that would ease it.

Retrospection had dampened her mood slightly and Bob noticed it. 'What's the matter, Sal?' he asked. 'You seem a bit sad suddenly.'

'Nothing is wrong, Bob,' she said. 'How could anything be the matter when I have you in my life?'

He suspected that she was recalling another engagement when she had been so badly let down. Indeed his own thoughts had veered off unbidden towards Kate and the miserable ending to their relationship. There would be nothing like that again for either him or Sal. They were meant to be together. He couldn't imagine ever hurting her or vice versa.

'Good. As long as you are all right,' he said, tucking her arm through his as they walked on companionably, the dog trotting happily beside them.

Because it was customary for the bride's parents to pay most of the wedding expenses, and they weren't around and Bob's people weren't very well off, the couple decided to foot the majority of the bill themselves. It seemed sensible, therefore, to opt for modest celebrations which they planned for the spring of the following year.

With arrangements put into place, they enjoyed their betrothed status and life went on as normal, only much enhanced, and the worrying Bernie Fox affair faded into the past though it could never be quite forgotten. Tommy continued to thrive and was a joy to them all as he started to sit up on his own and sprout a couple of teeth.

When Ann decided it was time she learned to drive

Sal offered to teach her, which caused surprise in a certain quarter.

'You, giving driving lessons, Sal,' said Dolly in a manner to suggest that her granddaughter had just announced her intention to sign up for work as a navvy on the Hammersmith Flyover building project.

'Yeah. What's wrong with that?' asked Sal, spreading marmalade on her breakfast toast.

'Why doesn't she have proper lessons like you did?'

'Because they cost money and I come for free,' Sal explained.

'I'm sure Bob wouldn't mind teaching her for nothing,' suggested her grandmother. 'I know it wouldn't have worked for you, Sal, being so close to him, but it would be all right for Ann as she isn't involved with him.'

'Gran, why do you not want Sal to teach me?' asked Ann, carefully easing porridge into Tommy's mouth as he sat in his highchair banging a spoon on the tray.

'It isn't that I don't want you to exactly . . . it seems a bit odd, that's all.'

'Because Sal is a woman?' Ann asked.

'Mm. You don't usually hear of women teaching anyone to drive, do you?' she said. 'It's a male job.'

'Then we'll break with tradition,' declared Sal. 'Sundays and Wednesday afternoons when the shop is closed. Is that all right with you, Ann?'

'Perfect, if you wouldn't mind looking after Tommy for me while I'm out, Gran,' was Ann's response. 'I'll only be gone for an hour or so each time.'

'Course I don't mind. I still think it's a funny old carry-on, though.'

'Women drove tanks and planes during the war, Gran,' Sal reminded her.

'Things were different in wartime,' Dolly pointed out.

'Well, I'm quite capable of teaching my sister to drive whatever times we're living in.'

'I know that. It just seems a bit strange for a woman to be doing that sort of thing.'

Sal laughed. 'Times are changing, Gran, and we have to change with them,' she said. 'Anyway I shall have to make a success of it now, won't I? To show you that I'm every bit as capable as any man at the wheel.'

'You don't have to prove anything to me, love,' said Dolly.

'I do to myself though.' Sal turned to her sister. 'So go ahead and apply for your provisional licence so that we can get started.' She paused. 'Meanwhile I have a favour to ask of you both.'

'Go on,' urged Dolly.

'Bob wants me to go with him to Devon to see his folks some time soon. I haven't seen them since we got engaged. So I'll need a couple of days off.'

Dolly looked at Ann and said jokingly, 'Ooh, I don't know about that, do you?'

'Well . . .' began Ann. 'She has offered to teach me to drive so I'd better keep on the right side of her.'

'Yeah, course it's all right, Sal,' said Dolly more seriously. 'I suppose we ought to meet his people, too, sometime as we're going to be related.

Sal frowned. 'Bob and I have been talking about that as a matter of fact but it won't be easy to arrange because we can't go there, all of us together, because of the shop, and they can't come to London.'

'Because of the animals?' asked Ann.

'Not really. They could get someone to see to them for a couple of days but they can't leave Joe.'

'Couldn't they bring him with them?' suggested Dolly. 'It might be difficult to get him up the stairs but we'd manage and it would be lovely to see them all.'

'He wouldn't come,' Sal told her. 'He won't go further than a mile or so from the house and he wouldn't even do that at one time.'

'There's some progress then,' said Ann.

'Very little,' said Sal sadly. 'It hurts me to see a young man stuck around the house so much.' She finished her toast. 'Anyway, I can tell Bob to arrange our visit to Devon then, can I?'

'Yep,' agreed Ann, 'and I shall get an application form from the post office for my provisional licence.'

Somehow the buoyancy of the atmosphere had deteriorated as the tragedy of Joe's situation lingered.

The endless long hot days, punctuated by balmy nights, that the summer of 1959 mostly consisted of, continued into September and the weather was glorious for Sal's visit to Devon. As always she received a royal welcome and huge congratulations on the engagement. The happy couple were given an electric toaster as a present from the family and Sal was delighted.

'Thought we'd better get you something modern, you living in London and all,' said Mavis. 'So I went into Exeter to see what was in the shops. We don't want folks thinking we are behind the times down here in the country. The toast pops up by itself when it's ready apparently.'

'We don't even have one of these at home yet,' said Sal, having offered profuse thanks. 'We still use the grill on the gas cooker. Ann and Gran will be very envious.'

'No using it before the wedding, mind,' warned Mavis lightly.

'We wouldn't dream of it,' Sal assured her.

Sal and Bob had left London very early on Sunday morning and were there in time for lunch, Mavis's glorious roast which lasted well into the afternoon because they all stayed around the table talking.

'There's only one thing I don't like about you two being together,' said Mavis.

'Oh?' questioned Sal.

'You live so darned far away,' she explained. 'So we don't see enough of you.'

'Yes, that is a problem,' said Sal, relieved that the objection wasn't personal.

'Anyway you're here now and that's what matters,' said Mavis and the conversation became general.

Sal adored being here because she felt very much a part of their family.

Later on towards teatime when Sal, Mavis and Joe were sitting around relaxing and Bob was in the barn talking to his father who was busy with his woodwork, Sal asked Joe if he fancied a walk and, much to her joy, he answered in the affirmative.

'I hear you've got a new friend,' she remarked casually as they headed along the winding lane, the hedgerows abundant with wild flowers, some dying off in the incipient autumn.

'Gloria, you mean?'

'Yeah. Isn't she the girl we saw in the village who you said you didn't like?'

'She isn't so bad when you get to know her. You'll probably see her while you're here so you can judge for yourself. She doesn't wait to be invited, doesn't Gloria. She just turns up whenever she feels like it.'

'She probably knows you'd never invite her.'

'And the reason I wouldn't is because I don't want her coming to see me because she feels obligated,' he explained, 'and if I start asking her to come round, that is what she will think.'

'Not necessarily,' Sal disagreed as they started up a gentle slope. 'It's what friends do, invite each other round. She probably comes because she enjoys your company. From what I've heard about her from Bob she isn't the traditional do-gooder type.'

'That was my orginal opinion. She was a right little cow at school. Full of herself and always in trouble for getting into fights with other girls and giving the teachers a load of cheek. Then, when she started coming to the house to see me, I changed my mind about her,' he said. 'She just appeared one day and said she thought I needed cheering up. So I realised that she must be one of these charitable sorts.'

'Which just goes to show that you shouldn't judge people too quickly,' said Sal. 'Though it could be that she likes you and that's why she comes.'

'I suppose I could call her a sort of friend now, and she does cheer me up in a peculiar sort of way.'

'Why peculiar?'

'She's very outspoken and bossy and not very complimentary,' he explained. 'She's always telling me that she's fed up with pushing me about in the chair and that I should be wheeling her around.'

Sal laughed. 'Obviously a girl with a sense of humour.'

'She really goes on at me,' he continued. 'She tells me to get out and get some smart clothes; says I'm getting to look like someone's dad.'

'Maybe she's got a point,' said Sal.

'Oh no, not you as well.'

'How long is it since you last had any new clothes?'

'Since before the accident.'

'Well then. Of course you'll look old-fashioned,' said Sal. 'Something new is definitely overdue.'

'I don't need anything since I never go anywhere,' he pointed out. 'Anyway, I don't have any money.'

'I'm sure Bob will be happy to help out,' she said.

'Oh yeah, I'm sure to want to ask for a handout and go round the town in a wheelchair,' he said with irony.

'Stop feeling so sorry for yourself. I'm sure Bob won't mind taking you into Exeter tomorrow to see if you can see anything you fancy, even if it's only a sweater or a jacket for the winter. I'll come too if you like.' She paused. 'Maybe Gloria can come as well if you want her to, seeing as she's been nagging you about getting some new clothes.'

'I am *not* going to Exeter, Sal,' he said firmly, 'so let that be an end to it.'

'Oh well, it's your loss.'

They carried on in silence for a while. 'It isn't that I don't appreciate your interest,' he said suddenly. 'It's just that everything is such an effort when you're where I am.'

'Mm, it must be,' she said sympathetically, steering the chair to the side of the road when she saw a tractor coming towards them. 'None of us can really imagine what it's like unless we've actually been in that situation . . . hang on, what's the tractor driver doing? Why doesn't he slow down and move over, the dozy devil. Blimey, Joe, he's heading straight for us.'

Seeing the tractor hurtling down the slope at them, Sal pushed the wheelchair as close to the side of the lane as she could then ran out instinctively waving her arms to warn the driver, realising too late that he had no control. Helpless and paralysed with terror she braced herself for what was to come . . .

'Hello Mrs B,' greeted Gloria, knocking on the kitchen door then walking straight in without waiting to be asked to find Mavis setting the tea table with a home-made Victoria sponge and some iced fairy cakes. 'Cor. They look lovely, can I have one?'

'Why ask when you've already taken one,' said Mavis as Gloria munched into a fairy cake.

'I like to be polite,' she said ludicrously.

'Joe isn't in,' Mavis told her.

'Not in?' she reacted in surprise. 'But he never goes out except when I force him into it.'

'Well he's gone out now.'

'Where's he gone? For a cross-country run?' joked Gloria to whom good taste was merely the flavour of a favourite food.

'That isn't very nice, Gloria.'

'Just having a laugh,' she explained chirpily. 'Where has he gone anyway?'

'Sal, Bob's intended, has taken him out for a breath of fresh air.'

'He's in good hands then so I'll have a cup of tea then I'll go for a stroll to see if I can find them.'

'It isn't teatime yet,' Mavis reminded her.

'No harm in having an early cuppa, just you and me, is there?' Gloria suggested.

Mavis shook her head. 'You're a rum 'un you are,' she sighed. 'But go on then, put the kettle on.'

'So who's this one for, Dad?' asked Bob of the doll's house that his father was crafting out of wood, the details so small and intricate it hardly seemed possible that they had been made with such shovel-like hands. The doors, windows and even a porch were dainty and perfect.

'One of the local farmers; it's his little daughter's birthday soon and he wants it for her.'

'These doll's houses are so well made, Dad, it's a pity you can't market them.'

'As I've told you before, son, it would spoil it if I did it for a living,' he said. 'It's my way of relaxing, just a hobby. Anyway it takes many hours to make one of these so you'd have to charge the earth if you looked for a profit and people don't want that, not when they can get a mass-produced one for a fraction of the price. So, as long as I cover the cost of the materials and a drink or two over the top I'm quite happy.'

'But it's so out of character for you,' Bob commented. 'You're the sort of man who likes to make a few quid.'

'Dreams son,' he said. 'Just talk. People like me only make money from working hard.'

'But you're always looking for ways to get rich.'

'Hope, boy, that's what drives me on, looking for that one deal that might work, because one of these days I hope I might just make some money without having to graft for it. The carpentry isn't work to me so I don't mind not turning a profit.' He stood back and looked at the results of his efforts, the little house almost complete, except for the painting and the furniture which would all be made by hand. 'Anyway my stomach is telling me it must be nearly teatime so let's go back to the house.'

And they left the barn together chatting in a friendly manner.

Watching the tractor hurtling towards her Sal shut her eyes tightly, every muscle in her body stretched to breaking point. When she felt herself pushed to one side, landing on the grass verge face down, she was dazed and could feel grazes but, much to her amazement, she was alive.

'You all right Sal?' said a voice close to her and turning she saw Joe also lying on the ground face down. 'Sorry if I was a bit rough but I had to give you a good shove to get you clear.'

Confused as to what had actually happened, she scrambled to her feet and saw that the tractor had come to a stop at the bottom of the hill and was in a ditch. The driver was already heading towards them looking worried.

'The brakes failed on the slope and the damned thing went its own way. I'm very sorry, miss,' said the man. 'Are you all right?'

'A bit shaken up but I'll live,' she assured him.

'What about young Joe?' he asked, looking in his direction.

'I don't know what state he's in,' she said shakily, noticing that the wheelchair was still where she had left it out of harm's way at the side of the lane.

'Can someone get me up and back into my chair please?' asked Joe. 'Never mind standing there chatting.'

Between them Sal and the man did so.

'You all right son?' asked the man.

'Yeah, no thanks to you, Bert.'

'You're right, and I'm very sorry, boy. I never expected the damned machine to let me down on a slope. I shall get it repaired right away,' said Bert, who was middle-aged with a leathery look of farming to his complexion.

'You're the sort of man to keep your farm vehicles

properly maintained as a rule,' said Joe. 'It was an accident so let's say no more about it.'

'It was my fault as much as anyone's,' said Sal. 'I shouldn't have run out in front of you. I acted on impulse. I was trying to make you steer the tractor away.'

'Oh well, as there's no harm done, it's best forgotten,' agreed Bert.

Sal nodded.

'You did well, son,' said Bert. 'If you hadn't acted so fast I dread to think what would have happened to your friend here. She certainly wouldn't be standing there ready to wheel you home.'

Joe introduced Sal to the man who was a neighbour of the Becks and a farmer.

Bert stroked his chin thoughtfully. 'I was under the impression that you never got out of the chair except for bed and essentials, Joe,' he said.

'I don't.'

'You got out of it quick enough just now though, didn't you?' he pointed out. 'You must have done or the young lady wouldn't be standing here now.'

'I can't remember what happened,' said Joe.

'Oh well, I've got to get back and see about getting my tractor towed back to the farm.' He looked at Sal. 'You look a bit shaken up, miss. Shall I go and get someone to take you both home?'

'Thanks, Bert, but I'll be all right. I'll have a sit-down on that tree trunk before we head back though.' She had spotted the remains of a tree on the grass verge on the other side of the lane. 'We'll be fine, honestly.'

'Right you are then.' He walked away up the sloping lane.

'Sandwiches as well, eh, Mrs B,' said Gloria as Mavis cut into a loaf. 'Just what I fancy.'

'I don't remember inviting you to tea,' said Mavis.

'I'm a friend of Joe's,' she reminded her. 'So I don't need an invitation.'

'You're a saucy maid, I know that much,' said the older woman. 'Anyway I don't know how you'll be able to manage any sandwiches as you've just polished off two of the cakes. Honestly, the damned cheek of it.'

'It pays to be cheeky,' said Gloria. 'You don't get anywhere in life if you sit back and wait for things to happen.'

'Mm. 'Appen you're right. But as you've invited yourself to tea, you can make yourself useful and wash those cups we've just used.'

'Yeah all right,' Gloria agreed cheerfully, taking the crockery over to the sink.

Stan and Bob came in.

'Is tea ready, love?' asked Stan.

'Nearly,' she said. 'But we'll wait for Sal and Joe to come back anyway.'

There was a tap on the open kitchen door followed by the entrance of their neighbour.

'Hello Bert,' said Stan. 'Have you come for a cuppa?'

'No, I've just called in to tell you that there's been a bit of an accident down the lane,' said Bert, who thought he ought to do his neighbourly duty and let them know. 'Your Joe and a young lady called Sal.'

Gloria swung round looking stricken. 'What's happened?' she asked.

'The brakes on my tractor failed and I was all over the road,' he began to explain.

'Where are they?' asked Gloria.

'A mile or so down the lane.'

He went on to explain that there was no damage done and they were both unhurt but Gloria heard none of it. She had bolted from the house with her hands dripping washing-up water while the others listened to the whole story.

Both Sal and Joe were feeling shaken after their near miss with the tractor so they sat in silence together for a while, Sal on the tree trunk, Joe next to her in his chair.

'Thanks for saving my life, Joe,' she said when she'd recovered a little.

'Think nothing of it,' he said, making a joke of it. 'I do that sort of thing every day of the week.'

'Seriously, Joe, what you did was amazing, risking your life as you did.'

'Now you're exaggerating. It wasn't that dangerous.'

'A tractor running into someone head on. I would say that was lethal. It was very brave of you.'

'I didn't think about it,' he told her. 'It just sort of happened almost despite myself. I suppose my instincts wouldn't let me just sit there and do nothing.'

'You realise that you used your legs.'

'No. Of course I didn't.'

'How did you do it then?'

'I'm not sure. It happened so fast. I suppose I just launched my body towards you to push you out of the way.'

'You must have stood up, even if only for a second or two, to be able to do that or you would have fallen straight over and not reached me.'

'I can't remember what I did but I couldn't have used my legs because I can't, can I?'

'You have done Joe; you must have been upright to have been able to thrust yourself forward as you did,' she pointed out. 'To push me clear.'

'It's all just a blur to me,' said Joe. 'I just remember lurching forward towards you then hitting the ground and I'll have bruises tomorrow to show for it.'

'But don't you realise what this means?'

'It doesn't mean anything,' he said.

'It means that if you did it once you could do it again.'

'Nah. When you act on impulse like that you don't remember which part of your body you actually used. Anyway, so what if I did stand for a couple of seconds. I wouldn't be able to do it again.'

'Bet you could.'

'I'm not going to take up the challenge,' he said in a definite tone. 'I know what I'm capable of. Whatever happened back then was just a fluke.'

A sudden loud interruption brought the conversation to an abrupt halt.

'There you are,' said Gloria, marching up to them and glaring at Joe. 'You're sitting there as large as life enjoying yourself while I'm worrying myself to a frazzle thinking you've been hurt. I could kill you, Joe Beck, for causing me such worry.' She scowled at him and Sal could see that she was close to tears. 'You've no right to have people fretting about you.'

'Oi, what are you going on about?' said Joe, looking at her sharply. 'Who said I'd been hurt?'

'Bert came to the house and said there had been an accident with his tractor and that you were involved.'

'And he actually said I'd been hurt, did he?' he asked.

'Well . . . he said there had been an accident.' She thought about it. 'I didn't wait to hear the rest. I came out looking for you then.'

'So you jumped to conclusions, as usual.'

'What do you mean as usual?' she blazed.

'You don't think before you speak,' he said. 'You just open your gob and out it all comes.'

'Why you cheeky bugger—'

'Hey you two,' interrupted Sal, observing the mutual overreaction. 'Calm down before you come to blows.'

'Well, he can be so annoying,' said Gloria.

'He's also a hero,' declared Sal. 'He saved my life.'

'What? How?'

Sal told her.

'Blimey,' she gasped. 'I didn't know you had it in yer, Joe Beck.'

'I haven't. Sal's making more of it than it actually was,' he said modestly.

Sal stood in front of him and lifted her arms. 'The tractor was that close to hitting me, and it didn't because

243

you pushed me out of the way. I am simply stating facts so stop denying it and enjoy your moment of glory.'

'Yeah, stop being so flamin' stupid,' added Gloria, taking hold of the wheelchair handles 'And let's go home. Your mum and dad will be wondering if you're all right. Tea is ready anyway.'

'You've invited yourself I suppose,' he said.

'Of course,' she confirmed as they made their way back to the cottage, Sal walking by the side, the two women having introduced themselves. 'I need nourishment having to wheel you about. You're no lightweight you know.'

'Nobody asks you to do it.'

'Somebody has got to make you go out or you'd rot away indoors,' she said. 'Still, now that you're doing heroics you probably won't be in the chair for much longer.'

'Who says?' he asked.

'It's obvious,' she replied. 'If you can fling yourself about all over the place, you can get out of that chair. I'm not wheeling you about if you can walk.'

'I can't,' he said.

'The least said about that the better at the moment I think,' suggested Sal. 'I think Joe is still feeling a bit overawed by what happened.'

'I'm fed up with you both going on at me,' he said. 'There hasn't been a sudden miracle. I haven't got the use of my legs back out of the blue.'

'All right, keep your hair on,' said Gloria.

As a farm truck approached, Sal fell back and walked behind them listening to their banter and deciding that there was more to Gloria than was immediately obvious. She clearly cared for Joe a great deal. Maybe just as a friend as everyone thought; possibly there was more, on her side anyway. As she was so confident and pretty and, according to Joe, in demand and promiscuous, why else would she bother with a man in a wheelchair?

That evening had a touch of magic about it at the cottage, Sal observed. The cider was flowing and there was a delicious supper of cold meats, cheese, home-baked bread and pickles.

'Good grief, another meal,' said Sal lightly. 'I shall be like the side of a house if I come here too often.'

'You town folk eat like sparrows,' declared Mavis.

'We certainly don't have as many meals as you do,' Sal told her. 'Lunch is a snack and tea is just a cup of tea and maybe a biscuit and supper is a cup of cocoa and maybe some bread and cheese. Dinner is our only big meal.'

'No wonder you're all so skinny,' said Stan.

'The word is slim, Dad, and it's all the rage in London,' put in Bob. 'And I love her just the way she is.'

'Hear hear,' added Mavis.

'I'm not fat,' said Gloria, who was still there. 'And I'm a country girl.'

'It's a miracle you aren't since you eat more than half a dozen horses,' said Mavis. 'When you're here anyway.'

'Anyway everyone,' began Stan, standing up at the head of the table. 'Will you all raise your glasses and let's drink a toast to the newly engaged couple. To Sal and Bob. All the best for the future and we're all looking forward to the wedding.'

There were cheers and general well-wishing then Stan added, 'I also think we should drink a toast to Joe who acted like a proper hero this afternoon.'

'Hear hear,' said Sal heartily.

'Don't start that again,' Joe protested.

'Shut up and drink your drink,' ordered Gloria.

'Oh well Joe, do what you're told, boy,' he said to himself but he was grinning.

Feeling the warm cheeriness radiating through the room, Sal's happiness was pierced with a sudden inexplicable feeling of loneliness for her sister and grandmother. They were holding the fort at home with no treats while she was having a whale of a time here, Gran on her own since Grandad died and Ann without the man she loved. And here Sal was being treated like royalty. In the midst of all this joy she was overwhelmed with sadness.

After the meal was over, such was her sense of urgency, she left Gloria helping with the dishes and told Bob she wanted to walk down to the telephone box in the village. He was surprised and said he'd take a stroll with her.

'Hello Gran.' After the operator had put her through she had been oddly relieved to hear Dolly's voice, as though some major catastrophe might have happened since she left home. 'It's me, Sal.'

'Sal, are you all right love?' Dolly asked, immediately concerned for the evening was advancing and also because long-distance calls were expensive and not an everyday occurrence.

'Yeah I'm fine. I've just rung to find out if everything is all right there.'

'Course it is, love. You shouldn't be worrying about us. You should be enjoying yourself, not spending your money on phone calls from far away.'

'I am enjoying myself but I'm thinking of you both as well,' she explained. 'Is Ann around?'

There was rustling and crackling down the line then Ann's voice said, 'Hello Sal. How are things in sunny Devon?'

'Lovely. How's Tommy?'

'He's fine; much the same as when you last saw him, since you've only been gone a day.'

'I just wanted to hear the sound of your voice.'

'Really? When you're away with your delectable taxi driver,' she laughed. 'You must be barmy wanting to ring home.' There was a brief pause. 'Not unless one of you is cooling off, of course.'

'Can't I ring home without you and Gran thinking something is the matter?'

'No, we are far too nosy for that. Anyway, are they being good to you down there?'

'Treating me like a queen.'

'Lucky thing. Well you won't get any of that sort of treatment here so don't waste time ringing us and make the most of it before you get back here and behind the counter.'

'Ooh there's the pips, 'bye.'

'Ta-ta.'

When Sal came out of the phone box she was sniffing into her handkerchief.

'What's the matter?' Bob asked worriedly. 'Has something happened at home?'

'No they're fine,' she assured him.

'So why . . . ?'

'I don't know what's the matter with me to come over all emotional like this,' she replied. 'It has something to do with being very happy I think; your folks making such a fuss of me and everything. Then I thought of home and came over all tearful. I mean Ann isn't going to have a boyfriend's people making a fuss of her, is she? And Gran doesn't have anyone special in her life. Not even her son since Dad went.'

'Ann is still young, she'll meet someone special one day, I'm sure,' he said.

'A woman in her circumstances? It isn't very likely,' she said sadly. 'It seems such a shame. She has a lot to offer.'

'Not everyone is prejudiced, you know,' he said.

'Not many men would want to take on another man's child, though, would they?'

'Some might not. Others wouldn't mind. It would depend how they felt about Ann, I suppose.'

'Mm.'

'You just never know what might happen,' he said, determinedly positive.

'That's true.'

'And as for your gran she would have had her moments

when your grandad was alive. She has you and Ann and she's happy in her own way.'

'I know, Bob. This is so ridiculous,' she said. 'I'm having a wonderful time and here I am in tears.'

'So dry your eyes and let's head back,' he said, slipping his arm round her.

As they approached the cottage garden, Gloria rushed out to meet them.

'You'll never guess what,' she said excitedly. 'Joe wants to go to Exeter tomorrow to buy some clothes. Can you take us in your taxi, please, Bob? I'm going with him because he's got no idea about clothes since he stopped having any new ones.'

'Joe, going to Exeter,' said Bob in amazement. 'He never goes into town.'

'I know but he wants to now; he just suddenly came out with it and said he needed some new gear. You could have knocked me down with a feather.'

'Me too,' said Bob.

'Good news isn't it?'

'Well yes . . .'

'It's a start anyway,' said Gloria happily. 'It's something for us to work on.'

Sal knew for certain in that moment that Gloria was more intelligent and caring than people gave her credit for.

'Of course I'll take you,' said Bob.

'Thanks, Bob. I'll go and tell him,' she trilled. 'Ooh, I'm ever so excited.'

As Gloria scuttled back into the house, Bob said, 'You

see, Sal, I told you anything is possible. That was the last thing I expected and if that can happen so can anything.'

'His actions this afternoon must have given him the confidence to want to go further afield and take an interest in his appearance again,' she suggested.

He nodded. 'Yeah, it could have something to do with that, though he still isn't walking of course.'

'As Gloria said, it's a start.'

'It's a positive sign, that's for sure,' he agreed.

As they walked across the yard together towards the kitchen door, Sal realised that her feelings of melancholy had dissolved completely. Bob was right, you really never did know what was going to happen and she would be very interested to know what might be on the cards next for Joe.

Chapter Ten

The full effect the increase in supermarkets was likely to have on small traders like the Storeys was still more of a threat than a reality and Christmas continued to be a bumper marketing opportunity for The Toffee Shop.

'We'll need plenty of boxed chocolates,' said Sal to the confectionery rep who always requested the Christmas order well in advance and came for it one Monday afternoon in October when the shop was quiet. 'We sold a huge amount of them last year, didn't we girls?'

'We certainly did,' confirmed Dolly who had brought in a tray of tea and biscuits for her granddaughters and the man from the wholesaler's.

'A lot of them were bought last minute by men who had forgotten to get their wife or girlfriend a Christmas present,' piped up Ann, who was unpacking a carton of packaged cigarettes at the back of the shop while Tommy was having his nap in the small downstairs sitting room.

'Don't knock it,' said Sal lightly. 'It was good for business. Anyway, they weren't all for last-minute gifts. A box of chocolates is still a real treat for most people even though the shortages and rationing are long gone.'

'I suppose so,' agreed Ann.

The chocolate order complete, the rep moved on. 'What about stocking fillers for the kids?' he asked.

'We'll need plenty of those,' said Ann. 'Tommy is hanging up his stocking this year.'

Sal and Dolly laughed. 'He isn't a year old till New Year's Eve so Christmas means nothing to him,' Sal reminded her.

'So I'll enjoy it on his behalf,' said Ann. 'He can have baby toys in his stocking and I'll eat his sherbet dab.'

They all chuckled and the rep went on to read from a list of kiddies' favourites and they discussed how many boxes of each they would need for the festive season, 'Gobstoppers, bull's-eyes, liquorice comfits, sweet cigarettes . . .'

'And double our normal amount of raspberry ruffles,' said Sal to complete the order. 'They always go really well at Christmas. Adults love them.'

'You eat most of our stock,' teased Ann.

'That's a lie,' Sal came back at her jokingly, though she couldn't deny being partial to them.

'It certainly is a whopping great fib,' added Dolly, smiling and turning to Ann. 'You'd better apologise to your sister or she might stop teaching you to drive.'

'She wouldn't do that because she enjoys seeing me suffer,' said Ann.

Ann's driving lessons were well underway. There were none of the arguments that often occur between relatives involved in this sort of activity but there were moments of hilarity when they had to stop and park because they were helpless with laughter. It wasn't that they didn't take the lessons seriously because they were both diligent in their purpose but whenever Ann made a corker of a mistake like crunching the gears or kangaroo-hopping when setting off from stationary, the tension of it made them howl with mirth. Even so Ann was making progress and it would be useful to have two drivers in the family when she eventually passed her test.

Now the rep was leaving with a nice healthy order in his attaché case, Dolly disappeared into the house as this wasn't her shift and Sal put a carbon copy of the order in a folder ready to be checked when the goods were delivered. She then went back to polishing the shelves and sweets jars as this was a slack period in the shop.

'Doing the Christmas order always gives me a premature burst of festive spirit. I feel as though it's here already,' Ann remarked, stacking the cigarette packets on to the shelves. 'I can almost taste the mince pies.'

'It is here as far as selling the stuff is concerned,' said Sal. 'There's no point in putting out seasonal stock on Christmas Eve, is there?'

'The season might well be here for traders but I doubt if anyone else has given it a thought yet.'

'Except kids of course. They'll be making their lists already.'

'Won't it be fun when Tommy is old enough to understand and pester us about it miles too early?' said Ann.

'I don't know who will be the bigger kid, Tommy or his mother,' laughed Sal.

'Me neither.' Ann was finding motherhood an absolute joy, especially now that her son was getting to be such a grand little character.

As it happened, Bob mentioned Christmas a few evenings later when he and Sal were walking home from the cinema having seen *On The Beach* with Gregory Peck and Ava Gardner.

'Mum rang me up today,' he said. 'She sends her love.'

'How are they all?' asked Sal with interest.

'Fine,' he replied. 'Joe is doing well apparently, since he's started back at physiotherapy. He can't do more than a step or two yet but he is using the crutches around the house more often instead of the wheelchair and he is really trying hard now and keen to get back on his feet. It will be a slow process but he seems to have accepted that at last.'

'That really is good news.' Sal had been delighted to hear that Joe was giving physiotherapy another try which they'd heard about soon after she and Bob had come back from Devon. He'd obviously been inspired by the incident with the tractor which had also given him confidence for the trip to Exeter while they were there. 'How's the notorious Gloria? Still bossing everyone about and generally making her presence felt?'

'From what I can make out yes, but because she is so good for Joe Mum tolerates her,' he said. 'I think she might even be getting to like her but she'd never admit it.'

'If Gloria makes life better for Joe, that makes her a star in my book,' she said.

'Exactly.'

'Did your Mum say if anything seems to be developing between them or are they still just friends?'

'She didn't mention it,' he told her. 'Why, do you think there might be?'

'It did occur to me naturally, especially as she's obviously very fond of him. She wouldn't spend so much time with him otherwise and make such an effort encouraging him in her own domineering way.'

'Mum would have said something if anything had changed in that direction,' he said. 'Oh yeah, not half. She might be getting to like Gloria but she'd soon change her mind if there was the slightest possibility of her becoming part of the family.'

'There is more to that girl than any of you give her credit for,' she told him.

'It isn't me who has anything against her,' he pointed out. 'As you say, she's cheered Joe up and that means a lot. But she's got a reputation in the village and Mum wouldn't want that for one of her boys.'

'Good job I'm whiter than white then, isn't it?' She grinned, kidding him.

'You can do no wrong in Mum's eyes, which reminds me, she was talking about Christmas and she wants to know if you and the family would like to spend the holiday with them in Devon. It will give the two families a chance to meet before the wedding and as the shop will be closed for a couple of days anyway she thought you might be able to make it.'

'That's really kind of her,' said Sal, rather taken aback

and not at all sure it was a good idea given the disparity between the two families. 'What a lovely thought.'

'But you don't fancy it,' he guessed.

'I'd love to go,' she told him. 'But I don't know about the others. We have always stayed at home for Christmas, and there's the baby to think of now. It's a very long way for a little one, especially in the middle of winter.'

'Yeah, there is that but he'd be taken door to door in the taxi,' he pointed out.

'As much as I'd love to come I wouldn't leave Ann and Gran at Christmas.'

'Mum and I both know that,' he assured her. 'And of course, I feel duty bound to go to see them for the holiday. I expect Mum thought it would solve the problem of us being apart and get the two families together at the same time.'

'It's a lovely idea and a very kind thought on your mother's part.' She recalled how quiet and dismal Christmas had been since they'd lost Mum and Dad. Last year had been abysmal with her missing Bob while he was in Devon and Ann being confined to bed. 'I'll mention it to them and see what they say.'

'A chance to go away for a few days to Devon, and you're not sure if we'd want to go,' exclaimed Ann incredulously when Sal spoke to them about it later that night after Bob had left. 'You must be off your head.'

'It's a long way for Tommy to travel in the middle of winter,' Sal said. 'I thought you might be worried about that.'

'He'll be fine,' Ann said with enthusiasm. 'It isn't as though he's newborn or anything. He'll be a year old by then. It'll be lovely to get away. Don't you think so, Gran?'

'I certainly do. It'll be a lot of work for Bob's mum, though, with all of us turning up,' said the ever-considerate Dolly. 'Are you sure she doesn't mind?'

'She suggested it so she can't do,' said Sal.

'Well I'm game,' approved Dolly. 'It will make a nice change and it will be good to meet your future in-laws.'

'That's decided then,' said Ann as though the matter was settled. 'You can go ahead and tell Bob to tell his mum that we'd love to come.'

'But I'm not sure if you'll like it,' Sal felt compelled to mention. 'They live very differently to us.'

'Oh really. In what way exactly?' Dolly was curious.

'They have animals,' said Sal.

'So what,' responded Dolly. 'We have Scamp who we love to bits so I suppose you could sort of call us animal people.'

'They have a lot of animals that more or less have the run of the house,' Sal explained.

Dolly did look a little perturbed at this. 'What, the goat and the cow and everything, all in the house?'

'No of course not, though the tortoise is sometimes indoors and a chicken was in the kitchen once when I was there because it was poorly.'

'We kept chickens during the war,' Dolly recalled. 'But in a chicken run in the garden; not in the house.'

'Theirs are outside in a chicken run normally,' Sal

explained. 'Unless one of them is ill or anything and needs a bit of comfort.'

'That's something then,' said Dolly.

'But I was mostly talking about their attitude to things, which is much more casual than ours,' Sal went on. 'As well as the animals they keep outside, they have three cats, and a couple of dogs as well. I know you're keen on hygiene, Gran, albeit not quite as fussy as Mum was, but it'll be no good you worrying too much about that sort of thing while you're there because they are much more relaxed about such things than we are. I don't want you having a fit if one of the cats jumps on to the table for instance.'

'Oh lor,' she said.

'And you'll have to pretend not to notice if Bob's mum drops a Brussels sprout on the floor and doesn't rinse it off before putting it in the saucepan,' Sal continued.

'I'll try,' agreed Dolly, though she did look somewhat concerned.

'They are clean-living people but they don't worry about the odd speck of dust and to them the domestic animals are part of the family so they are given more leeway than we give to Scamp.'

'There's an old saying about that sort of thing, something about eating a peck of dirt before you die,' said Ann. 'You'll have to remind yourself of that while we're there, Gran.'

'I'm not sure if Gran wants to go now,' said Sal.

'Well I do and we won't go without you,' Ann decided.

'So please say you'll come, Gran. It will be so good for Tommy to have some country air and he will love the animals, you know how he adores our Scamp.'

'I think Sal is trying to put me off,' said Dolly.

'Not at all; I'm just warning you ahead so that you know what to expect,' said Sal. 'It's a different sort of household to the one you are used to. Different; not wrong or bad.' She paused. 'The important thing to remember is that they are really lovely people and they will make us very welcome.'

'Hmm.' Dolly mulled the situation over for a few moments. 'All right then. Provided we can get a neighbour to look after Scamp, how can I say no?'

'Couldn't we take him with us?' suggested Ann.

'He wouldn't be happy with all the other animals because he isn't used to them,' said Dolly. 'The poor thing would be terrified.'

'You're right, Gran,' agreed Sal. 'Better if he stays here and I know of several people round here who would be only too happy to have him for a few days.'

'Devon here we come then,' said Dolly excitedly.

'Yippee,' cheered Ann.

The cottage glowed and glittered like a giant bauble with a lit Christmas tree in the window, paper chains and tinsel in abundance. The air was warm and fragrant with the aroma of fresh-baked sausage rolls and mince pies which welcomed the visitors when they arrived in the late evening of Christmas Eve.

Mavis, Stan, and Joe on crutches, were all at the door

to meet them and there was an excited outpouring of greetings and introductions.

Sal had warned Dolly and Ann about the Becks' different way of living but – because it was unimportant to her – it had never even occurred to her to mention in advance to their hosts about the colour of Tommy's skin. Bob obviously hadn't done so either because the look of shock on Mavis's face when they took the sleeping child from the car was savagely visible.

'Oh, I didn't realise,' she said, obviously embarrassed by her reaction but managing to recover with alacrity. 'We don't see many of . . . er those round here but he's a beauty and it'll be lovely having a little 'un in the house at Christmas. Come on in, everybody. Leave your bags where they are and Stan and Bob will see to them later on because supper is ready and waiting for you.'

Sal knew in that moment that they had done the right thing in coming and that this Christmas was going to be very special for them all.

It seemed to be one long round of eating, drinking and jollifications, Sal observed. There were presents galore; before breakfast, then more gifts off the tree after a long and delicious Christmas dinner following which they all watched the Queen's Christmas broadcast on the television. Everyone helped with the clearing up then out came the sweets which they were all too full to manage but did so just the same.

Gloria joined them in the afternoon.

'Everyone's sleeping off the dinnertime booze at my

place,' she explained. 'So I thought I'd come up here for a bit of life.' She spotted Tommy who was tottering around having recently found his legs, albeit rather precariously. 'Oh isn't he beautiful. 'Ello little 'un. Come to your Auntie Gloria. Come on. That's it.'

He walked unsteadily over to her and the two became instantly inseparable. She lifted him up and smothered him with kisses, which made him chuckle.

'What's all this,' said Joe, looking puzzled. 'I didn't know you liked kids.'

'There are lots of things you don't know about me, Joe Beck,' she said. 'I love little ones, always have. Not that it's any of your business, of course.'

With Tommy occupied with Gloria, Ann enjoyed the relaxation and Sal and Bob went for a walk.

'It's all going very well, isn't it,' she said.

'Very.'

'Is it worth giving up your bed?' she asked because his bedroom had been transformed into a family room for the visitors and he and Joe were on camp beds in Joe's room, his brother's bed having been moved next door for Dolly.

'You bet,' he responded.

'It's great that the two families have met and seem to get along. It will make things so much easier at the wedding,' she remarked. 'And if Joe continues as he is it looks as though he'll be able to come to the wedding as well as your parents.'

'Yes, I'm hoping he'll be my best man but the job involves a certain amount of organisation which might be difficult for him,' he said. 'I know he's a lot better but he's still on crutches and uses the wheelchair as well.'

'Perhaps your dad could help him with that part of it. Joe could be with you at the church and maybe your dad could do the rest.'

'We'll see.'

The afternoon was advancing and the air was raw and damp, the hedgerows muddy and bleak. 'Should we invite Gloria to the wedding, do you think?' she asked.

'Fine by me but I don't know what Mum would have to say about it,' he said.

'It would be nice for Joe to have someone with him.'

'Yes, you're right so we'll keep it in mind. We have to work out how we are going to put them all up.'

'All of that has to be organised,' she agreed. 'Once Christmas is over the time will fly and after the New Year we shall be able to say that it's this year. I get excited every time I think about it. That's why I like to talk about it so much.'

He chuckled because he loved her enthusiasm and tendency towards exhilaration. 'I know,' he said affectionately. 'But I think we'd better head back now, it's getting bit dimpsy as they say in these parts when it gets dusk.'

'Next Christmas we'll be a married couple,' she reminded him as they began the walk back.

'What a lovely thought.'

He couldn't wait. Courting was an exhausting and frustrating business. He was eager to wake up every morning with her by his side and have her there when he got back from work. He suspected that women were more romantic about weddings than men who to a certain extent viewed them from a practical angle. That wasn't to say that he didn't love her with all his heart and feel emotional about marrying her because he had those feelings. But he was looking forward to everyday life after the glamour and excitement of the wedding was over; living and loving with Sal by his side. They were going to live at his place initially with the idea of getting a mortgage on a place of their own later on. He didn't care where they were as long as they were together. Living apart when you were in love was a strain.

The cottage came into sight, exuding festive cheer. 'Meanwhile we've got the rest of this Christmas still to enjoy,' she said. 'It's turning out to be very special for us all. Your folks make brilliant hosts.'

'They'll be your folks too soon,' he reminded her. 'Mrs Beck. I hope you like the sound of it.'

'I really do,' she said. 'I've been practising my new signature already.'

'You won't be practising for much longer.' He smiled. 'You'll be doing it for real.'

'That Gloria is a proper little diamond,' said Ann when she and Sal were getting undressed for bed that night, speaking in hushed tones because Tommy was asleep. 'I could do with her around all the time. She's a natural with kids and kept Tommy amused all afternoon and evening. She even changed his nappy off her own bat. Because I could see that he was having a good time I relaxed and enjoyed myself.'

'She's very good with Joe too,' said Sal. 'She's made a world of difference to him. When I first knew him he never moved out of his wheelchair. Saving me from being hit with a tractor got him going but Gloria had made a difference even before then, and I don't think he would have come this far without her. It might only be a few steps but it's huge progress.'

'He wants to hang on to her then.'

'They're only friends apparently.'

'I think there's more to it than that even if they haven't acknowledged it yet.'

'I hope you're right,' said Sal. 'Those two would make a great team.'

'It's a smashing family you're marrying into, Sal,' Ann went on to say. 'Talk about a welcome; they rolled out the red carpet good and proper for us. Bob's mum has told me that I'm very welcome to come down to stay with Tommy independent of you if I fancy a break sometime.'

'She said the same thing to me,' added Dolly, who was already in bed. 'So when you've passed your driving test, Ann, we can leave Sal looking after the shop and head off to Devon with Tommy.'

'I know you're only kidding but I wouldn't mind,' said Sal. 'I'm sure Bob would help me out in the shop.'

'Anyway, this visit isn't over yet,' said Ann, yawning as she brushed her hair. 'It's been brilliant so far, hasn't it, Gran?'

'Lovely,' agreed Dolly. 'And after all your warnings about the animals, they haven't put a foot wrong, or should I say a paw. Not a cat on a table in sight.'

Sal was laughing as she got into bed. What a wonderful day it had been.

They arrived home in the late evening of Sunday ready to open the shop the next day. Tommy was asleep and they were all tired but the feeling of well-being remained because they had all had such a lovely time.

'If you go ahead and unlock the door and get yourself in, girls, I'll carry the baby in and come back for the luggage,' offered Bob.

Feeling sleepy from the long journey and chilled by the night air as she got out of the taxi, Sal said, 'Thanks Bob. We'll go in through the shop to save going round the back in the dark.'

Ann and Dolly were shivering and hugging themselves against the cold as Sal unlocked the shop door and hurried over to the light switch. They were all so eager to get upstairs they hurried through the shop without looking around. It wasn't until Sal went back to hold the door open for Bob and Tommy that she noticed that the shelves behind the cigarette counter were empty. Cigarettes, cigars, tobacco had all gone. They'd been burgled!

Further investigation showed that the stockroom had also been cleared out. The thieves had got in through a window at the back, well out of sight of the neighbours. They had broken the window but must have done so in such a way as to make little noise.

'Nobody seems to have heard or seen anything,' said

Bob when he got back from collecting Scamp from the neighbour who'd been looking after him.

'At Christmas time people are having parties and enjoying themselves indoors,' said Sal. 'They wouldn't hear much outside with all the noisy celebrations inside.' She patted the dog's head affectionately. 'It wouldn't have happened if you'd been here, would it, Scamp?'

'We couldn't have left him here on his own,' said Ann. 'He'd have been much too lonely.'

'Of course not,' said Sal.

'Cigarettes and tobacco are easy to sell and light to carry, that's why they didn't bother with anything else. There was no money in the till or they'd have had that,' said Bob.

'At least they didn't go upstairs,' Dolly commented. 'Nothing has been touched up there.'

'Oh well, I suppose we'd better report it to the police,' said Sal wearily. 'Or we won't be able to claim on the insurance.' She looked at her sister and grandmother. 'You two go upstairs and put the electric fire and the kettle on and get yourselves warm. I'll deal with it. I'll use the phone down here so I can describe the scene if the police want me to.' As she walked over to the phone, she turned and said to Bob, 'You'll be tired too after that long drive. You go on home and I'll see you tomorrow.'

'Not likely,' he said. 'I'll stay to give you some support.'

'That's nice of you but I'll be fine.'

'I'll stay anyway.'

She gave him a watery smile but she had been horribly affected by the burglary. She felt violated by the intruders.

Knowing that some uninvited people had been in here helping themselves was an eerie feeling. What a miserable end to such a beautiful Christmas!

'It will have been yobbos,' declared Nell who lived across the road. 'The buggers. They'd soon know about it if I got my hands on them, I'd wring their ruddy necks.'

'The police seem to think it might have been a more organised gang,' Sal told her. 'They took a lot of stuff so they would have needed transport to carry it and get it away from here. They must have parked near the back alley.'

'That makes sense, I suppose. And we were all too busy enjoying ourselves to notice anything,' said Nell, sounding apologetic. 'I did look over once or twice in daylight and everything seemed to be all right.'

'You weren't expected to keep an eye on the place, Nell,' Sal assured her. 'None of us expect this sort of thing to happen, not around here. In all the years The Toffee Shop has been here we've never had a break-in. If Scamp had been here, the whole neighbourhood would have known something wasn't right because he'd have barked the place down. That would have scared the living daylights out of the burglars and sent them packing.'

'You'll be insured I expect,' said Nell, who didn't think twice about enquiring into other people's private affairs.

'Yes, of course; we'll put in a claim and eventually we'll get some compensation, though you know how long-winded insurance companies are. It isn't the loss of stock so much as the thought that someone could do that to us. Knowing that strangers have been in here.' She shuddered. 'Ooh it sends cold shivers up my spine.'

'It'll do you no good to dwell on it,' Nell advised.

'I'm trying not to.'

'How's your gran taken it?' asked Nell. 'She's getting on a bit to have to cope with burglars.'

'You know Gran. She's a tough old thing,' Sal told her. 'But it must have upset her. It's shaken us all. But she's got Ann and me to look after her and we feel safe knowing that the dog is around. I will never curse having to take our Scamp for a walk on a cold winter's night again because he's such a godsend. It's made us all grateful to have him.'

Nell nodded.

'Thank goodness for the cash and carry,' said Sal. 'I went over there first thing this morning in the car to get some cigarette stock until the wholesaler can get a delivery to us. The burglars cleaned us out.'

Ann came into the shop and joined in the conversation. Other customers arrived and took part. News travelled fast around here and everyone wanted to have their say.

An elderly woman, a regular called Ethel, came in carrying a dish with a cloth over the top. 'Heard about your trouble and thought you might be off your food and not wanting to bother much. So I made you this and I know you'll eat it because my shepherd's pie is the best in London and you won't be able to resist it no matter how upset you are. It only needs warming up.'

Sal burst into tears.

'Ethel's shepherd's pie ain't that bad, ducks,' said Nell, making a joke of it because she knew that Sal was touched. 'Not as good as mine o' course but it's nothing to cry about.'

'Thank you so much Ethel,' said Ann, coming from behind the counter and taking the dish off her while her sister recovered. 'It is so kind of you.'

Sal wiped her eyes and came out from the counter too. 'Thank you Ethel,' she said, hugging her. 'You've restored my faith in human nature and made me cry in the process.'

This one kind gesture had put everything back into perspective for Sal. The robbery had overshadowed the warmth of the Becks' hospitality at Christmas and made the world seem cold and friendless. Ethel had made her realise that they did have people who cared about them. The neighbours might not always approve of the Storeys and enjoy a good gossip about them but they were there when they needed them. It wasn't just the Storeys against the rest of the world as it had seemed a few minutes ago. She also had her lovely Bob and their wedding coming up in a few months' time to look forward to. Her life was blessed indeed and it would take more than a few burglars to dampen her spirit.

A week or so later Nell came into the shop with a suggestion.

'I reckon it would do you two girls and your gran good to have a night out together, to help you forget about the burglars,' she said to Sal who was on duty. 'There's a Marilyn Monroe film on at the pictures.'

'Yeah it would be nice,' Sal agreed. 'But the three of us can't go together because of Tommy. Maybe I'll suggest that Ann and Gran go and I'll babysit.'

'I'll look after the little 'un if your sister will trust me with him; that's what I had in mind when I suggested a night out for the three of you. He'll come to no harm with me. I've had four kids of my own so I ought to know a bit about it. All left home now of course. I might as well sit over here watching your telly instead of being at home listening to my ole man snoring in the armchair.'

'Thanks very much Nell,' said Sal. 'I'll see what Ann has to say and let you know.'

'All right ducks,' she said, looking towards the sweet jars on the shelves. 'Give us a quarter of humbugs please.'

'Coming up,' said Sal.

The interesting thing about Nell's offer was the fact that she had been one of the most disapproving of the neighbours when Tommy had first arrived. She had made no secret of the fact that she was disgusted with Ann and thought her mother must be turning in her grave. Yet here she was offering to look after Tommy. Oh well, there was no accounting for the vagaries of human nature, she thought, as she tilted the sweets from the scales into a paper bag.

'So you're deserting me tomorrow night then,' said Bob a week or so later when Sal told him about the visit to the cinema which Ann and Gran had been all in favour of once Ann had managed to convince herself that Tommy would come to no harm with Nell.

'Yeah, sorry about that,' she said, seeing him off at the front door. 'It's the best night for Nell and as she's doing us a favour we feel we must try and fit in with her.'

'Don't worry about me,' he said in his usual easygoing manner. 'I'll have a night in and catch up on some reading. I've not done nearly as much since you and I have been together.'

'Me neither,' she confessed. 'We've both got more to do with our time now, though I still love to read and do so in bed when I can but not as often as I would like because I feel bad about having the light on in case it disturbs Tommy.'

He thought about this. 'Why doesn't Ann move into your parents' empty room with Tommy?' he asked. 'That would give you all a bit more space.'

'We're leaving the room as it is just in case Dad comes back,' she explained. 'We keep it dusted and aired but that's all.'

'Ann and Tommy could move back in with you if your dad came back,' he suggested. 'You'll be leaving home and moving in with me after the wedding anyway.'

'Exactly, so the problem will solve itself then.'

'And in the meantime you don't feel comfortable reading in bed, something I know you enjoy.'

'Actually it's a bit awkward in more ways than one,' she admitted. 'There's also the problem that when Tommy wakes up in the night it disturbs me as well as Ann. So we're both half asleep in the morning.'

'The wedding is still a few months away and it doesn't seem very sensible for the three of you to be cramped together in one room when there's an empty one across the landing, especially now that Tommy's getting bigger.'

'I can't disagree with you because from a practical point of view you are absolutely right. And I know Ann would like to do it because of space for Tommy and she feels guilty when he disturbs me in the night; she's still angry with Dad and doesn't think we should be considering him at all as he went off and left us but Gran and I both think it seems as though we are in some way betraying Dad if someone else takes over his bedroom.'

'But he isn't there, Sal.'

'It's what I feel, Bob, and it has nothing to do with common sense.'

'I understand that,' he responded. 'But your father has been gone for more than two years.'

'And you think that means he'll never come back, do you?' she cut in sharply.

'No, that isn't what I meant at all. I'm just saying that your sleeping arrangements aren't sensible as they are at the moment. I love you and because of that I don't want you to be feeling tired during the day when Tommy has had a disturbed night. It isn't right for you not to feel free to read in bed if you want to; not when there's an alternative. I know that reading is one of your big pleasures in life.'

'It's nice of you to be concerned.'

'You're the most important person in my life so it's only natural that I would be,' he said. 'Do you really

272

think that your father would be in any way upset at the idea of his daughter and grandchild using his room? From what I've heard about him he would be all for it.'

'Maybe.'

'Why not look at it this way. Living accommodation is desperately short in London and you have an empty room you don't use. Some people would give an arm and a leg for that,' he said. 'It's almost as though you're keeping the room as a shrine.'

'That isn't fair because it isn't like that at all.' She put him straight in a definite tone. 'It would seem as if we'd given up all hope of his coming back if we used his room. That is why it is out of use.'

He shook his head slowly. 'It's just a room, Sal, four walls and a few square yards that no one is making use of. Of course you wouldn't be giving up hope of seeing him again if you started using his room. You would be doing the sensible thing. I can understand you keeping it as it was for a while after he went. But Ann didn't have Tommy then. Things have changed and it makes sense to adapt to them.'

'Mm, I suppose you're right,' she finally conceded. 'It would be more convenient all round. I'll see what the others think.'

'Good.' He smiled. 'Now behave yourself tomorrow night. No flirting or getting drunk and disorderly.'

She laughed. 'I'm going to the cinema with my grandmother and sister, not to a hot London nightspot.'

'That's what you tell me,' he said, teasing her.

'I could say the same thing about you,' she responded,

extending the joke. 'You're telling me that you're staying in to catch up on your reading but you could have something else in mind altogether. A date with some gorgeous glamour girl for instance.'

'Why would I do that when I'm already engaged to the most gorgeous of all glamour girls?'

'Ooh, listen to you; you've got all the patter,' she said. 'You know exactly the right things to say.'

'Well,' he said, spreading his arms and grinning in a way he had that made him look like a wide boy and which she found very attractive. 'In my job I get plenty of practice.'

'You're a master at it too. I'll see you the day after tomorrow. Enjoy your night off from seeing me.'

'As if I would,' he said. 'But you enjoy yourself.'

'As if I could,' she came back at him and they both laughed, safe in the knowledge that their love was strong enough to withstand anything.

A glass of whisky and a good book was one of Bob's favourite ways of spending time, second to seeing Sal of course. It was the perfect way to relax. He mostly read factual history books and found the knowledge he absorbed interesting and also helpful in his work. Sometimes tourists hired him to take them around London and being able to tell them something about the places he was pointing out to them was very useful.

He was also beginning to enjoy fiction, Dickens in particular, and settled down to read one of his the following evening. Lying on the sofa with his head on a cushion and his drink on the coffee table beside him he was happily absorbed.

He was so relaxed that when the doorbell rang it made his nerves jangle for a few seconds. Maybe Sal had changed her mind about her girls' night out, he thought hopefully, as he made his way to the front door. He certainly wasn't prepared to see the person who was standing there.

'Hello Bob,' said Kate with a wide smile. 'Well don't just stand there gawping, man. Find your manners and ask me in.'

Chapter Eleven

It was the interval between the second feature and the big film, the lights were up and Sal was waiting in the queue for ice creams from the girl with the tray. The auditorium was crowded and noisy, the air infused with a mixture of cigarette smoke, cheap scent, liquorice allsorts and hair lacquer. Eagerly anticipating her turn to be served, it occurred to her how odd it was that the variety of ice creams in the shop at home didn't create nearly the same excitement as one bought and eaten in the cinema which always seemed to have a special deliciousness of its own.

'Here we are, girls,' she said, handing choc ices to Ann and Gran. 'We'll just have time to unwrap them before the film starts.' She glanced around. '*Some Like it Hot* has certainly pulled the crowds in.'

'They say it's really good,' said Dolly as she unwrapped the silver paper on her choc ice in eager anticipation of that scrumptious first nibble.

'With Marilyn Monroe, Tony Curtis and Jack Lemmon in it, it can't really fail,' Ann said.

'That's true,' Dolly agreed.

'Oh, by the way,' began Sal, having a sudden thought and deciding to mention it while it was on her mind, 'Bob was saying that he thinks it's a bit daft for us not to use Dad's room now that we have Tommy, instead of the three of us sharing one room. He reckons the sensible thing is for Ann and the baby to move in there.'

'Three cheers for Bob,' responded Ann. 'At last someone has seen some sense.'

'How about you, Gran?' Sal enquired with concern. 'I know that you and I have both thought we should keep the room as it is, ready for Dad to come back to, but I'm beginning to have second thoughts now that Tommy is getting bigger. We can always rearrange things again when Dad does surface.'

Her grandmother's look of anguish filled Sal with compunction and she regretted raising the subject but knew that it had to be done. 'I'm not suggesting that we abandon all hope of his return, Gran,' she added quickly. 'It just seems . . . well, it would be more comfortable for all three of us.'

'Yes, of course you must do it,' Dolly agreed swiftly. 'It's stupid having that room empty and the three of you squashed in together. We should have done it ages ago.'

'Are you sure it's all right with you, Gran?' asked Ann. 'Only it would be so much more comfortable for us.'

'Yes, you can go ahead with my blessing.'

'Thanks, Gran.' Ann laughed. 'No offence Sal, but what with Tommy waking you up and me feeling guilty about that and also on edge in case you turn the light on and wake him, the whole thing is exhausting.'

'Shush,' urged someone from behind when the lights went down and the audience fell silent as they stared at the screen.

Sal loved the glamour of Marilyn Monroe and admired her looks enormously but somehow her mind wasn't on the film this evening. All she could think of was the haunted expression in her grandmother's eyes when she'd suggested putting Dad's room back into use. Gran had obviously accepted that it was the right practical decision but Sal knew that it was another knife in the wound Dad had left when he'd disappeared. Life had to go on and there were realities to be faced. But it was hard to move on from a thing like her father's disappearance because it remained unsolved so they couldn't grieve or finally come to terms with it. All Sal could do was to make sure she helped Gran to keep the hope alive. But as time passed with no word from him a return was becoming increasingly unlikely.

Oh well, she must stay positive, and try to concentrate on the film for the moment which was funny and very entertaining. But try as she might, it failed to hold Sal's attention.

'You've got a nerve,' said Bob as Kate stepped uninvited into the small hallway of his flat.

'That isn't much of a welcome for someone you nearly married, is it?' she said, looking as striking as ever with her dark looks and long hair.

'Nearly being the operative word,' he pointed out. 'You chose Australia over me, remember.'

'You chose England over me as I remember it,' she came back at him.

He sighed. 'Well it's all in the past whichever way round it was. Are you back in England for good?'

She nodded.

'So what happened to the better life down under you were so keen on?'

'It wasn't for me so as soon as the two-year period was over and I could come back without having to pay the Australian government back the full cost of my fare out there, I got Mum and Dad to lend me the money for my passage home. I'm staying with them at the moment.'

He gave a dry laugh. 'Back at home eh. I bet that's going down a storm, I know how much you enjoy your parents' company, I don't think.'

'It's only temporary.'

'I'm sure it is,' he said. 'So why didn't you like Australia?'

'I didn't not like it. The country is absolutely beautiful and excitingly different to here but I just couldn't settle,' she replied. 'It was harder for me to adapt than I had expected.'

'No get rich quick schemes then.'

'No. Not that I could find anyway. I'm glad I went though. It was an interesting experience and at least I had the gumption to do it.'

'Meaning that I didn't, I suppose.'

'If the cap fits . . .'

'You know why I didn't go with you and it was not because of any lack of courage but I'm not going to argue about it or even discuss it. As far as I'm concerned the whole thing is over and done with. I am with someone else now and we'll be getting married soon.'

Up went her brows.

'Surely you didn't think I would sit around moping for you for more than two years, did you?'

'No, of course not.'

'Don't tell me you didn't find a sucker who you could train into a top-class meal ticket.'

'I won't even bother to answer that. Now where are your manners? Isn't it time you asked me in properly instead of keeping me in the hall?'

With an irritated sigh, he waved his hand towards the living room and she swept in.

'Still reading your boring old books then,' she commented, picking up a copy of *The Pickwick Papers*.

'Yeah, still doing it. Reading improves the mind,' he responded. 'You should try it some time.'

'My mind is fine as it is, thank you very much, and I see that you need a spot of anaesthetic to help you get through them,' she said, picking up his whisky glass and sniffing it.

'Not at all,' he said. 'I was enjoying a relaxing evening at home until you barged in.'

'Not seeing your lady friend tonight then.'

'She isn't my lady friend, she's my fiancée and she's spending the evening at the cinema with her relatives, not that it's any of your business.'

'You and I could never get enough of each other when we were together,' she said. 'You wouldn't have been at home alone reading your fusty old books in those days.'

'You wouldn't have allowed me to,' he riposted.

'Of course I wouldn't,' she admitted. 'I was far too passionate about you.'

He emitted an eloquent sigh. 'Have you come for any particular purpose other than to annoy me?'

'Yes, I have as it happens,' she replied. 'There's someone I'd like you to meet and I want to arrange it with you.'

'Oh? Wouldn't it have been easier to ring up?'

'I wanted to ask you in person.'

'Who could there possibly be in your life that you would want me to meet?' He gave her a studious look. 'Don't tell me you want me to give your new man the once-over.'

'Aah,' she said, tapping her nose mysteriously. 'You'll just have to wait and see, won't you?'

'Not really, no,' he said. 'Whoever it is I have no interest in seeing them. Now I'd like you to leave me in peace please.'

'Afraid of what might happen if I stay, are you?'

Another sigh. 'Oh grow up for goodness' sake, woman,' he said irritably. 'Just go away and leave me alone.'

But Kate was nothing if not persistent. 'Do you still have a day off on a Sunday?'

'Usually, yeah,' he replied warily.

'Good. I'll be round on Sunday morning about eleven o'clock,' she stated. 'I shall be here on the dot.'

'But . . .'

'I'll see you on Sunday,' she said, and hurried from the room and out of the front door before he had a chance to argue.

Angry and exasperated, he grabbed the glass of whisky and emptied it in one swallow. Why did he feel so threatened by Kate? She couldn't touch him now. Half an hour ago he had been happy and content, looking forward to his life with Sal. Now he felt as though he was on the verge of a catastrophe, though quite why he didn't know. It wasn't as though he was harbouring any remaining feelings of love for Kate. That much he was sure of. His reaction to seeing her again was one of pure trepidation. Still, she had a new man she was bringing to see him on Sunday so she wouldn't be harbouring any ideas of a reconciliation.

Sitting back down on the sofa he was quite unable to concentrate so got up, took his coat off the peg by the door and headed for the local pub. It wasn't so much the beer as the company he was in need of.

Sal was in high spirits when Bob saw her the following evening. She'd enjoyed the film last night but what she was most happy about was the fact that Ann and Tommy had moved into her father's room.

'I've got a bedroom to myself for the first time in my life,' she said with jubilation when they had a drink in one of the riverside pubs near Hammersmith Bridge. 'I shall go to the library as soon as I can to stock up on reading material.'

'Good I'm glad that's all settled,' he said.

'Thanks to you. I'd probably never had the nerve to suggest it if you hadn't twisted my arm.'

'I do have my uses then.'

'You bet.'

'You'll just about get accustomed to having a bedroom to yourself when you'll have to share one again, with me,' he reminded her.

'That's a bit different,' she giggled. 'Apart from anything else I know that you won't stop me from reading in bed.'

'I must admit that reading in bed isn't the first thing that springs to mind when I think of us as newlyweds,' he said with a wicked smile.

She grinned. 'I bet it isn't,' she said laughingly.

The jolly repartee petered out and an odd silence ensued. Bob stared towards the window, seeming lost in a world of his own.

'Is something the matter, Bob?' she asked. 'You seem a bit preoccupied.'

He'd been debating with himself all day whether or not to tell her about Kate's visit. Should he worry her with it when it wasn't absolutely necessary? But Kate was coming back on Sunday so he knew he must be straight with Sal.

'I had a visitor last night,' he told her.

'Oh really. It must have been someone important to make you so thoughtful.'

'It was my ex . . . er Kate actually,' he said, feeling unnecessarily guilty. 'She turned up out of the blue.'

Her reaction was sharp: an involuntary stab of fear. 'I thought she was in Australia.'

'So did I until last night,' he said. 'It didn't work out, apparently, so she's back home.'

'Why did she come to see you?'

He frowned. 'I didn't ask her to come if that's what you're thinking. I have had nothing to do with her since our relationship ended.'

'All right, no need to bite my head off. I wasn't suggesting anything. It just strikes me as odd for someone to turn up at their ex-fiancé's door.'

'It is odd but that's Kate for you,' he said. 'She isn't given to doing the acceptable thing.'

'So what now?' she asked, wishing that Kate had stayed out of the way down under. 'How did you feel seeing her again?'

'Irritated mostly. She came barging in and interrupted my evening.' He paused, looking at her. 'I didn't realise that I was still in love with her, if that's what you mean. Absolutely not!'

'Naturally I wondered,' she said. 'You were in love with her once remember.'

'I'm not now and can't imagine how I ever was.'

'It was a good test then. And she's gone now so why are you still letting the visit bother you?'

'She's coming back on Sunday morning,' he explained.

This was beginning to have a distinct air of threat about it, Sal thought worriedly. 'Oh really,' she said. 'Why would she do that?'

'She's bringing someone she wants me to meet. It

must be a new bloke though why she needs me to see him I have no idea.'

'If you really don't want to see her again why didn't you tell her straight?'

'Because she didn't give me a chance,' he replied.

'You could always make sure you're not at home,' she suggested.

'She'd come back another time until whatever it is she wants she gets.'

'Then tell her to get lost.'

'I have.'

'Then tell her again and make sure she listens.' She looked at him. 'Why has seeing her again affected you so much if you don't still have feelings for her?'

Because Kate's a troublemaker; because I don't want to see her ever again; because she always has an agenda, take your pick, he thought but it wasn't necessary to burden Sal with all of that so he just said, 'I don't still have feelings for her, I promise you. But because I am happy and in love with you, it annoyed me that she turned up. I was sitting there with a glass of whisky and book and she just swept in as though she owned the place.'

'You've told her about me, I assume.'

'Of course.' He pondered on this for a moment. 'I was wondering if you might be willing to be there with me when she comes on Sunday. Would you do that for me, Sal?' He paused then added, 'Please.'

'Why would you want me there?'

'Because you are part of my life and I want you to

be involved in everything that happens to me. You ought to be there with me,' he explained. 'Whoever it is she wants me to meet I want them to meet you too.'

'If you're sure that's what you want, of course I'll come over,' she told him.

'Thanks Sal.'

'Come on drink up,' she said. 'I think we both need a little fresh air to clear our heads.'

'Fresh is the right word for it,' he said, as they came out of the pub and walked along the slip road to the bridge, a freezing wind blasting across the waterfront and making the skeletal trees sway so that their shadows moved eerily in the pale glow of the street lights.

'It is a bit brisk but there is nothing more therapeutic than the Thames on a cold winter night,' she said, pausing on the bridge and looking out over the water, satin black in the moonlight. 'There is something so atmospheric about it.'

'Therapeutic,' he said in a teasingly derisive manner. 'Lethal is the word I would use. We'll both have frostbite by the time we've walked back to your place.' He was standing beside her with his arm round her. 'I prefer the Thames on a warm summer night.'

'Don't be so soft.'

'Just kidding.'

She turned and linked her arm affectionately through his. 'We're strong Bob, you and I. No amount of ghosts from the past will spoil things for us.'

'I know,' he said.

And they walked back to The Toffee Shop, heads down against the bitter wind.

The Storey women always had a lie-in and a cooked breakfast on a Sunday morning, and lingering over their eggs and bacon was all a part of the treat.

'So I'll go out driving with you, Ann, as soon as I get back from Bob's,' said Sal, tucking into some fried bread. 'I shouldn't think I'll be very long.'

'It strikes me as very peculiar, you going to meet his ex,' said Ann, spooning some egg into Tommy's mouth. 'Why does he want you to be there? More importantly, why is his ex-fiancée going to be there at all?'

'How do I know?' said Sal. 'I can't get into the woman's mind. And he wants me there because I am his other half and as such he thinks my place is by his side.'

'It's only right and proper,' Dolly put in. 'It shows how much he thinks of Sal and that there will be no funny business.'

'Mm, I suppose so,' Ann agreed. 'Weird, her turning up like that, though. It must have been a shock for him, the same as it would be if you answered the door and found Terry standing there.'

'Perish the thought,' said Sal. 'Kate has got some front, I'll say that much for her. Anyway, as soon as I get back we'll get you out on the road for some more practice. We'll be back in time to help you get the lunch, Gran!'

'All right dear. You must be getting quite good at driving by now, Ann,' remarked Dolly, sensing accurately that Sal didn't want to linger on the subject of Bob's ex-fiancée.

'She's improving,' said Sal lightly. 'It'll soon be time to put in for her test.' She smiled at her grandmother. 'She'll be able to take us all out for a run on a Sunday afternoon before long.'

'I can't wait,' said Ann, adding jokingly, 'but I don't know if I'll take you two with me. I might just take Tommy and drive off into the sunset.'

'No you wouldn't because you'd miss us too much, wouldn't she, Gran?'

'Not half, especially when she wants one of us to change the baby's nappy.'

'All right,' Ann conceded amicably. 'Anyway, it's a family car so I'd have to take you if you wanted to come.'

Normally Sal enjoyed the occasion of Sunday breakfast after the rush of weekday porridge and toast. She liked the fact that they chatted with the thought of the day off ahead to look forward to. But today it was spoiled for her by anxiety about what was to come. As much as she told herself that she had nothing to fear from Kate, her instincts told her otherwise.

'Shall I put the kettle on so that we can give her a cup of coffee or tea when she arrives?' suggested Sal.

'I don't want to give her the idea that she can hang around,' Bob replied.

'If she's bringing her new man with her, we'll have to offer them something. It's only good manners.'

'Go on then.'

Just as Sal turned to go into the cupboard-sized kitchenette the doorbell rang so she accompanied Bob to the door at his request. At first glance the very attractive woman standing there appeared to be alone until Sal's glance moved downwards and she saw a little girl, a most beautiful dark-haired child who looked to be about two.

'This is Lucy,' announced Kate, coming inside and offering no further explanation as to who the child was.

Bob introduced Sal to Kate, whose response was a curt 'Hello.'

'Is your friend not coming, Kate?' he asked.

'What friend?' she asked, taking Lucy's coat off.

'You said you were bringing someone you wanted me to meet. I assumed it would be a friend.'

'It was Lucy. My daughter.' She gave Bob a long hard look. 'Your daughter too, Bob.' She looked down at the little girl. 'Say hello to your daddy.'

Sal sat on a bench by the river. She couldn't face going home. Not yet. The wound was still too raw. She wasn't ready for all those outraged comments. 'Bob has a daughter? Well blow me down . . .' and so it would go on because Ann and Gran would be shocked and concerned for Sal. She'd left Bob's flat with the word 'daddy' echoing in her mind. That one word had made her feel like an intruder. A man and woman and their child. Surely there could be no stronger bond. It was obvious that Bob had been as surprised as she had but she hadn't waited to find out the details. Fighting for your man was one thing, depriving a child of its father quite another. She'd left right away. Vaguely she'd been aware of him asking her not to go but she'd carried on anyway. He and Kate had some serious talking to do and she, Sal, wasn't part of that particular conversation.

Deep in the pit of her stomach there was a dull ache of emptiness; an awful coldness. She was no stranger to emotional upheaval but this was more intense than anything she'd experienced when she'd broken up with Terry.

The bitter wind stung her face and the winter sunshine gave out no heat; it just shone on the river tinting it green, its stark beauty making her want to weep.

'What the hell are you playing at, Kate,' Bob demanded when the door slammed after Sal. 'You know as well as I do that Lucy isn't mine. How can she be? I haven't seen you for years.'

'I was pregnant when I left for Australia though I didn't realise it until I was on the boat. I was so busy getting ready to go I didn't notice that I'd missed a period and I put the sickliness down to nervousness about going.'

'You nervous,' he said contemptuously. 'That's a good one.'

'I'm only human, Bob. I get scared the same as everyone else,' she told him.

'I suppose so.' He looked at Lucy who was sitting on the sofa cuddling a pink fluffy rabbit and looking very sweet. 'Would she like a biscuit and something to drink?'

'Milk if you've got it please,' said Kate, 'and she's got a sweet tooth so a biscuit would be nice.'

Bob went into the kitchenette and provided the necessary, noticing again in a preoccupied sort of way, because he was still in a state of shock, what a beautiful child Lucy was.

Having settled the little girl, he sat down at the small, scratched and shabby dining table with Kate and said in a low voice, 'So she is definitely mine you reckon.'

'I've told you, she was conceived before I went abroad and there was no one else but you so she must be.'

'So why didn't you write and let me know?' he asked.

'Because you were on the other side of the world so there didn't seem to be any point,' she said. 'There was nothing you could have done.'

'I'd have known I had a daughter,' he said. 'Surely I had a right to that.'

'I was the one with the problem, Bob,' she snapped. 'I was away from home with a baby. It was very hard. Not only was I an immigrant, I was an unmarried mother as well. Not a popular combination. I was too busy dragging myself from day to day to contact someone who was too far away to help.'

'I could have sent you some money.'

'I did think of that but managed to survive without it. I took any job I could find and worked almost to the end of the pregnancy in a café. I managed to hide my bump by wearing loose clothes so no one knew about it.'

'And after she was born?'

'The woman I lodged with looked after her while I went back to work,' she explained. 'So I managed to keep us. I had already decided to come back to England when the two years was up so the thought of coming home kept me going.'

Hmmm. None of this sounded like the Kate he remembered. She wouldn't know how to grin and bear anything. But Lucy was a reality and was obviously well cared for so Kate must have faced up to motherhood. He wasn't finding the idea of fatherhood so easy to take in. It was one hell of a shock.

'Well, obviously I'll accept my responsibilities as her father,' he heard himself say, but it was as though someone else was speaking the words. 'We need to arrange for me to pay something towards her support on a regular basis, and I would like to see her now and then. But can we do that another time? Right now I need to go and put things right with Sal. The poor girl must be wondering what's hit her.'

'Yeah, OK,' she agreed amicably. 'I'll leave Lucy with Mum so that we can have a proper chat another time.' She stood and picked up her daughter's coat from the chair. 'I'll give you a ring to arrange it.'

As soon as he had seen them out, Bob grabbed his coat and tore out of the door and into his taxi, en route for Sal's.

'So,' began Sal after Bob had told her what had happened after she left. 'Where do we go from here?'

'Sorry to put you through this,' he said. 'It must have been a terrible shock. It knocked me for six too.'

They were in the living room at the Storeys' house.

Dolly was in the kitchen preparing the lunch and Ann, having been asked by her sister to have the driving lesson another time, had taken Tommy out for a walk so they were able to speak in private. Sal hadn't said anything to her grandmother and sister about the dramatic turn of events.

'Yes, I could see that when Kate came out with it,' she said. 'This might sound selfish, but what about you and me? Our future together. What will happen now?'

'I realise I'm asking a lot of you but I'm hoping we can carry on,' he said. 'I have agreed to help support Lucy financially but Kate won't be in my life.'

'Lucy is definitely yours then.'

He told her what Kate had told him about the conception. 'I'm fairly certain that Kate wasn't seeing anyone else at the same time as me so I'm in the frame, though I shouldn't speak about it like that because she's a lovely little girl and the innocent party in all this.'

'Yes, she is,' said Sal dully, feeling as though she had already lost him.

He must have sensed her concern because he leaned over and took her hand. 'It isn't every day a man discovers that he's a father and naturally I want to do right by the child. But there is nothing between Kate and me and nor will there be in the future.' There was a pause. 'I realise that having a child from a past relationship turn up in your fiancé's life is a lot for any woman to take on board; too much for some.'

'Naturally I'm not thrilled about it,' she told him straight. 'I want us to have our own family.'

'And we shall; God willing.'

'Obviously I'm not heartless enough to stop you from having Lucy in your life,' she went on. 'But it will take some getting used to. Kate must intend to let you play a part in the child's upbringing or she wouldn't have brought her to see you.'

'It's money she's after,' he said. 'Once she's got me to agree to that formally I probably won't see her for dust.'

'I'm not so sure but perhaps you'd better wait and find out what she has in mind when you next see her before you make hasty judgements,' she suggested.

'Maybe you're right,' he agreed. 'But meanwhile we must try not to let this spoil things for us.'

'We can't pretend it hasn't happened.'

'No, of course not, but it's an issue outside of what we have together, something from the past. It doesn't change things between us. It shouldn't do anyway.'

'I suppose not.' But Sal felt as though everything was different already.

Although initially Sal hadn't wanted to discuss the revelations of the morning with Ann and Dolly, it was rather a relief to talk to them about it over lunch.

'Blimey Sal,' was Ann's unrestrained reaction as she tucked into roast beef and Yorkshire pudding. 'That's a bit of a bombshell. Bob's got a kid. Good grief!'

'He didn't know anything about her until this morning,' Dolly reminded her sharply. 'It isn't as though he's been hiding her away or anything.'

'It's still a rotten blow for Sal though,' said Ann. 'What will you do?'

'Bob says it won't affect our relationship,' said Sal.

'Then he's living in cloud cuckoo land,' stated Ann. 'Of course it will affect things between you. Apart from the emotional side of things you're going to start your married life with a financial burden you hadn't bargained for.'

'That's a cold-hearted way of looking at it,' said Sal. 'Such a thing hadn't even occurred to me and wouldn't bother me in the least.'

'You say that now, but how will you feel when money that he should be spending on your life together will be going on a child from his past? You're bound to resent it.'

'Look on the bright side, why don't you?' said Dolly with irony. 'Bob isn't the first man to have this happen to him and he won't be the last. He and Sal will get through it together. She doesn't need you looking on the black side, Ann.'

'I just want her to be aware of the reality of it,' said Ann, then catching Dolly's eye and realising how thought-lessly hurtful she was being added, 'But I'm sure it will be all right. Bob's a good sort. He'll do right by you, Sal.'

'It isn't his fault this has come like a bolt out of the blue,' Dolly went on. 'He knew nothing about the child as the mother didn't bother to keep him informed. Had he known I'm sure he would have done the right thing at the time.'

'Which means he wouldn't be free to marry Sal now,' said Ann, trying to be more positive. 'So you could even say it worked out for the best.'

'The best would be no skeletons in the cupboard,' said Sal. 'But I can see what you mean.'

'So what's his ex like?' asked Ann.

'Good-looking and confident but there was something very cold about her,' said Sal. 'She was very full of herself. No warmth in her at all as far as I could see.'

'You're almost certain not to like her,' Ann pointed out. 'Ex-girlfriend and mother of his child; that's a recipe for dislike.'

'Mm. Perhaps you're right. I suppose I was naturally biased. But she is overconfident. I could imagine her running rings around Bob.'

'You'll have to watch her then.'

'If I get the chance I will. I am not going to give in without a fight; that much I do know.'

'There's no suggestion of your having to give in or otherwise is there?' asked Dolly. 'I mean, it isn't as if he's going to go off with her or anything. It's merely a matter of maintenance for the child I should imagine.'

'That's what she wants apparently,' said Sal, 'but I wouldn't trust her further than I could throw her.'

Bob wanted the maintenance issue settled speedily so he was glad when Kate telephoned a couple of days later to say she would be over to see him that evening.

'I can send you money by registered post every week or month to save us meeting up,' he suggested, having given her a cup of tea and looked at the birth certificate she had brought with her showing that Lucy was born in April 1958. Kate had emigrated the previous autumn. 'Though I would like to see Lucy every so often so we'd have to meet then, I suppose.'

'Is that all you're worried about, having to see me?'

'I am getting married to Sal and I don't think she'd be very keen on the idea of you and me seeing each other.'

She sipped her tea, fixing her gaze on him as she put the cup back into the saucer. 'You're not getting away with it that lightly, mate,' she announced. 'I want a whole lot more than a few bob every week from you.'

'Such as?'

'Marriage and all the respectability that goes with it for me and my daughter,' she informed him in an uncompromising manner. 'If you'd known I was pregnant at the time you would have done the decent thing because you're the type who would. It didn't happen then so you can do it now.'

He couldn't believe she could be serious. 'That's the most ridiculous idea I've ever heard.'

'Making sure that your daughter doesn't grow up with a stigma, that's ridiculous, is it?'

'Of course not,' he said. 'But I can't marry you. Even apart from anything else, I don't love you.'

'That's a minor detail,' she said breezily. 'Marriages have survived without a penn 'orth of love in them. All I want is for Lucy to grow up in a family and without scorn.'

297

'But people will already know she was born the wrong side of the blanket,' he reminded her.

'Not if we move away. Make a new start somewhere else,' she said. 'We needn't leave London; just go to another part where no one knows us.'

'Absolutely no chance,' he stated. 'It's the last thing I want.'

'What you want isn't important. It's our daughter we have to think about.'

'And to have her grow up with parents who can't bear the sight of each other because that's what would happen,' he said. 'We would grow to hate each other over time without the basic ingredient at the start. You think that would be better for her, do you?'

'We loved each other once.'

'We fancied each other,' he corrected. 'And that time has passed and it isn't coming back.'

'How can you put your own personal feelings above the well-being of a child?'

'How can you use a child to get what you want?' he came back at her sharply.

'I'm not using her, I'm just stating facts. You don't know what it's like, having everyone look down their noses at you,' she told him. 'It's even more painful to see them doing it to Lucy. She's too young to understand at the moment but as she grows up she'll realise what people think of her and be very hurt by it. And all because you're too selfish to do the right and proper thing.'

'You must admit you've left it a bit late to appear

demanding that I turn my life upside down for you,' he said.

'I've never been conventional.'

'That's no excuse,' he said. 'I'm with someone else now. I can't just leave Sal in the lurch and go off and marry you. I don't want to be with you, Kate. So no, I'm not doing it.'

'How can you reject your own flesh and blood?' she demanded. 'I've had a hell of a time on my own looking after her. Leaving her with anyone who wanted to earn some spare cash so that I could work to feed her.'

His conscience was beginning to bother him, despite himself. 'But if I help you financially you won't have to leave her to go out to work, and now that you're back with your mum and dad, you'll have them behind you. They probably adore having their little granddaughter around.'

'It drives me mad living with them, Bob, you know that very well. I need to be away from home and in my own place.'

He was beginning to get really worried now as his sense of responsibility closed in on him. He grew up in a loving family and his father was a vital part of his childhood. Little Lucy wasn't going to have that. 'With the best will in the world I can't afford to set you and Lucy up in a place of your own. I'm a taxi driver not a bank manager.' He waved his hand towards the room. 'Sal and I are going to have to live here in this poky little flat for a while until we can afford the deposit on a place of our own. I can't get you and Lucy accommodation as well.'

'That's easily solved if you do what I want,' she said. 'You marry me instead of Sal and you, me and Lucy get a place of our own.'

'You're unbelievable,' he said. 'Can't you see how impossible that would be? How many more times do I have to tell you, I am not the least bit in love with you?'

'And how many more times must I tell you that it doesn't matter? I am asking for respectability, not love. You could live your own life, come and go as you please . . .' She paused, giving him a sharp look. 'So long as you're around enough of the time to be Lucy's father . . . or to be seen as such.'

An awful sense of inevitability was beginning to creep over him. He remembered that dear little girl sitting on his sofa, so innocent and vulnerable. The images were tugging at his heartstrings. How could he let his child, his own flesh and blood, have a miserable life when he had the means to do something about it?

'I need to think about it,' he told her. 'Can you go now please? I want to be on my own.'

'Yeah, all right.' She gave a careless shrug, getting up and putting on her coat. 'I'll give you a call sometime tomorrow. I'll see myself out.'

As the door closed behind her, he sat in the armchair staring at the orange and blue flame of the gas fire and searching for another solution to this seemingly insoluble problem. There was no doubt in his mind that he would have married Kate had he known she was pregnant at the time; his conscience wouldn't have allowed him to do otherwise. But now he couldn't bear the thought of it. Even more painful was the thought of losing Sal. All their plans for the future would be shattered because of Kate's visit.

Then he was brutally honest with himself. It wasn't Kate's visit that had wrecked everything; it was his irresponsibility in getting Kate pregnant in the first place. They say that past sins come back to haunt you and his certainly had.

But none of it was Lucy's fault. She was a sweet child who deserved her daddy to be there for her.

'Don't expect me to be understanding about it because I can't be,' said Sal the next day when he told her what he felt compelled to do while they walked by the river in her lunch hour. He'd turned up at the shop and said he needed to talk to her and they'd both known it wasn't the sort of conversation they could have in front of Dolly and Ann. 'You have just broken my heart so all I can think about at this moment is myself. Selfish I know but that's how it is.'

'What choice do I have, Sal?'

'You can tell Kate to get lost and marry me as planned.'

'Sal, it's the child,' he stressed. 'You'd hate me if I didn't do right by her.'

'I couldn't hate you more than I do for not doing right by me,' she said, her voice rising to a shriek.

Her own pain and disappointment left no room for anything else. Bob's obvious distress went over her head because she was too immersed in her own self-pity to deal with it at this moment.

'Sal . . .'

'Don't touch me,' she shouted as he tried to put his arm round her to comfort her, the volume of her voice causing a man walking his dog to turn his head.

'Please,' begged Bob. 'Let's see if there is any way you and I can stay together.'

'So you're suggesting an affair now, are you?'

'No of course not . . .'

'You've gone down even more in my estimation now for thinking that I would become your bit on the side.'

'That wasn't what I meant but I shouldn't have said it,' he told her. 'But I am so desperate not to lose you I'll come out with anything. Kate and I will be leading our own separate lives so I thought maybe you and I . . .'

'You thought wrong, mate. You can't have us both and you've chosen her,' she raged.

'Only because of Lucy.'

'You've decided to go down that road so you and I are finished. You can cancel our wedding arrangements yourself. You've broken us up so you can do the dirty work.' She halted in her step and stared at him, all her shattered emotions culminating in a violent need to hurt him. Her hand whacked across his face so hard she could feel the sting. 'I'm going home now and I never want to see you again. I hope you rot in hell!'

As she walked away tears of anger and pain rolled down her face and she was too wrapped up in her feelings to care if people passing by looked at her with curiosity. Nothing had ever hurt her this deeply before.

★   ★   ★

Bob's feelings were similar to hers as he watched her stride away and knew he was powerless to change anything or even to comfort her. Added to the pain of losing her was dark overpowering guilt for hurting her so badly. It was his mess; not hers. She shouldn't have to suffer because of what he'd done in the past. But she *was* suffering and there wasn't a damned thing he could do about it. Any gesture of regret on his part would hurt her even more. Shoulders down and hands thrust into his pockets he walked away in the opposite direction.

After a few days of rage and self-pity, during which Dolly and Ann maintained a diplomatic silence though they knew what had happened, Sal began to take the broader, less selfish view and she knew she would have to see Bob one more time. So on Sunday morning she drove round to his place.

'Now that I've calmed down, I just wanted to tell you that although I'm still full of rage towards you for letting me down, I can understand why you had to do it. I'm hurting too much to wish you well with any degree of honesty but—'

A ring at the doorbell brought the conversation to an abrupt halt.

'Damn,' he said. 'I'll get rid of whoever it is.'

When he re-entered the room Kate was with him. 'What are you doing here?' she demanded of Sal. 'Didn't he spell out the message clear enough?'

'Don't speak to Sal like that,' admonished Bob.

'Well, she's got a cheek coming round here.'

Sal gave her a studious look; she saw the conniving glint in Kate's dark eyes and knew in that instant with absolute certainty that Kate was using Bob. Sal also guessed that Kate was capable of exploiting a child for her own ends.

'Bob, can you give us a few minutes?' Sal asked. 'I'd like to have a chat with Kate on my own.'

He looked surprised and rather concerned but said, 'All right, I've got some paperwork that needs seeing to in the taxi so I'll go and get on with that.'

'I don't know what you've got to say to me,' said Kate after he'd gone. 'But all I have to say to you is bugger off. You're not wanted here.'

'I shall have my say whether you like it or not,' Sal insisted. 'And I think you are using Bob for your own ends. In fact, I don't believe that Lucy is his child at all.'

'Oh yeah,' Kate said, looking guarded. 'And what would give you a silly idea like that?'

'*You* give me that idea. The way you are. I can see the hardness in your eyes.'

'You know nothing about me. This is only the second time you've ever seen me.'

'And that's quite enough, added to what Bob has told me, for me to know that you are not the type who would have suffered on your own when you found out that you were pregnant. If Bob really had been the father of your child you'd have pestered him with airmail letters asking for money at the very least. But you didn't choose to tell him about Lucy until she was nearly two years old which is odd by anyone's standards. Come on Kate, you don't expect me to believe that you wouldn't have been after him for support for all that time if Lucy really was his.'

'I couldn't care less what you think,' Kate said airily. 'Bob believes it and that's all that matters. I have shown him the birth certificate and you can't argue with that.'

'I admit I don't know how you got over the birth certificate side of it,' Sal said thoughtfully, 'but I do know that Bob isn't Lucy's father.'

'As long as Bob thinks he is that's all that matters to me,' Kate said, looking uneasy as she realised that she had slipped up.

'Thinks he is?' queried Sal.

'A slip of the tongue,' she came back quickly. 'Obviously I meant to say knows he is.'

'You got pregnant after you left this country, didn't you?' Sal gave Kate a studious look. 'So, what happened, did Lucy's father leave you in the lurch so you thought you'd come back here and try your luck again with Bob?'

'You can't prove any of this,' said Kate, narrowing her eyes on Sal. 'And Bob won't believe it. He's far too taken up with the idea of being a dad.'

'Too taken up with the duty he thinks is his more like,' Sal disagreed firmly.

Kate gave a careless shrug. 'The reason is irrelevant,' she said. 'He's doing the right thing, that's what matters.'

'The right thing for you, not for him or Lucy,' persisted Sal. 'You let him down badly before, the least you can do now is to leave him alone to get on with his life.'

'Let him get on with his life with you while my

daughter suffers the stigma of illegitimacy? Don't make me laugh.'

'Why don't you get her real father to do what he should?'

Kate met Sal's steely gaze. 'Bob is her father,' she said in an even tone, 'and you can't prove otherwise.'

'No, I can't. But the truth will come out eventually and your daughter will be the one to get hurt.'

'Time will tell,' said Kate. 'So now that you've had your say, clear off and leave Bob and me alone.'

Without another word, Sal walked out of the room and left the flat.

'As I was saying before we were interrupted, Bob, I hate you for what you've done to me but I can understand why you feel duty bound to go with Kate,' said Sal emotionally, when she found him by his taxi in the street.

'Sal, I feel so miserable,' he said, clutching a wad of papers attached by a bulldog clip.

Sal respected Bob for his decency and sense of duty even though she was convinced it was misplaced. But she was as flawed as any other human being and a worm of spitefulness rose up and made her glad that he was feeling pain too, while at the same time hating herself for it. 'Yes I know you do but I'm hurting too much to be able to feel sorry for you at the moment.'

'Of course, I wouldn't want that, I'm so sorry I've hurt you, Sal,' he said.

She knew that there was no point in her telling him about her conversation with Kate or what she believed to be true because he had to find out for himself or he would resent her for telling him. His sense of responsibility to the child was too strong for him to draw back at this point without concrete evidence that Sal didn't have. 'But I will tell you to be careful. Kate isn't to be trusted and I think you know that in your heart.'

'I'm not doing it for Kate, you know that,' he said. 'I'm doing it for Lucy.'

'Yes I do know that but my advice still stands. Goodbye Bob,' she said, her voice breaking.

'Sal, don't leave it like this.'

'What else can I do?' She spread her arms in a helpless gesture. 'You've made your choice. So there's nothing more for me to say.'

'I suppose not,' he agreed sadly.

'Cheerio Bob,' she said and hesitated no longer before walking away in a dignified manner, leaving him staring after her, helpless to change anything.

Chapter Twelve

'I am absolutely determined not to be destroyed by it,' Sal told Dolly and Ann that evening when they were sitting in the living room. 'I will cry alone.'

'Ooh my Gawd,' exclaimed Ann. 'That sounds a bit melodramatic. A bit like something out of one of those novels you read.'

'I suppose it does really,' Sal was forced to agree. 'But I'm sure I can rely on you two to keep my feet planted firmly on the ground if I get too theatrical.'

'It's what you've been doing for the best part of the afternoon, though,' said Dolly. 'Crying alone up in your room.'

'Yeah, but now I've stopped and if you see me feeling sorry for myself again, remind me of what I've just said about not being destroyed. Jilted once is bad enough; twice is a flamin' calamity and enough to knock the stuffing out of anyone for good and all. But I can't let that happen, not when we have a shop to run.'

'Don't worry. We won't let you sink into a trough, will we, Ann?' said Dolly

'Not likely,' agreed Ann, adding in a jokey manner. 'Not until she's got me through my driving test anyway.'

Sal managed a watery smile though her sense of desolation was almost physical. 'How long have we got left until the test?' she enquired.

'Six weeks.'

'Right, so we need to get you some extra practice in if Gran is willing to look after Tommy.'

'Course I will,' said Dolly.

'Thanks, Gran,' said Ann, and turning to Sal added with a sudden note of seriousness, 'Thanks for giving me your time, sis.'

'Don't start being polite to me just because of what's happened,' said Sal. 'That really will make me feel like a pitiful case. Anyway, what else will I have to do with my spare time now that Bob isn't going to be around?'

'Oh Sal,' said Ann biting her lip, full of empathy now. 'It's so rotten for you. I could kill Bob for doing this to you.'

'You're not the only one. Anyway, I need a challenge and teaching you to drive is certainly that,' she said quickly and as Ann moved towards her, she added swiftly, 'If you hug me I'll collapse into tears again so best not for the moment.'

Ann and her grandmother exchanged glances then Dolly said, 'How about I put the kettle on for a nice cup of tea.'

'Gran's answer to everything,' responded Ann with a

rueful giggle because her sister's sadness was so evident you could almost touch it.

'Or, alternatively, we could get the sherry and port left over from Christmas out of the sideboard,' Dolly suggested.

'That's more like it, Gran,' said Ann. 'We could do with a bit of cheering up.'

'There isn't enough to get us plastered,' said Dolly.

'It doesn't matter about that. A little tipple is all we need,' said Sal. 'I'll get the glasses.'

'The *Sunday Night Play* will be on the box later on so we can get as tiddly as possible with our limited supplies while we watch that,' said her grandmother.

As she went into the kitchen with her sister, Ann searching the larder for savoury biscuits to make the drinks more of a treat, her grandmother in the other room invading the sideboard for some light relief, Sal had to force herself to carry on because all she really wanted to do was to go to bed and hide away under the covers. But that wasn't an option under her self-imposed rules so she got the glasses from the cupboard and set them out on the table.

'The BBC Television Theatre please,' requested a man who Bob picked up in central London.

'Certainly,' said Bob, setting the meter and pulling out into the traffic. 'That theatre used to be the Shepherd's Bush Empire until the BBC took it over in 1953. We used to go there regular to see the shows before then.'

'Those were the days, eh. But live variety has all but finished in this country, more's the pity,' said the man. 'The box in the corner is the big draw now.'

'Are you in show business yourself then?' asked Bob, interested despite his own gloomy mood.

'I will be tonight,' he explained. 'I'm a guest on *This is Your Life* with Eauman Andrews.'

'Oh, very impressive,' said Bob.

'It is quite exciting,' said the man.

'I bet,' responded Bob as they came round Shepherd's Bush Green and pulled up outside the theatre, along with several other taxis and private cars dropping people off.

'Good luck,' said Bob as the man got out and paid him. 'Thanks.'

Bob watched him walk to the theatre entrance, well lit and bustling with people going in, a commissionaire on the door, fur coats out in force for the occasion. I bet there are plenty of famous faces in there tonight, he thought as another fare came up to his window and asked to be taken to Marble Arch. Driving back into central London along the Bayswater Road, Bob wasn't required to make an effort at conversation as the female passenger obviously wasn't feeling chatty, so he sank back into thoughts of his own parlous situation. Again he asked himself the same painful question: how could doing right by one person make you do so wrong by another?

He had to face the family with the news; that was his next ordeal. He was going to Devon early tomorrow morning to tell them about the latest development in his disastrous personal life. It wasn't something you could do on the phone; it was far too personal. Mum and Dad would be upset because they thought so much of Sal. How he missed her and wished they were still together, he thought as he approached Marble Arch at a bumper-to-bumper crawl in the heavy traffic.

The first thing Bob heard when he opened the cottage door was Gloria's strident tones coming from the kitchen.

'Come on Joe, just one more step . . .'

'I can't . . .'

'Yes you can, now come on, don't be such a sissy,' she urged. 'One more step then I'll let you sit down and you can have your crutches back.'

'You've got no heart.'

'And if you give up now you've got no balls.'

'Language, Gloria, please,' came his mother's predictable admonishment. 'I've told you before, we don't allow that sort of talk in this house.'

Bob smiled to himself. It was good to be home.

'Hello Mum,' he said, opening the kitchen door.

'You're here already,' whooped Mavis, rushing over and embracing him. 'I wasn't expecting you this early.'

'I got away sooner than I expected,' he said, omitting to add that he wasn't sleeping well so was only too glad to get out of bed and do something rather than lying there torturing himself with conscience and heartache about Sal.

'Sit yourself down, son, and I'll make some tea and get you something to eat.'

Bob looked towards Gloria and Joe, the latter now sitting down, flushed and breathless.

'Looks as though you're doing well,' he said, shaking his brother's hand in greeting. 'Your walking is really coming along.'

'I don't have a choice with her driving me on.' He looked at Gloria with disdain. 'She's a perishin' slave driver.'

'She's doing it for your own good,' said his mother who had obviously had a change of heart towards Gloria. 'So just be grateful that she puts up with your bad temper.'

'If you say so,' he sighed.

'I'll make the tea if you like, Mrs B,' Gloria offered. 'Then you can sit down and talk to Bob.'

'Thank you my dear,' agreed his mother to Bob's astonishment. The girl certainly seemed to have found a niche in the family after such an unpromising start. 'And make him a sandwich to keep him going till dinner while you're at it. There's plenty of cheese in the larder. He's partial to a nice bit of Cheddar.'

'Righto, Mrs B.'

'Is Dad at work, Mum?' Bob asked.

'Yeah, he's doing a painting and decorating job in Exeter,' she replied.

'He's managing to keep busy then.'

'Very busy, thank goodness. The better times seem to have found their way down here at last, though not in such a big way as London, of course. But there's building work going on in the town and people are splashing out and sprucing up their houses.' She looked towards Joe. 'Still, 'appen your dad will have some help before too long. Your brother is coming on that well lately.'

Bob frowned, wondering if Joe would be physically able to go back to manual work even if he did regain the use of his legs.

'Of course it will take some more time but he should be able to do some light jobs eventually, so they reckon at the hospital. Nothing too heavy obviously,' she said, sensing Bob's concern. 'He'll want to be working when he's able and odd-jobbing is all he knows.' She looked at Bob. 'But how's everything with you, son? How's Sal? It's a pity she couldn't come with you this time.'

'Er . . . actually Mum, I've got something to tell you about Sal,' he began in a hesitant manner. 'I was going to wait until Dad is here but as you've brought the subject up I may as well tell you now.'

'What's happened?' asked Mavis, giving him a sharp look. 'I hope you haven't been . . . er . . . misbehaving, Bob.'

'No, she isn't pregnant,' he assured her, wishing ardently that that was the problem. Then he went on to tell them what had been happening.

'Oh well, if you got Kate into trouble of course you must do the decent thing,' said Mavis, having listened to the story without interruption. 'But she went away and left you once so how do you know that she won't do it again when the mood takes her?'

'I don't.'

'So you have thrown your future with Sal away because Kate has taken it into her to head, all of a sudden, to come back into your life and claim paternity and demand marriage.'

'Only because of the child,' he said.

'I shouldn't rush into anything, son,' she advised worriedly. 'Support the little girl, yes, but hang back on the marriage until you're a little more certain that Kate isn't going to leave again.'

'Unfortunately Kate is making all the rules so I suppose we'll do it when she wants to,' he said. 'I'm the guilty party.'

'It takes two, remember.'

'But I feel to blame,' he said, 'though it's more a matter of feeling responsible.'

'As long as you're sure that the child is yours.'

'I'm as sure as I can be; I've seen the birth certificate. Which makes it my responsibility to make certain Lucy doesn't grow up with fingers pointing at her.'

'That Kate sounds like a real cow,' put in Gloria, who was sitting at the kitchen table next to Joe.

Mavis gave her a sharp look. 'All right, Gloria. If we need your opinion we'll ask for it.'

'I think you should tell Kate to go and take a running jump, Bob,' she persisted.

'I'm sure that Bob can manage his affairs without your advice,' said Mavis primly, reverting back slightly to her initial attitude towards Gloria.

'I was only trying to help, Mrs B,' she went on, unde-terred. 'I really like Sal.'

'We all do but that isn't the point,' said Mavis. 'Anyway, haven't you got a job to go to?'

'Nah. I'm not doing the lunchtime shift today,' said Gloria, who worked as a barmaid in a pub in Exeter. 'I'll be working tonight though.'

'Well, why not take Joe and go in the other room and play cards or something so that Bob and I can have a chat on our own,' suggested Mavis.

'Right you are,' agreed Gloria breezily, handing Joe his crutches. 'Come on then.'

And they left, Gloria still loudly encouraging him to walk without the crutches and him telling her to stop nagging.

'Now that they've gone, Bob,' Mavis began, 'I have to tell you that I'm very disappointed in you for getting into this mess. You've been well brought up and it shouldn't have happened.'

'But these things do happen, Mum, no matter how well brought up you've been. You know that.'

'With a bit of restraint they don't need to,' she said sternly. 'But it's done now so you have to take the consequences.'

'Exactly.'

'I can't pretend to like Kate,' Mavis went on. 'She never fitted in with us but I'm sure we'll do our best to make her welcome when you bring her here.'

This was an awkward moment for Bob because his marriage to Kate wasn't going to be a normal one and he doubted if she would want to go to Devon because she loathed the country and had never taken to his family. She had only suffered the occasional visit when they were together before to keep him happy because they had been planning to spend the rest of their lives together. It was very different this time around. It wasn't just the two of them now either; there was the complication of Lucy being his parents' granddaughter.

'Obviously your father and I would hope to see our first grandchild,' she said as though reading his thoughts.

'But I never thought it would be under such circumstances.'

'The thing to bear in mind is that none of it is Lucy's fault. She's just a little girl.'

'And we must all make sure she doesn't suffer because of her parents' irresponsible behaviour. Do you have any photographs of her?'

'No, I haven't, sorry. I'll ask Kate for some snaps and send them to you.'

'I'd like that,' she said.

He felt completely distanced from his daughter, probably because he hadn't seen her since Kate appeared out of the blue with her that time. When Kate had been to see him since, she came alone leaving the child with her grandparents, so as yet there was no bond between himself and Lucy. The whole thing felt oppressively odd, like an unfeeling business arrangement, as there was nothing left between himself and Kate. But his sense of responsibility towards Lucy was strong so he would do what he must with a willing heart and make the best of it for her sake.

'So, it's all changed for you then, Bob,' said his father when the two men went to the village pub for a pint before supper.

'Unfortunately yes,' Bob confirmed.

'You don't have to marry Kate, you know,' Stan went on. 'It hasn't become a law of the land so far as I'm aware.'

'It's the right thing though,' said Bob. 'And I don't think you'd be very pleased if I didn't do that.'

''Appen I wouldn't,' he agreed. 'But I know how happy

you were with Sal.'He took a long swig of his beer. 'Sometimes financial support for the child is enough.'

'It won't be in this case because she wants respectability,' said Bob.'Anyway I've burned my boats with Sal so there is no going back as far as she's concerned.'

'That doesn't mean you have to spend the rest of your life with a woman who isn't right for you.'

'I shall have to try to get along with her, for the sake of the little girl, won't I? She needs me,' said Bob.

'Easier said than done,' proclaimed Stan, taking a tobacco tin and some papers out of his pocket and rolling a cigarette.

'I'll just have to do my best, won't I? Anyway, that's enough about that. How are things with you? Mum says you've been busy.'

'Aye. I've been doing a lot of work in town after I put an ad in the local paper. People are spending money on their houses again and there aren't enough painters and decorators to keep up with the demand so I've been doing all right.'

'Mum seems to think that Joe will be back working with you before too long.'

'It'll be a long while yet,' said Stan, shaking his head and frowning. 'But I hope to have him back eventually. He's come on in leaps and bounds lately. Mostly thanks to Gloria. He complains about the way she pushes him to his limit but he's cheered up no end since she's been around.'

'I noticed that she seems to have become like one of the family,' said Bob. 'Mum seems to be quite fond of her now.'

'On and off. It still isn't all plain sailing between the two of them but I think your mother is beginning to accept how good she is for Joe,' said Stan. 'The girl is a bit mouthy and rough around the edges but she's wonderful with him. She seems to have taken his recovery as her own responsibility.'

'Are they still just friends?' wondered Bob.

'As far as I know,' replied Stan. 'I haven't heard any different but I'd have no objections if there was more.'

They lapsed into silence as they drank their beer then Bob said, 'How's the woodwork?'

'I haven't had time to do any lately.' He drew on his cigarette. ''Appen you'll be wanting a doll's house for your young 'un so I shall have to make time to do that.'

'That would be lovely, Dad,' said Bob but none of it seemed real. The beautiful dark-eyed little girl who had come to his flat seemed as remote to him as a child he might see in a film: a complete stranger. 'I think maybe we should go home after this one. Mum will have the meal ready and be niggled if we're too long.'

'Yeah, you're right boy,' he agreed, swigging his beer. 'Your mother is a force to be reckoned with when her dander is up so we won't risk upsetting her tonight.'

It was strange, thought Bob, but somehow the situation he was in seemed to distance him from his family. Even though Sal hadn't known them for long she had been very much a part of it and he knew that she would be missed. In his heart he was sure that when he did come home to see them he wouldn't be bringing Kate or Lucy. Such a thing would be anathema to Kate and as far as he knew there was no law that said grandparents had the right to see their grandchildren. He felt very lonely suddenly and wished more than ever that he still had Sal in his life.

It was a bright and breezy Sunday afternoon in April and Sal and her sister were out walking in Ravenscourt Park with Tommy in the pushchair while Dolly was at home taking a nap. Scamp was let off the lead as soon as they were safely inside the park gates and was racing around, tail wagging, ears back. Sal threw a stick for him and he tore after it with Tommy in hot pursuit. At sixteen months he was steady on his legs now.

'He's such a little sweetheart, that son of yours,' said Sal, watching him with pleasure. 'He cheers us all up.'

'And you've needed plenty of that lately,' said Ann.

'Not half,' she said with a wry grin. 'Still, onwards and upwards as they say. What I need is a new challenge. Apart from your driving lessons.'

'What about a new man?'

'Even if there was anyone interested, which there isn't, I don't think I would want to know, 'said Sal seriously. 'It's a case of twice bitten for me. I'm steering clear of that particular minefield for the moment.'

'It isn't a choice for me with my circumstances,' said Ann wistfully. 'But I sometimes wonder how different things would be for me if Tommy's dad and I had stayed together.'

'It's a shame about that,' said Sal, throwing another stick for Scamp and listening to Tommy's chubby laughter, the fresh air invigorating her. 'A pity too that the man doesn't even know about his son. He would be so proud and would love him to bits I'm sure.'

'Maybe,' admitted Ann.

'Why not contact him,' suggested Sal. 'Give him a chance to see Tommy.'

'After all this time, not likely. He'll have found someone else by now and the last thing he'll need is me turning up with a child. Look what happened when Bob's ex turned up with a kiddie. It wrecked your life as well as his.'

'Mm. But you wouldn't be demanding anything from him, would you? You'd just be giving him a chance to see his son.'

'It's too late, Sal,' she said. 'I made my decision and I have to stand by it.'

'You're not only depriving Tommy's dad, you're depriving Tommy too.'

'He isn't old enough to know anything about it,' said Ann.

'He will be though, eventually, won't he, and time flies?' Sal reminded her.

'Yes, and I shall have to live with that. But men don't want past affairs coming back to haunt them, it's a well-known fact.'

'Not all men are the same,' Sal pointed out. 'Some might object, others would be delighted to know they have a child. You can't judge them all because of some stereotype we've been brought up with.'

'True,' admitted Ann. 'But I'd rather leave things as they are so stop nagging me.'

'Fair enough,' agreed Sal, lapsing into her own thoughts

as her sister chased her son, making him squeal with laughter.

It was two months since she'd parted from Bob. She was still hurting but at least she'd regained her concentration which at first had been seriously affected. She could now lose herself in a book and had devoured plenty these past few weeks, making her one of the library's best customers. At least there was some respite from her painful thoughts now.

She was recalled to the present by her sister who was saying, 'Shall we head for the swings now?'

'Yeah, let's do that.' Sal swept her adored nephew up into her arms and kissed him. 'Tommy will love that, and bags I get to give him the first push.'

'You are a fool over him,' said Ann, smiling.

'I know I am,' confessed Sal. 'I don't have a child of my own so I share yours.'

They made their way companionably over to the playground.

Surprisingly for Bob, now that Kate had got him to agree to marry her and ruined his life in the process, she didn't seem to be pressing for an early marriage. Neither did she show any sign of wanting to move in with him until after the wedding which he guessed was because her parents wouldn't approve and she needed to keep on the right side of them to help with Lucy, especially as regards babysitting.

But when she called round to see him one day in April he realised that there was no lessening of intent.

'I don't mind living here in the flat for a while after we get married, until we can afford something better,' she said, casting a critical eye around. 'It isn't ideal for a child, of course, but I suppose it will do for a time.'

'Don't you mean when I can afford something better,' he corrected her.

'Same thing,' she said. 'What's yours is mine. That's what marriage is all about, isn't it?'

She was right, of course, and had he been marrying Sal there would have been no resentment. As it was there was plenty because he knew he was being manipulated and there didn't seem to be a damned thing he could do about it.

'Mm,' he said dully. 'If you say so.'

'And on the subject of us getting married, we need to set a date and put things in motion,' she announced.

'There's no immediate hurry is there.'

She narrowed her eyes on him. 'I hope you are not trying to back out,' she said accusingly.

'I'm a man of my word, you know that,' he reminded her.

'That's all right then,' she said. 'So you'll need to come over and see my parents sometime soon so that we can get everything sorted out.'

'Is that really necessary?' he asked. 'We don't need to make a big performance of it. You tell me the arrangements and I'll let you know if they suit me.'

'That just won't do, Bob. You'll need to reinstate your relationship with Mum and Dad as you're going to be part of the family.'

'Like you intend to do with my parents,' he said with irony.

'That's different. Your people are in the back of beyond and won't be involved in the wedding arrangements. Mine will be doing it all so you need to be on good terms with them.'

A now familiar feeling of suffocation squeezed hard. He wanted to run as far away from this situation as it was possible to go. But he knew he couldn't so he must try harder to get used to it and he needed time. 'There's no rush to make the arrangements, though, is there?'

Another sharp look. 'You're not going to wriggle out of this, Bob, no matter how hard you try,' she declared. 'Lucy needs you and you are going to do the right thing by her.'

'I've no intention of reneging on my duty. I just need time to adjust. Though I must admit I don't think it's going to be a very happy arrangement for either of us.'

'It will be what we make it,' she said firmly. 'We'll have to put plenty of effort in for Lucy's sake.'

'All right Kate,' he said with a weary sigh. 'I know exactly what's expected of me so there's no need to go on about it.'

'I'll arrange for you to come over to my place some-time soon so that we can set the ball rolling.'

Bob had got along well enough with Kate's parents in the past; he'd always felt rather sorry for them because Kate never tried to hide how irritated she was by them and he had often had cause to wince at the harsh and disrespectful way she spoke to them. Now, the idea of meeting them to make wedding plans filled him with dread. But he just sighed and said, 'Let me know when, and as long as I'm not working I'll be there.'

For some time Sal had been thinking that they needed to find new ways to bring in more business for The Toffee Shop to keep up with the increasingly ubiquitous supermarkets. They had to compete to stay in business in the changing world of retail. The idea came to her as she was about to fall asleep one night and she hardly slept a wink because of the excitement of it.

'I've had an amazing idea,' she told Ann and Dolly at breakfast the next morning. 'A way to bring in more business.'

'Oh no, not more work,' groaned Ann, cutting some toast into fingers for Tommy. 'We do enough hours as it is and I've got a child to look after outside of work.'

'The competition is really hotting up so we need to do something and I'll do any extra work that's involved,' Sal told her. 'I've nothing else to do with my free time so I might as well concentrate on the shop.'

'So what is the idea?' asked Dolly, tapping the top of her boiled egg with a spoon and removing the shell.

'A Saturday stall in Shepherd's Bush market,' she announced. 'Selling and promoting our home-made range of toffee.'

The idea was greeted with silence.

'Well, don't overdo the enthusiasm, will you?' said Sal with good-humoured sarcasm.

'Give us a chance to think about it,' Dolly came back at her. 'Who would look after this proposed stall?'

'One of us,' she replied. 'We could either take turns or I'll do it if you two don't fancy it.'

'I'm not sure if I'd want to do it,' said Ann with her usual candour. 'I've got Tommy to think of and I'm not having him out all day in the middle of winter.'

'You won't have to do it then,' Sal assured her. 'I'll look after the stall every week unless either of you fancy a break from the shop counter.'

'But if you're out all day at the market we'll be short-handed in the shop,' Dolly pointed out.

'I've been awake for most of the night thinking about the idea so let me tell you what I've worked out.'

'We're listening,' said Dolly.

'The first thing is to establish if we can produce more toffee and possibly add a couple of new flavours to the range; treacle or mint or something.' She looked at her grandmother. 'Obviously, Gran, I don't expect you to carry the extra workload on your own. I would do that or we could do it between us.'

'I might be a bit long in the tooth but I'm still capable of increasing the production of toffee. It won't be a problem for me.'

'As long as you ask for help if you need it,' Sal insisted. 'I don't want you getting worn out. You do most of the cooking and cleaning as it is.'

'I'm more interested in knowing what's going to happen in the shop while you're out at the market all day Saturday than asking for help with the toffee-making.'

'We take on a Saturday assistant,' she proposed.

'Now that really is a good idea,' said Dolly.

'There are always teenage school kids wanting to earn some extra pocket money,' Sal went on. 'Once we get them trained, it will make it easier for you and I'll be back at the shop before the last-minute Saturday rush. I'll make a point of being back by about half past three of four. Earlier if I've sold out.'

'You're very confident about the market sales, aren't you?' observed Ann.

'I have faith in our product, yeah, and that's all thanks to Gran,' Sal said. 'We all know how delicious her toffee is and this is an opportunity to get it more widely known. Anyway there's no point in starting something new with a negative attitude, is there?'

'I suppose not,' agreed Ann.

'Of course there isn't,' said Dolly. 'The idea is beginning to grow on me now.'

'What about you, Ann?' asked Sal.

'You know me, I'm not over fond of too much hard work but it does seem like a good idea and working the stall every now and again on a nice sunny day might be rather fun. It will be a change anyway.'

'We've got the car to take everything to the market.' Sal, was increasingly fired up. 'It's only a few minutes away in the car and when you've passed your test, Ann, you can help with the transport if you want to.'

'So I've already passed in your mind. The test is just a formality.'

'Yes, that's right,' confirmed Sal, adding with a wicked grin, 'With me as your teacher you can't fail.'

'Hey, steady on sis,' urged her sister lightly. 'It's me who's got to do the flippin' test and you never know how it will go on the day. Everybody says that about it. Nerves play a big part as does the mood of the examiner.'

'All right, so if you fail you try again and again until you do get your licence.'

'That's the spirit,' said Dolly.

'What are you trying to prove, Sal?' asked Ann.

'That no matter how many times I'm knocked down, I'll always get back up fighting. I may not have much luck with the men in my life but I might fare better in business because I won't be relying on luck. Plenty of effort and optimism is what will make this venture work.'

'I reckon your Auntie Sal is going to drive us all mad with her new scheme, Tommy,' said Ann, giving him another finger of toast and being rewarded with one of his heart-melting smiles.

'I will too and the very first thing to do is for me to go to the market and find out what the procedure is for getting a Saturday stall,' said Sal as though referring to a list in her mind, 'then if that looks promising, we look for a Saturday assistant.'

'What did I tell you, Tommy?' said Ann jokingly. 'She's started already and there'll be no stopping her now.'

He didn't understand what the words meant but he was able to respond to atmosphere and he did so by squealing with delight then emitting a hearty chuckle.

Chapter Thirteen

'I must say, Bob, that Kate's father and myself are delighted that the two of you have got together again,' said Kate's mother, a woman typical of her age and class with a fiercely neat appearance, grey hair tightly permed into symmetrical waves, make-up kept to a minimum and blouse buttoned up to the neck. 'We were both terribly upset when you parted.'

'So was I at the time,' he told her.

'Obviously the circumstances of your forthcoming nuptials aren't what we wanted for our daughter but at least you're doing the right thing for Lucy, that's the important thing.'

'It must have been hard for you when Kate went to Australia, Mrs Smith,' he remarked for the purpose of polite conversation.

'Heartbreaking,' she confirmed with emphasis. 'But that's life. You have to let your children go and if they choose to sail to the other side of the world there isn't much you can do about it.' She paused, looking at him.

'Your parents must have been delighted when you decided not to go after all.'

'I'm sure they must have been but we were all far too worried about my brother at the time to pay much attention to my plans,' he said.

'Yes, I think Kate mentioned something about your brother being injured in an accident,' she said vaguely. 'Is he all right now?'

'He's making progress, thank you.'

'That's good.' She sounded unemotional.

Bob had dropped off a fare in the area where Kate's parents lived so had called in to break the ice. But only her mother was at home.

'You must have been thrilled when Kate decided to come home,' said Bob, struggling to keep the dialogue going.

'Oh yes. It was more than we could have hoped for,' she responded, adding quickly, 'though we were very sorry it didn't work out for her in Australia, of course.'

'Naturally. Still, she was very keen to give it a try so she got it out of her system,' he said.

'Indeed.' Mrs Smith opened the sideboard drawer and took out a notebook and pencil. 'Anyway, Bob, as you are here we might as well make a start on the arrangements for the wedding. We can bring Kate and her father up to date later. Anything they are not happy with can be altered but I think we should make a few notes.'

'Suits me,' he agreed.

'Well, given the circumstances, we are thinking in

terms of a very small wedding; just family and a few close friends,' she announced. 'Is that all right with you?'

'Oh yes. The smaller the better as far as I'm concerned.'

'Obviously a church wedding wouldn't be appropriate,' she went on primly. 'So it will be at a registry office and a meal at a hotel afterwards; we can discuss which one when the others are around.'

'Yes, of course.'

'The first thing we need to decide on is the date,' she continued, taking her diary from her handbag and opening it. 'When would suit you?'

'Any time really,' he said, accepting his fate and trying to be gracious about it. 'I'm not fussy.'

'As it's going to be such a small affair it won't take long to arrange, and obviously the sooner the better. So what about a month's time?'

'That seems a bit quick.' Bob was struck with panic despite his good intentions.

'Not really,' she said. 'The sooner the better the way things are. Time is moving on and Lucy is growing up fast. She'll be two years old soon and before we know it she'll be old enough to understand these things. I don't see any point in waiting.'

'No, I suppose you're right,' he said with a sigh of resignation.

'Shall we say this time next month, as long as it suits Kate,' she said.

'All right then.'

'Good, I'll pencil it in.' She wrote it down then looked up. 'Now, the next thing is the financial side of it.

Obviously as the bride's parents we'll bear the brunt of the expenses but it's traditional for the groom's side to make a contribution.'

'Yes of course,' he agreed, but he had become more than a little preoccupied.

'Well, do you have any suggestions as to what you might pay for?' she asked.

'Er . . .' His thoughts were spinning as something she'd said lingered in his mind. 'What did you just say?' he asked.

'I asked if you had any suggestions about your financial contribution . . .'

'Before then.'

'I said this time next month—'

'No, no, before that,' he interrupted. 'About Lucy being two.'

'I just said that she will be two soon. Why?'

'It's May now so she's two already,' he said.

'No, not yet,' she stated.

'When is her birthday then?'

'End of June so no sooner will the wedding be over than we'll have to get cracking on her birthday celebrations.'

'But she was born in April.'

'No.'

'Are you sure?' he persisted.

'Of course I'm sure.' She frowned. 'Surely you don't think I would get my own granddaughter's birthday wrong.'

'Definitely the end of June,' he said.

'Yes, yes, for goodness' sake, Bob,' she said, beginning to object to his questions.

He stood up with a purposeful air. 'I'm sorry, Mrs Smith, but I have to go now.'

'Go? What on earth are you talking about?'

'I'm leaving.'

'But what about the wedding arrangements?'

'There will be no wedding; not one that I'll be taking part in anyway,' he informed her. 'Tell your daughter what you've told me about Lucy's birthday and she'll understand why.'

'But . . .'

'I really am very sorry Mrs Smith but I have to go now,' he said and, almost beside himself with fury, he left the house. He couldn't remember ever being this angry before. He'd been miserable and niggled since Kate's return. Now his head was blazing with real unrestrained rage and in a curious way it felt good to let go and feel it burn.

'I hope you weren't too hard on your mother for letting the cat out of the bag last night,' he said when Kate came round to his place the next morning when he was about to leave for work.

'Mum gets confused about birthdays,' she said.

'Oh per-lease. Don't insult my intelligence any more than you already have by trying to make out that your mother isn't all there,' he said. 'She is perfectly compos mentis.'

'All right, you're not Lucy's father,' she finally admitted.

'I know that,' he said. 'I'd have had to be superhuman as she was conceived well after you set sail for Australia. What puzzles me is why your mother didn't work it out for herself.'

She looked sheepish.

He narrowed his eyes on her suspiciously. 'She knows I'm not Lucy's dad, doesn't she?'

'I didn't dare tell her the truth because she would have disapproved,' she confessed. 'So I told her that you'd agreed to marry me and bring Lucy up as your own, even though she isn't. She thinks you already know you're not the daddy and are doing it because you're a decent bloke. That's why Lucy's birthday wasn't a stumbling block for her.'

He shook his head in disbelief. 'You are incredible, Kate, an absolute monster.'

'That's a bit strong,' she came back at him. 'I am just looking out for my daughter.'

'I would have found out the truth when Lucy's birthday came round in *June*.'

She shrugged. 'We'd have been married by then and I can't see what's so wrong with the idea anyway? We got along once, we could do it again.'

'I'd sooner spend the rest of my life trapped in the sewers,' he told her emphatically.

'All right, there's no need to be ridiculously dramatic.'

'There's every need,' he said. 'You casually come back into my life and feed me a pack of lies then, when you get found out, you have the brass neck to suggest that we play happy families. These are people's lives you're playing with, you know.'

'All right, all right,' she snapped.

'What about Lucy's father?'

'We split up,' she replied.

'I gathered that.'

'Why ask then?'

'I meant, why isn't he looking after you and Lucy?'

'Mind your own business,' she said.

'Surely he should be helping you,' he suggested.

In response she shrugged. 'I suppose you'll go running back to that Sal woman now that you've got me off your back.'

'We're not all like you, Kate,' he told her. 'We don't all think we can just swan in and out of people's lives. I gave up any right to be with Sal when I agreed to marry you. She told me there was no going back and I have to respect that.'

'How very honourable of you,' she said with withering sarcasm. 'You always were a bit too decent for your own good.'

'That's something you wouldn't know anything about, isn't it,' he said. 'Doing the decent thing.'

'All right, I'm no angel and I've never pretended to be,' she admitted. 'There was a time when you didn't mind that. In fact, I think you found it quite attractive.'

'I didn't realise how unscrupulous you were then but I do mind it now,' he said. 'Anyway, I have to go to work so go home and look after that daughter of yours.'

'Are you sure you don't want to be a part of her life? You'd make a smashing dad.'

'Maybe but not to Lucy,' he said, determined not to weaken and find himself agreeing to something he didn't want because he felt very sorry for the little girl. 'Perhaps you could try and patch things up with her father for her sake. If not, I'm sure your parents will give you plenty of support. I can't give you the respectability you want, Kate, because I can't allow myself to be used in that way and ultimately Lucy would be the one to suffer.' He walked to the door and held it open for her. 'So if you don't mind . . .'

'All right, I'm going.'

After he had ushered her out, he said, 'Despite everything, I do wish you well, Kate. I hope you get something sorted out.'

'I'll survive.' With a nonchalant shrug she went on her way.

Closing the door behind her, he reflected on what a near miss he had had. If Mrs Smith hadn't mentioned Lucy's birthday yesterday, he would have gone ahead and plunged into a disastrous marriage which would have been made worse when Lucy's birthday came round and he realised he'd been tricked.

But part of him was sad that Kate was in such difficult circumstances. For all her faults she was just a human being and he had once loved her. He knew somehow that she would be all right. Now he had to face up to the fact that he had lost Sal needlessly and he wasn't going to disrupt her life again by trying to get her back. That really would be selfish, so he had to carry on alone. And before he lapsed into a complete trough of self-pity he had a living to earn. He put on his jacket and left the flat.

Walking to the bus stop, Kate was philosophical about the way things had turned out. Bob had been worth a try and she would have got away with it if it hadn't been for her dozy mother who had been given a thorough trouncing about letting the cat out of the bag. Even Kate's careful alteration on the copy of Lucy's birth certificate had looked genuine enough to fool Bob. Not a nice thing to do but what was a girl to do when she got herself into this sort of mess? She had to be creative and Bob had seemed like the answer to her problems. It hadn't worked out so she was stuck with her parents for the moment. Their irritating ways almost drove her insane at times but, credit where it was due, they couldn't do enough for Lucy. That meant a lot to Kate. She was selfish and used people for her own ends but, despite her deviousness, she did love her daughter deeply and wanted to make things right for her.

She would send an airmail letter to her daughter's father, whom she had met on the boat to Australia, and ask him to send more money. Terry Granger was too much of a rat to give her the respectability of marriage but he did come up with dough when she needed it. I'll manage, she thought, as she hopped on to the bus.

Sal threw herself into the market project. All her energy was channelled into the new demands on her time and thoughts which pushed personal frustrations to the back of her mind. A Saturday assistant was found by word of mouth, a local schoolboy called Charlie who was keen to earn some extra pocket money. Saturday stalls were allocated on a first come first served basis but Sal was told that as long as she was at the market early enough there shouldn't be a problem.

Extra toffee was produced, and some weighed and bagged in advance, a pair of scales bought second-hand as well as a toffee hammer. A large blackboard with STOREYS' HOME-MADE TOFFEE chalked in big letters and a colourful oilskin cloth to put on the stall were all ready the night before.

'One good thing about it is that if you don't sell the toffee at the market we'll soon shift it here at the shop,' said Ann on the Friday night before the big day.

'Thanks for the vote of confidence,' said Sal, 'that's exactly what I need to hear just before my first day.'

'Honestly, Ann,' admonished her grandmother. 'You can be so insensitive at times.'

'Sorry,' said the tactless Ann. 'I only meant that nothing would be wasted. I was trying to be positive.'

'All right, we believe you,' said Sal cheerfully. 'We know you well enough to understand your own peculiar brand of logic. And you're right, we can sell it here though I hope I don't have to bring it all back.'

'You won't,' said Dolly reassuringly. 'You might have to be a bit pushy in your sales pitch though, love. When the punters come into the shop they want to buy from us; at the market they won't go there intending to buy our toffee because they don't know anything about it.

So it's up to you to inform them and make them realise that they can't do without it. When they've bought once they'll come back again and again but it's that first purchase you've got to go for.'

'Do you think I need to give them a taster?'

'Good idea. You could start the ball rolling that way on your first day,' suggested Dolly. 'But you must attract their attention or they'll just walk on by. You can't afford to be shy.'

'I'm beginning to wish I'd never had the idea,' joked Sal.

'You won't have a problem with the spiel,' encouraged Dolly. 'You'll be a natural.'

'Come and get your luvverly toffee 'ere,' she said in an exaggerated manner of a market trader. 'Is that the sort of thing you mean?'

Ann and Dolly were in fits. 'Not exactly dear. I don't think you've quite got the hang of it yet,' said Dolly. 'It'll come with a bit of practice.'

'In that case, this time tomorrow should see some improvement,' said Sal.

'I do hope so,' said her grandmother with a wry grin.

In the event, the thought proved to be worse than the deed. Once Sal caught the atmosphere of the market crowds she was out among them giving tasters and extolling the virtues of her wares like an old hand. 'Home-made toffee, fresh from the pan. Try before you buy,' she chanted. Some people bought as soon as the toffee hit their taste buds; others came back later.

'It will probably ruin my dentures,' said one elderly man who returned after a few minutes still chewing, 'but it will be worth it for that lovely mouth-watering taste, so give us half a pound, please luv, if you will.'

Sal had pre-packed the bags into quarter pounds so she gave him two and soon realised she hadn't done nearly enough as they ran out and she had to weigh every sale before taking the money which meant she had a permanent queue. Things were delayed further by the fact that they had wanted to display the toffee in the trays so it had to be broken into small pieces first with a toffee hammer before she could weigh it. Some people didn't wait. Panic set in as she couldn't work fast enough. She knew that this was a problem that needed addressing if she wanted to maximise sales. But it wasn't going to be easy.

'Either we bag all the toffee in advance, or I have some assistance, and as we can't spare anyone to help me on the stall it will have to be the bagging,' she said to her sister and grandmother later on when she got back to the shop, flush with success and eager to make the stall more efficient. The shop was quiet before the last rush of the day and when someone came in for a bar of chocolate Charlie served them.

'You need to have the toffee out on display,' opined Dolly. 'If we bag it all in advance the punters can't see what they're buying. We must show the goods off or it will be just like selling pre-wrapped stuff that they can get anywhere.'

'Mm, I agree with you, Gran, but I just can't work fast enough. Ideally I need someone to weigh up while I take the money or vice versa, only when I run out of pre-bagged toffee, of course.'

'A crowd attracts more crowds, isn't that what they say?' said Ann. 'So a queue is a good thing.'

'That's true. But if people leave because they don't have time to wait you've lost sales anyway.'

'There is that,' Dolly agreed.

'What about me?' piped up Charlie. 'I'd love to work on the market.'

'You're needed here,' said Sal. 'That's why we took you on to help while I am out.'

'It isn't flat out busy all the time here, though, is it?' he pointed out. 'It's frantic early then it's patchy. I could do a couple of hours down the market after the early rush here. Then come back a bit later on for the rest of the day. It's better than no help at all surely. I'd go on my bike. It wouldn't take long.'

Six eyes rested on him. Sal looked at her grandmother and then her sister.

'Could it work, do you think?' she asked.

'I'm sure we could manage for a couple of hours, aren't you Ann?' said Dolly.

'As long as I get the chance to take Tommy to the park,' said Ann. 'I don't want him stuck around the shop all day.'

'I'd be back by dinnertime,' promised Charlie.

'I won't let him come unless you're both happy about it,' Sal made clear to Ann and Dolly. 'I'm quite prepared to do the market on my own even if we do lose a few customers.'

'Let's give it a try this way,' decided Dolly. 'If it doesn't work this end, then you will have to do the market on your own, Sal.'

'Fair enough,' she agreed.

'Well done Charlie for suggesting it,' said Dolly.

'S' all right,' he said cheerfully.

'I'll go and unpack the car before the shop gets busy again,' said Sal.

'I'll help you,' offered the obliging Charlie and he followed her out of the shop towards the car parked outside.

As the summer progressed the Saturday market became part of the working week and was a huge success. Charlie proved to be a Godsend to Sal. He was quick and nimble, cheerful and good with the customers: a born trader.

'I reckon I should forget my O levels and go into the market game,' he said to Sal one day at the stall. 'It's a lot more fun.'

'Don't you dare,' she told him. 'You finish your education and get yourself a good job.'

'I s'pose I shall have to.'

'I'd never forgive myself if working for us were to lead you astray.'

'Don't worry, I'll do my O levels when the time comes. It would break my mum's heart if I didn't. I'm the first one in our family ever to get into grammar school.'

'I bet she's proud,' said Sal.

'I'll say. She's embarrassin' at times,' he said. 'But I want to do well even if the homework is a perishin' nuisance.'

'Good boy,' she said, smiling at him. He really was a likeable youngster and made her realise that not all teenagers were delinquent types as popular opinion had it ever since Teddy Boys had been in their heyday a few years ago and given the youth of the country a bad reputation. 'You'll go far.'

The success of the market stall meant more work on the production side of the toffee. Dolly and Sal used Wednesday half-day closing for this purpose and worked alongside each other at the stove with a heavy-bottomed saucepan each while Ann took Tommy out to the park if it was fine.

'The chocolate toffee has proved to be very popular on the stall,' said Sal, stirring butter and sugar together with a pinch of salt in the pan on the heat.

'Yeah, it's always a favourite,' said Dolly, testing the temperature of the evolving toffee with a thermometer and judging it to be ready as it turned amber in colour. She took the saucepan off the heat and poured the mixture into a greaseproof-lined tray. 'As did the almond one. The new demand has made us more creative in our recipes.'

'It has, though the original creamy toffee is still the most popular of all,' Sal reminded her. 'All our other varieties are based on your original recipe. It must make you feel really proud.'

'I don't really look at it in that light,' she said, modest as always. 'I'm just glad there is still a demand for it after all these years with so many new sweets coming on to the market. But yes, I suppose there is a little pride in that.'

'Good,' said Sal, stirring slowly and looking into the saucepan as the contents came to the boil. 'You deserve to be proud of yourself. All these years and Storey Toffee is still going strong.'

They fell silent and Dolly cleaned the saucepan and prepared to make another batch while Sal popped the thermometer into her pan to test the heat then emptied the contents into a tray and began melting the chocolate ready to spread over the top.

'Am I allowed to ask if all is well with the Becks?' enquired Dolly tentatively, putting butter and sugar into the washed pan ready to repeat the process. 'I noticed you had a letter with a Devon postmark this morning and guessed it was from Mavis.'

'Of course you're allowed to ask,' Sal assured her. 'I would have told you about it later anyway. Yes, it was from Mavis and they all seem to be all right.'

'Is that the first time you've heard since—'

'Since Bob and I split up, yes,' she cut in quickly because the subject had created tension. 'She says she hopes I'll go down to visit them when I can get away.'

'Oh, wouldn't that be a bit . . . ?'

'Inappropriate,' Sal finished for her, her voice trembling because the contents of Mavis's letter had had a huge impact on her. 'No, not really, because Bob didn't marry

Kate after all. He found out that the child wasn't his so called it off and is on his own again. That's why Mavis feels able to contact me.'

'I see.' Dolly pondered for a moment. 'I suppose you're feeling a bit hurt because he hasn't come rushing round to you.'

'I told him not to come back to me if it all went wrong and he's obviously taken me at my word.'

'But you wish he hadn't.'

'With my heart yes but with my head I'm glad because I've got my life back on to an even keel and I don't want all that emotional turmoil again. I've been hurt once too often.'

'I don't think Bob would hurt you again, dear,' said Dolly, returning the saucepan to the heat.

'I didn't think he would ever hurt me and he did so how do I know someone else won't come crawling out of the woodwork making demands on him?'

'It wasn't his child and it wasn't his fault that he hurt you,' Dolly reminded her.

'Mm, there is that,' Sal sighed. 'But things are best left as they are. I'm still getting used to the idea that he didn't marry Kate so I'm not really sure how I feel yet.' She spread a thin layer of the melted chocolate over the toffee in the tray and moved it to the back of the table with the others to cool and set. 'So how are we doing, Gran? Do I need to do another lot?'

Dolly looked at the growing number of trays. 'No, I think this will be enough for this session,' she said. 'I'll finish this pan and do the clearing up if you want to go to the library to change your books. I know you often do that on a Wednesday afternoon.'

'I haven't finished the books I've got yet,' she said. 'With all the extra work, I'm so shattered when I go to bed I fall asleep after a couple of pages.'

'That's a shame.'

'Oh no, I'm not complaining. I enjoy the challenge. I get a good feeling from working hard.'

Which was no substitute for what she'd had with Bob, thought Dolly, but had the good sense not to say so. 'You know what they say about all work and no play,' she ventured.

'I'll get back to reading, don't worry,' Sal assured her.

'Why don't you and Ann go to see a film one evening soon? I'll look after Tommy.'

'You're working hard too. So I suggest that you and Ann have a night out.'

'I'd rather stay with Tommy,' Dolly said quickly.

From the way she spoke it dawned on Sal that her grandmother would probably welcome a quiet evening on her own with Tommy in bed. Sal and her sister were, after all, of a different generation so inevitably had opposing views about some things despite the fact that Gran kept up to date. 'OK. If you're sure, I'll see if Ann fancies a night at the flicks. Meanwhile I insist on doing all the clearing up while you put your feet up and I'll make us a cup of tea.'

'Did someone say something about tea,' said Ann, clattering in with Tommy at her side 'I don't mind if I do.'

'Make yourself useful and put the kettle on then,' said her sister 'While I wash these pans.'

'OK.'

Seeing Tommy smiling up at her Sal couldn't resist picking him up and smothering him with kisses. 'Did you have a good time at the park, darlin'?' she asked.

'Yeth,' he said sweetly and Sal melted. She really believed that she couldn't love him more if he was her own.

Bob walked into Hammersmith Library and scanned the aisles but he wasn't looking for books. He was hoping for a glimpse of Sal who he knew often changed her books on a Wednesday afternoon at about this time. It wouldn't be good form to blatantly call on her and ask for another chance, after hurting her so badly, but if they just happened to meet maybe she would agree to at least talk to him, outside of these hushed walls.

Absolutely no sign so far so he went over to the history section and tried to engross himself in what was on the shelves while keeping an eye open for any new arrivals. Spotting a book that appealed to him he browsed through it, deciding to take it out on loan though as this wasn't his local library he would have to join. That would be a good thing anyway, as he was planning on coming back again in the hope of seeing Sal. The things you do for love, he thought as he walked over to the counter.

The Storey sisters went to see *The Apartment*, a romantic drama starring Shirley MacLaine and Jack Lemmon.

'Good film,' said Ann as they stood in the queue for chips on the way home, having promised their grandmother they would get some for them all for supper. 'It made us laugh and cry and it all turned out right in the end.'

'Unlike real life,' said Sal.

'Ooh, that's a bit cynical,' said Ann. 'Not like you at all, Sal.'

'It's true though. I mean take us two. Here we are still single and you're having to bring a child up on your own.'

'That's my own silly fault. And as for you and Bob, I don't know why you don't try and get him back before someone else snaps him up. He's a good-looking bloke Sal. He won't stay single for long.'

'If he wants to get involved with someone else that's his business,' said Sal.

'All right, there's no need to go all haughty about it.'

'Sorry. But it's all so unsettling. I mean I had all the pain when we parted. But I picked up the pieces and got my life back together again. Now he's back upsetting me all over again.'

'He hasn't been anywhere near you,' Ann pointed out.

'Not physically but knowing he's single after all makes me feel vulnerable.'

'You're obviously still in love with him so go and get him, girl.'

'Like you went and got your man . . .'

'That's an unfair comparison,' objected Ann. 'The circumstances are entirely different.'

'Next please,' said the counter assistant.

'Three bags of chips with plenty of salt and vinegar, please,' said Sal.

348

The sisters didn't return to the emotive subject but talked about Ann's forthcoming driving test for the rest of the way home.

Initially Sal found it difficult to reply to Mavis's letter because Bob seemed to be in the way. But once she got going the words just flowed.

'I would love to come and see you but, as you know, it isn't easy for me to get away, especially now that we've taken on the Saturday market.' She paused with her pen in her hand, imagining the cottage and being with them all, the banter between Joe and Gloria, and the relaxation she felt when she was there and added, 'But maybe I could manage to do it at the next bank holiday weekend in August if Gran and Ann don't mind. Please let me know if that would be convenient for you. Obviously I'd rather not be there at the same time as Bob so if he's going to be there please let me know and I'll arrange to come another time.'

She finished the letter and folded it into the envelope smiling. A break in Devon would be something to look forward to and there was no law that said you couldn't stay friends with an ex's family.

A bit unconventional perhaps but what the hell . . .

Sal wasn't at all surprised when Ann passed her driving test. She was supremely confident at the wheel as well as competent so Sal would have been astonished if the examiner had failed her.

'I'll be able to go to the cash and carry to save you

doing it every time,' Ann said, driving herself and Sal home from the test centre, eager to go out in the car without L plates and practise her new skills. 'And take the money to the bank.'

'Yes, it's going to be really handy for me having another driver in the family,' enthused Sal who had no qualms at all about her sister taking to the roads on her own.

'I'll drive us all down to Brighton one of these Sundays soon,' Ann suggested. 'Tommy would love a day at the seaside.'

'We'll remind you of that when the novelty of driving wears off,' laughed Sal.

'It won't,' Ann declared. 'Driving a car is freedom and I love the feeling.'

Sal agreed with her as it happened; there was a certain delicious sense of liberation in getting behind the wheel even if the London traffic was nerve-wracking at times. 'Yes, I know what you mean.'

'So where can I go in the car now?'

'Nowhere except home,' said Sal. 'We are both going to be behind the counter or toddler-minding for the rest of the afternoon. Gran's been holding the fort with Tommy as well as the shop while we've been out so we are going back to take over from her.'

'Fair enough.' Ann pulled up outside the shop. 'I might go for a little ride myself after we close. It doesn't get dark until late. I shall take Tommy with me. You and Gran can come if you like. I can show her how good I am.'

'All right clever clogs, we'll all go round the block with you so that you can show off.'

'But no telling me what to do,' said Ann lightly. 'I'm a qualified driver now and on a par with you so I want no bossiness.'

'I won't say a word,' promised Sal.

'You must have been very confident of passing your test,' observed Sal as her sister hooked the child seat for Tommy on to the back of the front passenger seat after they closed the shop that same day. 'You even got a kiddie seat.'

'I knew I would pass sooner or later,' she explained with a wry grin. 'And I guessed it would be before Tommy became an adult.'

'All right, don't be sarky,' said Sal, holding the child ready to put him in the seat. 'It doesn't look very sturdy.'

'None of them are. Most people don't bother and just sit their kid on the seat.'

'It doesn't look very comfortable either. No wonder people let their kids sit in the ordinary seats. In you go Tommy,' said Sal, sitting him in with his chubby little legs either side of a partition in the centre so that they dangled at which point his lip trembled and he began to scream.

'Ooh, he doesn't like that one bit,' said Ann.

'I don't blame him either,' said Sal, 'I wouldn't want to be strung up in that thing.'

'Take him out then, Sal, and sit him beside you or have him on your lap,' said Ann.

'I think I'd better,' she agreed.

'What a waste of money that was,' said Ann. 'Someone

ought to invent a decent kiddie seat. Something with some sort of a safety element. I'll have to persevere with it, though. He might be all right when he gets used to it.'

'There there darlin',' said Sal, getting him out of the seat and sitting him on her lap. 'We're all going for a nice little ride to show you and your granny how clever Mummy is.'

He was all smiles now.

'It's all a bit of a performance just to go round the block, isn't it?' said Dolly, who was in the front passenger seat.

'Careful, Gran,' said Sal jokingly. 'This is Ann's big day. We mustn't spoil it for her.'

'Come on then, show us what you can do. I've left our meal in the oven so I don't want to be out for too long.'

Ann got in and started the engine. 'Right. Look out London, here we come,' she said with a flourish and the car moved away without a sign of a stall or a shudder.

'Well done,' said Sal. 'If you keep at it long enough you might get to be as good as I am.'

'Ha ha,' Ann came back at her as they headed towards the town. 'I was better than you by my third lesson.'

'Now now you two,' Dolly intervened. 'You don't need to compete over this.'

'It's just a bit of fun, Gran,' Sal assured her.

'To you it might be a joke,' said Ann good-humouredly, 'but I'm deadly serious. Driver of the Year 1960. That's me.'

They all joined in the fun and Tommy chuckled like mad. Sal couldn't help thinking what a lovely atmosphere there was between them all. Considering that the three women spent so much time together they very rarely had any serious disagreements. Naturally there were times when they irritated each other just by drawing breath and there was an occasional heated argument but never anything that wasn't resolved fairly quickly. Sal considered herself to be very blessed. She might not be lucky in love but she was well compensated in other ways.

Maybe they could all go to Devon if she decided to go at the bank holiday. They'd love that and she was almost certain that the Becks would be all in favour. Yes, that was a good idea so she would mention it to the others at a more convenient time. Meanwhile Ann was going round Hammersmith Broadway like a veteran. She really was a very confident driver!

Chapter Fourteen

'Do you have the cash and carry list ready for me, Sal?' asked Ann one afternoon a few weeks later.

Sal nodded, picking up a piece of paper from behind the counter and coming out into the shop. 'I'll just run through it with you quickly. Paper bags large and small, two boxes of Mars Bars to tide us over, wine gums and chews if they have them, various cigarette brands as listed, and anything you see that you know we need that I've not put on the list.'

'Will do.' She took the list.

'You need our trader's card or you won't get in.' Sal hurried to the back of the counter and got the card out of a drawer. 'So are you all set?'

'I'm ready and raring to go.' Ann glanced down at Tommy who was holding her hand. 'We're looking forward to our little outing, aren't we, darlin'.'

'Yeth,' he said, rewarding them with one of his joyful grins.

'Ooh I could eat you,' said Sal, picking him up and

hugging him. 'You enjoy your outing with Mummy and I'll see you when you get back.'

Ann laughed. 'We're only going a few miles down the road,' she reminded her lightly. 'Anyone would think we were emigrating the way you're carrying on.' She clamped her hand over her mouth in an exaggerated manner. 'Sorry sis, I forgot that isn't a word we use in this house.'

'Don't be so daft,' said Sal. 'I'm well over that. So go and get the stuff and don't be all day. We're waiting for it.'

'All right, don't nag.'

Dolly appeared and together she and Sal went outside to see them off, smiling and waving.

'Any service here today?' asked one of their regulars on her way into the shop.

'What can I get you, Hilda?' asked Sal, hurrying back inside followed by Dolly.

Ann was enjoying herself immensely, driving around Shepherd's Bush Green and on to the Uxbridge Road towards the cash and carry warehouse at Acton. Unlike many new drivers, heavy traffic didn't worry her in the least because she was so comfortable at the wheel. Tommy was in the back, the child seat having been deemed a dead loss and discarded. She could see him in the driving mirror and he was as happy as could be, listening to her singing nursery rhymes to him.

She adored the stage he was currently at. For her, personally, it was far more rewarding than the baby time because he was such fun and gave so much back. It was hard to believe that he would be two at the end of the year. Even more difficult to recall was how much she hadn't wanted a baby when she had realised that she was pregnant. He was her whole life now.

'Hickory Dickory Dock,' she chanted for the umpteenth time because it was his favourite.

'Agen,' he demanded when she reached the end.

'You'll give Mummy a sore throat with all this singing,' she said with a smile in her voice.

'Agen,' he persisted, squealing with delight.

She was distracted by a car in a side turning ahead, the driver determined to nudge his way out despite the steady flow of traffic on the main road. Surely he would stop and wait until it was safe. He must know it wasn't his right of way. But she had yet to learn that not all drivers obeyed the Highway Code to the letter and, much to her astonishment, he put his foot down and shot out at high speed. She slammed on her brakes as hard as she could but she felt the impact as the car went into the side of her vehicle at around the same time as the dull jolt of one behind hit the back.

Shocked and confused as she was, the only thing that registered was the sight of Tommy, who had been thrown into the front and was lying on the floor in a sea of broken glass, his screams ripping the heart out of her. There was blood too; lots of it. She tried to get to him but was wedged against the steering wheel.

'Help me someone,' she cried frantically, tears streaming down her face as her son's shrieks rang in her ears. She managed to open the car door. 'Help, help,' she yelled in a strangled voice. 'It's my baby. Please help . . . someone . . . please.'

The sight of her nephew lying still and helpless in the hospital cot swathed in bandages and with a drip in his arm supplying intravenous fluid upset Sal more than anything else ever had. Her own personal traumas were as nothing compared to this.

'Thank God you're here,' said Ann, throwing her arms round her sister and weeping when Sal and Dolly arrived. 'Oh Sal, he's lost a lot of blood and they don't know if he will make it.' She went to her grandmother. 'Oh Gran, please make him better. Please don't let him die.'

'Shush, shush love. Don't even think about that.'

'It's all my fault,' she sobbed. 'I was driving the car. I should have been more careful. I must be overconfident.'

'Now don't punish yourself,' advised Dolly. 'From what we've heard from the police who came to the shop to tell us what had happened, the accident wasn't your fault. The other driver came out of a side turning at speed when they should have waited, and went straight into you. There were plenty of witnesses. Anyway, don't worry about that side of it now.'

The three of them stood by the cot looking down at Tommy, so still and silent. It wasn't official visiting time but because the child's condition was critical Sal and Dolly could stay as long as they liked and Ann wasn't expected to leave his side. A nurse swept in with news that the doctor would be along to speak to them soon.

'You should have heard him screaming when it happened,' sobbed Ann. 'It broke my heart. But I'd give a lot to hear it now. At least I'd know he'd still got life in him.'

'He's only sleeping so soundly because they've given him something to calm him and keep him still so that the drip stays in place,' said her grandmother. 'He'll be making a noise soon enough, don't worry.'

'We hope,' said Ann miserably.

'Now come on love,' said Sal kindly. 'Don't even think like that. He'll come through it.'

'Maybe I should have put him in the child seat,' she wailed.

'There's no safety aspect to those seats at all; they are only a convenience,' Sal reminded her. 'He might have been even more badly hurt if he'd been in it, you never know.' She looked at her sister, who had a couple of dressings on her face. 'What about you? Are you all right?'

'Don't worry about me. Just a couple of minor cuts; nothing at all. Oh Sal. Why don't they do something? They've been talking about a blood transfusion so why don't they get on with it instead of just leaving him. I've given them his blood group which is different to mine. I was told that at the time of his birth.'

'They'll give him blood when the time is right if that's what he needs; they're probably discussing it right now,' said Sal. 'I know it can't be easy but you must try to calm down. They'll do everything they can for him. They're professionals; they know what they're doing.'

Sal had been beginning to worry when Ann had been

late back from the warehouse and when two policemen had appeared at the shop her legs had all but buckled. She and Dolly had closed the shop and the butcher in the parade had driven them to the hospital in his car. Now she didn't know how to comfort her distressed sister because things really didn't look good for Tommy. But she mustn't show how scared she was because Ann needed a positive influence at the moment. Perhaps they would all be more able to cope if they knew exactly what the prognosis was for Tommy no matter how devastating the news might be.

It transpired that there was a problem with the blood transfusion Tommy needed because his was a rare blood group. As his mother wasn't a match his best chance was his father. When Ann explained her personal circumstances, the doctor asked if the father could be contacted.

'No not really, I'm not in touch with him,' she explained, anguish making her irritable and unreasonable. Why didn't they get on and make her boy better instead of pestering her with questions? 'I haven't seen him for years.'

The doctor looked grave. 'It would help your son's chances considerably if we could find a suitable blood donor and his father really is his best hope. But speed is of the essence. He needs the blood urgently.'

Because Ann's mind was dulled by distress, she couldn't see beyond the obstacles. 'I'm sorry but I can't get hold of him,' she said. 'I don't have a phone number for him. I don't even know where he is now.'

'You've got the address of where he was when you last saw him though, haven't you?' Sal cut in.

'Oh yeah, I know where he lived then,' she said. 'It's in the Notting Hill area, near Portobello Road.'

'That isn't far so give the details to me and I'll go and see if I can find him. You can't leave Tommy. If his dad has moved on, someone might know where he is.'

'Would you do that for me, Sal?' said Ann, finally glimpsing hope.

'Of course I will, give me the address and some directions and I'll go right away.'

'It would be a great help,' urged the doctor.

Sal took a notepad and pencil from her handbag and handed it to Ann. 'Write the details down and I'll be on my way.' She looked at Dolly. 'Can you stay here with her, Gran, until I get back? I'll be as quick as I can.'

'Will do.'

It was almost dark when Sal came out of Notting Hill Gate station and walked down Pembridge Road and into Portobello Road towards Westbourne Grove. The area was no more than a few miles from where she lived but it was like another world, run-down and shabby with a threatening feel to it, probably because the Notting Hill riots had left such a stain in the public consciousness.

Terraced rows of large houses rose broodingly either side of her and she guessed they were the multi-tenanted properties rented out to immigrants for inflated rents that Ann had told her about. A group of black youths in fedora hats stood in a group outside a café talking and smoking and Caribbean music drifted out from a basement as she passed.

She found the house she was looking for and rang the bell. A man of West Indian appearance opened the door and gave her a steely gaze.

'Yeah?' he said in a questioning manner.

'Is Thomas here please?' she asked.

He weighed her up thoughtfully. 'He might be but he won't want to have no white trash woman knocking at his door,' he told her.

She managed to let the insult go over her head because she knew a little of the reason for it. 'It's very urgent. If he's here, please let me see him,' she begged.

'He won't have nothin' to do with no white women,' he said. 'Not since one treat him bad. So be on your way.'

'I don't want money.' She put her foot in the door as he tried to close it. 'If I don't get to see him a little boy will probably die. Please, I'm begging you.'

He opened the door a little wider and stared at her as though mulling it over. 'All right,' he said at last, 'there's no need to make such a drama of it. Wait here.'

'Hurry please,' she said. 'It really is very urgent.'

The dilapidated door slammed behind him, leaving her standing outside the run-down building, her heart thudding against her ribs. Had she not been nauseous because her nervous system was shattered by Tommy's condition, she might have enjoyed the spicy aroma of curry emanating from the house. As it was it made her feel worse. Hurry please, she urged inwardly. Get a move on for God's sake. But the door remained firmly closed.

Tommy stirred a little then went back to sleep. It was painful for Ann not to be able to pick him up. Such an action would dislodge the needle in his arm so all she could do was lean down and stroke his brow, very gently so as not to disturb him. Never in her life had she felt so helpless. Her mouth was so parched with nerves she could barely swallow.

'I'll stay with him if you'd like to stretch your legs and get some fresh air,' said Dolly.

'I'm not leaving him, Gran,' she responded predictably. 'I could really do with a cup of tea though. I'm that dry.'

'There's nowhere we can get one,' said Dolly. 'I'll go home and get a Thermos flask when Sal comes back.'

'Where is Sal?' Ann fretted. 'Shouldn't she be here by this time?'

Dolly looked at the big round clock on the wall of the ward. 'She's not been gone an hour yet. Bear in mind that she has to find the place, speak to the bloke and then get back.'

'Yeah, o' course,' said Ann dully.

A nurse walked neatly on to the scene, took a look at Tommy then ran her eye over the two women and offered to make them a cup of tea. That one small act of kindness touched Dolly and the tears began to flow. She'd managed to hold back until now in her concern for Ann.

'Thank you, Nurse,' she said, wiping her eyes. 'That's very nice of you.'

'A pleasure,' the nurse said and hurried away.

Drying her eyes, Dolly looked at the doors of the ward, willing Sal to appear. But as yet there was no sign of her.

At last the door of the house opened and a tall West Indian man appeared.

'I'm Thomas. You wanna see me?' he said in a questioning manner, his voice deep and velvet with the lyrical sound of his homeland.

'I'm Ann Storey's sister,' she told him. 'I understand that you were very close to her at one time.'

She could see him frowing in the dim light from the street lamp and he moved back towards the open door. 'I did know her once, yeah, but it was a long time ago and I want nothin' more to do with her. So go away and don't come pestering me again.'

'Please,' she said, grabbing his arm firmly as he started to go inside.

'Hey, take your hands off me,' he objected. 'Why is she sending her sister after me anyway?' He narrowed his eyes at her. 'If she has something to say why hasn't she come herself?'

'Because she's at the hospital.'

'She is ill?'

'No, not her,' she replied. 'Her son – *your son* has been injured in a car accident and his condition is critical.'

'*My son*,' he exclaimed. 'I have no son.'

363

'Yes, you do and he's a very sick little boy at the moment,' she explained.

'She had a child and she didn't let me know,' he said, sounding angry.

'She thought it best at the time.'

'How can it be best when a man gets deprived of his own flesh and blood?' he exploded.

'She made the decision . . .'

'And now because it suits her she wants me to know,' he said angrily.

'That isn't how it is. Not at all,' Sal tried to explain. 'Please don't be angry. We are desperately worried; that's why I'm here.'

'You turn up here without being invited and tell me I have a child and I'm not supposed to be angry,' he said heatedly. 'A complete stranger arrives on my doorstep and tells me about some kid that might not even be mine.'

'He is yours, believe me,' she assured him. 'You only have to look at him to know that.'

'So now he is ill you come to tell me,' he said, fiercely critical. 'Why, why now? Is it because you want me to see the child before he dies?'

'No, not at all. With your help he might live. I'm here because he needs a blood transfusion and he has a very rare blood group,' she explained. 'The doctors think his father is the best hope of a match. We need your blood, Thomas, and we need it urgently.'

'I've heard some stories in my time but that is the sickest of the lot,' he said because the enormity of the situation was hard for him to take in so he wasn't allowing himself to believe it. 'You are a stranger to me, so go on your way and leave me alone.'

'Please, I'm begging you,' she said, crying now. 'I'll get down on my knees if it will help.'

'Now you're being stupid.'

'It really is a matter of life and death,' she persisted. 'Will you let a little boy die when you have the means to save him?'

In reply he went inside and slammed the door.

Sal rang the bell and banged the knocker then used her fists to beat on the wooden door until they were sore. People in the street were standing around watching, though she guessed that noisy disturbances were no novelty in this neighbourhood. 'Please help us,' she shouted through the letter box. 'Don't let a child die when you can save him.'

Eventually, when there was no response at all, Sal turned and headed towards the station, tears streaming down her face. She had to go back to the hospital and tell her distraught sister that she had failed to bring little Tommy a lifeline.

Standing in the hall near the front door of the multi-occupancy house, Thomas was trembling in reaction to what he had just heard. Residents were standing at their doors listening to what was going on; some were on the stairs, others on the landing. He was used to the lack of privacy around here. They were crammed in like animals, ten or more people to a room, so he paid little attention to those looking for some spectator sport.

His mind was on something far more important: a sick child whom he had just refused to help. He'd always thought of himself as a decent human being so how could he have done that? What did it matter if he wasn't the biological father or what he felt about the child's mother? He might just have the chance to do something worthwhile in his life.

He opened the door and scanned the street for the sight of Ann's sister and just spotted her in the distance. He tore after her before she disappeared round the corner.

'Oi, get off of me,' cried Sal, feeling someone touch her arm from the back and assuming it was one of the many youths hanging around the streets in this seedy corner of London.

'It's me,' he said and turning she saw Thomas. 'Sorry I was so hard on you back there. Of course I'll give my blood if it's found to be a match.'

For the first time since her nephew's accident, Sal glimpsed a tiny ray of hope.

'I knew in my heart you would be a good man,' Sal told him. 'My sister wouldn't have thought so much of you if you hadn't been. My name is Sal.'

'Yeah, she mentioned you.'

She could see why Ann had fallen for him. Wow! He was one good-looking bloke; tall with an athletic build and the warmest dark brown eyes she had ever seen, except perhaps in his son.

'The shock of hearing her name again caused me lots

o' pain,' he explained. 'She just finished with me and I never knew why.'

'I'll leave it to her to tell you all about that,' she said diplomatically. 'Right now we have to hurry.'

'Come on then,' he said, quickening his pace.

They were half running when they got to the tube station and rushed in.

At the hospital things moved at speed after Sal and Thomas arrived. A special emergency blood test was done and Thomas found to be a match for his son. The medical team worked quickly to set up the transfusion and, at last, the doctor had a positive prognosis for the little boy.

As Thomas was with Ann at the bedside and being very supportive to her, Sal suggested that she and Gran go home.

'I'll come back later with a flask of tea and some sandwiches for you when I've seen to the dog,' said Sal. 'But I'm going to suggest that Gran stays at home and gets some rest.'

'Yes, I think you should, Gran,' agreed Ann. 'Thanks for being so good both of you.'

'We're your family, what else would we do?' said Gran.

'See you later,' said Sal and she and Dolly made their way out of the ward.

'Thomas seems like a nice enough sort of fella, doesn't he?' Dolly remarked.

'Very nice,' confirmed Sal. 'He saved Tommy's life and that makes him a star in my book.'

★   ★   ★

'Thank you, Thomas,' said Ann, who had been deeply moved to see him and was still feeling a bit shaky. 'I will be for ever in your debt.'

'What else would I do with my blood but give it to someone who needs it, especially if that someone is my son,' said Thomas, feeling emotional at seeing her again. 'Why didn't you tell me you were pregnant Ann?'

'I knew we couldn't have a future together and I didn't want you to feel trapped because I was having a baby,' she explained. 'So the only thing I could do was to end it.'

They were snatching a few private moments in the corridor outside the ward while the nurse was attending to Tommy.

'How could you think I wouldn't want my own child?' he demanded.

'It isn't as simple as that and you know it,' she said. 'You've been on the sharp end of prejudice since you arrived in England and so have I since I had Tommy so we both know that black and white doesn't mix. The whole thing was doomed for us.'

'We could have tried to make it work. Mixed marriages aren't common, I admit, but they aren't completely unknown. But you went ahead and made the decision without even bothering to find out how I felt about it.'

'Honestly Thomas, it didn't seem as though that was what I was doing at the time.' She thought back over that period. 'I really did believe that I was doing right for you by just slipping out of your life with my problem. It's well known that men usually want to run a mile in that situation.'

'Some men might,' he said. 'Others would like the chance to make their own decision when they are given the facts.'

'Sorry,' she said, pale with exhaustion. 'I really did have your best interests at heart.'

'Now isn't the time to discuss it,' he said, preceiving her weariness. 'I can see that you're very tired.'

'It's been a long day.'

'I can stay with Tommy if you want to go home to get some sleep,' he suggested.

'Thank you but no,' she said. 'I must be there when he wakes up in case he's distressed. He'll need his mum.'

'If it's all right with you I'd like to stay anyway,' he offered.

'Of course you can stay. He's your son. You've every right. Now that it's all out in the open and you know about him you are welcome to play a part in his life when he's better if you would like. I know you've missed almost two years but better late than never.'

He looked at her bleakly. 'I'm going back to Jamaica so it really is too late,' he told her.

'Oh Thomas,' she said. 'Why?'

'Isn't it obvious? My kind aren't wanted here.'

'So you're giving up.'

He shrugged. 'If you like.'

'Oh well, it's your decision,' she said wearily, too mentally tired to discuss it further at the moment. 'Come on, let's go back into the ward. I don't know how long they'll let you stay now that Tommy is out of danger but let's wait and see.'

He followed her through the doors and they seated themselves either side of the sleeping child.

It was odd, thought Bob, how you could see something a hundred times without interest and one day it leaped out at you with new significance. This was how it was for him with a notice on the board in Hammersmith Library where he was on a Wednesday afternoon, again hoping to see Sal. It was a timetable of evening classes at various schools in the borough starting in the autumn.

History of England – 7.30–8.30 Monday evenings

He stared at it again and again remembering how Sal had suggested he went to classes to learn more about the subject for which he had a passion. He'd hated the idea then. Like many people with only a basic education, he'd always been rather in awe of the classroom and thought that formal learning was out of reach for someone like him. But why shouldn't he give it a try? It was available for anyone and he didn't have anything better to do on the evenings when he wasn't working.

Making a mental note of the details, he waited a little longer in the hope of seeing Sal, then made his way home. At least he'd decided to do something positive with his spare time, he thought, his spirits rising as he left the library. It had taken a while but he had acted on Sal's advice at last.

★   ★   ★

Tommy was in hospital for two weeks and they were all very careful with him when he came home because of the head wound, though Sal was amazed at how quickly his strength and vitality returned. Ann hadn't worked in the shop since the accident, having been with Tommy at the hospital, and she continued to take time off to devote her energies exclusively to him on his return home. Sal and Dolly were happy to do her shifts for her and generally give her their support.

This did mean however that Sal had to write to Mavis Beck to explain the situation and tell her that she wouldn't be able to make it to Devon at the Bank Holiday after all.

'I feel that Ann still needs my support here,' she wrote in conclusion. 'The whole thing has upset us all terribly and we feel we want to be near Tommy. I can't tell you how grateful and happy we are to have him home. I will come as soon as I can spot an opportunity. I really do want to see you all and would welcome the break.'

She signed and folded the letter and put it into an envelope ready to post.

'So when do you leave?' Ann asked of Thomas as they walked by the river with Tommy one day in late August. Ann was wheeling the empty pushchair while the little boy trotted along beside them noticing everything that moved and squealing with joy at any dogs he saw and the ducks on the river.

'Next month.'

'That soon?'

'Yeah.'

'Oh well, at least you've seen something of your son and if you give me your new address I'll send you some photographs and keep you up to date with what he's doing and how he is.'

'I would like that.'

Thomas had visited his son a few times since he'd been home from hospital and all the talk between him and Ann had been about Tommy. Their own feelings for each other and what they had once had together hadn't been mentioned. While her little boy was so sick she hadn't been able to think about anything else but she knew, as she always had, that she was still in love with his father. It was irrelevant now, of course. She had made her choice over two years ago and he had plans of his own.

'It's a shame you're going, though, as you seem to have taken such a shine to Tommy,' she remarked.

A group of youths was walking along the towpath towards them and as they drew near they started to taunt them.

'Nigger lover,' said one to Ann.

'Trash,' said another.

'Hey, don't talk to her like that,' said Thomas, taking a swing at one of them.

'Leave it,' she urged him. 'They aren't worth it.'

Sensing the hostile atmosphere, Tommy started to cry. Ann picked him up and tried to comfort him.

'Black bastard,' said one of the boys, pointing at the child.

Thomas was a strong man and he really went for them

now. He grabbed one boy and held his hands behind his back. 'Any one of you come near me and he goes in the river,' he threatened.

'Let it go, lads,' said Thomas's hostage. 'I don't want a bleedin' ducking.'

The boys walked on and Thomas let his captive go, giving him a hefty shove to help him on his way.

'That is why I have to go back,' Thomas told Ann, sounding distressed. 'That sort of thing.'

'I never thought of you as the type who would run away,' she said.

'I'm not running away,' he protested. 'Just going home to my own country.'

'You could always stay and fight back. I can't run away from that sort of thing. I have to stick it out for Tommy and me. I've had my fair share of abuse but I've had plenty of kindness too; not every white person behaves like those louts.'

'Why you so keen for me to stay?' he asked. 'You don't want me in your life.'

'I want you to stay for Tommy,' she replied. 'He's your son and you obviously adore him.'

'I have just told you, it's too late.'

'I also want you to stay because I'm still in love with you. I never stopped,' she burst out without prior intention, putting Tommy into the pushchair. 'Your son and I need you. On your terms though. We can see as little or as much of you as you want. No strings. No commitment, not unless you want it.'

'Why you do this to me?' he said in a low voice so

as not to alarm the child. 'You go out of my life, then just when I get it back on course you come back and try to ruin my plans.'

'I don't want to ruin anything for you,' she said ardently. 'I'm just telling you how I feel.'

'You should have told me that a long time ago.' His voice was rising. 'Now you're just causing more trouble for me because it's too late. I'm going back home to Jamaica and that's the end of the matter.' He leaned over to his son in the pushchair and kissed his head. 'So long, son.'

Without another word, he walked away towards Hammersmith Bridge and Ann didn't try to stop him. She didn't feel that she had the right. Albeit with the very best of intentions she had made a decision she now knew to be an error of judgement and hurt him deeply. There must be no more pain inflicted on him by her hand. He had saved her son's life. That was enough to ask of anyone.

Bob was having some cheese on toast before leaving for work one day in August when the phone rang and the operator told him there was a long-distance reverse charges call from Devon and would he accept the charge. This was standard procedure when his mother called.

Having gone through the greetings, she assured him that she and his father were both well and that Joe was now managing to walk a little on his own without the crutches.

'That's marvellous news, Mum,' said Bob.

'He still has to use the crutches quite a bit though, so he isn't out of the woods yet.'

'He will do for a while I daresay. You can't expect miracles, though putting one foot in front of the other is a miracle when you think of what he was like at one time.'

'Mm.'

'So why do I sense that all is not well with him?'

'Gloria has stopped coming round and he's very down about it,' she explained.

'Did they fall out then?'

'Not as far as I can make out. She came one day and said she wouldn't be seeing him any more,' she told him. 'She wouldn't give a reason apparently. But you know what Joe's like. He won't talk about it.'

'They weren't actually courting, were they, Mum?'

'They were supposed to be just friends but it was obviously a lot more than that.'

'They did seem to be fond of each other when I've seen them together.'

'Whatever it was it's all over now.'

'Pity.'

'We thought so too.' She paused and there was a lot of hissing and crackling on the line. 'Are you working this weekend, or taking it off as it's bank holiday?'

'Probably working. Why?'

'Well, you know I said you couldn't come because Sal was coming, well she can't make it after all so you're welcome to come if you like,' she told him.

'I see.'

'The Storeys have had a bad time,' she went on. 'Sal's sister had a car accident and the little boy was seriously injured. It was touch and go for a while apparently.'

'No!'

'He's all right now but Sal doesn't feel able to go away at the moment. Tommy is better but her sister needs her to be around,' she explained. 'Naturally it's shaken them all up'

'I have to go now, Mum.' He paused, sensing that his mother would welcome some extra support because of Joe. 'But I'll come and see you at the weekend.'

'That will be lovely, son,' she said and the pleasure in her voice assured him he'd made the right decision.

'But I really must go now, Mum, because there is something I need to do right away. Look after yourself. Love to Dad and Joe,' he said. 'See you all soon.'

He replaced the receiver, left the cheese on toast half eaten and hurried from the flat.

The shop was busy just prior to closing when Bob went in clutching a large bag with the head of a soft toy poking out of the top. Sal was serving sweets and Dolly was on the cigarette counter. Bob waited in the sweet queue while Sal broke some toffee and weighed it up. Intent upon what they were doing, neither of the women noticed him.

'A quarter of toffee please,' he said when his turn came.

'Oh.' Sal's eyes widened and she coloured up. 'I didn't realise you were here.'

'I've just heard about the accident and naturally I'm concerned so I thought I'd pop over to see how Tommy is doing,' he explained.

'So you don't actually want the toffee.'

'I do.'

'Which flavour?' she asked, meeting his eyes. 'We've increased our range since you were last around these parts. Vanilla, walnut, treacle, mint or original creamy toffee.'

'Very impressive,' he said.

'We think so,' she said, still waiting for his answer.

'Original please.'

'Coming up.'

'Mum has just told me about the accident,' he said as she weighed the toffee. 'That poor little boy. You must have been out of your minds with worry.'

Sal nodded. 'He's fine now but we are all keeping a very close eye on him.'

'I came as soon as I heard.' He lifted the bag up and put it on the counter whereupon a fluffy dog with long ears fell out. 'I got this for him. I hope he'll like it.'

'That's lovely,' said Sal, giving him the toffee. 'Why don't you go through to the house and give it to him yourself. Give Ann a shout to let her know you're on your way up.'

Bob was imbued with a sense of well-being. He hadn't realised just how much he'd missed being a part of this family. 'Thank you,' he said, making his way through to the back.

'Your change,' called Sal but her words went unheard.

★　　★　　★

377

'I hope you don't mind my turning up,' said Bob.

'Course we don't. It's good to see you, Bob,' Dolly assured him after they'd closed the shop and were all sitting in the living room drinking tea, Tommy trotting around hugging his new toy. 'I still haven't forgiven you for what you did to Sal but she's managed to survive without you so we must put that in the past where it belongs.'

'Gran,' admonished Sal. 'You're being really embarrassing.'

Bob gave Sal a reassuring look. 'You're right to mention it, Dolly,' he said. 'I deserve more than a verbal rap on the knuckles. A clout round the ear would be more appropriate.'

'How is your family?' asked Sal with a swift change of subject.

'Mum and Dad are fine and Joe is coming on in leaps and bounds; he's even walking a little without sticks but he's just had a blow in that Gloria has disappeared off the scene and apparently he's devastated. I think Mum is worried that it might cause a setback because Gloria was such a strength to him.'

'What happened then?' Ann enquired. 'Did they have a falling-out?'

'I don't know the details,' he told her. 'Mum just said that Gloria turned up and said she wouldn't be seeing him again.'

'That's a real shame,' said Sal, puzzled by this news because Gloria had seemed to be so fond of Joe, despite her bossy and sometimes offhand attitude towards him.

'My thoughts exactly,' said Bob. 'I had planned to work this weekend but I've decided to go down there to see what's going on. I think Mum could do with some moral support.' He grinned at Sal. 'I had been banned from the place because you were going down there but as you've cancelled I've been given the green light.'

There was an odd silence,

'Have I said something?' he asked, perceiving a sudden awkwardness. 'It's all right, Sal. I can quite understand your not wanting to be there at the same time as me, given what happened.'

'It isn't that, Bob—' she began.

'It's that we didn't even know that she was planning to go or, more importantly, cancelled it,' Ann cut in.

Sal looked sheepish. 'I didn't get round to mentioning my plans to go because I only said I might try to go at bank holiday when Mavis mentioned it in her letter . . .'

'It's the other bit that I'm interested in,' said Ann. 'The cancellation bit. Why did you cancel?'

'Obviously I wouldn't go away and leave you and Gran after what's happened.'

'Tommy has fully recovered,' Ann pointed out.

'Yeah, but we're all still a bit fragile.'

'No we're not. We're back to normal and I'm not having you cancelling a visit to people you think a lot of on my account, especially when it's completely unnecessary.'

'But—' began Sal.

'But nothing,' interrupted Ann hotly. 'If you want to stay in Devon until Tuesday I'll cover for you in the shop. It's time I got back to work properly anyway. Tommy will be fine in the shop with me or the back room or the garden if it's nice weather, with his toys.'

'I would have been back by Monday night anyway,' she said. 'And I wouldn't have gone until closing time on Saturday, having done the market, so you and Gran wouldn't have had to do extra work. But it's all academic as I'm not going.'

'So you cancelled just because you think we will fall apart if you're not here.'

'Of course not. I was just trying to be supportive.'

'You've given me your support in spades and now you're overdoing it. Gran and I and Tommy can survive for a long weekend without you, isn't that right, Gran?'

'Course it is,' confirmed Dolly.

'I can't go now anyway,' Sal objected. 'I've told Mavis I won't be going and Bob is going instead.'

'I'll stay away if you want to go,' he offered.

Dolly and Ann exchanged looks and sighed in unison.

'Oh for goodness' sake. Why on earth can't you both go?' asked Dolly in exasperation. 'Mavis has plenty of room.'

'Isn't it obvious?' said Sal.

'Not to me it isn't,' said Dolly. 'You were once together, now you are not. It isn't the end of the world.'

'I'm sure you are both sufficiently adult to be able to be in the same house for a couple of days without killing each other or making other people feel uncomfortable,' suggested Ann.

'I'm game if you are, Sal,' he said.

'Our car is still off the road after the accident,' Sal remembered. 'But I could get the train I suppose.'

'I shall be driving an empty cab down there and you're very welcome to come along with me,' Bob offered.

'There you are,' enthused Dolly. 'You'll be in the back so you won't even have to talk to him if you don't want to.'

'I've told Mavis I won't be going so she won't be expecting me,' said Sal.

'That's easily solved,' said Bob. 'I'll ring the village pub and leave a message. She'll be delighted to have us both there. You know how she enjoys a crowd. Joe will be pleased to see you too. He has a soft spot for you.'

'They'll think we're back together.'

'We'll enlighten them as soon as we get there,' he said. 'Problem solved.'

'You're just putting obstacles in the way,' said Dolly. 'So stop making such a fuss.'

'Why do I feel as though I'm being bullied?' asked Sal.

'Probably because you are,' said her sister. 'In your own best interests.'

'But the whole thing is bizarre.'

'Something a bit offbeat is good for us all now and again,' declared Ann. 'If you want to go to Devon, Gran and I will be very happy about it. If you don't want to go then stay here. But don't stay here on my account.'

'I still feel a bit selfish going off.'

'It's a couple of days in Devon, not a month in Spain. You deserve a break. You do, after all, run the business and do the majority of the work. Gran and I will have a nice quiet time without you coming up with new ideas for the business with the threat of more work. We shall take Tommy to the park and down by the river.'

'Looks like you've made up my mind for me,' said Sal.

'Someone has to in this case,' said Ann. 'Unusual for you to be a ditherer. You normally know your own mind.'

Bob stood up. 'I must go and do some work as I'll be taking the weekend off.' He turned to Sal and said in an even tone, 'Are you coming to Devon or not?'

'Yes, I'll come.'

'What time shall I pick you up then?'

'Ann and I will do the last part and the cashing up so you'll be free to go when you're ready as soon as you get back from the market,' Dolly told Sal. 'We'll have Charlie in the shop to help with the last-minute rush.'

'What time?' repeated Bob.

'About half past four.'

'I'll be here on the dot,' he said. 'Cheerio all. See you on Saturday.'

And after giving Tommy a valedictory hug he went, leaving Sal simultaneously apprehensive and excited.

Chapter Fifteen

'Splitting up can be a double blow,' remarked Bob as they headed out of London on Saturday, Sal settled in the back of the taxi. 'Because you lose a family too and if you've become fond of them, you miss seeing them.'

'We've both suffered in that way,' she said. 'But you seem to have wormed your way back into my family's good books quite successfully.'

'That isn't fair,' he came back at her. 'I couldn't not come and see Tommy when I heard about the accident, could I? I think a lot of him, you know that, and I had to be sociable to the others while I was there. Anyway, you've no room to talk since you and my mother seem to be quite friendly.'

'When Kate went out of your life Mavis felt it would be all right to contact me again. She made the first move and I responded, that's all.'

'And on the subject of Kate—'

'I'd rather not talk about her,' she cut in.

'I just wanted to explain.'

'There's no need,' she told him with a weary sigh. 'You did what you had to. I understood that and got over it. So, let's just leave it at that.'

'I hated hurting you.'

'But you went ahead and did it anyway,' she said. 'So let's not go back over old ground. Just make sure your mother knows that there is nothing between us now. I don't want her getting her hopes up unnecessarily.'

'Will do,' he said and they lapsed into silence.

The evening air was infused with the cool, ambrosial scent of autumn when they arrived at the cottage, abundant with heart as usual. Mavis had prepared a tasty meal of meat pie and vegetables followed by apple tart and custard.

'So it's back on between you two then, is it?' Joe blurted out when they were all sitting round the table.

'No, it isn't,' said his mother who had been put in the picture by Bob almost on arrival. 'And don't be so rude as to mention it, if you please.'

'Why are you both here then?' he persisted.

'Because we both wanted to come,' replied Sal.

'And there isn't no law against a man and a woman going visiting together,' said Mavis. 'It don't mean that something has to be going on between them.'

'Course it doesn't,' Stan added in support. 'So hold your tongue, Joe. You don't like it if anyone asks personal questions about you and Gloria, do you?'

'No I don't,' Joe was quick to respond, 'so don't get any ideas about that, Bob.'

There was an awkward moment before the conversation resumed. They were all eager to know about Tommy, and Sal complimented Joe on his progress with walking. But the tension was palpable and she realised that she had made a big mistake in coming here at the same time as Bob. An early departure would upset her hosts so somehow she would have to try and make the weekend as bearable for them all as possible.

Later on Sal had an opportunity to speak to Joe alone when he went out into the yard after supper. She found him leaning on the gate with his crutches propped up against it, staring out over the fields which were suffused with a luminous glow from the moon.

'Well done on the progress you've made,' she said. 'You've come on in leaps and bounds since I last saw you.'

'I do what I can,' he said. 'Sorry I embarrassed you earlier.'

'You didn't embarrass me. It's obvious you would think that Bob and I are back together, given the circumstances. I shouldn't have come at the same time as him. It was bound to create an atmosphere.'

'It seems a bit peculiar that you're not together when you're both here, that's all. We'll probably get used to it.'

'There will be no need because next time I'll make sure I come at a different time to him,' she told him.

'Either that or make it up with him and get back to normal,' he suggested.

'No chance,' she said. 'Too much has happened.'

'He only finished with you because he was tricked into it,' he pointed out.

'Maybe but whatever the reason, it didn't hurt any the less. I got through it somehow and I'm not prepared to let myself be that vulnerable again.'

'I'd have Gloria back tomorrow if she'd have me. And it was her who gave me the elbow.'

'What actually happened, Joe?' Sal enquired. 'Had things not been good between you for a while?'

'Things were great. We were getting on better than ever, I mean *really well*, you know, we got to be more than friends,' he said. 'She seemed as keen as I was and I was on top of the world. My life had turned around; my walking was improving and I had a girlfriend I adored. Then she arrived at the cottage one day and wouldn't even come inside. She said she wanted to talk to me at the door. Then she came out with it straight off. "I'm very sorry but I won't be seeing you again, Joe, and I don't want you to try to contact me because I won't change my mind." Just like that. There was no explanation; nothing. She just turned and ran back across the yard and disappeared down the lane.'

'And because she was so definite about it you didn't try and contact her?'

'That's right. She seemed to be upset when she was telling me and I didn't want to make things worse for her,' he explained. 'But I can't believe she ended it because she doesn't care for me.'

'No, neither can I,' said Sal thoughtfully.

'Maybe I'm just fooling myself,' he said. 'I mean what other reason could there be?'

'I don't know Joe, I really don't,' she said, adding silently, *but I intend to find out.*

The next morning after a late breakfast, when she'd helped Mavis with the dishes, Sal decided to go for a walk, making sure they all knew she didn't want company. She strode out towards the village, disappointed to find it deserted. Determined to pursue her course, she sat on a bench and waited until someone appeared; a man with a dog as it happened. She approached him and got the information she needed then headed towards a row of cottages on the outskirts of the village and knocked at the door.

'Sal,' greeted Gloria, smiling initially then narrowing her eyes suspiciously. 'What are you doing here?'

'I just wondered if we could have a chat.'

'Joe's sent you, hasn't he?'

'No. None of them even know that I'm here.'

'You're back with Bob then.'

Sal shook her head.

'So why are you in these parts?'

'I came to see the family,' replied Sal. 'Big mistake as it happens because everyone assumes the same as you, that we must be back together or thinking about it at least. It's making the weekend a bit difficult to be honest.'

'What do you want with me?' asked Gloria.

'A chat,' Sal said. 'Just us girls together as we are both ex-girlfriends of the Beck brothers and have something in common. Perhaps we could go for a walk.'

A man's voice boomed out from inside. 'Who is it at the door, Gloria?'

'Just someone to see me, Dad,' she shouted back. 'I'm going out. Shan't be long.'

She slammed the door behind her and she and Sal headed out of the village into the country.

Bob, Stan and Joe were in the village pub for a pre-prandial pint. Apart from the landlady there wasn't a woman in sight, this being Sunday lunchtime.

'It's nice to have you with us, Joe,' remarked Bob, the three of them sitting at a table rather than standing at the bar as usual out of consideration for Joe's difficulties. 'I think it must be the first time since before the accident.'

'I do sometimes come down for a pint with Dad these days,' said Joe.

'He's done well,' said his father. 'We don't want him slipping back because he's missing Gloria.'

'I'm not missin' her,' denied Joe.

'Ooh, not much,' said Stan, swigging his beer. 'You've been going about with a face like a strangled chicken ever since she disappeared off the scene.'

Joe shrugged but didn't say anything.

'You could at least have tried to get her back,' suggested his father.

'She asked me not to.'

'You should have tried anyway,' Stan went on. ''Appen that's what she wanted, you to go after her. Women like a bit of coaxing.'

'No, Dad, that wasn't what she wanted.'

Stan turned to Bob. 'Then there's you, treading eggshells around Sal when you obviously want her back. What's the matter with the two of you? Why don't you sort yourselves out? There was never any of this malarkey between me and your mother.'

'Perhaps they were simpler times, Dad,' said Bob.

'They were very hard times, boy,' said Stan. 'We didn't have a ha'penny to bless ourselves with but at least we knew what we wanted as regards our womenfolk.'

'So do we,' said Bob.

'That's why you broke it off with Sal 'cause of some woman claiming paternity, because you knew what you wanted, is it?'

'I had no choice.'

''Appen you didn't but that's all finished with now so why don't you get Sal back?'

'Because she won't have me,' Bob replied. 'I couldn't expect her to after what I did.'

'That isn't what I've seen since the pair of you arrived yesterday,' said Stan. 'So you made a mistake, put it right.'

'She was hurt before, Dad, by someone else so she's bound to be wary.'

'That isn't none of your doing so if you want the girl go and get her. Ask her for another chance.'

'I have to respect her wishes.'

'Which is what you'll be doing if you try to get her back,' Stan persisted.

'She doesn't want me back, I've told you.'

'Rubbish,' snorted Stan. 'I didn't think I would rear two

such hopeless sons. Joe lets Gloria go without a fight, and you, Bob, can't see what's staring you in the face. So, Sal might take a bit of persuading but it's what she wants, I would put money on it if I was a betting man. Anyway, what sort of a fella just gives up without even trying?'

'In case you haven't noticed, Dad, times have changed since you were young back in the Stone Age.' Bob grinned wryly. 'Nowadays we don't bully women into doing what we want. We consider their feelings.'

'You cheeky young bugger,' objected Stan, grinning too. 'For that you can buy me another pint.'

'Seeing as you're such an expert on the subject of women, it strikes me as odd that Mum wears the trousers in our house,' Bob commented.

'She thinks she does,' was Stan's reaction. 'That's the art of a happy marriage. You let the women think they're the boss but you make all the rules and get your own way.'

'So you won't be afraid of facing Mum if we're late back for dinner then,' said Joe.

'Ah, that's different,' Stan came back at him. 'That's just a matter of consideration.'

'Which is what we are showing when we leave the women in our lives be when they ask us to.'

'No, that's just lack of spirit,' said his father.

'I give up,' said Bob with a sigh and a slow shake of his head as he stood to fetch the drinks.

'You've had plenty of practice at giving up as that is what you've done with Sal,' his father pronounced.

'Same again, Joe?' asked Bob, bringing the frustrating conversation to a close.

'Yes please.'

Bob walked to the bar feeling irritable. What made it even more infuriating was the possibility that his father might be right.

Sal and Gloria had walked out of the village and were sitting on a tree stump on the edge of a copse; they were engrossed in conversation, mostly about Stan and Mavis and how fond they both were of them.

'You always know where you are with them,' said Gloria. 'Mavis was a bit hard on me at first — I'm not exactly a lady, am I, and it's only natural she would be protective of her son — but I think she got to like me in the end.'

'I'm certain she did,' said Sal.

'I miss going to the cottage a lot,' sighed Gloria wistfully.

'Do you miss Joe too?' probed Sal.

'Oh not half,' she replied.

'No chance of your getting back together then?'

'Nah.'

'It's a pity because you made such a great couple,' said Sal. 'He is obviously very fond of you.'

'Huh,' Gloria said with a dry laugh. 'He wouldn't be if he knew what I am really like.'

'But you always seem so open and natural; never any airs and graces. Don't tell me you have a dark side to your nature.'

Gloria gave Sal a close look. 'I suppose you could say that I do.' Her near-black eyes were full of sadness. 'I haven't been honest with Joe and that's why I had to end it.'

'Am I allowed to know in what way you haven't been honest?' Sal asked tentatively.

'I must admit it would be a relief to talk to someone about it because no one else knows but I can't risk Joe finding out because he'd be devastated and I've hurt him enough already.'

'You can trust me if you do want to talk,' Sal assured her. 'Whatever you tell me will stay between us, I promise.'

Gloria stared at her hands, picking her nails nervously. 'Well,' she began slowly then added in a fast staccato manner: 'I was the cause of his accident. It was me who ran out into the road and made him swerve.'

Sal was too stunned to speak.

'I knew you'd be shocked,' said Gloria, sounding worried. 'I wish I hadn't told you 'cause now you'll hate me as much as I hate myself if that's possible.'

'I don't hate you but I'm wondering why you didn't come forward to stop all the rumours about Joe being drunk in charge of the motorbike?'

'I was too scared,' she confessed miserably. 'Even apart from the fact that I thought I would be sent to prison for causing an accident I was supposed to be indoors that night. I'd been out late the night before and my dad said I was getting myself a bad name in the village for seeing a lot of different boys so he forbade me to go out. But when he and Mum went to the pub I sneaked out to see a boy. I was running home to get back before Mum and Dad when the motorbike came along. I thought I could get across the lane before it reached where I was but they go at such a speed those things

. . . it only just missed me before it hit the tree. Anyway I saw the lights of a car coming so I knew that the motorcyclist would get help. Then I disappeared across the fields in the dark and ran straight home.'

'Oh Gloria,' said Sal, unable to hide her distress.

'I told you it was a really terrible thing, didn't I?' she said. 'Of course, I didn't know who was on the motorbike at the time but news soon got round the village and I found out it was Joe and there was talk of someone running across the road, and they wanted that person to come forward. I kept trying to pluck up the courage to own up but I just didn't have the nerve. The longer I left it the harder it became, especially when I heard that Joe had lost the use of his legs. This thing was weighing me down. Then I saw you with Joe in the village one day and I got to thinking that maybe there was a way I could compensate in a small way for what I'd done.'

'So you went to the cottage to cheer Joe up and help him start walking again,' surmised Sal.

'Exactly.'

'Well, you succeeded so that should ease your conscience a little,' said Sal, glad to find a positive aspect. 'Everyone knows it was your support that got him this far and you cheered him up no end.'

'I was happy being with him too.'

'So why end it?'

'When he started to walk a bit without crutches I thought my job was over but things were complicated because we had feelings for each other by this time so for a while I just couldn't bring myself to do it.'

'Was it absolutely necessary to end things?'

'Oh yes,' she said without hesitation. 'I couldn't go on living a lie. It would have been wrong.'

'You could have told him the truth.'

'It would have broken his heart.'

'You've done that anyway.'

'Yeah, I suppose I have . . . and my own. Anyway, if I did come clean Mavis and Stan would never forgive me and I don't blame them. That would cause a family upset.'

'Would they have to know about it?' asked Sal. 'If Joe was able to forgive you why bother them with it?'

'I'm not gonna tell any of them about it so we'll never know,' stated Gloria. 'It happened and I can't change that.'

'You could get Joe back though,' advised Sal. 'If you love him and you want to be with him, it's worth a try. Tell him the truth about the past and how you feel now. You have, after all, compensated in part for what you did by getting him to walk again and cheering him up when he was so down.'

'But he'll think I only did it because of guilt, which I did at first.'

'So explain how your feelings for him changed when you got to know him better. It isn't possible to predict what the outcome of your confession might be because none of us can judge how another person will react to anything. But I think you'll feel better in yourself if you are honest with him, no matter what happens as a result.'

'I want him back,' Gloria said ardently. 'I'd love to be with him properly with everything out in the open.'

'In that case I think you'd be wise to do something

about it,' said Sal. 'Maybe he will be angry at first but once he knows how you feel about him now, he might well come round. If you don't try you won't know, will you?'

Gloria thought this over. 'Everything you say is true but I'm such a coward.'

'That's the last thing you are. You wouldn't have gone to the cottage and spent so much of your time with a disabled stranger if you were. You didn't know you were going to fall in love with him. It must have been a burden at first.'

'No, not really and that surprised me. I'm not a patient person so I thought I would be hopeless with him. But somehow my brash way of doing things seemed to work.'

'You put a lot into it and it must have been hard just turning up at the cottage that first time so let's not have more talk about your being a coward.'

'You don't hate me then.'

'Of course I don't,' Sal said. 'We all make mistakes and you've tried to make up for yours. Now you've got a chance to put things right.'

'I'll think about it.'

'Meanwhile I'd better get back. Mavis might need a hand in the kitchen.'

Taking Sal by surprise, Gloria threw her arms round her and hugged her. 'Thanks,' she said simply. 'You've been great.'

'I hope it works out for you both,' Sal said.

They walked back to the village in comfortable silence broken only by casual conversation. It occurred to Sal that she was the least qualified person to advise anyone on their love life since hers was such a disaster. Problems were usually easier to solve when they were someone else's.

During lunch an uncomfortable atmosphere hung over everything and Sal blamed herself entirely. She shouldn't have allowed herself to be persuaded into coming with Bob because it was definitely the situation between the two of them that was causing it. Everyone felt awkward with them being here but not together, and Joe's down-beat mood didn't help.

Mavis and Stan did what they could to make things normal but somehow it didn't come off. There were awkward silences galore and false laughter at Mavis and Stan's brave attempt at humour.

Sal decided that this couldn't go on so as soon as she had finished helping Mavis with the dishes and the Becks senior were settled in their easy chairs Sal beckoned Bob to the kitchen and suggested rather forcibly that they go for a walk.

'It's raining,' he objected.

'Just a bit of drizzle,' she said. 'That won't hurt you.'

'All right, I'll get my jacket on the way out.'

Sal donned the raincoat she had brought with her because the weather had been unsettled for a while and they headed off across the yard.

'You're energetic today aren't you,' he said. 'Walking this morning and again this afternoon.'

'It's only an excuse to get you on your own,' she explained as they headed down the lane. 'And don't get the wrong idea.'

'That's a pity,' he said drily.

'Don't be flippant. Your poor parents are suffering because of us. We shouldn't be here at the same time and it's making for an awkward atmosphere.'

'It is hard going, I must admit.'

'So either we leave right now. Or we make more of an effort for the rest of the weekend,' she suggested sharply.

'Oh Sal,' he said, halting in his step and turning to her, suddenly very emotional. 'Let's end this rift right now. I really am sorry I hurt you so badly. You know I didn't want to be with Kate. If I could change what happened I would. I'll get down on my knees and propose to you all over again if it will help. Please give me another chance.'

Annoyingly Sal's eyes filled with tears and all the resolve she had built up since they had parted melted away. She wanted to be with him so much that it hurt. Being alive in itself made you vulnerable. Trying to protect yourself against pain was just a waste of life, she now realised.

'Did you keep the ring?' she asked, remembering the magical day when they had gone to the West End to buy her a diamond solitaire.

'Of course.'

She gave him a studious look. 'You've got it with you, haven't you,' she said.

'Er . . .'

'You have . . .'

'A chap has to have hope and there was never going

to be a better chance than a weekend in the country with you.'

Despite herself she laughed. 'I ought to make you go down on your knees for being so sure of yourself.'

'That's the last thing I was,' he said, going down on his knees anyway, there in the lane. 'Hopeful is a whole lot different.'

'Get up, you fool,' she said, 'before we have another near miss with a tractor.'

They were both laughing as she helped him up, too wrapped up in each other to notice a young woman with wild dark hair climb over a gate from a field and head towards the cottage in the rain.

It was smiles all round back at the cottage.

'Thank the Lord for that,' said Mavis when Sal showed them her ring safely back on her wedding finger. 'I've wanted to bang your heads together to make you see sense this weekend.'

'Me too,' added Stan.

'All we want now is for Joe to come back with a smile on his face and we can all get back to normal.'

'What do you mean?' asked Bob. 'Where is Joe?'

'Out with Gloria,' said Mavis. 'She came to the door and said she wanted to speak to him in private so they've gone out. They won't have gone far because he didn't want to use the wheelchair. They're probably over in the field.'

'That sounds promising,' said Bob.

Sal was struck with nerves for Gloria as she had

apparently taken Sal's advice. Despite her own happiness she was worried for her and for Joe who would initially be hurt.

'They might be a while,' she said.

'How long can it take to kiss and make up?' said Mavis. 'He'll be back for tea. Especially as it's raining.'

Sal doubted it. There were complicated issues being discussed over in the field at the moment, and they might take time to resolve, despite the weather.

'Typical Bank Holiday weekend washout,' grumbled Ann as she and Dolly headed back from the park in the rain on Sunday afternoon with Tommy in the pushchair under the storm cover. 'They put on these open-air events, a Punch and Judy show, a few kiddies' rides, music in the bandstand and down comes the rain and everybody goes home soaked to the skin.'

'It is a bit of a British tradition, I must admit,' agreed Dolly.

'Still, Tommy had a go on the roundabout and the swings before it turned wet so that was something, I suppose. The Punch and Judy show held his interest for all of half a minute.'

'He isn't old enough for that sort of thing yet. There'll be plenty of other times,' said Dolly. 'The best is yet to come for him. He's becoming more knowing every day. Christmas will be great fun this year.'

'Yes it will,' said Ann with enthusiasm.

'When is it his father goes back to Jamaica?'

'Next month.'

'Never mind, love,' said Dolly. 'Tommy can't miss what he's never had, can he?'

His mother could miss what she had had, though, thought Ann, but said, 'We'll have a cup of tea and some of your lovely sponge cake when we get in. That'll cheer us up.'

They trudged on through the puddles until they reached Perry Parade.

'Someone's sheltering in our shop doorway,' remarked Dolly. 'And I don't blame them either in this weather.'

'As long as they move to let us through, they can stay there for as long as they want,' said Ann as they approached The Toffee Shop. 'It's quicker to go in the front through the shop rather than go round the back in this weather.'

'Excuse us please,' said Dolly as Ann steered the push-chair into the shop doorway while her grandmother got the keys out, paying no attention to the person taking shelter. Dolly glanced up at the man, who was neatly dressed in a raincoat. 'Horace,' she gasped in amazement. 'Horace, is it really you?'

'Dad,' exclaimed Ann, adding quickly and angrily. 'About bloody time too.'

The others had started tea when Gloria and Joe finally came in soaked to the skin but wreathed in smiles.

'I hope whatever you had to talk about was worth getting your death of cold for,' said Mavis drily.

'It was Mrs Beck, I promise you that,' said Gloria, beaming.

'Go and get yourselves dried off before you sit down for tea,' urged Mavis. 'You'll get rheumatism when you're old if you let the damp get into your bones.'

'I think we'll take that chance, because we have something to tell you and it can't wait, wet clothes or not.'

And without further ado she started talking, explaining about her talk with Sal that morning and how that had inspired her to make a clean breast of things to Joe. Sal hadn't expected her to tell Mavis and Stan about her part in Joe's accident but she did; out came the whole story, ending with the news that Joe had decided to forgive her and they were now a couple. Nervously Sal waited for Mr and Mrs Beck's reaction.

'Well I can't pretend it isn't a shock, Gloria,' said Mavis. 'Apart from causing Joe serious injuries you let people think that the accident was his fault for being drunk.'

'I know,' she said remorsefully. 'It was a terrible thing to do. What else can I say?'

'But credit where it's due, at least you tried to make up for it,' Mavis went on. 'And Joe has come on a treat with your help.'

'I know he can never have back the years when he was confined to the chair,' said Gloria. 'But I will try to make him happy, I promise you.'

'We'd never have got together if it hadn't been for the accident,' said Joe.

'And as for people thinking it was Joe's own fault because of drink, let them think what they like,' said Stan ardently. 'This need never go outside of these four walls.'

'The thing is,' began Joe, sitting down with his crutches

beside him. 'Gloria and I are going to be together whatever happens.' He looked from one parent to the other. 'But obviously we would like your blessing. If I can forgive her, I'm sure you can find it in your hearts to do the same.'

'I think you'd both better go and get dried off then come and sit down for your tea then, don't you?' said Mavis.

'Shall I put the kettle on for more tea, Mrs Beck?' offered Gloria.

'If you would, dear,' said Mavis, smiling. 'If you're going to be one of the family again, you might as well remind yourself of where everything is. But get your wet coats off first, both of you.'

'Will do,' said Gloria happily and tripped lightly from the room.

After that the rest of the stay was a joy. No more awkward silences but plenty of laughter and none of it false. Sal was sad when it came to an end.

'It was quite a weekend,' remarked Bob on the journey home. 'Mum and Dad must have thought all their birthdays had come at once with both their sons getting sorted out.'

'Yeah, I'm really pleased it worked out for Joe and Gloria,' said Sal. 'I always thought there was more to that girl than was immediately obvious.'

'I did sometimes wonder why she suddenly turned up out of the blue to help Joe,' he said. 'I'd never have guessed the reason in a million years.'

'Nor me but I knew, somehow, that she hadn't given up on Joe because she didn't care for him,' she said. 'That's why I went to see her.'

'It's just as well you did or they might never have got back together.'

'They would have if it was meant to be.'

'I thought you didn't believe in all that stuff about fate,' he reminded her.

'A girl can change her mind, can't she?'

'And thank God you changed your mind about me,' he said. 'By the way, I haven't told you, I took your advice and signed up for evening classes.'

'It took you long enough but good for you.'

'I only did it to fill in the time,' he explained. 'Now that we are back together, I may not bother to go.'

'Yes you will,' she said. 'I shall make sure of it.'

'I love it when you're bossy,' he said, laughing.

They did a lot of laughing on the way home and Sal was in high spirits when they arrived back at the shop, keen to tell the others the good news, that her engagement was back on. So her mood was hugely dampened when Ann came out to meet them with a face like thunder.

'Thank God you're back,' she said.

'Why, what's happened?'

'Come inside and see.'

'You go on up, Sal,' said Bob. 'I'll bring your case.'

Sal was shocked and delighted to see her father in equal measures.

'Where have you been?' she asked, hugging him when he stood up to greet her.

'He's been refusing to tell us anything until you're here,' said Ann furiously. 'Disappears then comes back without a word of warning and expects us to roll out the red carpet for him.'

'I thought it best if we were all together before I try to explain . . .' he began apologetically.

'And togetherness with your family is something you'd know a lot about, isn't it?' said Ann sarcastically, 'having buggered off and left us without so much as a word.'

'He hasn't wanted any special treatment and you know it,' Dolly put in, defensive of her beloved son. 'He's expecting nothing from us. He isn't even staying here even though he does actually own the place.'

'I'm staying in a boarding house,' he explained to Sal in his usual quiet manner. 'To save any disruption here. Things have changed since I've been away.' He picked Tommy up. 'For the better too.'

'Enough of that old flannel,' Ann said sharply. 'You've got some explaining to do. So start talking.'

'Ann, don't speak to Dad like that,' admonished Sal. 'Whatever he's done he's still our father so show some respect.'

Bob appeared with her suitcase, judged the mood of the company and said, 'I'll see you tomorrow, Sal.' He made a diplomatic exit.

'Dad, the last time we saw you was the day of Mum's funeral so I do think we need to know why you went off like that without a word,' said Sal.

Ann took her son from Horace and sat him on her lap as their father started speaking.

'I was in a mess emotionally and I couldn't be strong for you as I should have been so I just had to get away.'

'But you were rock solid,' Sal reminded him. 'Everybody said how strong you were, dealing with everything and helping us all get through the funeral.'

'On the outside maybe; inside I was actually falling apart,' he informed her.

'Did you plan to leave?' Ann demanded.

'God no,' he replied. 'It took me weeks afterwards to realise the enormity of what I'd done.'

'Why didn't you come back when you did realise?' Ann wanted to know.

'Like I said, I was messed up and not thinking straight,' he tried to explain. 'That night after the funeral I felt as though I couldn't go on without your mother. I felt strange and unreal and I couldn't stop crying. I couldn't cope with you all needing me. I just couldn't do it. I felt so weak and useless, I knew it was only a matter of time before I let you all down.'

'You did that all right,' snorted Ann.

'Stop interrupting Ann, for goodness' sake,' warned her grandmother.

'So when you were all asleep I threw some things into a case and left, having no idea where I was going. I walked to the station and waited for the first train into central London. I didn't know where to go. Anywhere would do. So I got a train to Margate and that's where

I've been ever since, working as a confectionery rep on the South Coast and living in a boarding house.'

'While we were all worried sick about you here, you were doing very well for yourself.'

'Living from day to day and scratching a living is what I've been doing and feeling more miserable by the day. I was ashamed and hated myself for letting you down but I didn't have the courage to come back. You girls always saw me as the strong quiet one in the marriage; the one you could turn to.'

'Mum ruled the roost and you let her.'

'Ann,' rebuked Sal. 'Don't be so rude.'

'Ann is right,' said Horace. 'I did let Joan push me around most of the time. I never felt worthy of her you see.'

'Why?' asked Sal.

'Because I wasn't the sort of man she wanted. She worshipped her father and no one would ever come up to him in her eyes. She wanted me to be like him but I never could be.'

'What was he like then?'

'An overbearing bully of a man; he died when you two were little so you won't remember him,' he said. 'Your mother adored him. What I saw as bullying, she saw as strength.'

'Why did she marry you if you weren't what she wanted?' asked Ann.

'You can never really know someone until you actually share your life with them and by that time it's too late,' he said. 'Anyway, she loved me in her own way and was a good wife even though I was a disappointment to her.

Despite everything I was devoted to her and her death practically finished me off. I knew you were all suffering but I couldn't claw my way out of the trough I was in. In desperation I went to see a doctor and he said I was suffering from clinical depression and gave me some tablets that calmed me a little. But I knew I wouldn't ever feel right until I'd made my peace with the three of you. It's only now I've felt strong enough to come and see you.'

'Oh Dad. You poor thing,' said Sal tearfully, wrapping her arms round him. 'It's so good to have you home.'

'We've missed you,' added Dolly, sniffing into her handkerchief. 'Get your things from the boarding house and come home.'

'But things have changed here . . .' he began.

'Nothing that can't be sorted out by a little rearrangement,' said Sal. 'Ann and Tommy can move in with me again and you can have your room back.' She turned to her sister. 'All right with you, sis?'

Despite herself Ann was a little wet-eyed. 'Of course,' she said thickly.

'It won't be for long because I'll be moving out soon,' said Sal. 'I'm getting married.'

Dolly and Ann stared at her. 'So Devon worked its charm and it's all on again with Bob then,' said Dolly.

Sal nodded.

'Thank God for that,' said Ann, hugging her sister.

'It's turning out to be quite a day,' said Dolly.

With her father back working in the business, Ann was able to reduce her hours which suited her because it

wasn't so easy having Tommy around the shop now that he was a toddler; he was into everything and needed her attention. It made it more difficult for her financially though, since she earned less. She was planning on finding a job outside the family business when Tommy started school but that was a long way off and she had to pay her way until then. Still, she was luckier than many women in her position in that she was able to live rent free and had a supportive family.

Being only human, she couldn't help feeling a stab of envy for her sister, who finally had her wedding planned. Ann felt especially lonely knowing that Thomas would have sailed for Jamaica by now.

She was mulling all of this over as she pushed Tommy on the swing in the park one afternoon in September, the grass carpeted with fallen leaves and the air infused with the earthy chill of autumn.

'I went to the shop and your sister said I would find you here,' said a voice beside her and she turned to see Thomas.

She stared at him, mystified.

'You didn't really think I could go away and leave you once you had come back into my life, did you?'

'But it was all booked . . .'

'I sold the ticket,' he explained. 'If you'll have me, from now on it will be the three of us. You, me and our son. Together we can be strong.'

And now she really did believe that there was nothing she couldn't face with him by her side.